The Mission

Books by HANS HABE

The Mission
The Wounded Land
The Countess
Ilona
Devil's Agent
Off Limits
Our Love Affair with Germany
Black Earth
Walk in Darkness
Aftermath
Katherine
A Thousand Shall Fall
Sixteen Days
Three Over the Frontier

HANS HABE

The Mission

A Novel

TRANSLATED FROM THE GERMAN

BY MICHAEL BULLOCK

Coward-McCann, Inc.
New York

Dedicated to the memory of
PROFESSOR HEINRICH NEUMANN
Chevalier de Héthárs

INSTEAD OF AN INTRODUCTION

THE American edition of this novel appears after editions in twelve European languages. None of these editions carried an introduction.

In a letter sent to me a few months before the publication of this book in America, John J. Geoghegan, President of the Coward-McCann publishing house, wrote in part: "About half the population of the United States is under twenty-eight years of age."

This sentence evoked certain reflections. America—in spite of everything—is a happy country. It has a right to be proud of its past. It has a right to forget the terrible things that happened in Europe.

This novel takes place in Europe in 1938, a year before the Second World War. It describes the beginning of the death march upon which six million Jews set out. The tragic end of this march is stamped upon the mind of every young American. The bloody outcome is well known, but here, however, we are dealing with its inception in 1938. By this time Hitler's persecution of the Jews was ready to go into high gear.

On January 30, 1933, Adolf Hitler came to power. On February 27 the Reichstag burned. On October 14 Germany left the League of Nations. The law of the jungle was established.

The annihilation of the Jews had been—from his youth—the aim of the paperhanger from Braunau. He had proclaimed it in *Mein Kampf*. Hitler's anti-Semitic program was to win him the German people, whose anti-Jewish tendencies had already clearly shown themselves during the German Baroque period. He also regarded anti-Semitism as a skeleton key by means of which he could penetrate the anti-Semitic mind in other European countries.

7

Immediately after his seizure of power Hitler began to carry out his program.

On April 1, 1933, a boycott of all Jewish shops and businesses was proclaimed in Germany. The slogan ran: "Whoever buys from Jews places himself outside German society." In the same month, all Jews were dismissed from state service.

In May of the same year, unnoticed by the world, the first concentration camps were set up. Among these were the terrible names of Dachau and Oranienburg.

In September 1933 the Reichskulturkammer was established. Anyone who did not belong to it was shut out from German cultural life. Jewish writers were not allowed to publish, Jewish painters were not allowed to exhibit, Jewish musicians were not allowed to give concerts. Dr. Josef Goebbels spoke of "Jews and Jews' lackeys." A "Jews' lackey" was anyone who, though not a Jew himself, supported the Jews.

By 1934 Jews were to all intents and purposes outlawed. Anyone who committed an offense against a Jew was free of prosecution. Jews could leave the country only on certain conditions. The export of "Jewish capital" was forbidden. Numerous prominent Jews were arrested and thrown into prison or concentration camps. Many who were later released—in particular during the Olympic Games—had to pay a "ransom."

In June and July the action *"Juden unerwünscht*—Jews unwanted" was systematically carried out. At the entrance to towns, on the gates of swimming baths, hotels, restaurants and shops appeared notices: *Juden unerwünscht*. Every day in Germany fifty to a hundred and fifty Jews were killed or maltreated. National Socialist youths in SA uniforms lay in wait for the Jews outside the synagogues. Brutality was the order of the day.

On September 15, 1935, the Nuremberg Laws were promulgated. "Jew" had ceased to be a religious definition. Now there was only a Jewish "race." Anyone who had Jewish grandparents came under the Nuremberg Laws. Jews were forbidden to enter public establishments. No Jewish family was allowed to employ an "Aryan" maid. Where Jews were permitted to enter a park at all, they had to sit on "Jews' benches."

In the years 1935 to 1938 anti-Jewish measures were continually intensified. Sexual intercourse between Jews and non-Jews was punished with severe prison sentences, later with death. Jewish children were not allowed to attend "German" schools. Papers like Hitler's *Völkischer Beobachter* and Julius Streicher's *Stürmer* announced the "final solution" of the Jewish problem. The inmates of the concentration camps, the number of which had increased tenfold since 1933, were 85 percent Jews. Where Jews were murdered "illegally," in about 75 percent of the cases, proceedings were quashed. Where proceedings were initiated, they ended in over 90 percent of the cases in the murderer's acquittal. Although the Führer of the Third Reich declared that it wanted to "get rid of" the Jews, Jewish emigration was made so difficult as to be almost impossible. In the year 1937 alone, over 10,000 Jews were arrested for ostensibly infringing the currency laws; their property was confiscated. Jews who were admitted into other countries were allowed only in exceptional cases to take more than ten Reichsmarks with them. Even Jews who possessed perfectly valid exit visas were frequently arrested at the frontier. At the end of 1937 Dr. Goebbels announced to his Führer that the "legal elimination of the Jews from German life was complete." This meant that illegal measures for the "solution of the Jewish problem" could now be embarked upon. It was the signal for mass murder.

On March 11, 1938, the brown hordes, greeted with jubilation by the majority of the Austrian population, marched into Hitler's Austrian motherland. Austria became the "Ostmark," the eastern province of Germany. The acts of brutality committed in Austria surpassed those in Germany. Over 80 percent of Vienna's Jewish population was "provisionally" arrested. Old men, women and children were forced to scrub the streets and the walls of houses to eliminate the patriotic Austrian slogans that had been painted on them before the entry of the Germans. Common criminals were released from Austrian jails to make room for the arrested Jews. Over a hundred Jews were "shot while attempting to escape." The concentration camps set up by the Fascist regime of the Chancellor Dr. Kurt von Schuschnigg, for example the transit camp of Wöllersdorf, were filled with Jews.

In 1938, the year in which the action of this novel takes place, the National Socialist regime had resolved not merely upon war with the civilized world, but also upon the annihilation of the Jews. Mass deportations—in October 1938, 23,000 Jews were deported to Poland—and the "Crystal Night" of November 9, 1938, during which the majority of German synagogues were burned down and 40,000 Jews put in concentration camps, had already been decided upon. The "final solution," which in Germany alone claimed 180,000 Jewish victims, in Czechoslovakia 243,000, in Poland 2,600,000, in Rumania 220,000, in Hungary 200,000 and in Holland 104,000, was underway. On January 30, 1939, Hitler spoke in the Reichstag of the "annihilation of the Jewish race in Europe." The gas ovens were heated, the Apocalypse had begun.

How much the world knew of all this in July 1938, when the man whom I call Professor Dr. von Benda set out for Évian-les-Bains on Lake Geneva, will be shown in this book. Compared with what we know today, the world's knowledge was probably slight. But human cognition is made up of both knowledge and imagination. Imagination is no substitute for facts, but neither are facts a substitute for imagination. The duty to exercise imagination is no less than the duty to learn.

HANS HABE

Ascona, Switzerland
Winter, 1966

The Journey to Évian

And it shall be for a sign unto thee upon thine hand, and for a memorial between thine eyes, that the Lord's law may be in thy mouth: for with a strong hand the Lord brought thee out of Egypt.

EXODUS xiii, 9

I

A fictionalized recounting of the tragic Evian Conference held in 1938 at which Hitler, through an unofficial representative, offered the release of 40,000 Austrian Jews at $250 a head.

THE frontier town was called Basel; its name comes from the old Roman Basilea, but in that summer of 1938 Basel ought rather to have been called Babel.

Never, perhaps, since the time that men set up boundaries to protect themselves and their families, their goods and chattels, from their neighbors—for we all judge others by ourselves—perhaps never since they built walls and dug moats to preserve intact their individuality and their sovereignty, that is to say their vanity and their arrogance, never did the word frontier station better correspond to the idea behind it than in the year when to the east of Basilea darkness was settling in. The frontier station formed a triangle between three countries or rather between three worlds; neutral Switzerland, a country dozing away half awake, half asleep in the centuries-old security of its happy freedom, France which had not yet recovered from a victory won twenty years before and which, being on intimate terms with God, trusted in His goodness, and the new Germany, that had spread its boundaries far and wide and was in the process of extending them all over Europe and the world. These three worlds reached into the midst of this frontier station.

For anyone who wished to, it was not hard to see the frontier station's threefold character. One could see Swiss customs officers, dignified and somewhat absentminded, difficult to distinguish from soldiers in their uniforms, because, for their part, Swiss soldiers did their best to look no more martial than customs officers; French *douaniers* loitered about with damp cigarettes in the corners of their mouths, wearing blue uniforms that had probably never been pressed since the days of Captain Dreyfus, frontier guards resembling discharged veterans; and

then German policemen, armed revenue officers, customs officials, SA men, thronged the streets as though Basel already belonged to them and as though they only tolerated this Babel
because so many railway lines converged here and so many
railway lines went out from here into so many sick countries
that were waiting for the German cure.

The train had been standing for over an hour. The man
who was looking out of the window of his first-class compartment on the German side of the station was about sixty-five,
of medium height, with short hair not yet quite gray and a
fleshy but well-shaped nose on which sat a pair of rimless spectacles. A commonplace appearance, one might think, but a
closer look revealed that the eyes were a good twenty years
younger than the pale, lined face, as is the case with people
whose brain functions independently of and longer than the
body. One also observed a certain authority which radiated
from within, and finally one noted that the almost lipless mouth
was not, as seemed at first, hard or crabbed, but rather shaped
as though the lips had turned inward in the course of concentrated thinking. The man was wearing a comfortable traveling
suit of the best material, too comfortable in fact: it must have
been cut by a first-rate tailor; however, he had apparently not
reckoned with a sudden loss of weight, but the traveler did not
look like a man who would run to the tailor over every detail.
The traveler smoked incessantly as he watched the SA men
who had planted themselves alongside the carriage, as though
beside a prison van about to leave the prison yard.

There was also another gentleman in the compartment; he
did not look out at the platform, but sat by the door with his
eyes fixed on the corridor. He had introduced himself soon after
they left Vienna—an Austrian Jew named Steiner, Jakob
Steiner, until recently a well-to-do textile merchant in the
Rothenturnstrasse, now glad to get out of Austria with little
more than ten marks in his pocket; but he was not even certain
about this, that was why he had confided in his traveling companion, as people in distress often do, referring again and again
to this last minute on the inhospitable soil of his homeland. His
anxious loquacity was not as imprudent as it might have seemed
under the circumstances; he had recognized the elderly gentle-

man as the distinguished university professor, Dr. Heinrich von
Benda, the world-famous surgeon and specialist in diseases of
the kidneys and urinary tract, head of the department of the
General Hospital in Vienna that had been named after him, a
co-religionist and member of the same race, whose recent arrest
had caused mute dismay in the already dismayed city. Little
Herr Steiner, either because he was too preoccupied with his
own affairs, or because respect forbade him, had addressed no
questions to the Professor and the Professor, although he listened with sympathy, had neither mentioned how he had escaped the clutches of the Gestapo nor how he had managed to
obtain the race exit permit that was unobtainable even for
gold.

The train stood in the German station so long that it might
have been shunted onto a siding. The glass dome seemed as if
it would break in under the heavy July sky, but neither of the
two men dared to open the window; the men in uniform reminded them that even in a first-class prison it is prohibited to
open the window.

Finally the guards entered the train, and ultimately they
approached the compartment. Their uniforms were of many
colors, ages and styles, but there could be no doubt as to who
the masters were. The men in brown pushed the others aside,
looked over their shoulders, treated them with suspicion or
condescension; the older ones were merely supernumeraries,
tolerated and intimidated representatives of an abdicated decency.

As the door of the compartment was flung open, little Herr
Steiner rose with that solicitous politeness which is intended
to captivate officialdom, but only serves all the more surely to
arouse its brutality. With a glance at the travel documents
which Herr Steiner held out to the entering men like a child
giving the teacher an excuse note, two SA men threw themselves upon the emigrant's meager baggage, flung his suits,
shirts and shoes on the plush seat, turned his pockets inside out
and ordered the trembling man to take off his jacket. One of
the SA men, with a beery face, and sweat dripping off his red
cheeks, had planted himself in the doorway with arms folded, as
though to prevent little Herr Steiner from escaping, although

freedom was eternities away, at least a hundred yards. Another had taken possession of his toilet case and was having fun with it. Slowly and libidinously he was squeezing the contents of a tube of toothpaste onto a hair brush, muttering something about the jewels that Jews notoriously smuggled out of the country in toothpaste.

While one of the older officials half hesitantly, half with obedient zeal, frisked the little man, a third SA man inspected the other traveler's passport. Immediately attention was diverted from the textile merchant; the passport went from hand to hand, the official and the SA men nudged each other, whispered, exchanged meaning glances. Obviously they had been expecting the traveler, were informed of his arrival and had received special instructions as to his treatment.

"You're traveling on a special mission, Herr Professor," said the SA man, and the simple statement had about it that ring of fraternizing impudence which small men display when their official position permits them to sit in judgment on those greater than themselves. At the same time it had a certain ring of respect of which the subordinate soul cannot so easily divest itself; but both were combined with a concealed irony expressed in the emphasis placed upon the "Herr Professor."

The Professor nodded; he did not look at the SA man, however, but kept his gaze on little Herr Steiner, who stood there in his shirtsleeves and now, when he seemed to have been forgotten, stared wide-eyed with all the greater fear.

It was at this instant that the dubiousness of his mission dawned on the Professor with frightening clarity. He was sorry that he had not confided in his traveling companion, had not responded to his trust with trust; he wished that his passport too would be examined with penetrating closeness, his baggage also rummaged through; he was tempted to tell little Herr Steiner now, in front of the SA men, what brought him in such a shamefully comfortable manner out of the land of terror and into the promised land of freedom. But there was no opportunity; the officials had already handed back his passport, given no more than a fleeting glance at his cases and left. Only one of them, the one with the beery face, seemed to have changed his mind. He returned, tore the door open and called out to the Professor, *"Auf Wiedersehen."* Only two words, but the man might just as well have stuck out his tongue, the words sounded scornful—"Good-bye, but I don't imagine I shall ever see you again!"—or threatening: "You just wait till we meet again!" The door slammed shut, the glass rattled, but Professor von Benda smiled, because he felt that these two words, at least these, would justify him in the eyes of little Herr Steiner.

"It's like this, Herr Steiner . . ." he began, but he stopped at once, because he read in his traveling companion's eyes—the textile merchant had long since begun picking up his scattered things—a suspicion which a few sentences would not dispel. A few sentences or more—there were now tens of thousands of Steiners, scattered over the globe, a Diaspora in the Diaspora, and he would not be able to go to all of them and say: "It's like this, Herr Steiner . . ." And even if he could, he wouldn't be allowed to finish the sentence. He was ashamed of his weakness, like someone who finds a burden too heavy as soon as he has taken it onto his shoulders.

At the Swiss station Herr Steiner quickly took his leave, and as the Professor gazed after him it seemed to him that the little refugee was also running away from him. He stood hesitantly, and immediately afterward was greeted by a man who gave his name as Stechlein and introduced himself as an official of the German Consulate in Geneva.

The gigantic young man with light blond hair falling over his forehead belonged to a type which in the past the Professor had never met, but which now kept emerging everywhere, as though certain regimes kept certain types up their sleeve in order, at the right moment, to unleash them throughout a country or a nation. The Professor had been in the habit of maintaining a certain distance in his behavior toward people, a distance that was reduced only in the case of his friends and his closest collaborators; now there seemed to be people who treated him distantly, and although the distance remained the same its reverse direction was a new experience for Heinrich von Benda. Stechlein did not lack politeness, but it was the politeness shown toward a traveling Zulu chief, an exotic blackamoor of whom one could not be sure that at home he did not eat human flesh.

Stechlein led the Professor to a waiting limousine. The town was quickly crossed and left behind. The Swiss valleys stretched lazily in the sun of the July afternoon; the expression they "bathed" in the sun was fitting, for they looked as well nourished, as carefree, as totally unoccupied as the sun-hungry holiday-makers. Near Neuchâtel, which Herr Stechlein insisted on calling Neuenburg—a perfectly legitimate name which nevertheless expressed a forcible seizure—the road narrowed and they drove between vineyards that were nature and yet not quite nature, since every trunk, every branch, every vine, betrayed the hand of man. The landscape, although it was not unlike the hilly country by the Wachau or the Mosel, appeared to the Professor entirely new and unfamiliar, as though in a free country the landscape too was different.

The car, driven by a silent chauffeur, was making its way to Geneva; so Herr Stechlein had told the Professor, without waiting for his acceptance. The Évian Conference, the Professor's goal, had been postponed by a day because of the late arrival of some of the delegates.

"The usual sloppy incompetence. But you won't mind that, Herr Professor." No, he wouldn't mind that, replied Heinrich von Benda, but he would like to go on to Évian next morning —he said that for no reason, said it merely to demonstrate that he had not yet entirely lost his own will, or rather had regained it. Certainly, just as the Herr Professor wished, said Herr Stechlein. He would have to speak to the Consul in Geneva first, but there would be no difficulty about continuing the journey. "Only I must ask you to keep in continual contact with me. I will give you my private number. You had better ring me from the post office, under no circumstances from your hotel. I must ask you not to forget for one moment that you represent the Jewish Community and nothing else."

"I have never supposed that I represented the Greater German Reich," answered the Professor.

During the rest of the journey he gazed out at the landscape.

Professor Heinrich von Benda, at that time simply Heinrich Benda without the "von," was born in a cheap Viennese apartment house whose appearance had not changed at all since its

construction, unlike the street in which it stood. The latter—
Omen est nomen—had taken full account of the vicissitudes
of history. Situated in the Leopoldstadt, a predominately Jewish quarter, the street was called Prateraugasse in 1873, the year
in which Heinrich was born; in 1929 it was rebaptized Hein-
rich-von-Benda-Strasse; nine years later it received the name
Frauenfeldstrasse after an old militant of the Party. The boy's
father, Herschel Benda, who called himself a vehicle renter—
in reality he only owned two cabs, one open and one closed,
which he drove himself, and four horses, two of them white—
Herschel Benda moved to the little north Hungarian town of
Alsószatmár on the Russian frontier, where he leased the
restaurant for third-class passengers. The boy, the only survivor
of three children—his mother had died early—was brought
up by one of his mother's sisters, the lucky one of the family
one might say, who had married a well-to-do Vienna dispensing
chemist. This man, a converted Jew and driven by other ambitions, sent Heinrich Benda to the university, predicting for the
boy a great future, which was perhaps meant to fulfill his
own secret hopes. Heinrich Benda did not disappoint him. He
was barely twenty-four when he qualified as a doctor of medicine *summa cum laude;* only six years later he received the
title of honorary professor. For a time he was spoken of as
the favorite pupil of the great Zuckerkandl, but, later, it was
said that Zuckerkandl had been the teacher of the great Benda.
As early as 1909, when he was thirty-six, Heinrich Benda was
nominated professor; he was the youngest professor in the
monarchy, and at thirty-nine the first man ever to become an
imperial councilor at this young age.

This career was all the more astounding because even during the reign of Emperor Francis Joseph I, which, after a
bloody and violent beginning, was marked by a certain liber-
alism, Jews were discriminated against within the limits of
practicability. Heinrich von Benda's rise would have been
hampered or at least considerably delayed if the learned surgeon had not made a revolutionary discovery in the field of
chronic nephritis, especially nephritis of the secondary con-
tracted kidney. Thereafter he was inundated with invitations
to the world's leading universities, including Oxford and Ley-

den, Harvard and the Sorbonne; and since everyone wants
what everyone else wants, Vienna was determined not to lose
the famous urologist. In addition—and undoubtedly linked
with this—Professor Benda, besides other members of the il-
lustrious imperial family, was permitted to treat His Majesty
the Emperor. Relations between the monarch and the doctor
were the subject both of authenticated stories and of amusing
anecdotes, which made the rounds of the Viennese coffee-
houses.

It was around this time that it was suggested to the Professor that he should become converted to the Catholic faith—
racial prejudices were not yet demanded, people contented
themselves with religious ones. To the general surprise, the
Professor flatly rejected the proposal—surprising indeed because at that time to change one's religion was as customary as
to move from one house to another—but also because no one
had thought of Heinrich Benda as a "good Jew." He never had
been a "good Jew"—he had quickly forgotten his school
Hebrew, maintained a relationship with God that required
no intermediary, felt himself a doctor, an Austrian, a Viennese,
in that order, and last of all, a Jew. If he nevertheless refused
to accept standing baptism, this was entirely in keeping with
his character, in which humility and pride existed side by side
in perfect harmony. He believed that he could do nothing that
was not predestined in the councils of God—this was his humility; but he was far too proud to regard opportunism as anything but servility. He was convinced that the monarch needed
Professor Benda more urgently than Professor Benda needed
the monarch.

His Majesty accepted the Professor's refusal in silence; indeed, as subsequent events were to show, it must have wrung
from him a certain admiration. In 1912, when the Emperor
had laid down to die and yet, with the Professor's help, most
cheerfully rose again, he astonished those around him by expressing the wish to elevate Professor Heinrich Benda to the
nobility. In the Austro-Hungarian monarchy no other doctor,
even of the right faith, had enjoyed such a distinction, and for
a highly irrational reason: because His Majesty was of the opinion that a man "who messed about in one's backside" couldn't

be a nobleman. Whether because of the Emperor's offensively low opinion of the doctor's status or his all too high opinion of the noble's, the Professor once more declared that he attached no value to receiving the august favor. Thereupon a lively exchange began between the Hofburg and the imperial councilor's villa in Hietzing, since it was quite unthinkable that His aged Majesty should be apprised of the Professor's ingratitude.

Then the problem solved itself. After the Professor had paid a visit to the Schloss Schönbrunn—it was 1915 and the Emperor was weighed down by the burden of the war that had been forced upon him—the monarch expressed the wish that the Herr Hofrat should ask a favor. Naturally the Emperor was convinced that the well-informed Professor would request the title of nobility. Either because on the spur of the moment he could think of no other way out, or because he had long since planned the joke, the Professor replied that he himself had received more honors than, in his humility, he deserved, but he knew an old man to whom the imperial favor would give great happiness, gilding the evening of his life. If his father were raised to the nobility the monarch could be sure of the Professor's gratitude. It speaks for the Emperor that, although he misunderstood his doctor's presumptuous request, he nevertheless responded to it with a hearty laugh.

"So you don't want to be the first of your line," he said. "You want to start off as the second generation to bear the title of nobility. What is your father's name, Herr Hofrat?"

"Herschel Benda," replied the Professor.

"Does he live in Vienna?"

"No, in Alsószatmár."

"Fine. Then in future he will be called Herschel Benda, Chevalier d'Alsószatmár." Thus Herschel became a nobleman and the ancestor of the knights of Benda. He died the following year, the same year as the Emperor; his tombstone bore in simple letters the words: HERSCHEL BENDA, CHEVALIER D'ALSÓSZATMÁR, INNKEEPER AND VEHICLE RENTER, and the tombstone would still proclaim the fairy story of a better world, if the Jewish cemetery at Alsószatmár had not been destroyed by wild hordes in 1941.

Long before the memorable episode at Schönbrunn, when

he was still a young doctor, Heinrich Benda married the daughter of a well-to-do Jewish banker, who bore him a son, Felix,
and two years later a daughter, Elisabeth. The marriage lasted
twenty years and was as uneventful as only happy marriages
can be. Then the Professor's wife died of the Spanish flu that
followed, like a second earthquake, on the heels of the First
World War. Like many great men, Heinrich von Benda proved
to have little talent as a father. He showed such an unjust
preference for his daughter, a beautiful, sickly and unusually
gifted girl, over his reserved, complex and cantankerous son
that Felix could not help regarding his father as coldhearted
and himself as superfluous, neither of which was true, or only
in the sense that Heinrich von Benda could not bear to be
alone, but at the same time had no need of society. He had
lived alone with his wife, now he lived alone with his daughter; he could not divide himself with more than one person.

Felix was not the only one who had difficulty in understanding Heinrich von Benda. He was an artist—all great doctors
are, for if it were not so, all doctors would be equally equipped
and one would be as good as the other—he was an artist, was
possessed and, like most artists, often displayed apparently
schizophrenic behavior. When you heard him talked about by
those who worked with Professor von Benda—doctors, nurses,
students, laboratory assistants—you observed recognition turn
into admiration, admiration into love. They praised his modesty, kindness, directness, were ready to answer his call at any
time of the day or night, to stay with him and stand by him;
he insisted on operating personally on the mother of a nurse,
and on the son of a laboratory assistant and grumblingly thrust
aside all payment, all thanks; he actually paid secretly for a student's studies and gave him private lessons. On the other hand
one heard that he unceremoniously threw out hypochondriacal
patients who wasted his time, kept highly placed personages
waiting for hours for no visible reason, admitted patients who
had just arrived before others who had been waiting a long
time; failed to respond to invitations and often did not even
apologize for his absence.

The fear of fears, the fear of wasting time, dominated vast
areas of his being. He wasn't an egotist, as Felix contended,

or at least had the good excuse that his time did not belong to him, so he could not give it away. He who stands protectively in front of "his" time is merely, so far as other people are concerned, standing protectively in front of himself. The theft of goods and money is punished by imprisonment, whereas hardly anyone thinks anything of stealing other people's far more irreplaceable time; the theft of one's own and other people's time is looked upon with favor, it makes the thief popular, whereas to be miserly with one's time makes one most unpopular. Thus many people thought the Professor unworldly, indeed an eccentric; in fact he was bound to create this impression because he liked to deal with the world on his own, without the intervention of society. He read a great deal, and not only the latest scientific publications; he was one of the few people in Vienna who had a subscription to the London *Times*. He rented a box at the Opera and the Burgtheater; twice a month he listened to an opera, with the same frequency he saw a play. His favorite pastime, however, was his porcelain, which did not remain unnoticed in the world of collectors, for, without neglecting old pieces of another manufacture, he had specialized in Viennese porcelain of the eighteenth century. Chocolate cups, pipes and *trembleuses* of du Paquier porcelain, comedy and canapé figures, a number of family groups from the state factory, along with gods, heroes and emperors from Sorgenthal, were the highlights of his collection.

Few people knew Professor von Benda, few could explain the oddities of his character. He was an eccentric, for he was happy. Up to 1938, the year when history suddenly stepped out of the pages of history books, Heinrich von Benda was in the habit of saying that the death of his wife had been the only tragic event in his life. That man is happy who believes that destiny fulfills a useful purpose and that he himself has a useful part to play in the scheme of things—Heinrich von Benda believed both. Although he knew that disaster and misfortune may befall one, he first looked to see whether perhaps he had failed to assist kind fate; if nevertheless disaster and misfortune befell one without any such failure, they were simply due to blind chance. Since he was happy, his need for love was small. His two-volume work, *Nephrosclerosis and Other Dis-*

eases of the Kidneys, was the standard textbook of modern urology in every university; he cared little about his personal popularity or unpopularity. His pride, related to arrogance, but as different from it as one brother from another, sprang not from his continual rise, not from the recognition he had won, not from the perpetual honors and confirmations, but from the absolute sense of his own necessity.

He was not surprised to discover, at the age of almost sixty, that he was in love with a girl of twenty-seven, nor was he surprised that she returned his love and became his wife. When he told Bettina that he had been waiting for her, he had no fear of being ridiculed; on the contrary, he explained his feelings by his age. He had attained the pinnacle of his professional career, was, if not wealthy, at least well-to-do. His children were married. Since he called out into himself, an echo must clearly answer him. Let the malicious and disgruntled speak of panic at the prospect of a closing gate. He knew better, knew that a door had opened—a thousand times he had opened the door between his consulting room and his private apartment and then closed it again. Now he left the door open, that was all.

Bettina Wohlgemuth came of a well-known Protestant family, or rather the family had become well known through Bettina's father, one of the favorite portrait painters of the turn of the century. The gentle, dark-haired and dark-skinned girl, two years younger than Benda's daughter, had had artistic ambitions of her own and when the Professor met her, she was preparing for the final examination at the Academy of Fine Arts. She renounced the examination and her career: she was fully occupied brushing off the dust that had accumulated during thirteen years of the Professor's bachelor life. Five years later, in the cold early spring of 1937, when a boy was born, the very image of his mother—they baptized him Heinrich, he was to bear his father's name and be raised in his mother's religion—Heinrich von Benda was more intensely aware than ever of his happiness; not that this feeling was new, or that it took him by surprise. It was the autumnal fruit of an old tree, and when, if not in autumn, should trees bear fruit? Only when he thought of his other two children was the Professor sometimes seized by a malaise, because it seemed to him as though they were not his children at all, as though he had now become a father for the first time; yet he was reassured by the thought that it is evening and night which bear morning within them, that men should not have children until they can devote themselves to them.

The political events of the last few years, which finally led up to the trip to Évian, had not passed by the Professor without having left their mark. He was no *homo politicus;* he followed developments with attention, sympathy and a certain concern but dispassionately, because he couldn't for one moment envisage a revolution in Austria. It was true that the torchbearers of doom were already marching through the streets of Vienna, everywhere members of the illegal party were to be seen in their white stockings and leather shorts, and drunken wearers of brown and purple shirts did battle in taverns and meeting halls, but the Professor thought that the baroque stage scenery in front of which these incredible events were taking place was bound in the end to swallow up the squalid future. Anti-Semitic demonstrations and riots were the Sunday pastimes of a youth born blind; many people shouted *"Heim ins Reich!"* and *"Ein Volk, ein Reich, ein Führer!"* and *"Heil Hitler!"* and *"Juden hinaus!"* but the din of the street rarely penetrated over the tall hedges of the Hietzing villa. Two or three times screaming groups broke into the lecture hall where Professor Heinrich von Benda was teaching, but they were put to flight by his students. It is true that some of them obeyed the demand to boycott the "Jew's" lectures, but the hall was in any case too small for the number of those thirsting for knowledge. The Professor believed that the best way to respond to vulgarity was to ignore it.

Hofrat von Benda, as everyone said, had remained extraordinarily young. But old age leaves no one untouched; it seems to attack first those cells that produce imagination. He did not believe in the deadly outcome of the pestilential evil because he could not imagine it. Austria, he thought, had survived so much history that it would also survive this hysteria; he was seriously convinced that the human hand can set up frontier posts against epidemics, that the bacilli would halt at boundary stones.

There was no lack of warning voices, even in his own house. It should have struck him that Bettina heard more, knew more than he, that their friends confided many things in her which they concealed from him. Hesitantly and cautiously she tried to talk about England, France, even America, to persuade him to lecture abroad, if not to emigrate, but he reassured her, interrupted her, sometimes becoming impatient and angry when she reiterated her warnings. Whether that which was hastening toward them with the inevitability of catastrophe was beyond his imagination, whether he could not renounce his faith in his country and his people, or whether it was a matter of a more personal, entirely unconscious process—namely the fear that outside his habitual environment he would become as old as he was and be no more than an old man with a young wife and a small child—he clung more than ever to an optimism that is often the only thing left to old men.

Then came those March days in which the Austrian chancellor, till then the grotesque caricature of his German model, realized, too late, that his secret idol would cast him aside, that the jaws were already open to swallow the little fish which the waves were washing toward the great whale. In the Ballhausplatz they looked around desperately for allies, and when the name Benda cropped up, they did not hesitate to send the president of the Jewish Community to the internationally famous Professor; but Heinrich von Benda found this belated zeal ludicrous, indeed repellent. The chancellor and his "Fatherland Front," till now so impudent, so sure of themselves, could doubtless continue without him.

On the 11th of March, 1938, the German troops crossed the Austrian frontier to the tumultuous acclaim of the population of the "Ostmark." On the 13th of March the *Anschluss* was effected; on the 10th of April it was confirmed by a plebiscite.

Professor Heinrich von Benda was arrested on the 15th of May, a Sunday.

The Professor was fetched from his bed by the SA at six in the morning and taken to the police prison on the Rossauer Lände. His arrest surprised rather than frightened him, if only because he felt as unfamiliar in the role in which he was now cast as though he had been dressed up in carnival clothes. He did not imagine himself to be immune to dangers, diseases and the blows of fate; he had made no pact with the dark powers and had received no safe-conduct from the bright ones, but he was convinced that for each individual destiny held ready certain particular dangers, diseases and corporal punishments, just these and no others. That he could be arrested and carted away like a criminal, without a word of explanation, seemed incredible to Professor Heinrich von Benda, even while it was happening.

The company that awaited him in Cell 21 increased the feeling of unreality, for it actually was company in the best sense of the word. If he had been locked up with vagrants, murderers, thieves, he might have realized more quickly that the law was no longer in force, neither the law of the land nor the law of his own life. But the fact that he was sharing the narrow cell, scarcely large enough for a single prisoner, with a lawyer, a theatre director and an official of the Jewish Community, that is to say with men whom he was accustomed to meet in the street or in public places, completely convinced him of the unreality of the experience. The almost comical nature of the situation —for this was how Professor von Benda experienced it at first —was brought into relief and emphasized by the behavior of his fellow prisoners. Armin Silberstein, the president of the Jewish Community, assumed the task of introducing the gentlemen to one another—"Herr Rechtsanwalt Doktor Schönglas, Herr Professor Hofrat von Benda," "Herr Theaterdirektor Grünwald, Herr Professor Doktor von Benda"—with as much ceremonious politeness as if they were in the foyer of the State Opera House. The distribution of the beds—two bunks were fixed one above the other on each wall—was also carried out according to the rules of extreme politeness. "No, Herr Professor, of course you will sleep down below"; "Please, Herr Doktor, do use my pillow"; "I shall be perfectly all right without the blanket, Herr Rechtsanwalt."

The idea that he would be spending the night here, indeed several days to come, seemed to the Professor unbelievable, and this feeling did not change when he learned that the theatre and cabaret director had been here a full seven weeks, that

the advocate had been arrested a fortnight ago; only Herr Silberstein, in the *terminus technicus carceris,* had been "jugged"
the previous day. With the exception of Dr. Schönglas, the
lawyer, none of them had been interrogated.

It was not until the midday meal—four tin bowls were
pushed in by a warder—that the dull pane of glass before
Heinrich von Benda's eyes, through which he had till now been
looking at events, gradually began to clear. He sat at the little
table with Silberstein; the two others had settled down on
their bunks. Dr. Schönglas and Fritz Grünwald, cabaret director and comedian, were discussing the food, which was
rather more plentiful today, a Sunday; were evaluating the
warders, the older and the younger, the kinder and the more
brutal; appraising the lavatory, whose flush Herr Silberstein, a
genius, had managed to repair; and this everyday conversation,
this unusual, incredible, monstrous conversation that was accepted as perfectly normal, this discussion between convicts
adjusted to their lot, first awoke the Professor to a consciousness of reality. He could not bring himself to ask his cellmates
the reason for their or his arrest; he didn't want to start a criminals' conversation about "what did they get you for?"—but the
comedian, who had understood the Professor's mute question,
turned to him and said, "They're locking up the cream of
Jewry, and we are the cream of the cream—but that's no reason to feel flattered. When we go out for exercise you will see
that the Rossauer Lände is filled with the cream of the cream
to the roof."

With this and similar *bons mots* Fritz Grünwald tried
throughout the next few days to entertain his cellmates, though
assuring them that in his case this was in no sense gallows humor: "This is the only sense of humor I ever possessed; people only applaud a clown when they're sure something is hurt-
ing him." Fritz Grünwald's wit was not new to the Professor;
without knowing him personally, he had often applauded the
comedian. When the little, lean man with the bald bullet head
and the thick, black-rimmed spectacles appeared on the stage
of the Simplizissimus he had always been greeted with grateful laughter. During the past year hecklers had repeatedly interrupted the performance, even releasing swarms of mice on

the stage and in the auditorium, but this had not perturbed
Fritz Grünwald. "In fact I was rather reassured by it," he now
declared to the Professor. "All my life I was never quite sure
whether I wasn't winning applause from the wrong gallery.
You know, Jewish jokes are a revolver that has the unpleasant
characteristic of firing simultaneously forward and backward.
I looked at the mice and thought, You are very welcome messengers; obviously my jokes are being understood correctly by
friend and foe."

The Professor quickly took a liking to Grünwald. Behind
prison walls the everlasting exchange of deceptions, which we
call social life, becomes difficult if not impossible; since all ac-
quired traits of character are useless, the prisoner quickly dis-
cards them; since he is robbed of his will, his will to humbug
is also paralyzed. The Professor found his surmise confirmed
that the comedian's wit concealed a Talmudic philosophy and
his humor a courageous melancholy. Grünwald's primary character traits appealed to him enormously.

For Armin Silberstein, on the other hand, the president of
the Jewish Community, the same who had come to see him
a few months earlier, Heinrich von Benda with the best will
in the world could feel no similar sympathy. He had always
had an antipathy toward organizers, delegates and committee
workers; if they represented a religious or humanitarian association his involuntary aversion developed into a rational distrust. If only the president of the Jewish Community hadn't
been a Jew! This was a paradoxical and probably rather dubious thought which worried the Professor. He himself was so
much of an assimilated Jew that he felt the word assimilation
to be purely historical and even then offensive. He found it
hard to accept the Jews from the east of the former monarchy
as his brothers—no, he would never have said anything against
them, if opportunity offered he would have taken them under
his protection, he even felt admiration for their proud isolation
and their hopeless obstinacy, but he simply couldn't feel broth-
erly toward them. At the same time he knew that his mute
aversion sprang from self-defense and this in turn was a concession to anti-Semitism. He condemned the anti-Semites but
feared to be lumped together with the eastern Jews by the anti-

Semites. At this point Heinrich von Benda was able to reason with himself, was able, by passing judgment on himself, to rein in his feelings, to which he had previously given no thought. In particular he observed the manner in which he identified himself with the alien Jews, in the sense that he wished them all to be shaped in his own likeness, that is to say with all those virtues which for centuries people had denied the Jews. Armin Silberstein, by contrast, seemed made for the anti-Semitic caricaturists. He was an eastern Jew with red hair and a red beard, a guttural voice and expansive gestures, with sad, protruding eyes that did not light up even when, as all too often, he told jokes and stories. Silberstein had come to terms with prison life in a way that intensely annoyed the Professor; annoyed him because Silberstein had never expected anything else from the *goyim*—an expression as repulsive to the Professor as any anti-Semitic swearword; annoyed him because his readiness to suffer had nothing heroic about it, but only an almost cowardly resignation; annoyed him, finally, because Silberstein's ability to obtain little advantages for himself and his cellmates appeared to the Professor a sign of the capacity for compromise which people attributed to the Jews and in which he wanted no part.

With the third of his new colleagues, Dr. Hugo Schönglas, the Professor quickly felt at home. The huge man with the physique of a gorilla and the skull of the Golem was one of Vienna's most celebrated defense lawyers, a stalwart fighter of tremendous forensic gifts and at the same time a notable theorist whose polemical writings against the Supreme Court had aroused attention far beyond the frontiers of his country. He came from an old Viennese family; his father had been a High Court Judge; his figure, not unlike Professor Benda's, was fitted for the growth of legends around it. It was said that he represented the poor out of pure love of justice and at considerable self-sacrifice, while the rich asserted that for them Dr. Schönglas's fees were "exorbitant." Dr. Schönglas could not come to terms with the injustice that had been done to himself and his cellmates. It was touching to see how he, who had never had a very high opinion of the law, now could not grasp its treachery, clung to formalities, drafted protests and pleas, talked about going on a hunger strike and contemplated all sorts of adventurous actions, threatened the warders and planted himself in front of them with clenched fists.

None of the prisoners heard from friends or relatives or learned of the events that were taking place outside the prison. During exercise the Professor caught sight of old acquaintances —doctors, lawyers, politicians and industrialists. They were driven around in a circle among murderers, burglars and thieves. He listened to the endless conversations of his cellmates but spoke little. The apathy that had come over him frightened him, like the symptom of an unknown disease. It was bound to be unknown to him, since only prisoners experience it: a state like death, in which all the life instincts appear to be paralyzed and which nevertheless springs from a life instinct, since life behind bars is only endurable when it is dozed away in a state resembling death.

During the day the Professor had little time to think of his wife and his child, for behind prison walls every hour of inactivity is so skillfully apportioned that although the prisoner finds existence too long, he finds the day too short. At night, when he lay awake on his bunk—little Grünwald above him breathed as softly as though even in his sleep he was considerate toward the others; Silberstein snored with an angry growl; Dr. Schönglas threw his massive body this way and that, the timber cracked at every joint—when the moon broke in through the bars, the Professor thought of Bettina and Heinrich. But in the unreality there was no outside and inside, no fixed points to which he could have clung, the self-evident became unattainable and the probable boundless; dead men appeared and behaved gaily, the living sank down into the grave; even freedom and imprisonment were indistinguishable, so that the Professor often wondered whether Bettina could set him free or whether he had to set her free.

Not until the fifth day did the Professor wake from his lethargy, become aware of where he was and what had happened to him. On that day Dr. Schönglas once more, this time for an insignificant reason, revolted against a warder, a middle-aged man who till now had treated the prisoners neither well nor badly, rather indifferently and as though they weren't there at

all. As other warders did from time to time, this man addressed
the lawyer with the familiar *du* when he told him he hadn't
washed out his bowl properly, or something of the sort. But
that morning Dr. Schönglas had worked himself up into a mood
of rebellious depression; his cellmates had already felt that
there was something in the air; he couldn't endure the humiliation a moment longer. He answered back, not saying anything
he wouldn't have said before, but this time also addressing the
warder as *du*. The warder hit out, striking the lawyer in the
face twice with the flat of his hand.

They stood against the wall as though paralyzed: the comedian with his face twisted, as if the blow had struck him, the
president of the Jewish Community white and helpless, wondering how he could grab Dr. Schönglas's arms and stop him
from striking back; but Heinrich von Benda clutched at his
heart, ashamed of doing so but unable to master the impulse,
because his heart had been seized by an agonizing contraction.
Nothing happened, at least nothing that any of the witnesses
had expected. The warder left, the key turned in the lock,
the three stood against the wall staring at Dr. Schönglas, who
stared unwaveringly at the door. Thus the three men stood
motionless, until Dr. Schönglas began to cry, a dry sob shook
his body, his lips moved, struggling with the weeping or with
a curse for which he could find no words, lips twisted in pain,
complaining, accusing, shivering, twitching like those of a
whipped child that doesn't know whether to cry; but not a
sound left his mouth, he remained mute, while a transformation took place in him. In a few seconds he changed before the
eyes of the others; his chest caved in, his shoulders collapsed,
his arms grew longer and longer, the tips of his fingers seemed
almost to be touching the floor. In the middle of the cell stood
a sick, wounded, mortally injured gorilla.

Silberstein was the first to recover himself. He led the lawyer to his bunk as though leading a blind man, pushed him
down, sat beside him, tried to talk to him. But only when the
Professor sat next to him did Dr. Schönglas speak his first
words: "I didn't hit him, I didn't hit back!" The rest of the
day he ate nothing; he remained lying on his bunk, his face to
the wall; he didn't undress, he lay like this all night.

That night the prison on the Rossauer Lände seemed to come to life. Cries for help, screams of pain, animal howls, echoed through the building; groans and whimpering came from the nearby cells; boots tapped on the stone floors, a shot rang out, the lights of the cars driving in and out of the yard passed across the ceiling of the cell. None of the prisoners in Cell 21 closed an eye, none of them dared to move, none dared speak. And when they were taken out for exercise next morning the yard was black with black uniforms: the SS had taken over the police prison.

At about five in the afternoon they came for Fritz Grünwald. He was entertaining his cellmates with imitations of a dozen well-known Viennese personalities, comedies simultaneously of character and of situation, for he pictured the first words each of them were likely to have uttered when they heard the news of the *Anschluss*. He was just giving an uncannily lifelike imitation of a folksy comedienne specializing in dialect acts, a fat, motherly woman from the outskirts of Vienna, dripping with kindness and *Gemütlichkeit* of the golden Viennese heart, who, according to Grünwald, must undoubtedly have stepped forward to the footlights when she heard the great news and cried out, "Give a cheer, folks, Hitler's here!"—then the door opened and the warder stepped in and took Grünwald away.

Grünwald did not come back, neither that day nor the next. In the morning the warder, an elderly and almost humane man, told them Herr Grünwald was in the next cell, in solitary confinement. The three men didn't believe it, and their anxious disquiet increased when they looked for Grünwald in vain during the next exercise period; also his meager belongings were not fetched from the cell, as would no doubt have happened in the case of a simple transfer.

Heinrich von Benda was the first to hear Grünwald's voice. It was next morning, at about five o'clock; dawn was already breaking behind the bars. The Professor woke with a start, sat up, thought he had awakened from a nightmare and was still hearing its echo. Fritz Grünwald was screaming. Now the two others were awake, were sitting up, listening. A man yelled, then a second man yelled. "Swine, Jewish swine!"—

"Did you fuck her, you Jewish swine?" They could hear every word, every obscenity, the whistle of the blows, the screams of pain, the yells of the torturers, the whistle of the blows.

The three prisoners hurriedly dressed, all at the same time, although this was contrary to agreement and routine. They couldn't move about in the cell and kept getting in one another's way. "We must do something," said the Professor—for the first time he urged the others to do "something," and they discussed what they ought to do, but they were like three shipwrecked men on a raft in the middle of the ocean discussing which port to make for. The Professor began to hammer on the door, ashamed of doing something that would only calm his nerves, or worse still, his conscience, while he knew very well that no one would hear his hammering, no one would answer it. Now it was quiet in the next cell, and also in theirs.

When the door opened, they saw a pair of black uniforms, seemingly without heads, they heard a voice: "Better call it an accident—in his cell." Grünwald was kicked into the cell; before that, it seemed, they had been carrying the slumped body under the arms. Grünwald fell with his face on the floor and lay without moving. The bolt of the door was pushed shut. Schönglas and Silberstein carefully lifted Grünwald and laid him on the bunk. He was in stockinged feet; his vest and underpants torn and blood-soaked, the man an empty blood-drenched sack. Little Herr Grünwald lay quite silent. Only when they laid him on his back did he utter a groan; his back was bleeding from the wounds cut by the whiplash.

A strange, icy calm took possession of Professor von Benda —icy, yet not as strange as had appeared to him for an instant. In this one instant he had been on the point of saying, "We must call a doctor," a sentence he had not uttered since his early youth. For a moment he had forgotten that he himself was a doctor, but now he knew it again, and for a short while he acted as impersonally as a doctor who cannot do justice to his profession in any other way. He took off his jacket, rolled up his shirtsleeves, knelt down beside Grünwald. He examined the wounded man—pulse, heart, lungs, neck, kidneys, liver—but he did it only out of a sense of duty or habit; after the first fleeting palpitation he knew that here the doctor's art,

as laymen call it, had come too late; he knew that Grünwald
would die. He had seen hundreds of people die, but although
he had never become accustomed to death, death had nevertheless taken him into its confidence, death whispered to him
whom it already possessed and would not release. He looked
into Grünwald's little face, from which all traces of life had
vanished. The bone of the fine nose was broken, one eye closed,
a bloody lump, and because the blood had run from both corners of the mouth, the lips formed a half circle that ended at
the point of the chin, like the weeping mouth of a melancholy
sun in children's drawings. The Professor looked into the
face and remembered that he had never seen the comedian
without glasses; when he washed, Grünwald was in the habit
of turning away, as though afraid of being caught without his
thick horn-rimmed spectacles. The Professor had the feeling
that Grünwald recognized him, that he was returning his gaze
gratefully and beseechingly, but this might have been an illusion; the dying always have a grateful and beseeching look.
He did not rebel against his inability to help, as he had rebelled for a lifetime; it almost reassured him to know that he
would have been just as unable to help in the operating room,
under the arc light, with all his instruments at hand, surrounded by anesthetists, assistants and nurses. The lawyer and
Silberstein stood behind him holding cloths and sheets in
readiness; Dr. Schönglas brought a bucket of cold water, but
the Professor stood up and shook his head. He took the coarse
horse blanket and carefully spread it over Grünwald. "He's
dead," said the Professor, although Grünwald was not yet dead
—he did not die until the words had drifted away. There was
nothing to be seen of one eye, but the other was wide open,
and as the Professor closed it he was surprised to see how light
it was.

They were standing in silence around the dead man as the
door opened again and the warder entered.

"You're coming with me," the warder said to the Professor.

"He's dead," said the Professor to the warder.

"You haven't seen anything," the warder said to the prisoners, and as he said it he looked at the dead man, as though

this applied to him too, to the dead man. Then he turned to the Professor and said, "Bring your junk with you."

The Professor packed his little bag.

Outside, the prisoners were at their morning work. They were sweeping and scouring and scrubbing the floor, which only grew even filthier under their rags and brushes and brooms. The Professor's shoes became wet in the dirty water; no one looked up at him; he recognized this man and that, but even they did not look up. He walked quickly and asked himself why he felt no fear. He had never pondered whether he was brave, at least not in a physical sense, for physical courage was not a characteristic one either possessed or did not possess; it was a condition depending upon circumstances, it came upon you or abandoned you, sometimes you could conjure it up, even if it was alien to you, and often it arose entirely of its own accord. The Professor had been burdened with responsibility from early life, but responsibility was the antidote to fear; that man alone was brave, in the truest sense of the word, who had no responsibility and yet was not afraid. The Professor did not know exactly what he was responsible for now, but it seemed to him that he was responsible for Silberstein and Dr. Schönglas and for the prisoners who were scrubbing the floor and for the dead man in Cell 21.

In the room to which the Professor was taken there was only a bony man of tubercular appearance. He was wearing a double-breasted jacket that was too short and too tight, with wide lapels and the Party badge in the buttonhole. He sat behind a filthy desk under a picture of the Führer which, being too big for its frame, bulged out of it.

The man pushed a sheet of paper across to the Professor and told him to sign it.

Heinrich von Benda took his spectacles from his nose, put them in his breast pocket, and drew out a second pair, his reading glasses. The sheet of paper was a duplicated release form on which the Professor's name had been filled in, together with the date of his birth, the date of his imprisonment and also that day's date, the date of his release. The form further stated that the undersigned remand prisoner, Benda, Heinrich, No. 17884, confirmed that he had been treated with complete correctness, had suffered no injury to health or possessions, that therefore he voluntarily renounced all claim to damages, that he would spread no rumors, slanders or other lies, especially none that might damage the reputation of the German Reich, of German justice or the German community. The Professor read the faded lines, read every word, and as he read Fritz Grünwald looked over his shoulder. A number of excuses for his treachery occurred to the Professor—that he had no alternative, if he did not want to end up like Fritz Grünwald without benefiting anyone; that he had a wife and child and pupils and patients; that this signature did not bind him to anything except perhaps to a necessary freedom—but he dismissed these excuses almost as despairingly as one usually calls them up. He knew that he was going to sign, he would sign, but he would not lie to himself. As he ran through the form for the second time the temptation of heroism came upon him, for an instant Heinrich von Benda savored the sweet senselessness with which heroes become intoxicated. But his common sense was stronger; he was immune to senselessness and heroism. Yet he delayed signing the lie in order at least to make the man with the badge aware that he could not be so sure of his victory over human dignity.

The man was quite sure of his victory. He took no notice of the Professor, busied himself with his papers, smoked his cigarette, and did not even look up. "You've been lucky. The Duke of Windsor made a personal appeal to the Führer on your behalf. Incidentally, you're forbidden to practice medicine. Once a week, on Monday at nine, you are to report at your local police station."

Forbidden to practice, thought the Professor, and he almost laughed. The man with the badge, or the Führer behind him, could no longer forbid him to practice; that had already been done by Fritz Grünwald, the comedian who lay dead in his cell and whom they would shovel into the ground by the prison wall.

He signed.

When he was at the door, the man called out something

after him. The Professor turned around. His little suitcase
stood in the middle of the room in front of the desk. He took
the suitcase and left.

Outside, in the freedom that was no longer worthy of the
name—the walls of the prison had merely been moved back
to coincide with the frontiers of the country—Heinrich von
Benda discovered a new meaning for an old word. "Disappeared" was the word, and it had become a terrifying syno-
nym for many others. When no one answered a telephone
call, when a telegram could not be delivered, when a letter
was returned unopened, people did not say "gone away" or
"not at home" or "moved," they said "disappeared."
    Elisabeth, the Professor's daughter, had disappeared along
with her four children—four girls. Had she and her husband
and daughters left for Palestine? This had been Bettina's hope;
she had gone every day to the house in which Elisabeth had
lived, but she could give the Professor no such consoling
news. If she had emigrated, Elisabeth would have said good-
bye to her stepmother, with whom she was on the most
friendly terms, other occupants of the house would have
known, the authorities would hardly have denied it. On the
other hand the occupants of the house knew nothing of any
arrest. One morning the Berenson family wasn't there anymore, they had disappeared, as they said with a shrug of the
shoulders.
    That Elisabeth had vanished without trace, had dissolved
into nothing, filled the Professor with all the more somber
foreboding because a tragic end was somehow in keeping
with her nature. It was difficult in her case to cling to that pious
hope which is often based on nothing more than the impos-
sibility of imagining the tragic end of a joyful being. Since her
earliest childhood tragedy had oppressed Elisabeth, now
thirty-five, like a circling thunderstorm. An exceptionally
talented pianist, she had almost been an infant prodigy, but
when, barely nine years old, she had been about to give her
first concert, she was stricken by a mysterious fever; when she

recovered she had lost, not her talent, but her courage. She
made a successful debut later in the hall of the Vienna
Music Society, but soon after this she met the banker Oskar
Berenson in Berlin—he called himself a banker, but in reality he merely dabbled in all kinds of financial manipulations
of a speculative and, so it seemed to the Professor, dubious
nature. The gentle, almost ethereal girl, with such a fine,
fastidious taste that there was something decadent about it,
married the robust, aggressive, in the most offensive way primitive upstart, and for his sake renounced her career. She gave
him four children to the accompaniment of unspeakable agony
and vanished into a world alien to the Professor. Four years
ago, however, after their flight from National-Socialist Germany, Elisabeth reappeared in Vienna and in the Professor's
life. It was chiefly due to Bettina that the relationship between
father and daughter once more became warm and close—with
one limitation, characteristic of Elisabeth's life which, like an
ancient Greek temple, seemed to be bordered by broken columns. Her marriage had broken, but like those columns remained an entity in its broken parts. Elisabeth was one of those
women who like to transfer their self-esteem onto their
husbands and to defend this pride that they have bestowed
all the more vigorously the less cause they have to do so, with
the result that pride becomes transformed into obstinacy, into
the stubborn and foolish wish to prove the best to the world
that had expected the worst. The more she knew how little
value Oskar Berenson had, the more stubbornly she defended
him or her own error; she refused to allow a divorce to demonstrate what everyone knew, and she—best of all—refused until it was too late. The planned emigration to Palestine, for
which Berenson had been working, could only take place
jointly, *en famille;* what personal destiny had torn was knit
together again in the most unnatural way by world events.
Where had she gone, where had she vanished?

Many of those after whom the Professor inquired had disappeared. It struck Bettina, although he himself scarcely
noticed it, that in this respect too he was not the same man he
had been before his arrest. With a few exceptions his true interest had been centered exclusively upon his closest family

and his patients. Now, suddenly, he was interested in everyone, forgotten friends, acquaintances whom he scarcely knew—maybe he regarded them all as sick, maybe he felt responsible for people who were as unknown to him as Dr. Schönglas, Silberstein and Grünwald had been before.

He worried about others, and others worried about him. The pattern of this concern for his fate was full of surprises that aroused in him doubts as to his knowledge of human nature. Men and women whom he had taken to be friends avoided the house in Hietzing; many people upon whose strength of character he had counted proved to be fickle; almost total strangers gave him veneration, solidarity, even love. Although the Professor was now in his sixty-fifth year he learned for the first time that it is not necessarily the most lovable people who are most deserving of love and that in a lifeboat one is better off with a few sturdy sailors than with passengers from the luxury cabins.

He didn't admit it to himself, but in the beginning he also approached Bettina shyly, with restraint and a distrust that was directed more toward himself than toward her. He had taken the place of her father, she the place of his daughter; for when Elisabeth entered into the incomprehensible marriage with Oskar Berenson he had lost his child. These had been the secret machinations of fate; Bettina needed a father, but Heinrich von Benda needed a child. It is not always weakness that clings to strength—strength just as often clings to weakness. Now the Professor had to admit to himself that he had fostered Bettina's dreamy helplessness, childish dependence, elfin playfulness combined with a roguish cunning. With her blue-black hair parted in the middle and combed straight back, with her enormous blue eyes in the heart-shaped face, with her slender, boyish body upon which the birth of the child had had no effect, she really did resemble the elves which her famous father had painted around the turn of the century—curiously enough long before her birth. Not that Bettina was incapable of seriousness. On the contrary, she was serious in the unusual manner in which children are serious; she took almost everything seriously, games, questions, character and logical consistency. Thanks to the role of father which he played, Heinrich von Benda had been made doubly aware of his age, but precisely the admiration, adoration, indeed deification which Bettina bestowed upon him, the glorified father image that he saw in her eyes, had kept him young. This is not so surprising considering that fatherhood consists only secondarily in being a certain age, but primarily in a happy responsibility. The Professor knew that for Bettina he was a father but not an old man, not a support but a pinnacle, not a statue but a model. The birth of the boy had made no difference to this; now he had two children who needed his protection, Bettina perhaps even more than Heinrich, for how was a child to succeed on her own in being a mother?

Not until he was in prison did Heinrich von Benda become aware of his age, for it is humiliation that old age finds most difficult to bear. In the night after his return home when he took Bettina in his arms, he asked himself for the first time whether he was not an old man who was sharing his bed with a young woman. Everything was the same, only it was not the same. In vain did he tell himself during the next few days that he could not be so petty as to consider himself less because outer circumstances were trying to debase him. He himself— who was that? One speaks of the surface of the water, yet no one has ever seen it, because it does not exist; it is part of the water, there is no depth without surface and no surface without depth. The status he had possessed, the work he had accomplished, the fame that had crowned him—these were not like clothes one could take off and yet remain the man one was; they were like the skin that one cannot take off without bleeding to death. He himself—who was that? The master who dealt with life and death, to whom his patients looked up, to whom his co-workers listened, and the man who took his wife in his arms had been one: from the mirror image of the day flowed the vigor that poured itself out during the night—vain to talk about the unimportance of the mirror image, as if one remained the same when the mirror image changed. He himself—who was that? He who is used to leading another by the hand does not remain the same when he himself has to be led.

The Professor did not allow himself to be deluded by

friends, nor by himself, nor by Bettina—by her least of all.
She acted with skill, intelligence, even with a certain tender
cunning. Although she looked younger, she was after all in
her mid-thirties and had that maturity which is all the lovelier
the earlier it reaches its peak. During these days, since the
Professor only rarely left the house and avoided contact with
strangers, she had to fulfill the function of one of those peri-
scopes that often project above the water or the earth as the
only visible sign of an existence beneath them; only through
them can those living under water or earth see. Bettina acted
as though she were only an instrument; what she learned she
presented to Heinrich von Benda as a mere fact, he alone was
to interpret her experiences. She acted as though she were
even more in need of help than previously—but lies do not
become better, and often they become worse, when they are
merciful. When she returned from the *Kommandantur* she
told him, almost like an adulteress, that she had been shop-
ping; she kept silent about her clash with a high official who
had suggested to her that she should leave the "old Jew"; she
did not complain about having been kept waiting at the Passport Office, as though she were one of the hundreds of sup-
plicants besieging this office.

If the Professor could not know such details, he did know
that she was not telling him everything, that she kept quiet
about many things, and at times deceived him. He woke every
morning with the resolution to help her and himself. Powerful patients all over the world remembered their savior, colleagues and universities promised their support, ambassadors
of foreign governments gave him to understand that entry
visas were waiting for him. Nevertheless it was only after long
hesitation that he made up his mind to sign an application
for an exit permit which Bettina had brought him and cautiously placed before him. How could he leave the country,
he said, as long as he had no certainty as to Elisabeth's fate?—
but probably this was only an excuse. He was seeking the lost
past, without which he could not imagine the future; and this
worry about the future was a sign of old age, for the shorter
the remaining time, the more valuable it appears, so that it is
not so much youth that thinks of the future as age, as that to

the aged the future appears hopeless once the past has been lost.

Bettina was afraid. She was the periscope through which Heinrich von Benda saw the world, but this periscope was not an inanimate instrument, it had its own eyes. When she put the application in front of him, she had to do so without betraying her anxiety, which would either have made him aware of his helplessness or even have aroused his suspicion that she did not want to live with him here. He was neither amazed nor upset when his application and request were answered by an unexplained, but apparently final negative; and her bewilderment grew when he received the refusal almost with satisfaction. It was now too late to tell him that she loved him for his own sake, that what was lost meant nothing to her, that his age was as indifferent to her as those external attributes of happiness which, because he was a man, he had believed himself to be obliged to bring her; she should have said this while the renunciation was still voluntary, while he still possessed something besides himself.

Bettina had secrets from the Professor, but he also had his secret, no less dangerous because it had the tenderest origin. The pain around the heart which he had first felt when the warder struck Dr. Schönglas had recurred two or three times with varying degrees of intensity but always extremely painful. Were these nervous convulsions a rebellion of the vegetative nervous system, a myocarditis caused by arteriosclerosis or an incipient angina pectoris? The Professor could not have said with certainty even if he had been a heart specialist. Apart from an occasional cigar, he had not smoked since his student days, but in prison he had started smoking again and now, as though to make up for lost time, he smoked twenty, thirty, even forty cigarettes a day—without doubt an expression of his nervous tension, but reassuring in so far as he could explain his condition by the sudden onslaught of nicotine. To go to a heart specialist for an electrocardiogram would have been the simplest thing, but the Professor dismissed this idea because, in the midst of his enforced passivity, he was obsessed by the need to remain always in a state of readiness. It was true that in reality he had nothing to do, but as in his early years when he had worked in hospitals he scarcely dared

to take off his clothes, as though he might be called at any moment. Once, on a Monday, on his way home from the nearby
police station, he went into a chemist's, wrote out a prescrip-
tion for nitroglycerin and hid the little round pills in the
domestic medicine cabinet. At the next attack, he decided, he
would take the medicine, as a means of diagnosis in reverse:
if the drug acted, then the diagnosis was definite—angina
pectoris, oppression of the chest, constriction of the coronary
vessels that supply the heart muscle with blood, arteriosclerosis or a cramp with a neurotic basis. Nevertheless he let the
next attack pass without making use of the sedative, and he
totally concealed his condition from Bettina. Work, prestige,
wealth, fame, had cast over him a shroud of invisibility under which his age had disappeared. Was illness, even self-pity,
to reveal what was hidden under this hood? He grudged himself the leisure that had been vouchsafed him at the wrong
moment; he did not curtail his cigarette ration, he did not
avoid excitement, he offered clandestine resistance.

June was hot and sultry that year. In the garden of the
Bendas' villa the lilac bloomed in every color: white, mauve
and also that dark purple tone which Heinrich von Benda
loved; along the garden fence stood the chestnuts that had lit
their red candles. The Professor looked out through the open
window and wondered at nature's blossoming indifference.
The house, although unchanged, appeared to him strange because, ever since he could remember, it had been only a part
of his life, but now it was supposed to fill his life entirely.
For men of his type time is like a currency that becomes value-
less when too much of it is in circulation. He tried to shake off
his lethargy, even tried to feel fear, like someone who inflicts
a wound on himself in order to find out whether he is awake
or asleep; but only rarely—when he made up his mind to
speak straight out to Bettina—did he come near the causes of
his condition. "Up to now," he said to her once, "the hospital
ward was split up into individual beds, now I see only
the whole ward: if I can't help all of them I don't know what
use it is to help a few only."

Summer drew nearer. When Bettina was at home, the Professor acted as though nothing had happened, or as though

what had happened was a mistake, or as though what happened did not concern him personally. For years he had carried around with him the idea that one day, when he stopped teaching and healing, he would complete a book on which he had already done a good deal of research and which he planned to call *Acute Nephritis and Its Chronic Sequels.* Now he could have finished the book, but he couldn't even set to work on it; he dealt with time like someone who has to steal the fruit in order to enjoy it. If he heard Bettina's footsteps approaching, he hurried to the desk like a schoolboy caught idling, leafed through books and papers, and once or twice actually announced that he didn't want to be disturbed. He played for hours with little Heinrich, who toddled to and fro on uncertain legs, or bounced the child on his knee, but when Bettina came he quickly left the nursery. Instead of emerging from the nursery, as in the past, as if it were a fountain of eternal youth, he felt that he grew older as he sat on the carpet, an old man who possessed nothing but the treasure of old men, a superfluity of hours.

If Bettina was out of doors, in the hostile city, he walked restlessly up and down. He too was seized by fear and thought out plans for flight—flight offered the only way out, because the refugee, unlike the emigrant, does not have to recognize his persecutors. He collected the mail from the garden gate, pulled down the blinds—the blinds stuck, as always, but he did not want to call the servant and could not adjust them himself. Since his youth he had been too occupied with kidney stones, uremia, blood transfusions, protein tests and surgical instruments to understand about jammed blinds. In the street, beyond the chestnuts, marching Hitler Youths or SA or SS men sang, and sometimes only a maid sang. Not everyone loved his chains, but for most people freedom was a luxury they could dispense with. The Professor picked up a porcelain plate, Johann Joseph Niedermayer, *ca.* 1775, looked at it absentmindedly, and asked himself if he felt sorry for himself, "self-pity" as the contemptuous expression has it; the contempt seemed to him hypocritical, because even pity for others is only pity for oneself. Why had he only now begun to think about himself, since precisely now it mattered nothing what

conclusions he reached? They had forced a release certificate
into his hand in the Rossauer Lände, and the lilac was giving
off its scent, and the girls were singing, and the post was functioning, and the porcelain stood in the glass case, and friends
demonstrated their loyalty, and in the night he felt Bettina's
cool feet, but he was a trapped animal which, once it is behind
bars, differs in no way from other animals: lions and asses, and
leopards and sheep—all the same behind bars.

One day the Professor remained alone in the house with
little Heinrich. It was getting on for evening. Bettina had
hurried to a friend who thought she had heard something regarding the whereabouts of Elisabeth. When the Professor
entered the semidarkness of the nursery, through whose curtains the evening sun was casting its last rays, Heinrich had
been sleeping for some time. The Professor stood beside the
cot and stared at the sleeping child, stared at the pink cheeks,
the obstinate mouth, the little fingers that were moving in a
dream. But this time he was overcome by neither sentimental
emotion nor melancholy nor pity; his lips formed themselves
into an ugly word. He murmured "son of a Jew!" He began to
speak so loud that he almost woke the child. "Heinrich Benda
Junior," he said, "son of a Jew, son of the Jew Heinrich Benda,
half-Jew, Jew's son!" He repeated the ugly words, like curses
and yet full of tenderness, attacker and protector in one person, mouthpiece of devilish scorn and mouthpiece of divine
wrath.

Finally his excitement abated and he drew up a chair and
sat down by the bed. He looked at the sleeping child through
the bars of the cot and he realized that his child was also in
prison. He felt ashamed. It seemed to him that he had only
loved himself, that he had forgotten Bettina and the child. His
love for Bettina came over him with a happy violence of which
he had considered himself no longer capable. His mood
changed, as with someone who has spent long enough counting
his wrinkles in the mirror and makes up his mind to accept his
face. The extraordinary destiny that had always been kind
still favored him; it had merely disguised itself for an instant
to frighten him. The hospital over which he had ruled almost
as long as he could remember was called the General Hospital,

and the name ought to have struck him long ago. They had driven him out of the General Hospital, but the whole world had become a general hospital, and he was still Professor Heinrich von Benda. He stood up and went downstairs through the garden to the gate and toward Bettina. He felt young again; his heart too was young and he thought of going into the bathroom and destroying the nitroglycerin. During the night of the twenty-first of June at one-fifteen the telephone on the Professor's bedside table rang. He had been sleeping with anxious watchfulness; even before switching on the light he reached for the telephone.

The call was from the Reich Governor's home. "The Governor is ill and wishes to see you. A car will call for you in fifteen minutes."

Bettina had switched on the light. The Professor asked for the number that had called and rang up himself, to make sure there was no mistake. Sure enough, the Hofburg answered. The car, said the Governor's secretary, was already on its way to Hietzing.

Bettina put on a dressing gown; while the Professor dressed they discussed what the call might mean. The Professor packed his doctor's bag, which he always kept in readiness, although it was a long time since anyone had disturbed his night's rest. He considered whether he should give Bettina instructions as to what to do if he should not return home, but he was tired of making wills.

One of the Governor's cars brought him to the Hofburg. There had been a cloudburst in the evening; the Heldenplatz, in which a few weeks earlier the Führer of the German Reich had received the homage of his fellow countrymen, looked like an abandoned, dimly lit high baroque ballroom.

The suite in the Leopoldine Wing, to which the Professor was led up the "Swiss Steps," was furnished in the rococo taste of the Empress Maria Theresa and her son, the second Joseph. The Professor remembered his professional visits to the dying Emperor of the dying monarchy.

In the Governor's bedroom, apart from the patient, there were only his secretary in SS uniform and a man in civilian clothes who introduced himself as a doctor; he gave his name, but the Professor did not catch it. It was a severe renal colic, explained the doctor, the third within a few days, the X-rays showed a urate calculus, evidently there were also others, irrigation of the pelvis of the kidney— "They are oxalate calculi, Herr Hofrat"—had proved fruitless, an operation must be seriously considered. A few hours ago, continued the doctor, he had given the Governor an injection to which he had reacted surprisingly well, nevertheless the patient had expressed the wish to consult the Professor before daybreak.

How much of this declaration was correct the Professor could not easily decide, but it was clear to him after a few minutes that he had not been brought here for a medical consultation. No renal colic, however serious, demands an immediate operation unless, which was certainly not the case here, uremia has set in. If an injection had been given it would have been morphia or a morphia preparation, but the patient showed none of the signs of any such medication. No doctor with a trace of sense, finally, would have discussed such a painful situation in the presence of the patient. Moreover it did not take a diagnostician of Heinrich von Benda's caliber to recognize that the man on the lace pillows of the imperial rococo bed was in no danger of his life.

The Reich Governor was half sitting up in bed. Heinrich von Benda had often seen pictures of him—almost daily the papers published photographs of this obscure Viennese lawyer who had led his country home into the Reich and was now reaping the fruits of his speculation. In the pale blue pajamas bearing the excessively large embroidered monogram A.S.I. the man looked incomplete. It occurred to the Professor that uniforms do not make people uniform but perhaps rather conceal their uniformity; in his pajamas the Governor had actually lost his collective personality. True, he was pale, but even apart from this his thin face in which the lines were too clearly visible, as in primitive drawings—the nose too large, the forehead too high, the eyes too regularly placed, the lips too curved—resembled the face of a figure of milk glass such as one buys at annual fairs and places of pilgrimage. Also—an unparalleled error if an attempt was being made at deception —the Governor hadn't taken off his rimless glasses that seemed somehow part of his glassy face, which anyone seriously ill would most certainly have done. The Professor's suspicions grew when the Governor gestured to his secretary and doctor to leave. Now he was certain that he had been called in so that later he could be accused of a medical error, perhaps even of attempted murder by poisoning, and thus be removed from the protection of his friends abroad.

He was soon to learn better. He was suffering from kidney stones, said the Governor, and he had also been given an injection, but that was not why he had sent for the Professor. In fact he wanted to take the opportunity of discussing with him a matter that he had had on his mind for a long time but which it was impossible to talk about in his official chambers. "Our conversation is strictly confidential," he said. "Even my immediate entourage must be led to believe that it concerns my health. I must command you to maintain absolute secrecy. Sit down."

Such an introduction might have introduced a confidential atmosphere, but this was by no means the case; the air, on the contrary, had become more threatening, as though the Governor had merely wanted to indicate what consequences a breach of confidence might have for his nocturnal visitor.

"The American President," he began, "has called a conference for the solution of the refugee problem, which is to meet on the fifteenth of July in Évian-les-Bains on Lake Geneva." He let the name of the French spa melt on his tongue like a delicacy. "The conference, in which thirty-two states are taking part, is called a conference for refugees, but in reality its one and only aim is to save the Jews. The President is of Jewish origin—his family used to be called Rosenwald. Naturally the President can't impose the Jews on the American people, eighty percent of whom are of German blood; therefore the other states are to be persuaded, compelled or blackmailed to accept a certain quota of Jews. Do you understand me, Herr Hofrat?"

Yes, said the Professor, he understood, although he could not understand why the Reich Governor found it necessary to tell him all this, and moreover under an oath of secrecy.

"Nothing can prevent us," continued the Reich Governor,

"from dealing with the Jews within the Reich. Nevertheless
we welcome the Évian Conference. Or rather, we should welcome it if we had proof that it was not merely to serve the
purpose of propaganda to stir up hatred against the Reich.
Do I express myself clearly?"

"Perfectly," replied the Professor ironically, but the man
in bed pretended not to notice. The longer the Governor
spoke, the more clearly Heinrich von Benda felt that he had
not been sent for in order to be humiliated, indeed that the
others were somehow dependent upon him. He had heard
nothing about the conference at Évian, but the news filled
him with such satisfaction that he had difficulty in hiding his
feelings. While he had been in prison, while he had been shut
away from the world in his house, the world had come to its
senses, had resolved, late but at last, to oppose with its united
strength the monstrous crime that was about to be committed.

"You must bear in mind," said the Governor, and he spoke
like someone who on the one hand has prepared a speech, but
on the other is delaying coming to the point, "that the Jews
have plundered our people and are still in possession of stolen
goods to the value of around nine hundred million dollars. To
permit the Jews to take this capital away with them would be
to permit the thief to get away with his haul, but it would also
mean allowing the Jewish war against us to be financed with
German money. The Conference will therefore have to face
the fact that we want to get rid of the Jews, but that this can
only be done after we have confiscated their property.
Secondly, the Conference would be well advised to speak of
a European Jewish problem—Europe knows the Jews and
therefore wants to kick them out. In Hungary, Rumania and
a few other countries laws dealing with the Jews are already
being drawn up; the other European nations will follow suit.
We have no interest in handing over the Jews from the Reich
without being certain that one day we shall find a Jew-free
Europe."

Although the Professor was preoccupied with thoughts of
himself and his puzzling role, he could not help observing the
man in the rococo bed, a man such as he had never met before. He remembered that the Governor had a clubfoot, and

almost ashamedly he thought of the primitive idea of the
Devil, the God-be-with-us, as Austrian peasants called him.
"God made him, and therefore let him pass as a man"—the
Devil was at times considered human. The Devil lay in the
bedroom of the Leopoldine Wing, his rimless spectacles on his
nose, speaking singsong Viennese, delivering a monologue
about Jews, millions and the future of Europe.

"Thirdly—to come to the real point, Herr Hofrat," said the
Governor, nevertheless breaking off, as though this third
thing, the point, was a hurdle which even the Führer's Governor could not take in his stride. In Germany, he went on,
there were about three hundred thousand Jews, and a further
hundred and eighty thousand or so in the Ostmark; the number of Jews in the whole of Europe amounted to another five
or six million. "At the present time the German Reich disposes of some half million Jews. The Führer, in whose name
I speak, is willing to hand the Jews over to other countries if
these countries are for their part willing to indemnify Germany for the damage caused by the Jews." The Évian Conference, the Hofrat must know, was counting its chickens
before they were hatched, since no power in the world could
force the German Reich to let its Jews go. In other words—
the Governor drew a deep breath—the German Reich was
prepared to come to an agreement on an export tax, two hundred and fifty dollars per person, not excluding women and
children, but in the case of families with several children, irrespective of the number, the German Reich was prepared to
accept a round figure of one thousand dollars per family. And
one more thing. The German Reich had no interest in permitting the emigration of individual Jews—"It goes without
saying that two hundred and fifty dollars would not be too
high a price for people like you, Herr Hofrat"—the Reich
Government wanted to hand the Jews over "as a whole or not
at all." Two hundred and fifty dollars per head, at a rough
estimate, would amount to about one hundred and twenty-
five million dollars, but the German Reich would not demand
payment in advance, it did not expect the impossible, and it
would be perfectly willing to discuss payment by installments:
"Here are the goods, here is the money." On the other hand,

the foreign countries would not be prohibited from protecting the other Jews of Europe against all eventualities and showing their good will by setting up a Jewish fund "of, say, three to four hundred million dollars," a measure which would, for example, benefit the four hundred thousand Jews of "so-called Czechoslovakia."

The Professor was overcome by the same kind of feelings he had when he was arrested, feelings not unlike his reactions to the pictures of certain modern painters: Salvador Dali, Wilfredo Lam, Chagall, Max Ernst, Carrà, Giorgio de Chirico. People, objects, figures, could be recognized in these paintings, but not in the original, true meaning of the word, since recognition implies remembrance; they were composed of parts of reality, but not in such a way that the parts formed a reality; reality was evading control and while maintaining its contours was given over to nightmare or hallucination: a man split in two, a hand with seven fingers, horses hooves on a woman's legs, insects the size of elephants, the transparent belly of a pregnant woman, a flying cow, a house built of shadows. But common to all these pictures was emptiness; even if the canvas was filled with colors and forms and lines it was still empty. Man came out of nothingness and returned into nothingness, a wanderer on marble tiles, a paralytic on the slide, a blind man on the rainbow. The Professor saw the rococo bed and the spectacles and the portrait of the children of Maria Theresa and the hands on the sheets and the darkness outside the windows, but all this appeared to him empty, meaningless and disconnected, a desert into which a furniture van had disgorged its desolate load. He now knew why the Reich Governor had sent for him, but he did not want to ease his task and he pretended not to know.

"Do you mind if I smoke?" he asked.

"Please do."

The Professor lit a cigarette. "If I understand you correctly, the German Reich wants to sell its Jews. For two hundred and fifty dollars a head."

"A Jewish life ought to be worth that much to world Jewry. Do you know Armin Silberstein?"

"I was in prison with Herr Silberstein."

"I have ordered his release. Silberstein is in the picture. He will ask you to go to Évian as representative of the Jewish Community. The Reich Government has refused to take part in the Conference. You will be representing exclusively—I say, exclusively—the Jewish Community, but members of the Conference will quickly realize that we should not have given you an exit and currency permit if we were not pursuing some particular purpose. You will remain in touch with our Geneva consulate. One of my men will visit you before your departure."

The Governor removed his glasses and rubbed the bridge of his nose. The Professor felt that he was seeing the Governor's eyes for the first time; they were blue and somewhat glassier than the lenses of his spectacles.

"What prevents the Reich Government," asked the Professor, "from making contact directly with the foreign governments?"

"Since you are very well aware of the answer I shall save myself the trouble of giving it to you. Moreover a Jew will be far better able to describe the situation of the Jews."

"I have not agreed, Governor."

"You are not a worse Jew than Silberstein, Herr Hofrat. When it becomes evident during spring cleaning that a line of merchandise has become superfluous, it is either sold or destroyed. And I must also emphasize another thing. We shall naturally refuse to accept Jewish money. If the foreign governments call a refugee conference they must also pay the price for the Jews."

The Governor put his glasses on again and dropped back into the pillows. The Professor followed his eyes. The frescoes on the ceiling depicted shepherds and shepherdesses at wanton play. A euphoric feeling came over the Professor at the thought that he had only hated, only feared these criminal overlords, that he had not despised them enough. It was the jailer himself who had opened the window on the world for him. The representatives of thirty-two countries were gathering in Évian. The Führer and his governors could not destroy the Jews without at least suggesting a deal, half a million Jews for a hundred and twenty-five million dollars. Here are the goods, here is the money. Perhaps the megalomanic regime was already coming to grief, perhaps it already bore within it the seeds of bankruptcy. Confiscated millions, but in a currency that was no longer negotiable, like stolen notes whose numbers are known to the police. The regime could not get by without its opponents' currency. Ransom money. When the kidnapper demanded a ransom he bowed before the law. Once the ransom was paid the law bowed before the criminal. Évian-les-Bains. The famous kidney spa, no coincidence. *"Évian lave les reins."* Perhaps Évian did not only wash kidneys, perhaps consciences could also be washed clean in Évian. If he accepted the mission, he would have the opportunity of speaking to the representatives of thirty-two nations. He thought of Fritz Grünwald. Should he not dare to do for half a million people what he would certainly have dared for one?

He was not averse to accepting the mission, he said, but he must make three conditions: the release of his cellmate, the lawyer Dr. Hugo Schönglas, the cessation of the persecution of the Jews during the Évian Conference, and an exit permit for his wife and his child.

"I can promise you the first two favors," replied the Governor. "The third 'condition' I cannot fulfill. You have my word that your wife, who is in any case an Aryan, will be unharmed—your wife and your child will be unharmed. On the other hand you will understand that we must have a guarantee that we shall see you again, Herr Hofrat."

"Under those circumstances I must have time to think it over."

"One of my men will call on you tomorrow."

Dawn was already breaking when the Governor's car brought the Professor to Hietzing. Now that the tension was beginning to recede, he felt once more the oppression in his chest that heralded an attack, but he resisted it as in his youth he had resisted an illness that threatened him before an important operation. The oppression gave way slowly, but the pain did not supervene, and from this Heinrich von Benda drew his medical conclusion: an illness which the will was able to resist could not be so bad, at all events it was not of an incurable, a fatal, nature. He no longer believed he was fatally ill.

Like someone who is on the alert, Bettina had dressed immediately after the Professor's departure. She was waiting for him in a light skirt and a summer blouse; her features showed no worry or fatigue, she looked young and enchanting.

They went into the library, the Professor sat in the armchair by the window, she settled herself on a cushion at his feet and looked up at him expectantly—expectantly and with a smile of relief.

Contrary to his return from prison, when he had spared her many grim details, the Professor concealed nothing. The details were still fresh in his memory and he repeated every word the Governor had said, described the person and deportment of the man of glass, not without a slight shudder, but he withheld any comment. He wanted to hear an unprejudiced verdict, wanted to compare it with his own. Her questions and remarks, quickly interpolated so as not to interrupt him, reassured him, because her indignation at what she heard resembled his own, was of the same fabric. That Bettina was free from the poison of anti-Semitism he had known, but he was grateful that she did not exaggerate in the opposite direction, as is often the case with those who wish only to see the Jews in a favorable light, in an attempt to see them different than they are and to salve their own consciences.

When he had finished, she jumped up, spoke of a sign from destiny, sat down again—but he started with dismay, for he felt she had only heard one side of his story, the one relating solely and alone to him and his journey. Yes, a sign from destiny, but she meant that differently from what he had at first thought. Since all the laws of decency had been broken, she said, he too was not bound by any, least of all by such a monstrous promise, the only important thing was to leave the country as quickly as possible and never to set foot in it again.

"There must be some misunderstanding," he replied. She couldn't seriously suppose that he would use the journey to Évian to escape, gambling with the existence of half a million human beings. Existence, the Governor had said, but he had meant life, life itself; the regime would use his flight as an excuse for revenge on an unheard-of scale, for a St. Bartholomew's Night without parallel, the night of the long knives, the total destruction of unwanted merchandise.

She looked at him as one looks at a child. He was so young and she so old! Old men had no time, therefore they emptied to the dregs every glass that was offered them; since they had no time they acted without skepticism and without reflection, as the young are wrongly said to do; since they had no time to lose they wanted to cheat mortality with a little immortality. How was she to dissuade him from his insane plan? She loved him not least for the courageous resistance with which, without consideration for himself, he had flouted old age, but here he was risking not his health, not his night's sleep, not a few years of life, but life itself.

She had thought of all that, she said cautiously, and she didn't mean that he should declare himself a refugee and emigrant the moment he had crossed the frontier; he must play the game to the end. Here he interrupted her.

"And what about you and Heinrich? You don't imagine . . . ?"

"Alone with Heinrich I shall manage," she replied. "In a few weeks we shall be with you. They won't dare to touch the daughter of Wolfgang Wohlgemuth. What thousands of Jews have succeeded in doing under the most difficult circumstances, I too shall succeed in doing."

"You don't understand. It's a chance that won't recur. Half a million people, perhaps more . . ."

"That's slave trading!"

"What's the alternative? They're going to wipe out the Jews."

"The world won't allow that. Didn't you say, yourself, the Conference means that the world won't permit it?"

"The world wants to save the Jews, therefore thirty-two nations have answered the President's call. But do they know what is happening here and what they have to do in order to save the Jews? I shall bring them the key to the prisons and

camps of Europe, those that have been built and those that
have only been planned. It is contemptible to offer human
beings like merchandise, but in freedom the merchandise will
be transformed into human beings. The nations of Évian will
pay with money—never has anything more contemptible been
used for a better purpose."

How could she tell him that he, more than thirty years
older than she, knew nothing about human nature? He who
was a Jew could not know what the others thought about the
Jews. She had never told him that her father, if he had been
alive, would have opposed their marriage; she had never told
him about the drawings which she had found in her father's
studio, of the loathsome caricatures that had completely
spoiled her father's work for her. What miracle did he expect
from the thirty-two nations? Did he really believe that they
were just waiting to sacrifice a few hundred million dollars to
save the Jews? He kept talking about half a million people,
but they were half a million Jews. Who would take them in,
who would pay for them? And what curse was this that forbade her to open his eyes, simply because he was a Jew and she
was not a Jewess? She had never seen him as different from
herself, yet now they were different, because there was something about which she could not speak. She would have liked
to fall on her knees and beseech him to think only of her and
himself, but that was the last resort. She still wanted to employ
reason and persuasion.

"Whether you sell or buy Jews," she said, "it's almost the
same. You can't play the role of the intermediary. You can't
let this repulsive bargain be·justified by the use of your name."

How many great deeds have remained unperformed, he
thought, because the women were too proud of their men.

"I know, I know," he said. "They chose me because of my
name. They want to use my name, but there's nothing to prevent me from speaking only in the name of the Jews. What
would Fritz Grünwald say if he heard that Professor Heinrich
von Benda thought himself too good to save the Jews?"

She contradicted him. She had often influenced him, but
she had done it cautiously. Now there was no time for cau-

tion. "What makes you think the offer is meant honestly? It may be that Hitler is only offering to sell the Jews because he is sure there will be no takers—and then the rejection will be attached to your name, people will say you should have known the gentlemen weren't running any risk: either they will get the money or they will say the world doesn't want the Jews any more than they do."

"That's precisely what I must make clear to the other countries. Évian cannot, Évian will not refuse."

A touch of anger came over her. "You forget who you are," she said. "You're a doctor, the greatest. Are you Moses, that you want to lead the Jews through the Red Sea?"

He almost answered with violence that she had no right to impute vanity to him, but for an instant he wasn't quite sure whether he was moved only by the fate of the Jews, or whether he did not want to escape from the deathly passivity that is called old age. Or was he really confusing his mission, which Pharaoh's governor had entrusted to him, with the mission which, thousands of years ago, the Egyptian had entrusted in the night to Moses and Aaron: "Rise up and get you forth from among my people, both ye and the children of Israel . . ." He dismissed the thought, laid his hand on Bettina's head and said, "I'm only a doctor, I know. But half a million patients who are sick to death have fallen into my lap. I should look ridiculous in my own eyes if I bothered about a few kidney stones."

Outside the light was spreading out like blue milk. The Professor felt no fatigue; after many wasted days, a day was breaking that must not be wasted.

"And what about me? And Heinrich?" she asked, refusing to be pacified. "You imagine you're thinking of us, but that's just what you aren't doing. What is to become of us if you come back from Évian defeated? They will say you were merely spreading horror stories—you don't know them! And if you come back having scored a success, or what you call a success, we shall not be allowed to cross the frontier until the last of the 'goods' has crossed it."

"I have no choice, Bettina. They are keeping you and the child here as hostages."

"When you come back we really shall be hostages. We two and you as well."

He tried to refute her arguments. He was like a man being tormented by a jealous woman. His torment is mixed with joy, pride and vanity, so that what is irksome also fills him with satisfaction. He had been sure of her love, but really only because he had been so sure of himself. He had often doubted whether tenderness could replace passion, whether intelligent enjoyment could take the place of tumultuous desire, whether sure moderation could be a substitute for happy chance; but he had heaped up so much wisdom and understanding and care on one side of the scales that the other, however heavy, shot up like an empty bowl. Now he was receiving the proofs of her love quite spontaneously, but this was one more reason for dismissing all plans, indeed all thought, of flight. He was ready for any audacity, but not for the slightest move which, if it failed, might have meant a permanent separation. He allowed her to wring from him no more than the promise not to leave with the irrevocable resolution to return; he promised to let events run their course freely and to make his decisions dependent upon them, not to make the choice between the ultimate consequences of his mission and his personal escape until he was in Évian.

"But now I must work," he said rising—and Bettina observed half happily, half in dismay that he, who after his arrest had been a different man, was now becoming himself again. He began to prepare for his trip to Évian with the same vigor of will with which he had formerly run his hospital. Although it was barely seven o'clock, he rang Silberstein and asked him to come and see him, left a message at the hospital asking his former secretary to call him as soon as possible, rang a devoted student and sent him out in search of statistical material. He spoke to Frau Schönglas and requested that her husband should come and see him as soon as he was released, and sat down at his desk to draw up a list of foreign personages with whom to make contact on his arrival in Évian. He did not forget what Bettina had said. Much of it seemed to him justified, much of it likely, her doubts reinforced his own; but where a disease was so advanced, when a fatal outcome could be prevented only by a bold intervention, the minutes were precious, an operation was the only solution.

The morning sun found the Professor still at his desk.

The Way into the Wilderness

And the Lord said unto Moses, Wherefore criest thou unto me? Speak unto the children of Israel, that they go forward: But lift thou up thy rod, and stretch out thine hand over the sea, and divide it: and the children of Israel shall go on dry ground through the midst of the sea.

EXODUS xiv, 15, 16

II

THE President of the United States, initiator and pa-
tron of the international gathering, insisted upon being
informed personally of all questions relating to the
Évian Conference. On the same day on which he was about to
wish his special envoy good-bye and give him his final instructions, he received a report from the American Embassy in
Berlin. It said that the Jewish Community in Vienna intended
to send an observer to Évian and to accredit him to the Conference; astonishingly enough, an exit and currency permit
had already been issued to this observer by the Reich Government. The coded telegram gave the name of the famous
surgeon and kidney specialist Professor Heinrich von Benda
and at the same time warned against any illusory optimism
evoked by the Germans' cooperativeness. The President left
the telegram on his desk in order to discuss it later with
his Ambassador.

The special envoy was led into the President's study in the
west wing of the White House at five in the afternoon. Although he was an elderly man he strode rapidly toward the
desk, so as to prevent him from rising—a difficult task for
the President who had never quite recovered from the aftereffects of a polio attack which he had suffered seventeen years
before. With a grateful smile the President stretched out his
hand to the Ambassador over the top of the desk and asked
him to pull his chair closer; he inquired after the Ambassador's health and complained of the humidity, that very
special humidity that becomes the torment and the topic of
conversation of the inhabitants of Washington during the
summer.

While the President began to speak of the Conference with

63

an astounding knowledge of the facts, the Ambassador tried
to overcome the distrust which he had always felt toward this
man. The President had kept him waiting four years for a new
and important mission, and now he had entrusted him with
the most thankless of all. Nevertheless the Ambassador felt
no resentment, he was merely on the alert. The President was
a Pied Piper and a snake charmer, and he, the Ambassador,
was an upright man. He regarded charm, that indefinable
virtue, with a certain aversion; moreover the President was
one of those people to whom it is difficult to say no, for which
reason one later regretted having said yes; and not infrequently
one was angry with him because one was ashamed of having
been able to offer so little resistance to his charm. In a country
without an aristocracy, the President came of an aristocratic
family; his face had a noble beauty and unmistakable character. In his melodious voice vigor and melancholy strangely
harmonized; he had suffered enough to understand others,
yet not enough to have been weakened by pain—it was impossible to know what nature had in store for a man to whom
she had shown so much favor. In addition, the President was a
politician; he guided public opinion by listening to it, so that
idealism took on the more garish colors of opportunism, and
his humanity might very easily be influenced by the next election. Ever since he had received his mission, the Ambassador
had been wondering why the President had turned his attention to the misery of the European refugees, and why he had
called the Conference. The simple answer—that the President was concerned to protect or save the victims of persecution—did not satisfy him; he would have felt more reassured
if he could have discerned behind the President's idealism
some of the solid realism that would better have corresponded
with his own picture of him.

The President knew all that. He distrusted an idealism
which was not at the same time practical: it was easy to demand love of human beings and then to go into the jungle and
surround oneself only with such harmless creatures as wild
animals. The humanitarianism that did not reckon with man,
with his egotism, his treachery, his compromises, was no humanitarianism at all. Was there any cheaper popularity

than that gained by a moral demand that obviously could not be put into execution? *"So when this loose behaviour I throw off,/ And pay the debt I never promised,/ By how much better than my word I am,/ By so much shall I falsify men's hopes . . ."* The President often had to think of the Shakespearean prince; he considered contempt for man to be not incompatible with the desire to change him, a Machiavellian humanitarianism to be no paradox, indeed to be the *"realità effettuale delle cose"* and men as evil only *"when they are not made good by the compulsion of necessity."* He had paid for the confidence which the masses placed in him by the suspicion of the men who were permitted to look into the machinery of politics. Provided he succeeded in making his purpose clear to the Ambassador, it mattered little to him that the Ambassador did not understand his motives.

The Ambassador reported to him on the technical preparations for the Conference. As he spoke, he looked at the President's desk, which resembled the window of a toy shop. Everyone knew that Falla, the black Scotch terrier, was the President's favorite; in the course of his six years' reign the President had received innumerable Fallas—Fallas of china and glass and bronze, of leather and wood. Among documents and folders there also stood other toys—letter openers in the shape of daggers, models of old coaches, pens with batteries, musical cigar boxes. The Ambassador was already finding it hard to resist feeling touched by this sight—the President must have been cheated of his childhood, perhaps that was why he had the power to move hearts.

"Don't underestimate the difficulties, Mr. President," said the Ambassador, after hearing that the Conference would undoubtedly elect him its chairman. "We are speaking of half a million German and Austrian Jews, but the exodus from Czechoslovakia has begun, Hungary and Rumania will follow; the involuntary migration of the peoples . . ."

"You are already reckoning with a Hitlerian Europe, Mr. Ambassador."

"The Jews are reckoning with it. So are the participants in the Conference. Human charity has an antipathy to high numbers."

"I thought cynicism was my privilege," smiled the President, and the Ambassador was struck by this strange smile. The President seemed to smile only with his slightly protruding full lower lip, while his thin, hard upper lip remained unmoved.

"The world regards our humanitarianism with distrust," said the Ambassador, "and I fear this also has to do with numbers. We have raised our quota for the admission of German and Austrian refugees to twenty-seven thousand annually—a drop in the ocean. People will say that with goodwill we could solve the problem on our own."

"Tell that to the Senator from Mississippi or the Representative from Utah!"

Now the Ambassador smiled too. "I shall have to explain to the delegate from Guatemala why our generosity is prevented by the Senator from Mississippi."

The President wondered whether he ought not to send a younger, more active diplomat to Évian. True, the Ambassador was only a little over sixty, barely six or seven years older than himself, but in the last four years, since his recall from Athens, the Ambassador had aged. His features reminded the President of the old stone Indian to which tourists made pilgrimages in the mountains of New Hampshire. Four years of rest. Leisure was indispensable to men in their middle years, as though a man had to recover from a tumultuous youth and prepare himself for a tumultuous old age; but leisure enticed youth into imprudence and age into dying. It had not been easy to find the right man. The Ambassador was a diplomat of experience and high reputation; he was a God-fearing Catholic, but not narrow-minded or bigoted; he knew the Europeans as well as the Latin Americans, and he was proof against that admiration for the German dictator which was now becoming more prevalent in the United States.

The Ambassador had opened his briefcase and was glancing at his papers. "Thirty-one states," he said, "have now finally accepted. So there will be thirty-two including ourselves. Nine European—England, France, Switzerland, Belgium, Ireland, Holland—and the three Scandinavian countries. The Soviet Union has refused the invitation."

"With what explanation?"

"The Soviet Union is not in the habit of giving explanations. Since Marxism has already explained everything they have no need of explanations."

"We didn't count on Italy. Has the Vatican replied?"

"The Holy Father will send an observer."

"That means a refusal. Without explanation, I presume. The Catholic Church has already explained everything."

"Pius XI is eighty and seriously ill. He pointed out the 'Omens of Disaster' in his encyclical of May, nineteen hundred and thirty-two." The Ambassador continued quickly. "Divided Spain is sabotaging the Conference, the Loyalists fear concessions to Franco, Franco fears concessions to the Loyalists. The Little Entente and the Balkans are standing aside—they either have anti-Semitic governments or they fear Germany. The German Reich looks upon the Conference as a hostile act. That is illogical—"

"Not at all," interrupted the President. "It confirms my surmise that Germany doesn't want to get rid of its Jews, but to destroy them."

"I must speak frankly to you, Mr. President," said the Ambassador, without reacting to the comment. "In the European countries there is disastrous unemployment. France is flooded with Spanish refugees. Palestine could absorb a considerable contingent of Jews, but England has no interest in strengthening the Zionists and tilting the balance in that divided country against the Arabs. The nineteen Latin-American states are in economic difficulties, some of them have influential German minorities, many sympathize with Hitler, almost all of them feel envy and the traditional aversion toward us. Where there is no race hatred, as in Brazil, Haiti or the Dominican Republic, there are religious prejudices. There remain Canada, Australia and New Zealand; but the refugee question will offer them a welcome opportunity of demonstrating that solidarity with Britain which is for the most part so shaky."

The President was impressed by his Ambassador's skeptical honesty. People said that he liked to surround himself with mediocre yes-men; in reality he disliked being surrounded by mediocre no-men. There was an opportunism of skeptics that was no less cynical and at the same time more time-wasting than the opportunism of the *claqueurs*. The Ambassador was skeptical, but obviously did not fear unpopularity. The President had the feeling that he had made the right decision when he chose this cool old man who was not driven by ambition and as incapable of enthusiasm as of opportunism.

"You're trying to discourage me," said the President.

"No, I should like to ask you for concrete instructions, Mr. President."

"What do you mean by that?"

"At least you and I must be agreed as to our attitude toward the German Reich. If we are out to administer a rebuff to it, we shall probably isolate ourselves from the remaining participants in the Conference and be little help to the victims of persecution. If, on the other hand, we want to save the greatest possible number of victims, then we must avoid a moral condemnation of the German Reich, for a practical contact with the Reich Government will have to be our aim. We must not give utterance to the idea that Germany is out to exterminate the Jews, we mustn't even hint at it; otherwise we should appear to be aware of the hopelessness of our undertaking and to have arranged it purely as a political maneuver."

"Let us not speak so scornfully of politics," rejoined the President earnestly, but not without playing on the strings of his seductive cordiality. "To me politics, in the best sense, is the compulsion which the powers of justice exercise upon the powers of evil to lure them out of the darkness."

How simple, thought the Ambassador, the tactical operations of his divisional commanders appear to the chief of staff as he works out strategy on a large-scale map! What did the President want? Did he want to save forty or fifty thousand Jewish families from extermination, or was he striving for a condemnation of Germany, which might, possibly, not help a single Jew?

"I asked you earlier," the President continued, "whether you presupposed a Hitlerian Europe. You would have every reason to do so. Whether we become involved in a war next

year, the year after next or in five years' time, war is in any case
inevitable. Europe is a sinking ship. Sooner or later we shall
have to come to its rescue. Czechs, Poles, French and British
will have to defend themselves in order to give us the chance
of defending them. The Jews, on the other hand, and Hitler's
political opponents, can neither delay the war, nor will they
be able to help us in the war. We have no excuse for delivering
them up to annihilation, not even the dubious excuse of our
national self-interest."

"So you agree with me?" said the Ambassador, relieved.

"I agree with half your argument. Our first aim is to save
as many refugees as possible. Spare Germany's sensibilities so
long as you have the feeling that we can come to an agreement
with the Germans. Once this hope vanishes, then let our restraint vanish. An agreement or condemnation. The maximum aim humanity, the minimum aim politics."

A secretary, accompanied by the black Scotch terrier wag-
ging its tail, brought tea and dry pastries. The President bent
down and petted his dog. The heat had abated somewhat. Dusk
was falling over the White House; from outside came the reassuring swishing of the lawn sprinklers.

After the secretary had left, the President handed the Ambassador the telegram which he had kept for him.

"What do you think of that?"

"It's very odd," said the Ambassador.

"Do you know the name?"

"I remember that the Professor operated on the Queen of
Greece."

"Ought it to make us see things more optimistically?"

"I don't know. There are numerous prominent Jews outside
Germany. Why not one of them? Why an Austrian? Probably
Professor von Benda is not traveling on orders from the Jewish
Community, but on orders from the Reich Government. I'm
afraid the Germans are already operating on the second line,
the line of politics. It could be that they have found a willing
tool in the person of the Jewish representative, perhaps an
agent."

"I have ordered the Secret Service to keep the Professor under surveillance. Nevertheless, I can see another possibility. If the Germans wanted to make a proposal to us, who would be more suitable to transmit it than a prominent Jew?"

"Perhaps," said the Ambassador. "Perhaps." He placed the cablegram with the other documents, closed his briefcase and rose.

In the car that carried him through the steaming city to the station, he pondered once again on what the President had said. He saw before his mind's eye the President's long, narrow face, marked by pain, beautified by wisdom and coarsened by powder. It wasn't easy to resist this man. Humanitarianism to the limits of politics. Politics when there was nothing to be achieved by humanitarianism. To save human beings and, if they could not be saved, to use human beings. Man under the microscope, and humanity, small and far away, through the wrong end of an opera glass. It was difficult to bow to this logic, even more difficult to oppose it. A long and thorny path led from necessity to knowledge, from knowledge to action.

On Lac Léman, directly facing Lausanne, lies the spa of Évian-les-Bains, whose name is derived either from the Latin Aquianum or from the Celtic Ev. The 3,500 or so inhabitants, since the French are proud of their Celtic origin, prefer the second version, but Aquianum or Ev, the town owes its fame and prosperity to its healing waters. That the French of Évian are very special Frenchmen, that is to say very specially French, needs no explanation, since all frontier dwellers always display and preserve the national characteristics of their country most emphatically. But Évian is a frontier town in a double sense: it is held by Switzerland in a pair of tongs from east and west, with the lake forming the empty space between the tips of the tongs. On the opposite, northern bank of Lac Léman the vineyards of the canton of Vaud run down to the lake; to the west the Swiss frontier and the city of Geneva are only a few miles away. In 1591 the citadel and fortress of Évian offered heroic resistance to the attacking Genevois for five days. To the east it is no more than seventeen kilometers to the village of St. Gingolph; immediately after this, one is in the canton of Valais, so famous for its delightful wines. The beauty of the countryside, which to the south is overtopped by the peaks of the Haute-Savoie, snow-capped until far into the warm season, has contributed as much to the popularity of its healing springs as the excellence of its almost Swiss hotels and the attraction of its casino, in which many a citizen of neighboring but morally stricter Switzerland has been permitted to make reparation for the damage inflicted by the Genevois siege. It was less to its gaming tables than to its natural charms that Évian-les-Bains owed its choice as the venue of the conference of the Comité Intergouvernmental des Refugiés called by the President of the United States in 1938, since statesmen have always—as the examples of Carlsbad, Vienna, Verona, Utrecht, Geneva, Yalta and Locarno bear witness—preferred to solve the problems of suffering mankind in the most pleasant and under the best possible touristic conditions.

Heinrich von Benda arrived in Évian on the 5th of July. He came from Geneva, where he had spent one day at the Hôtel de l'Écu.

His stay in Geneva had been overshadowed by his telephone conversation with his son. Dr. Felix von Benda had been living since his earliest youth in Paris, where he had studied at the Sorbonne and worked, not without success, as assistant to the famous laryngologist Professor Lamartine. True, the Professor had made contact with Felix while still in Vienna, but it had not been easy—Jews were forbidden to make phone calls abroad, the Professor's telephone was tapped—but for nearly three weeks he had heard nothing from Felix. Immediately on his arrival he had asked to be put through to Paris. Trembling, with a pounding heart, he had waited for the connection, for he hoped to receive a sign of life from Elisabeth. If Elisabeth had succeeded in escaping from Germany, she would certainly have contacted her brother; if she was in freedom, Felix must know. But even before the Professor dared ask, Felix had already inquired after Elisabeth; he had heard nothing from her. In despair, robbed of his last hope, the Professor had put down the receiver. Father and son had arranged that Felix should come as quickly as possible to Évian—though to Felix's questions as to what brought him to Évian and how he had managed to get an exit permit the Professor had answered evasively. The following day, after being received by the German Consul-General in his private apartment, the Professor had traveled on to Évian.

The Hôtel Splendide, where a small but comfortable room awaited the Professor, was full to overflowing. The Hôtel Royal, a far more magnificent hotel under the same management situated on a hilltop, had been almost completely occupied by the thirty-two delegations, so that the spa visitors, with a few select exceptions, had taken refuge in the Hôtel Splendide situated lower down and close to the town. This second building was a spacious box made up of three broad wings, such as were popular during the early 1870's and around the turn of the century, dominated inside by red and green plush, both of them pretty weatherworn. To the left of the lift and the porter's lodge lay the bar and dining room, the latter bright and friendly but of a bourgeois monotony that suggested the sort of food found in a better-class *pension*, while the bar, like bathrooms in old hotels, gave the impression of having been tacked on later; this impression was reinforced by the shiny white paint on the unsuitable-looking bar, which looked thoroughly out of place, and the tired wine-red upright piano. To the right of the porter's lodge were the lounge and the writing room which, even though they were flooded with sunshine, had a depressing atmosphere, because they were intended to serve as a quiet refuge for the old and sick.

However, the Professor quickly discovered that the hotel was not primarily populated by people seeking healing from the baths or salvation from the gaming tables. It was now the headquarters of a "second line" of participants in the conference, or rather of camp followers, journalists, representatives of all kinds of private committees, of religious and humanitarian organizations, professional or voluntary, zealous or overzealous observers, photographers, propagandists, diplomats of nonparticipating governments and probably also agents of various secret services.

After the Professor had taken a bath he put a call through to the American delegation at the Hôtel Royal. One of the Ambassador's secretaries noted the Professor's request to be received by His Excellency as soon as possible on an urgent matter, and assured him that he would let him know the same day whether the Ambassador, a very busy man, could receive him. Then Heinrich von Benda left the hotel to go for a walk around the town.

His mood vacillated between elation and despondency. Even if the American secretary's reply had been no more than polite, he could not help being impressed by the effort that had gone into the preparation for the Conference. Those buried in the pit of silence had no idea that their knocking had been heard, the shipwrecked had no idea that rescue ships were speeding to their aid from all sides through the fog. There were not merely ships with thirty-two different flags. In the hotel lobby the Professor had seen Chinese and Indians, had met famous personalities from every country. Did this hotchpotch of languages mean that this time the world was setting out to build the Tower of Babel with the bricks of understanding? Although no national interests were at stake and only worries, difficulties and conflicts were to be obtained in return for compassion, labor, effort and cost were not being spared. At the same time, however, his thoughts circled continually around Elisabeth, and although he refused to abandon the hope of finding her here in the free world, he nevertheless felt like a doctor who discovers the healing serum on the very day on which his own child is beyond help.

On the slightly sloping road down to the town, the Professor noticed after only a few paces that a young man—fair-haired, tall, at most twenty-five years old—had attached himself to his heels. To be sure the German sheepdog—as the Professor baptized him—kept his distance; but when the Professor stopped he stopped; if the Professor looked at him, he turned away as though discovered; in a word, he behaved as crudely as people entrusted with such a crude task always do. The Professor resolved to take no further notice of him.

The Professor also observed the everyday activity of the little town with mixed feelings. From the green glass cupola of the Casino, reminiscent of a railway station, waved the tricolor, as though to declare the *grande nation's* pride in its roulette players; even now, in the afternoon, impatient gamblers crowded the broad steps. Outside the little cafés, sun-tanned

people were sitting over milky-green apéritifs; on the promenades by the lake old men and women were moving as slowly
as though seen by a slow-motion camera; one-horse carriages
whose backrests were covered with lace doilies were trotting
over the astonishingly clean asphalt. The smell of the lake
water mingled with the slight but constant smell of sulphur
and chocolate, that twin scent typical of old therapeutic baths;
architecture and gardens recalled the beginning of the new century—*Évian à ses enfants* it said on the overdramatic war memorial; a light breeze moved the empty swings on the terrace
of the secessionist bath house—but the Professor asked himself
why this hothouse of the past had been chosen as a place in
which to discuss the terrors of the present.

He wanted to walk down the Rue Nationale, Évian's relatively short main street, first on one side, then on the other,
but he slowed down and came to a stop; the short distance
seemed to him too far. Was he surprised by this sudden, almost
painful fatigue? He remembered what he had still been able
to do half a year ago, but that was different. If one continues
what one has done for a lifetime, the law of inertia, paradoxi-
cally enough, lends support to diligence, whereas a new undertaking demands youthful vigor. At least, thought the Professor, he would cut down on his smoking—fifteen cigarettes
a day, five in the morning, five in the afternoon, five in the evening, a strict ration, mild cigarettes, Egyptian perhaps or Turkish. He must not fall ill, not now, so close to the goal.

He walked on, looked at the pretty shop windows, especially
those offering ladies' clothes, ladies' shoes and all sorts of feminine accessories, wondering, as he looked at almost every item
on display, how it would suit Bettina. He had been too generous with the hours of his work, too thrifty with the hours of his
love. It is not the shortness of the remaining years that is the
curse of old age, but the shortness of those that are gone; it is
not the future that is too short—for who can tell its length?—
but the past, a whole past of missed opportunities. He stood
in front of a *couturière's* window—draped silks, a dress thrown
over an antique chair, a handbag placed as though left there by
chance—and remembered a visit to a Paris fashion show. He
had been surrounded by the delighted twittering of birds, Bet-

tina had once or twice grasped his hand and with red cheeks had drawn his attention to this, that or the other choice item; yes, he had said with a smile, she could order what she liked, but all the time he had been thinking about a difficult operation and an incompetent assistant whom he had to dismiss. Homesickness for Bettina overcame him with such force that he forgot everything else. If she were now to appear at the end of the Rue Nationale, who knows whether he would not desert with her, forgetting his mission and the shipwrecked? If he was thrifty with the money he had been permitted to take out and to change, a bare minimum—thrift could be learned, it was to begin at once with the cigarettes—he could perhaps bring Bettina back this green, high-necked, close-fitting and yet very discreet dress—green was her favorite color, precisely this green —but then he would have to save every penny, although he had long since forgotten how to save. On the last day, not before, he would see if he could afford such an extravagance.

His feet were aching, and in his left arm he felt the alarming, dull, slightly painful contraction. He did not continue his walk, but went over to the newspaper stand, opposite the Café Muratore, in the little square on the corner of the Rue Nationale. Because of the Conference the newspaper stand was richly larded with foreign papers—the *Journal des Nations* and the *Journal de Genève,* beside them *The Times, Le Temps,* the *Corriere della Sera,* a few American papers and the *Völkischer Beobachter.* As he selected only a few papers, bearing his vow of thrift in mind, he became aware that the young man was once more standing beside him, choosing with exaggerated interest from among the colored postcards, but the Professor merely asked himself whether the man had also been spying on him outside the fashion shops and, who knows, had guessed his thoughts.

He sat down at a table outside the Café Muratore. The whole of the first page of the *Journal des Nations* was devoted to the Évian Conference and immediately the barometer swung over to fine weather. The paper, as the Professor knew, was close to the secretariat of the League of Nations; it would not speak in such lofty tones of tomorrow's opening if great things were not being prepared with prospects of success. He surreptitiously folded the swastika-decorated title page of the *Völkischer Beobachter* and began to read the leading article, entitled "Where Are the Jews to Be Sent? Thoughts on the 'World Conference' at Évian," signed by Alfred Rosenberg. "In Palestine there are assaults, strikes, shootings and hangings," began the article. "Meanwhile the realization that the Jews can never be assimilated is growing throughout the world. The German people are firmly resolved to lead this problem to its only logical solution and to prevent those conditions from ever recurring again which were possible during the last few decades through the false tolerance and weakness of earlier generations. And where the situation has not yet come to a head, a similar development is taking place for the whole world to see (Poland, Hungary, etc.)."

Heinrich von Benda had reached this point in his reading when he heard himself addressed. He looked up and became aware of a lady at the next table whose features looked to him familiar, although he could not place her. The lady—about sixty, tiny, with two round red patches on her cheeks, not made up exactly to her best advantage and looking, with her faded elegance, almost as if she had stepped out of an old picture postcard of the watering place—was sitting alone, but there were two ice-cream bowls in front of her; evidently her companion had just left her.

Didn't the "Herr Hofrat" remember her, she cried, fortunately blurting out the supplementary explanations immediately afterward. Frau Direktor Lederer from Vienna—"my late husband, as you will remember, was director of the Veit Magnesite Works"—the Herr Hofrat had operated on her son in 1920, the 24th of October, 1920, to be exact, and had saved the boy's life; yes, he too, her only son, was here, had just gone over to the newspaper stand, he too, Ludwig, would be delighted, "such a pleasure, Herr Hofrat"—and then the lady began to assail the Professor with questions. How long had he been "outside," when had he escaped from the Nazis, were his family also "outside" and well and was the Herr Hofrat here for the cure or actually—"Well, what a piece of luck!" —practicing in this excellent kidney spa? The young Lederer, Ludwig Lederer, came back at this moment—a sickly-looking, lanky man in his late thirties—and now his mother deluged him, whose memory seemed somewhat imperfect, with the most generous biographical data concerning the Herr Hofrat, Herr Professor Heinrich von Benda, the "pride of the Vienna School of Medicine." The torrent of words which accompanied the introduction saved Heinrich von Benda from giving any relevant answers, but he had to answer one or two questions so as not to appear as distant as he normally would have been; however, this made him aware that he was skating on the thinnest of ice. To mention the reason for his trip to Évian, or even to speak of his mission, was forbidden him. He was "outside," it was true, but he was by no means one of those who had escaped to the "outside." How could he explain that his family were well, but still in Germany; that he, like Frau Lederer and her son—"What a happy coincidence!"—was also staying at the Hôtel Splendide, but neither as a doctor nor as a visitor to the spa. How could he tell the gratefully talkative lady that, perhaps in a few days, he intended to do the incredible, impossible and unheard-of, namely to go back "inside," and this with the intention of ransoming half a million Jews for the round sum of one hundred and twenty-five million dollars.

The young man, the Professor's shadow, was still standing by the kiosk deeply immersed in an English newspaper, which he held up in front of him partly like a protective screen and partly like a sandwich board. As he caught sight of him something else came into the Professor's mind. He was like a man suffering from an infectious disease who is nevertheless moving freely about among people. Who knew what this bloodhound might not report tomorrow and whether harm might not come to the Lederers, mother and son, or their relations in Vienna, as a result of this meeting with him, Professor von Benda, pride of the Vienna School of Medicine? He said good-bye quickly, almost hastily, paid as he left and returned to his hotel.

Here many new guests had arrived, there were trunks everywhere, in the lounges groups had formed and were discussing things in whispers, a new table had been placed in the writing room on which the first press communiqués of the Conference were beginning to pile up.

Since that night on which he had been called to the Reich
Governor, Heinrich von Benda had almost forgotten that he
was a surgeon, a scientist and a practicing physician, and that
in the field of politics he was a stranger and unskilled. From
his early youth he had not only despised dilettantism but had
considered it a dangerous evil, and now he himself was a dilettante who, with the rashness of a dilettante, was about to perform an operation upon which hundreds of thousands of
human lives depended. He gazed into the bewildering turmoil
of the hotel and began to ask himself whether he would be
able to get a hearing, whether brazen secretaries would not
turn him away and put him off with fine words, whether the
wheel of the Conference would roll on over him, whether he
would not be ground to dust by an unknown technique.

Finally he found a seat in the farthest corner of the writing
room, sat down and lit a cigarette. It was not a mild cigarette,
it was the thirtieth or fortieth that day, he had a bad conscience,
but he told himself that worrying about his health might be
more injurious to it than an excessive consumption of nicotine;
also he knew of no other means of mastering the burden of
fatigue. The next moment his attention was caught by a page
to whom he beckoned, and it seemed to him a good omen
that the boy had actually been looking for him. The telephone
message he had been expecting had come. The American Ambassador would be pleased to see Herr Professor von Benda
that same evening at seven-fifteen in the Hôtel Royal, Suite
108.

After Heinrich von Benda had assured him that he could speak
English, if not perfectly at least fluently and without much difficulty, the Ambassador dismissed his interpreter.

The Professor felt it appropriate to say a few words about
himself, but the Ambassador saved him from this embarrassing
necessity with a few flattering phrases. The name Benda, he
stressed, was widely known in America. At the same time he
apologized for his unduly formal evening dress: the French
Ambassador, the representative of the guest country, had invited participants in the Conference to a reception.

From the outset the Professor had resolved to hide nothing

and to be absolutely frank with the representative of the American President. He considered it superfluous, indeed tactless, to refer to his own arrest and release, but he came all the quicker to his meeting with the Reich Governor. He repeated the conversation in the Hofburg as fully and precisely as his memory allowed, going into the greatest detail when he came to the proposal. Here, for the first time, he mentioned his own role, emphasizing that he had been moved by the desperate plight of the Jews to accept the mission that had been so strangely entrusted to him.

After the first polite words, the Ambassador had not spoken again. He was wearing an old-fashioned dinner jacket and a stiff shirt with a high collar; in this social armor he looked even stonier than usual. He did not encourage the Professor with a single word, a single question, a single movement; indeed it seemed to Heinrich von Benda that the Ambassador had adopted first an astounded, then a defensive and finally a hostile attitude. As though weakened by his interlocutor's stubborn silence, the Professor's voice grew lower and lower; no sooner had he thrown one cigarette away than he lit a fresh one; finally he broke off in the middle of a sentence.

"I should like to ask you one or two questions," said the Ambassador after a pause. "In whose name are you speaking, Professor?"

"In the name of the Jewish Community."

"I cannot suppose that the Jewish Community has Jews to sell."

"The Jewish Community is fully informed. I have come to Évian on its instructions."

"Am I to understand that you passed on the Reich Governor's proposal to the Community, who for their part have sanctioned it?"

"If you wish, Your Excellency."

"But you have no power to speak for the Reich Government?"

"Naturally not."

"And to whom is your proposal directed? To the Conference or to the United States?"

"To the world," the Professor retorted irritably. "It can

make no difference to the Germans whether they receive the ransom from one or from several nations, and I assure you that it is a matter of indifference to people in mortal danger whether they are ransomed by one country, by several or by all the participating states."

"I am afraid, Professor, that I must acquaint you with certain diplomatic usages. To be worthy of the name, a proposal must be addressed by one definite authority to another equally definite authority. A diplomatic mission is like a registered letter that cannot be delivered without exact addresses—the sender's as well as the recipient's. The Jewish Community, which has accredited you to the Conference as an observer, cannot—even if it spoke for all the Jews in Germany—make any offer, because although it represents the Jews it does not dispose of them. The 'world,' to which the indeterminate proposal is made, is a wide concept; it is not to be found in the diplomatic vocabulary."

"I turned to you in confidence, Mr. Ambassador," said the Professor. He had reckoned with every possibility, but that his mission might come to grief on formalities, on usages, on the diplomatic vocabulary, as the Ambassador put it, had never occurred to him. He knew that nowadays papers had a high value, visas and passports and release certificates and safe-conducts and the father's and grandmother's birth certificates, but that even a sinking ship radioing for help had to show its papers—harbor documents, discharged cargo, the captain's birth certificate, the seamen's testimonials of good conduct—this was something he would not, could not, accept. "I didn't consider it necessary," he continued, "to refer to the secret nature of my mission—that seemed to me self-evident. A secret mission cannot be made subject to the same rules as an official one. The Jews of Germany and the occupied regions are saying through my mouth: We see a way, small though it may seem, of escaping certain annihilation. I didn't expect you to write out a check for several hundred million dollars, but I can assume that you will inform the President and the Conference of my mission."

The sharp tone in which these words were uttered did not offend the Ambassador. He felt sympathy for the famous doctor who now sat before him as a supplicant; indeed he feared that pity might overcome him and lead him to thoughtless actions. At the same time he was aware of the danger that threatened him, as the President's special envoy and as the chairman designate of the Conference, from a side from which he had least expected it. Between humanity and politics he had decided in favor of humanity. To save twenty or thirty thousand Jews, if not more, was no mean aim, and if he could persuade the delegates to raise their countries' immigration quota this could only be done in agreement with the German Government. The latter would have to release at least a part of the confiscated Jewish capital; refugees were not liked, Jewish refugees even less, Jewish refugees who were beggars least of all. And now this Viennese Professor had come along and upset the whole carefully conceived plan by talking about a mass exodus, of hundreds of thousands of Jews, perhaps of millions, by mentioning sums that no one had thought of and that were not to be found in any budget, by throwing into the scales, through his appeal to the world's morality, an element of unparalleled immorality.

"I am honored by your confidence," said the Ambassador, "and I hope I shall not disappoint it. Shall we therefore examine together and quite unofficially what the German Reich is aiming to achieve by this curious proposal? You know that confiscated Jewish capital amounts to about forty million dollars. Any payment to Germany—instead of, on the contrary, demanding payment from Germany—would mean sanctioning the illegal confiscation."

"Is the Conference meeting to demand money from Germany?"

"The release of Jewish capital is not the primary aim of the Conference, but it would provide a solid basis for solving the emigration and immigration problem."

"So it is still a question of money . . ."

The Professor opened a fresh packet of American cigarettes. He had no more matches on him—the Ambassador leaned forward to give him a light. He did so with a gesture that seemed to say, You shouldn't smoke so much, old man. The faces of the two old men were for an instant quite close together; each

saw the other's wrinkles, the tired skin, the experienced eyes
as though under a microscope.

"Your whole mission is based on money," said the Ambassador; he did not sound contemptuous, but sad. "And you are
indignant when I speak of money. The participating states are
not asking for money, they are asking at most that the Jews
should be restored their own property. Is that the same as the
bargain which . . . ?" He stopped. "Assuming there really
is a state in Europe, in the twentieth century, that wants to sell
human beings as slaves were once sold in the marketplaces.
I cannot believe it, Professor, but let us assume so. Do you know
that the League of Nations maintains a special department to
combat the trade in human beings? The League of Nations
does not distinguish between traders and buyers, it condemns
the one like the other. You must admit that the principle is
correct, for without buyers there would be no traders."

The Professor remembered his conversation with Bettina.
What is the alternative? he had asked; he had not found any
better argument since then, he could not ask the Ambassador
any other question.

"You speak of certain annihilation," replied the Ambassador.
"Don't imagine that I underestimate the desperate plight of
the Jews. The President doesn't underestimate it either—why
else should we be meeting here? But however inhuman the
new German regime may be, however abysmal its aims, Germany is in the heart of the civilized world, and all the signs
are that it is trying to win the acknowledgment of this world.
Here we come back to the purpose of the Reich Government.
I don't doubt that the Reich Governor threatened you with the
extermination of the Jews, but it is obvious that the brutality
of the threat must be related to the sum demanded."

"In Hitler's prisons people are being beaten to death every
day," answered the Professor. He had made no mention of his
own experience, no mention of Fritz Grünwald.

"That is why the President has called the Conference."

It was becoming increasingly clear to the Ambassador that
even before the Conference was opened he would have to
protect it from this desperate and obstinate old man. The
Germans—who could tell?—had perhaps smuggled him into
the fortress of Évian as a Trojan horse. Intergovernmental

Committee for Refugees, the Conference was called. Any reference to Germany or the Jews in the title had been avoided. All over Europe intolerance was in the saddle, intolerance, Europe's apocalyptic horseman. Yes, everyone knew that it was about Germany, about the German Jews. But the word refugees was a neutral concept that offended no one; there was no need to say where they came from; it was enough to find out where they were going. If this Professor from Vienna started hawking Jews from door to door here in Évian, if the press got hold of this manifest sensation, then it would be all up with the humanitarian character of the Conference, then it would be solely a matter of prestige and principles and politics, the enemies of humanitarianism.

"You can believe me, Professor," he said, "when I say it would not help those in distress if we were to respond to this blackmail. Trade in human beings is new to Europe, but political blackmail is a phenomenon that confronts us every day. Don't ask what happens when one refuses to yield to blackmail. Any resistance to blackmail contains a frightful alternative. Most wars come about because one of the two parties has refused to yield to blackmail, and history then asserts that the war would not have broken out if tribute had been paid to the blackmailer—but does history investigate what would have happened if the other party had decided to reward the blackmailer?"

"Do you think it's really like that?" the Professor interrupted him. "Would I be sitting here if it were? Less than half a year ago German troops crossed the frontier of my country. Hadn't my country's government been blackmailed? Hadn't the world yielded to the threat of war? Was the lofty principle that one should never reward a blackmailer really adhered to?"

"The Austrian people welcomed Hitler with cheers."

The Ambassador felt a little ashamed of his answer, an entirely rhetorical answer as he knew, and as he uttered it he was again touched by pity for the old man, who suddenly seemed to him much older than he was himself, although for years he had been unable to imagine that anyone could be older. Nevertheless it was not pity that moved him as he began to speak again. He didn't know precisely whether he was advancing political arguments in order to justify his pity, or whether political arguments merely permitted him to get out of the affair with dignity. In any case, the Ambassador remembered that he had not come to Évian as an emissary of humanity, of that indefinable "world" of which Professor Benda had spoken, but as the special envoy of the United States, a quite definite political power with quite definite political interests. The maximum aim, humanity; the minimum aim, politics. There were chess pieces, pawns in particular, that stood in one's way throughout the whole game, but at the very end changed into decisive pieces, a castle for example. Would a good player renounce such a piece? It was not impossible that despite all the goodwill of the participating states, the Conference might be wrecked on Germany's resistance, and then it would be appropriate to refer back to the unheard-of proposal—not in order to accept it, but in order to unmask the blackmailer.

His doubts and objections, the Ambassador declared, did not mean that he refused to report his conversation with the Professor to the President under all circumstances, to the Conference under certain conditions. A secret mission, the Professor had said. It must indeed be taken as such. Through the Jewish Community in Vienna or in some other way—the Ambassador lowered his eyes—the Professor could certainly get in touch with Berlin, could ask the German Government if they were prepared to make a definite proposal and, in the event of its acceptance, to guarantee delivery of the Jews. "I must emphasize that the proposal cannot be a subject of the Conference, but even a conference of diplomats"—he smiled—"is made up of human beings. Therefore the question could be discussed unofficially—but of course only if the German Government decides to convey its request through an accredited representative. That we should prefer the task to be officially entrusted to you, I need not stress."

Heinrich von Benda felt that in the course of the conversation the gulf between him and the Ambassador had grown wider and wider. He felt it almost physically, as though an abyss had opened up in the middle of the room. The Ambassador had moved further and further into the distance, had grown smaller and smaller, an old man sitting bent forward in an easy chair on the other side, on the edge of a deep ravine into which he stared fixedly. The old man in the easy chair stared into the ravine and saw something that only he could see, and perhaps the old man in the easy chair had a fishing rod in his hand and was waiting for a fish to bite. Heinrich von Benda could have taken hope from the Ambassador's last words, he had gone a long way from harsh repudiation to cautious conciliation—the Professor could not have expected more from this first conversation. Nevertheless he had the feeling that he had suffered a defeat, the same feeling he often had after an operation that had laid bare an incurable cancer in the human body: it was no consolation that it was not the operation that had been unsuccessful, but man that had proved to be an unsuccessful creation. The Reich Governor had spoken of human beings as of merchandise. The idea had horrified the Ambassador, but if human beings beyond the dark frontier were not merchandise to him they were nevertheless an amorphous mass. He could perhaps picture the Jews and their suffering and their distress, but he could not picture Fritz Grünwald, could not picture that the Jews, the amorphous mass, consisted of innumerable Fritz Grünwalds.

He didn't show his thoughts. The only thing that mattered now was that nothing final should happen, that the discussion should not be broken off, should not peter out in the sand. Although he had no idea of his next step, in particular did not know how he was to persuade the German Government to emerge from its cowardly reserve, he nevertheless promised to get into immediate touch "with Vienna," and he noted with a certain relief that the Ambassador said good-bye to him with the wish to be kept *au courant* with developments.

He passed through the lobby of the Hôtel Royal as though sleepwalking, assailed on all sides by a confusion of tongues worthy of Babel. Gentlemen in dinner jackets and ladies in evening dress were pushing their way in close ranks toward the lounges, in expectation of the buffet to which the French Ambassador had invited them that evening.

Fatigue, exhaustion, had rapidly overcome the Professor, or was it the flight into sleep which is sometimes available to the more fortunate of the unfortunate? He had gone to bed soon after dinner and had fallen asleep.

When he awoke, the phosphorescent hands of the clock showed two in the morning. He had slept deeply and, he believed, dreamlessly; he was therefore all the more dismayed by the pain that woke him. Together with the pain that had spread over his chest and radiated into his back, he felt a desperate hunger for air, not to be compared with any other feeling he had experienced before, because it was not hunger for something definite but for life itself. He knew very well that the two things, the pain and the shortness of breath, went together, but it seemed to him that he could defend himself against the pain if only he could overcome the shortness of breath. But this proved impossible, as hopeless as the defense of a fortress whose defenders are surprised by the besiegers just at the moment when they are rent by internal conflicts. He sat up and breathed deeply, as though he hoped to fill his lungs with a single breath, to take in and retain a belated supply of oxygen. For a few seconds he felt relieved, but the pain became more violent and lancinating, as though the heart could not bear the sudden access of air. He had sometimes reassured his patients with Greek and Latin expressions—not frightened but pacified them, because they liked to hear mellifluous names for their illnesses, names that had evidently come down from the remote past—but to no avail he called his shortness of breath dyspnea. The magic did not work on him, one could also die of mellifluous afflictions. Fear for one's life, sense of destruction—these expressions formed part of his everyday vocabulary, but he had not understood them until the things they described had come upon him. He was amazed how exactly he was able to observe himself, and even more that the terminology was apparently false, or at least did not apply to him. He certainly felt that something destructive, over which he had no power, was attacking him, but he was not afraid, did not think of death; fear of losing his life was submerged in the effort to escape destruction.

He felt for the light switch, an everyday gesture that filled him with a painful fatigue. Now that the little room was immersed in a feeble light—was the light feeble, or were only his eyes feeble?—he wondered whether he could get up and go over to the window. All at once there were two people in the room, Heinrich von Benda who lay in bed struggling for air, and Professor Benda who was considering whether he could advise his patient to get up. The pain in his chest, that spread to his arm and from there to his left shoulder, was so violent that he had to bend forward, but the pressure on his stomach and diaphragm made the shortness of breath even worse, his respiration shallower and more irregular; and since he feared the difficulty of breathing more than the pain, he laboriously straightened up again. Would he reach the window? The window drew him magnetically, and the night outside became a haven which he must reach at any price. He tried to estimate the distance between the bed and the window, and as he did so a long-forgotten picture from his childhood came back to him. In the house of his uncle, the dispensing chemist, he had shared a room with his two cousins and, as the youngest, he had been given the bed in the drafty position under the window; for years he had felt this to be a humiliating discrimination. Now he longed for his childhood bed; he ought not to have rebelled against the humiliation, then he might still have possessed a bed under the window. Two paces, at most three. He decided to take a chance, threw back the bedclothes, sat on the edge of the bed, pondering his actions carefully, as though under the eye of Professor Benda; a short pause after the effort, a rest before embarking on a fresh venture. He could no longer draw a deep breath, but he breathed all the more rapidly, abruptly, gasping for air like a hungry dog for a dangling bone. His chest rose and fell; he could not stop, although the pain grew even greater with the alternate arching and sinking of the vault of the diaphragm. The distance between the bed and the window increased, the window seemed to him unattainable, but he rose nevertheless and advanced toward it.

Now he was overcome by fear and despair, this time for an external reason. The two casements of the window were ajar, to be sure, but the window had been open, so that the air of the cool summer night must already have been coming into the room—he could not attribute the lack of air to the smallness of the room, could not expect any alleviation from open-

ing the window. Nevertheless he opened the window wider still,
leaned out, tried to give himself up to the illusion that his lungs
were able to draw more freely from a larger reservoir. In fact
the pain and shortness of breath abated for a moment, just long
enough to enable the brain to function more undisturbed. He
thought of Bettina, of the child, of his uncompleted mission,
of the consequence of a stroke, of paralysis, of his sudden
death. But whether it was that nature placed herself protectively between him and his thoughts, or whether his despair
demanded greater strength than at that moment he possessed,
his thoughts became more indifferent and did not penetrate
into his soul. The shortness of breath had decreased, but the
pain returned with redoubled violence, an unknown pain, or
so it seemed to him and rightly, since the pain changed with
each stage. If till now it had been a diffuse pain that had
squeezed his whole chest in a coat of armor from which his
arms tried painfully to free themselves, now he felt as though
thousands of ants of anguish had carried the pain to a single
anthill; now he knew exactly where his heart lay and that it was
the size of a clenched fist; his heart was a fist inside a clenched
fist, was situated behind the breastbone and ended in a point
between the fifth and sixth rib. Professor Benda ordered the
patient Benda to go to the washbasin, take off his pajamas, turn
on the tap, plunge both arms in the water and let the hot water,
as hot as he could bear it, run over his arms, especially the left
one. The tugging and drawing in his shoulder and upper arm
died down, but neither the panting hunger for air nor the pain
that came from the anthill diminished. When he straightened
up, because the bent posture had robbed him of air again and
his forearm was as red as a lobster, his eye caught the wall mirror, and it was probably at this moment that Heinrich von
Benda made up his mind at last and for the first time to take
Professor Benda's advice and pick up the little box of nitroglycerin pills that lay on the glass slab.

The effects made themselves felt almost at once. The pain
broke up, literally separated and ran in different directions;
first it spread over the whole torso, over shoulders and arms,
but it was in flight, merely fought a weak rearguard action,
finally disappeared completely, and only his exhaustion re-

minded Heinrich von Benda of the battle that had raged in his chest.

He dared not stretch out, dressed again, pulled the armchair effortlessly to the window and sat down. Angina pectoris, Professor Benda told the patient, angina pectoris, probably very far advanced. Expectation of life? A foolish question, as you know very well, my dear von Benda. Completely uncertain, even more uncertain than it normally is at your age. Of course the attacks, more or less frequently, at more or less regular intervals, may be repeated for years, not a pleasant prospect, but still better than the other possibility, namely that the next one may prove fatal—prove fatal, a more tactful way of putting it than simply to say "end in death." In any case this largely depends upon you, my dear von Benda. Naturally, absolutely no smoking, not another cigar, not another cigarette; that must stop once and forever. No alcohol, but you don't drink anyway; well, there would be no objection to an occasional glass of red wine or the odd glass of whisky. As much movement as possible in the fresh air on level ground, excessive effort is to be avoided. And above all, no excitement. No excitement. Excitement is poison, my dear von Benda.

Heinrich von Benda wrinkled his forehead, told Professor Benda roughly to depart. Admittedly, Professor Benda had been very useful to him while he was having the attack, but now he was beginning to talk nonsense, to talk the psalmodic language of doctors. It would be better if he would go away and leave him in peace.

He breathed deeply though cautiously, testing himself. He thought of Bettina and his son and Elisabeth. The Professor had to admit that he had been talking nonsense; but the Professor was no longer there, he had left Heinrich von Benda to his thoughts. The man at the window was overcome by an insurmountable longing for his wife, a longing that had been wafted to him by the wind of death but had not been wafted away again with it. Heinrich von Benda had arranged with Bettina that he would telephone her only in an extreme emergency; to get a connection was difficult, he was short of money, the phone was tapped. What had they meant by an "extreme emergency"? In no case must Bettina learn of his condition. Suppose he had died? For a fleeting instant he thought it would have been better for her and the child, but the idea, dictated by self-pity, was reprehensible. She loved him as he loved her—the single, simple truth among a myriad dubious truths, half-lies, half-truths, voluntary and involuntary complications. She knew everything about him, was probably also aware of his condition and for that reason had advised him to flee. Now he had the best excuse for flight: everyone had the right to die in peace. Everyone? That would include Fritz Grünwald, and the Viennese Jews, the German Jews, the Polish and Czech and Hungarian Jews; everyone meant also those whose mothers and fathers had prayed in the wrong houses of God. During the last hour he had not thought about his conversation with the Ambassador; now it seemed to him as though it lay far back in the past, as though it had taken place weeks or months ago—a phenomenon that he had noticed after previous attacks. Each time you look across into the next world, your eyes are dimmed for this world, after every step you take toward death a wall goes up behind you, the walls behind you stand increasingly close together, the distances you have passed over become larger. This concerned no one but himself, was entirely his own affair. Well then, what was that about the Ambassador?

He pulled his dressing gown more tightly around him; the night air was cool but it did him good. Perhaps he really hadn't been dreaming, but in his liberated subconscious he must have continued the conversation with the Ambassador. It was difficult not to get excited while you were asleep. The Ambassador had looked at him so strangely, with pity or askance, probably askance. Professor Heinrich von Benda from Vienna who is offering half a million Jews for two hundred and fifty dollars a head! Had not Bettina been right when she warned him how people would look at him? Was it coincidence that she and the Ambassador from the distant foreign country had said almost the same thing? What had brought him here, what was driving him on, who had he become? Did he want to be Moses and lead the Jews through the Red Sea?

He was not a religious man, and even an hour ago, when he had been close to death, in the cowardly hour of distress and easy divine revelation, he had not thought of God, had not called upon Him, had not implored Him, had made no promise to Him. Moses without God? But what do we know about the conversations between Moses and the Lord? We only know what that other prophet cried out at the ninth hour upon the cross: *"Eli, Eli, lama sabachthani?* My God, my God, why hast thou forsaken me?"* Prophet or son of God, and these words had come down to us: "My God, my God, why hast thou forsaken me?" It occurred to Heinrich von Benda that on his arrival he had discovered a Bible in German in his nightstand; a zealous Bible society distributed them everywhere to hotel guests, who no doubt required edification. He stood up, found the Bible still in the same place, sat down again in the armchair, and opened it. Exodus, chapter xiii. "And Moses said unto the people, Remember this day in which ye came out of Egypt, out of the house of bondage, for by strength of hand the Lord brought you out from this place. . . . This day came ye out in the month Abib." Abib, the month of ears of corn, a month in spring, March or April, the Professor couldn't remember exactly. The Lord had commanded Moses to raise his hand, and when Moses had raised his hand the waters parted. Should that comfort him, Professor von Benda? Did the waters part when he raised his hand, and why did they not part now, since the need was greater than in the house of bondage in Egypt? Had he only claimed to be Moses, or was he Moses without God, because God was dead?

He put the Bible aside. The clock pointed to four, the hour of approaching morning and the climax of crises in hospitals. The Professor's room faced east; by day he could see the northeastern bank of Lac Léman, where Vevey and Montreaux lie. The sky was growing light. The trilling of a bird fell silent; it had realized that it was still too early to sing. Heinrich von Benda shivered. He closed the window, or rather brought the two casements into contact, went back to his bed, and sat down gingerly on the edge. A great deal had happened since he had left his bed, for there is no greater step than that between illusion and knowledge. He looked around the sparsely furnished room and noted that the light really was dim, he hadn't merely imagined it. Bettina and Heinrich were still

asleep, and in the Hôtel Royal the reception was perhaps at
an end, and the Rossauer Lände was loud with the pain of the
tortured. In the hospitals the young doctors were sitting around
the steaming coffee, and in the wards the agony of the dying
was beginning. What would tomorrow bring? Should he ring
the German Consulate in Geneva, speak to the American Ambassador again, try to find other allies? Should he wait for a
voice, raise his hand, hope for a miracle? He didn't know. He
only knew that he mustn't die.

The Évian Conference was opened on Wednesday the 6th of
July, 1938, at four in the afternoon in the so-called Grand
Salon of the Hôtel Royal.

The thirty-two delegations—consisting of about two hundred people including attachés, advisers, experts, and secretaries—had already been in conference the whole morning.
The discussions took place in the delegates' apartments, in the
lounges and in the gardens of the hotel. Most of the delegates
preferred the summer park on whose beautifully kept lawns
tables, chairs and sunshades had been picturesquely arranged.
The park and hotel lie only about three hundred yards above
Évian, but the hill falls so steeply down to the little spa that
the park, framed in thick clumps of flowers and beds of blossoming roses, forms a terrace with an uninterrupted view of
Lake Geneva, the city of Lausanne and the mountains of
Vaud. The hotel, whose semicircular wooden balconies are
reminiscent of the artistic Spanish bird cages of the seventeenth
century, has something of the lavish elegance of the turn of the
century about it, a grace that contains nostalgia and a feeling
of farewell and combines elements of grandeur with a con-
quering bad taste.

As is almost always the case with international conferences,
these morning consultations were concerned primarily with
questions of procedure, which can always give the practiced
observer an indication of the future course of the conference.

Two groups had already crystallized during the morning
hours: those who thought the Conference might create a commission, an office, perhaps a permanent organization to devote
itself to the problems of the refugees within the League of

Nations, housed nearby; and a second that was in favor of establishing a new and independent committee concerned solely with refugee questions. Naturally the High Commissioner for Refugees and the General Secretary of the venerable Nansen Office were present. The latter especially, who was at the same time the chief delegate from Norway, threw himself ardently behind the move to create a department within the League of Nations, since he feared that the setting up of an entirely new and independent commission would lead to confusing demarcation difficulties, the division or diminution of his own budget and of course also a certain competition with his time-honored office. Even on the first day, however, it became clear that, although he was vigorously supported by the British, he was on the losing side, because the United States, which did not belong to the League of Nations, was strongly opposed to any incorporation within the hypertrophied body in Geneva.

Another subject was thornier and had to be handled with the greatest diplomatic tact. The refugees from Germany and Austria who had already managed to cross the frontier had their own representative bodies, associations and aid committees, more or less recognized by some governments, and these had sent delegates to Évian. One of them, Artur Rosenberg by name, but in no way related to the Third Reich's racial ideologist of the same name, had requested that his and other associations should be admitted to the Conference, which after all, so he argued, was there to discuss the refugees from National Socialist barbarity. A splendid unanimity, perhaps promising agreement later over other, more important matters, prevailed among participants in the Conference that sunny morning. The intervention of refugees in the Conference was to be prevented from the outset, and this for many, well-considered reasons. For one thing, remarked the Swiss delegate, the chief of his country's political police, the admission of emigrants would unnecessarily antagonize the German Reich; second, Paraguay's envoy convincingly argued, it would be impossible to admit one association without likewise accepting other, more or less private committees. But the American Ambassador settled the question. He possessed certain information, he said, indicat-

ing that Germany had permitted individual Jews to come to
Évian; if they were allowed to take part in the discussion it
would be impossible to prevent Berlin, either directly or via the
Gestapo, from being informed of the progress of the Conference at an unsuitable juncture. By midday Professor von Benda,
who also spent his time in the Hôtel Royal, where he made
the acquaintance of Artur Rosenberg, had learned that, like
many other people, he was welcome in the lobbies, lounges
and gardens of the fine hotel, but could only observe the actual
deliberations of the Conference from outside.

This prohibition, issued with absolute politeness and without personal animosity, applied, of course, only to the secret
sessions. When the Conference was meeting in public, entry
to the Grand Salon, provided there were sufficient seats, was
not forbidden to the Jewish representatives any more than it
was to the wives of the delegates, the notables of the town and
finally to the international press, which included the representative of the *Völkischer Beobachter* and similarly interested
newspapers. Whether there would be any public sessions at all,
apart from the opening and closing ceremony, appeared doubtful, since complete agreement over this procedural question
had already been obtained that morning. If the Conference
was to proceed without complaint, if the delegates were to
speak with uninhibited frankness and the possible impression
of a division of opinion was to be avoided as far as the outside
world was concerned, the Conference must meet behind closed
doors.

The solemn opening of the Conference took place punctually at four in the afternoon. In the center of the room stood
a horseshoe-shaped conference table covered with green baize
at which the chief delegates—three ambassadors, thirteen en-
voys, three ministers and thirteen other high diplomats, all in
black—had taken their seats, while their assistants occupied
the two rows of chairs immediately behind them. Three further rows had been reserved for the audience. Here, in the last
row, Heinrich von Benda had been given a seat between an
old lady and a Hungarian journalist.

The hall was high, but only of medium size, a lounge that
was certainly not intended for such a serious, one might almost

say macabre, occasion. The light walls, decorated in both the classicist and the secessionist style, were topped by a fresco ceiling on which stood the proud initials of the hotel framed by lacelike scrolls; the healing springs, parks and promenades of the town of Évian-les-Bains were also depicted, half realistically, half idealized, leaving one with the impression of being in an emporium rather than a conference hall.

The session was opened by the French Ambassador as the representative of the host country. Immediately after him the American Ambassador rose and extolled the humanitarian aims that had moved the President of the United States to call the Conference. America, he said, had already raised the quota for German and Austrian immigrants to 27,370 persons per annum; his government was certain that it would meet with understanding and sympathy among all the participating states. "I need not emphasize," said the Ambassador, "that the discrimination against minorities, the pressure that is being brought to bear upon them and the disregard of elementary human rights contradict those principles which we have come to regard as the standards of our civilization. We have heard from time to time of the disastrous consequences of the flooding of the international markets with certain goods which is known as 'dumping.' How much more disastrous, gentlemen, must it be if there is an involuntary and chaotic 'dumping' of large numbers of unfortunate human beings."

A cold shudder ran down the spine of Heinrich von Benda in the last row of seats. The American President's special envoy was speaking words founded upon noble intentions, but was he not also speaking of the persecuted as though they were merchandise, was not he too comparing them with the cheap and superfluous objects that some countries, particularly those of the Far East, had been pouring out on the markets of recent years?

The American Ambassador's speech was greeted with polite cheers; now the United Kingdom representative rose to speak. His lordship, member of the House of Lords and Chancellor of the Duchy of Lancaster, was a man who, whatever figures were contained in his coat of arms, could very well stand as an image of Britain. His lean figure, strongly marked cheekbones with the hollow cheeks, the protruding upper lip with two large incisors, the reddish-blond, thin hair surrounding a high forehead, betrayed the Englishman even at a distance, while his careful enunciation, his shy and at the same time unconstrained gestures, the cut of his double-breasted suit and his college tie indicated a family of high lineage.

The chief British delegate extolled the humanitarian aims that had moved the President of the United States to call the Conference. It had always been a British tradition, he said, to offer asylum to those persecuted for religious or racial reasons. On the other hand, he went on, he must point out that the United Kingdom was not "a country of immigration." "Britain is a highly industrialized country, densely populated and at present engaged in a difficult fight against unemployment." The same applied, if to a lesser degree, to Britain's overseas possessions. At the same time they were certainly in a position to take a limited number of refugees, more particularly young people willing to take part in the process of industrialization. Whether the Conference could begin work with good prospects of success depended primarily upon the refugees' country of origin—he avoided using the word Germany. "No country," declared his lordship, weighing his words and carefully stressing certain of them, "can be expected to take people who have been robbed of their means of existence before even embarking on their emigration. Nor can private associations be expected to replace those means of which the emigrants have been deprived in their country of origin." The resettlement of refugees, he concluded, had a chance of success only if the refugees were permitted to bring their goods and chattels with them.

It was fortunate, thought Professor von Benda, that he was forbidden to make his voice heard at this meeting. If he had been allowed to speak, how could he have resisted the temptation of asking his lordship on this very first day, at this solemn hour, whether the refugees from the Spanish Inquisition, the Protestants of Flanders and Brabant, the Huguenots, the aristocrats fleeing from Robespierre's guillotine, and Kosciusko and Mazzini and Kossuth, who died in exile, had been allowed to bring their "goods and chattels" with them, whether a regime that set out to carry off women and murder children did not naturally also rob "minorities" of their "means of existence," whether one could really expect furniture vans to cross the snow-covered Swiss Alps, that had become the grave of so many refugees, whether a human being was only worth as much as the money he carried in his bag.

Meanwhile the French Ambassador had begun to speak, this time in his capacity as representative of the Republic—a pale, thin man who possessed a fine intellectual's head, strikingly beautiful hands and the noble diplomatic language belonging to the nation of Talleyrand. His Excellency extolled the humanitarian aims that had moved the President of the United States to call the Conference, but he was manifestly the realist among the representatives of the Great Powers, because he immediately began to quote figures—France had already taken in 200,000 refugees and she was a country with forty million inhabitants for whom a total of three million foreigners represented even without this an almost insoluble problem. With an elegance to which the clumsier representatives of the Anglo-Saxon nations could not aspire, he did what they, if far less skillfully, had also done—he threw the ball into the court of the other participants in the Conference. He pointed out what services immigrants and also refugees had rendered the younger states of the world, the two Americas and especially Australia, so that the countries of these continents would doubtless welcome the refugees with open arms.

After the American Ambassador had been unanimously elected chairman, the Conference declared its wish to get down to the real work, and since diplomatic work is best carried out *in camera caritatis,* the public was asked to leave the hall. The Professor left the Grand Salon with the other nonparticipants.

Heinrich von Benda had the feeling, as he entered the crowded lobby, that the American Ambassador was gazing after him. He was not suffering from an illusion. The conversation he had had with the Professor the previous evening had not left the Ambassador's mind. He had informed the President, in a coded cablegram, of the Reich Government's strange, suspiciously indirect proposal, but he expected no answer to his report; he had to deal on his own with the problem that had arisen so surprisingly. To the Ambassador, who had long experience with diplomatic conferences, this was above all a question of procedure. The general assembly would very soon break up into committees and subcommittees, and this was a good thing, because the more people spoke the less they said. The important thing now—during the night the Ambassador had considered various possibilities—was to persuade the Conference to elect a committee empowered to negotiate with the Germans, or the "country of origin" if the participants preferred this phrase, or at least to sound out the intentions of the "country of origin." Once such a committee had been formed responsibility would no longer rest exclusively on his, the Ambassador's, shoulders; then the committee could hear Professor von Benda and, who knows, receive the German Reich's proposal. The Ambassador looked around—old stale diplomats, young ambitious diplomats, fair Anglo-Saxons, dark Latin Americans, overbred aristocrats and broad-shouldered Socialists; which of these, the Ambassador asked himself, was best fitted to act as chairman of the committee, to whom could he skillfully, with extreme caution and without betraying his true purposes, pass the ball?

Now the Conference was in "secret" session, and the Australian delegate, his country's minister of trade and customs, had asked to speak. Certainly, he began, the honorable representative of the République Française had rightly spoken of the blessings brought to the distant continent of Australia by immigration, but he had overlooked the fact that it was the British immigration that had so admirably contributed to Australia's standing and prosperity. "Up to now," he cried, "we in Australia have had no racial problem, and we do not wish to create one now."

A racial problem? The American Ambassador made no reply, but it seemed to him at that moment that he had little reason to be glad about his flattering election to the chair. The old man from Vienna, who had sat facing him yesterday evening and was now no doubt waiting outside the curtained glass doors for the result—what would the Professor have thought if he could have heard the Australian's speech? To the Minister sent by Australia—the Minister for Trade and Customs; why just this one?—the Jews were a "race"; he used the same vocabulary in which other words also appeared—foreigner, intruder, subhuman on one page, blood, soil, Aryanism, master race on the other—the Jews were a race and probably political refugees were a race by themselves, a foreign race, to which belonged all those who did not correspond to his own conception of nation, state and government. Poor old man, thought the old man in the chairman's chair, but he did not consider it appropriate to intervene, at least not at such an early stage.

His British lordship expressed his gratitude for the uplifting words in which his Australian colleague had described British immigration into Australia. He himself wished first to clarify a matter of principle. When the American President called the Conference, he must certainly have had in mind more than the problem of asylum. "First things first" was an old and well-tried English principle; it would be best to deal first with the emigrants who had already succeeded in escaping. A not inconsiderable proportion of the refugees had left their country of origin illegally; these emigrants were now in foreign countries without money or papers, a regrettable state of affairs which little could now be done to remedy, but which contained within it a further danger. Others might learn from the bad example and place the countries of asylum in "an embarrassing situation." Before starting to encourage emigration or immigration it must be unequivocally stated that the emigration and immigration must take place according to the correct forms; asylum could be afforded only to those who did not prove themselves from the outset unworthy of asylum by disregarding frontier, passport and immigration regulations.

Applause from several quarters. No one could read behind the stony mien of the Chairman. He had long since realized that high politics, or what people understood by high politics, had entered Évian. The loyalty of the colonies and dominions was not as solid as was pretended in London. But Évian was a sidetrack, and it didn't cost the colonies and dominions much, cost them at most the lives of a few million Jews, to demonstrate their solidarity with the mother country, just as it didn't

cost England much to hold back the troublesome stream of
foreigners from the countries of the Crown. On the Ambassador's desk lay a memorandum from the Jewish Agency for
Palestine stating that the number of Jews in the Holy Land
had risen between 1918 and 1937 from 60,000 to 416,000, that
the country of the Jews was entirely capable, if given support
in solving its irrigation problem, of taking in 240,000 Jews at
once and another half million in the course of time. The simplest solution, certainly, but also the most complicated. A million Jews in Palestine—that would mean for England, at war
with the Jews of Palestine who were demanding independence, a suicidal import of potential enemies. Was there not a
proverb that said that only the stupidest calves choose their
own butcher? That very morning *The New York Times* had
reported a bomb attack in Haifa under the headline TWENTY-
THREE DEAD IN ISRAEL UPRISING—twenty-three dead and also
a British soldier had been injured. To be sure, Jewish intellectuals in Berlin, merchants in Frankfurt, artisans in Vienna,
Jewish women and children in other parts of Europe had
little to do with those Maccabees who had grown out of the
meager soil of Palestine—but at this point the problem became so complex that one dared not think about it, let alone
attack it. Who were they, these Jews? Were they symbols of
intolerant persecution, the believers of a religious community, European minorities, American citizens, a nation in Palestine, disillusioned German patriots, the salt of the earth,
human beings like any others, or, who knows, members of
a particular race of which the Australian minister for trade
and customs had spoken?

In the meantime the Ambassador had almost automati-
cally called upon the Haitian envoy to speak, the only Negro at
the Conference table, a corpulent man with a shiny bald patch
and a brilliant white waistcoat, his country's commercial attaché in Paris who had been given the title of envoy extraordinary and minister plenipotentiary especially for Évian.

If the Conference was to be crowned with success, as
all *"hommes de bonne volonté"*—he spoke in French—wished
with all their hearts, then they must come to terms with certain
realities.

The gentlemen around the green table nodded their agreement, because nothing arouses more unanimous agreement at international conferences than the commonplace to which no objection can be raised and which everyone can interpret in his own way.

The realities, the corpulent man continued, demanded honest collaboration with Germany—he said *"l'Allemagne,"* not *"pays d'origine."* Germany was a state in which the rule of law prevailed. The Conference would be ill advised to act as though the Jews of Germany and what used to be Austria were actually in danger of their lives. On the other hand, for reasons which it was unnecessary to go into here, they were in danger of having to forfeit their material possessions, but precisely this might be prevented if a sensible agreement were reached with Germany. The Jews of the German Reich were reputed to possess two hundred million dollars, a considerable sum, certain German sources even put it at seven hundred to eight hundred million. If they could take this with them, their welcome would be ensured. Moreover there was a further consideration which he could not honestly conceal from the Conference. He might be considered to speak for most of the small Latin-American republics when he pointed out the important, continually increasing and fruitful commercial relations between these countries and Germany. It was scarcely in the interest of the great and wealthy states to delay or prevent such a healthy development through precipitate steps defamatory to the German Reich. It was true that Germany had refused the invitation to Évian, but it was a matter for the Conference, he said, to set up a committee to investigate German intentions and, if it proved possible, to maintain contact with Berlin. Here, he concluded, he was making a concrete proposal on which he asked the Conference—he bowed to the Chairman —to vote.

Now it was up to the American Ambassador to proceed tactically, that is to say with tact. Earlier than he had expected, the demand for the establishment of a committee to negotiate with Germany had been made even if not by the right man and not for the right purpose. His eye fell on the delegate from Colombia, who was sitting only a few chairs away from him.

In reality this was not the chief delegate from the republic on the River Magdalena; he had fallen ill and his place had been taken by the government's legal adviser, a university professor from Bogotá. Why hadn't the Ambassador thought of him straight away? The little bald-headed professor was known throughout the diplomatic world for his acute commentary on international law and for his contribution to the legal structure of the League of Nations; he was an authority; he was a liberal thinker and on top of that—a gleam of light at last—a Latin American, so that he would enjoy the confidence of no less than nineteen Latin-American delegations.

The Ambassador seized his chance. Whether they wished to act upon the suggestions of the honorable representative of Haiti in their entirety or only in part, he said, there could be no doubt that a committee must be set up to sound out German intentions—only the full assembly of the Conference would have the right to negotiate directly with Germany. He seconded the proposal, put it to a vote and at the same time, although this was not necessarily part of his function, he proposed that the honorable delegate of the Republic of Colombia should be elected chairman of the new committee. Speed was essential and if the chairman were elected now he could suggest the other members of his committee to the plenary session tomorrow morning. With this vote—without doubt an excellent result for this first afternoon—he, the Chairman, would like to adjourn the meeting until tomorrow. "It is getting close to eight, gentlemen, and the stomachs of diplomats speak no less loudly than any other stomachs."

A *bon mot* that neatly concluded the first day's work—but the Ambassador wasn't hungry. After the vote and as he made his way laboriously to the elevator between the waiting journalists, who bombarded him with questions, he managed things so as to be standing beside the delegate from Colombia. He invited him to dine with him in his private suite.

There he informed him of the strange affair which he called the "Benda Mission."

In the Hôtel Splendide two telegrams were waiting for the Professor, both in English: a very lengthy telegram from the

University of Boston offering him a professorship; a briefer one from the Montefiore Hospital in New York offering him the position of head of the surgical department. He also found a visiting card waiting for him; the correspondent of *The New York Times* had been to see him. From these messages the Professor concluded that the American press had reported his presence in Évian.

He had eaten a light breakfast and only a sandwich for lunch. "Full board," as the expression goes, had been paid for him at the Hôtel Splendide—whether by the German Government directly or through a middleman he didn't know. In the middle of the day he would have had to come down the narrow mountain path that linked the two hotels and then climb back up to the Hôtel Royal again, but wisely he had not trusted himself to perform this strenuous walk. Although he had grown up in Vienna, where lunch is the main meal of the day, and was accustomed to good food, he had told himself that after a heart attack, if he could not confine himself to bed, at least moderation was called for; also he wanted to spend as little money as possible, since he didn't know how long the Conference would last and he remembered the green dress in the shop window. Furthermore Heinrich von Benda looked with a certain humor upon the thrift which was imposed upon him by the currency regulations and which he now ordered himself to observe in even greater measure; he felt in no way oppressed or to be pitied because of the meagerness of his means, indeed he discovered, to his surprise, that poverty had a rejuvenating effect on him. It was an atavistic feeling, a memory that rose up from student days long past. Wealth had come with the years; the unworried freedom to spend money as he thought fit had been an accompaniment of age. It was quite fun, or at least so he told himself, to turn every bank note over twice before spending it. This was no frivolous attitude; the Professor knew very well that real poverty was neither fun nor rejuvenating. Behind the game that he played with thrift lay the consciousness that a telephone call to grateful patients, foreign friends, would have brought him any sum he wanted; but again it was not so simple, for he was determined to return home after the Conference and how could he then repay his debts, and if he borrowed money would he not have to reveal at once that, against all good sense, he intended to return home?

As he made his way to the dining room he became aware once again—and all the more so because of the cables he had just received—of his curious situation. Similar messages had piled up on his desk in Vienna before this. But then he had been a prisoner, the significance of the flattering offers had not been much greater than that of the laudatory obituary speeches that never call a dead man back from the grave. From Évian he could have answered the telegrams, in fact sooner or later would have to do so—but what was he to answer? That he had deserted his profession, that he had thrown the work of a lifetime overboard, that he was no longer interested in scientific research, that he was nothing but a Jew, and thus precisely what the new masters wanted him to be? In Vienna he had resolved to bring all his contacts into play, to ring the Duke of Windsor and the Aga Khan and the Queen of Greece, and had drafted in his mind an appeal to the Rothschilds, the Strausses, the Warburgs. Seen from close to, what he had passionately planned looked fundamentally different. They would all believe that he was concerned for his own safety or with a begging campaign for the refugees or at best with an appeal against the inhuman regime. Whom could he let into his secret, since he could not let everyone into his secret? How could he tell them that he was here for one single reason? He was here to offer Jews for sale with the added proviso that only governments were allowed to be the purchasers?

In the crowded dining room he had been assigned to a small table by the window. He still had no appetite, and the long menu embellished with alluring epithets made him feel nauseated. Not that he had been feeling ill; on the contrary, all day he had felt no pain and only every now and then a slight drawing in his left arm and under the armpit, so that his memory of the agonizing night was beginning to pale—a typical phenomenon with illnesses that do not continually announce their presence, but leap upon the unsuspecting in the form of sudden attacks. He began to indulge in all sorts of illusions. He tried to persuade himself that medicine recognized certain, or rather uncertain, illnesses grouped under the general name "pseudo-angina," diseases of the stomach, rheumatic pains and hernias of the diaphragm in particular, whose symptoms resembled those of angina pectoris and yet were not followed by the same serious consequences. He made up his mind to order a light lunch and not to think of his condition.

The glass doors were open and a cool breeze that had risen from the lake brought airy relief after the sultry, premature high summer day. The public seemed to the Professor a very motley collection, as though aboard ship, for unknown reasons, the first, second and tourist class passengers had been assembled together in one dining room. Beside gentlemen in dinner jackets sat others in sports and business suits, beside ladies in low-cut evening dresses were others wearing simple day frocks and tailormade costumes. To his surprise, even in this conglomeration of nations, social classes, health seekers and Conference supernumeraries, the Professor could clearly distinguish the refugees. Their clothes betrayed the tailors and dressmakers from "over there"; they wore their dresses and suits with a painful care, fearing that in the future they would not be able to replace them with anything equally good; they talked to the waiters and waitresses in low voices, with an anxious politeness, as though conscious all the time that those who served them were the possessors of French passports and hence beings of a higher order; they treated their marriage partners with a cautious tenderness, as is the way with people who have no one but each other. The tables of the emigrants, for the most part elderly people, were quiet islands in the quite turbulent dining room, where page boys were forever seeking individual guests, mostly newspaper correspondents, who were called to the telephone from Paris, London, Brussels and Oslo.

One of the pages came over to the Professor's table and handed him a telegram. It had been sent from Paris and read: Arriving late evening, can only stay overnight. Felix.

The Professor felt his heart, which registered every emotion like a seismograph, grow heavier and more burdensome; a hard thumb seemed to be forcing itself in between his ribs and preventing him from breathing. He asked the page boy to let him know the moment a visitor arrived for him, left the dessert untouched and lit a cigar. After all, he thought, cigars, whose smoke is not inhaled, had done him no harm in the past and would not cause him any trouble now.

It was due to the page, who had called out Professor von Benda's name in an indecently loud voice, that attention was now directed toward him; at several tables—they must have been the refugees' tables—there was whispering, people leaned forward to see better, which caused the Professor to stare down at his plate and hastily to sign the check. As he left the dining room he had to push past the table of Frau Lederer and her son; he greeted them as he passed, but he had a vague feeling, like a bad aftertaste, that his greeting was answered shortly and with embarrassment.

He remained in the lobby only long enough to tell the porter that he would now be in the lounge when wanted; but in spite of the briefness of his stop he noticed a strikingly fair-haired man who was hovering about him, obviously not unintentionally. The coarse-looking young man, recognizable as a German by his overwide hips and shoes that did not go with the rest of his clothes, followed the Professor into the lounge, where he sat down close by him with clumsy and unnecessary obviousness. The Professor now remembered the shadow who had followed him in the streets of Évian and had also popped up time and again in the park of the Hôtel Royal—but as he was wondering whether the Gestapo, like miners, worked in day and night shifts, something quite grotesque happened. At this moment the day shadow entered the lounge, looked around searchingly, took in the Professor and the night shadow with a glance, wrinkled his forehead and went over to the long table in the middle of the room on which faded daily papers, crumpled magazines and dreary specialist periodicals lay at everyone's disposal but to no one's advantage.

The Professor's thoughts oscillated between the imminent visit of his son and the day that was just drawing to a close. One thought was as distressing as the other. He had not seen his son for four years, in the last fourteen years they had met only sporadically. From his early childhood Felix had wanted to be a doctor, but when he had passed his final examination from high school and a decision about the future became urgent, he made his choice dependent upon an astonishing and quite unexpected condition. He wanted to become a doctor, but not in Vienna. Heinrich von Benda respected his son's resolve. He thought it was due to his natural pride and ambition which rebelled against studying at the same university in which his father played such an important, indeed dominant role; no doubt Felix did not wish to take any unfair advantage either as a student or in his career. Later Heinrich von Benda realized that the young man who set out for Paris was moved by these motives, but not by them alone. Felix wanted, at any price, to leave his father's house, for he imagined that his sister Elisabeth had claimed the whole of his father's love; he was fleeing from the Byzantine veneration shown everywhere to his father's name and which raised it to the status of a monument, so that only the name Benda mattered, while the Christian name Felix appeared totally superfluous; but he also left because he wanted to take revenge on his father. During the following years the Professor often asked himself whether in reality Felix ever wanted to be a doctor at all; perhaps he only wanted to appear free from vacillation. If following in his father's footsteps was a symbolic tribute to his father, at least it should not be paid to his father in person and under his eyes. For the first few years Felix used to spend his holidays in his father's house; then he more and more frequently made excuses and returned for only short periods to Vienna. As soon as he had received his degree he politely refused the material support which Heinrich von Benda had been giving him on the most generous scale. He managed as best he could on his own, though often very badly, as his father learned, refused with thanks his father's offer to help him set up in private practice and contented himself with the career of a hospital doctor, though he did succeed in rising to the position of first assistant to the Paris laryngologist, Professor Lamartine.

As he now sat waiting for Felix in the unfriendly green lounge, Heinrich von Benda wondered why his son had never aroused great emotions in him, not even strong feelings of a negative kind. He hadn't been a good father, in any case not good enough, but it wasn't that alone. Felix—this was nearer

to the truth—never did the wrong thing, he merely didn't do
the right thing the right way. His actions were so irritatingly
correct that any false step was out of the question, so that love
was relieved of all worry; but at the same time Felix was convinced that his actions constituted a criterion for others; he
knew the limits of his talents as few people do, but this fine
modesty was coupled with intolerance toward all those who
saw their own limitations less clearly; he felt little or no resentment at other people's lack of cordiality toward him, but he
himself was cordial toward no one. Eight years ago he had
married a French girl strictly brought up in the Catholic faith,
from an excellent but poor family; he had two daughters,
whose photographs he sent to their grandfather, without ever
bringing them to Vienna in spite of repeated invitations, and
when the Professor visited Paris, shortly after his marriage to
Bettina, Felix refrained from more than a single, thoroughly
formal invitation. The birth of little Heinrich was the first and
only occasion on which Felix "behaved badly," or at least appeared to do so; he sent a telegram of congratulation, but never
again mentioned mother and child in his letters that arrived
regularly every six weeks. Felix "behaved badly," but it was at
precisely this moment that the Professor took him to his heart,
either because in this expression of human weakness he for
the first time discovered the human element in his son, or else
because for the first time he became aware of his own mistakes
and omissions.

All this passed through the Professor's head while the lounge
was filling up to the last chair with a disquieting medley—re-
porters, a rabbi from New York, a Protestant bishop from
Paris, ladies from all kinds of aid and welfare organizations,
the former chief editor of the *Vossische Zeitung*, German and
perhaps other agents, emigrants, diplomats, old ladies and a
young pipe-smoking monsignor who was said to be the Holy
Father's envoy.

Although he tried to convince himself that the Conference
had only begun today, indeed only this afternoon, the Professor felt as though he had already lost a great deal of valuable
time and as though it was not least his own fault that it had
slipped through his fingers. Time and conscience had always

played in Heinrich von Benda's life the role of opposing sisters that fought and at the same time supplemented each other —if time ran away, conscience tried to catch up with it; conscience felt responsible for the conscienceless squandering of time, hated the thoughtlessness of time, but tried to replace the loss which time caused and through which time itself became poorer; the more time went on the loose, the more domesticated became conscience. And yet Heinrich von Benda had done everything he could. That morning he had gone to the post office and from there, taking every precaution, had rung the Geneva number of Herr Stechlein, had reached him and arranged a meeting for the following day without, of course, giving him any detailed information about his conversation with the American Ambassador. He had written Herr Silberstein a lengthy letter and sent it to Vienna express and registered, had made the acquaintance of a few international correspondents in the Hôtel Royal and learned something about the course of the secret Conference session. Finally and at a late hour he had spoken to an attaché of the Colombian Republic and asked him to arrange a meeting for him with the chairman of the special committee. Nevertheless the Professor was depressed that he had not had a single important conversation that day, nor apparently had moved a step nearer to his goal. He ought not to have left the Hôtel Royal, not just then; negotiations over the fate of the refugees were doubtless going on continuously in the lounges, bars and private suites; he ought to have wandered about there, made new contacts. Chance was a whore, but even whores had particular beats; perhaps, who knew, the one and only man, the man who held the key, might be among those surrounding him here, and yet he had failed to make the acquaintance of just this man; perhaps, who knew, just one of these men was waiting for the redeeming word in order himself to be able to utter the redeeming word; perhaps, who knew, he himself was too old, too immobile, too inexpert and too lacking in ideas to fulfill his task.

Again and again the Professor looked at the door, from the door to the clock, then again at the door. Was it joyful excitement that had taken possession of him, or did he fear the meeting with his son? It is hard for fathers to be honest. His sojourn in freedom was of short duration, and it was not certain that the meeting with Felix would not be their last. What would they talk about? Not about matters of indifference; dishonesty could not go that far. As soon as he had rung Felix, he had made up his mind to tell him everything. He had no other reason for this than that he must either lie or tell him the truth. From the point of the lie the point of the truth is just as easily reached as vice versa, but there is no path from the lie to the truth nor from the truth to the lie. One point can be reached from the other only at a single jump, without transition; the two points are infinitely far apart, but the will can bridge the distance in a single second, so that on the other hand they are quite close together. Since there is no path between lie and truth, there is also no middle way, no meeting point where the two might come together; if the slightest adjective or the slightest elucidation is added to the words truth and lie —half-truth, white lie, harmless lie, mitigated truth—the concepts change into their opposites or their characteristics, although enfeebled, become doubly visible. But would the son understand the father? No sooner had he reached his majority than Felix had become French, and like most new citizens he was French body and soul; eight years ago, on marrying the French girl, he had been converted to Catholicism and apparently was a practicing Catholic—would his son understand him? No, his son would not understand him, thought Heinrich von Benda, would perhaps ask him why he, who had never been a good Jew himself, had now taken upon himself the cause of the Jews, that the new Shylock, who was selling a pound of flesh, was no less Shylock than the one who demanded it—oh yes, he knew all that himself, why did he have to hear it all over again from the mouth of his son?

Then Felix appeared in the lounge doorway. His father had recognized him more quickly than he had recognized his father. The two men embraced.

"We'll go to my room," said the Professor. "It's small but we can drink a bottle of wine in peace." He said nothing about the two young men who were watching the reunion between father and son with poorly concealed interest.

He had set out early in the morning, said Felix as they walked toward the elevator, had been traveling all day and must set off again early next morning, because he could not be away from the hospital longer. "I've taken a room with a family, the hotels are all booked up. But I've got plenty of time—all night if you like."

In the elevator they spoke of unimportant things and as they talked the Professor reproached himself for not remembering exactly how old Felix was. Thirty-six, thirty-seven? He worked it out in his mind—1900, 1901, 1902. He remembered the day of Felix's birth exactly: the eleventh of October. It must have been the 11th of October, 1901. He didn't want to examine Felix directly; he studied him in the mirror of the elevator. He had the feeling that Felix had aged a great deal; he found it difficult to identify this middle-aged man with his own child, with the child and young man of the past; people you hadn't seen for a long time were like trees from whose tops you could no longer see the roots. The dark blond hair that Felix had inherited from his mother—he looked like her: the same fine, anemic face, the same absent eyes, the same slender, bent figure, and also the same tendency to age early—had grown thinner. Seen from the back Felix had a bald patch; it was strange to have a son who was balding.

"You haven't heard anything from Elisabeth?" asked the Professor, after the waiter had brought a bottle of Beaujolais and left again.

"Nothing."

The Professor related the circumstances of her disappearance; they speculated on various possibilities, but in the end could only cling to the hope that Elisabeth had somehow managed to reach Palestine.

"How's your wife?" asked the Professor.

"Well, thank you. She isn't working in the laboratory any more but is devoting herself entirely to the children."

"Marie-Louise is six now, isn't she?"

"Yes."

"And Denise four?"

"Yes. People say she is getting to look more and more like me. How is your wife?"

"You can imagine. But she is courageous, extraordinarily courageous."

He waited for Felix to inquire about his half brother. Felix tasted the wine, drank to his father.

"How's your own health?" he asked.

"Not bad. Events have taken it out of me a bit."

"Couldn't your wife and child have left with you?"

"There would have been no point. I'm going back myself."

"So you said on the telephone. I couldn't believe you meant it."

"I think I'd better tell you why I'm here."

"*Le Matin* says this morning that you have come to Évian as a delegate of the Jewish Community."

"The newspapers don't say anything about my special mission?"

"I've only seen *Le Matin*. There was nothing else in that."

"I'd like to hear your opinion."

His chin in his hands, Felix von Benda listened to his father's story attentively. What he heard angered and shocked him and he had difficulty in suppressing the old, unreasonable feeling, which he had long since banished to his subconscious, that his father was never, and despite all appearances never could be, right; but he made an effort to understand the old man. His father had asked him an objective question; he wanted to answer it objectively. For an instant, too, he felt a certain satisfaction over the belated frankness, born of necessity, with which his father approached him. But his father wanted to hear his opinion, he had to concentrate on the circumstances of the incredible mission, had to try to form a clear clinical picture. Meanwhile, the longer the Professor talked, the more difficult his son found it to separate the mission from the man to whom it was entrusted. He was like a doctor at the sickbed of a close relative: love is not helpful to diagnosis. Love! However much Felix struggled against it, he could not help being overcome with pity for the old man who was so unsure of his cause that he confided in his son. With that precision which he always brought to bear on any problem, Felix dissected his own pity and noted almost with relief that pity does not always spring from love—often you only suffer with someone in order to measure your own happiness against the other's unhappiness—but he came to the conclusion that he really did feel with the old man; an unfamiliar warmth rose in him, against which he once more tried to struggle, because it enveloped his judgment in a warm cloud.

Through the half-open window they could hear, fortunately only faintly and as though tired by its journey through the treetops, the music of the orchestra that was now playing on the hotel terrace.

"Do you really want to know what I think about all this?" Felix asked when the Professor had finished.

The Professor nodded.

"It could be a disaster if America or the Conference considered your proposal," Felix began. He had now complete control of himself once more, and was able to express his arguments as soberly as if he were speaking to or of a stranger. Obviously his father didn't understand what had been happening these last few years, he said; after all, so far as he knew, his father had never bothered about politics before Austria's *Anschluss*. "We have tolerated Hitler—forgive me if by 'we' I mean above all, France—therefore he is counting on our tolerance. This autumn at the latest he will invade Czechoslovakia."

The Professor lit a cigarette, drew on it a few times, then put it out again.

"This time the Germans will be making a mistake," Felix continued. "The patience of the world is at an end, they have no other choice than war. The alliance between Britain and France has rested since the end of the World War on the foundation of the Little Entente; if the Great Powers were to abandon Czechoslovakia it would be all up with them. Hitler has been lying to the world long enough with his 'willingness to negotiate'; moreover, in order to maintain Germany's pseudo-prosperity, he must start a war of conquest."

"Then the Jews of Germany, Austria and Eastern Europe are lost," the Professor broke in. "Hundreds of thousands, perhaps millions."

As he uttered the sentence the Professor was surprised to see how strangely he had become one with his mission, so that the question of war or peace scarcely touched him any more, so that his anxious concern now related only to the Jews, with whom for a lifetime he had felt nothing in common. Was he really a Jew before everything and merely had not realized it, or would he have felt the same for other tormented people, people in danger, or was it merely part of his character that he did nothing by halves, nor three-quarters, nor was even satisfied with ninety-nine percent, but only with perfection?

The persecution of the Jews, said Felix, was symbolic of the regime and the things it was planning. He came back to the inevitable war. Hitler and his propaganda machine pretended that the Jews were stirring up war, but in reality it was tragic how little they were doing to stir up resentment—tragic because they ought to be urging war, yet feared it more than anyone else because of the Jews in Hitler's hands. The world was doing everything to save the Jews—"France alone has taken in two hundred thousand refugees, Jews and others"—but the most important thing of all was that the now inevitable war must on no account be lost. "If we don't want to lose it, we must play for time. If Hitler felt secure the war would have broken out long ago, and all he needs to feel secure is a few hundred million dollars. Read last Sunday's *Le Temps*. Germany has no oil, no adequate food reserves, no foreign currency. Germany cannot buy anything and has nothing to sell but Jews."

"If I understand you correctly," said the Professor bitterly, "time is to be bought with Jews."

"You can put it like that. But in reality the problem hasn't arisen until now. Only your mission raises it. You must understand France, France and the rest of the world. For every Jew whom we ransomed with dollars we should be supplying Hitler with one machine gun or its equivalent. You know how many people one machine gun can mow down. One Jewish family —one tank. Machine guns and tanks and bomber planes . . ."

The Professor remembered the discussions he had had with the sixteen- or seventeen-year-old boy. Even then Felix's cold logic had placed him in difficulties; his sharp, rapidly associating intelligence had impressed him even then, but even then he had found it remarkable that reason and logic, Felix's particular reason and logic, had never convinced him. He had never believed that Felix would make a great doctor nor did he believe it now, only now he knew the reason. The discrepancy between heart and understanding was too great; with understanding alone one can only make the right decisions, never the great ones.

"The annihilation of the Jews is certain," he said. "The war is probable but not certain. How would you act if you were convinced that you could with certainty save a few hundred thousand people? Would you bother your head about the not necessarily certain consequences of your actions?"

"I should," replied Felix. "Perhaps you think I'm speaking as a Frenchman and a Catholic . . ."

"Certainly not consciously . . ."

He had known the conversation was bound to end like this, the Professor thought. Felix was not speaking as a Frenchman or as a Catholic, he was only speaking like someone who lived outside. German or French, Jews or Catholics—that was not the great difference; outside or inside—that was the great difference. There would never again be a bridge between those who had been outside and those who had been inside.

Felix went to the window. He felt that he had talked too much about Hitler, France, war and the persecution of the Jews and too little about his father. He had spoken like a stranger, not because his father was a stranger to him—he was was less of a stranger to him now than he had ever been—but because he wanted to spare the old man. He said, "The purchase of Jews would be immoral even if Hitler used the money to build houses," but he didn't like his sentence, because it was bound to sound like a criticism of his father; that was exactly what he hadn't wanted.

The Professor did not seem offended. "What is the alternative?" he said. "Are the Jews to be exterminated because it is unethical to ransom them?"

"Perhaps there isn't any alternative. But why you . . . ? Why did you, of all people, have to take on this mission?"

"Does that matter?"

"You're a great doctor. People say there's no greater alive today."

The Professor's heart tightened. It was not that his son had called him a great doctor for the first time, even if with the reservation that was part of Felix's nature. Heinrich von Benda was not troubled by such vanity, although it was far harder to achieve prestige in the eyes of his son than in the eyes of the world. What made him happily excited was the thought that he might have misjudged his son, that Felix was capable of tenderness, that the son only feared for his father.

Quickly, as though ashamed of having felt moved, Felix began to talk about the war again. The Germans would reduce towns and villages to ashes and rubble, and women and children would be killed, and one day it would be written in the history books that a Viennese Jew, a doctor named Heinrich von Benda, innocently and in good faith to be sure, but blindly, had contributed to the universal misery. "Don't you understand? Jews can't act like other people." For two thousand years mankind had not forgiven the Jews for having crucified Christ, but that Christ had forgiven the Jews, the Jews as much as all mankind, that He had redeemed them, that He had built His church upon love and forgiveness, that He had died for them as much as for all other men and that He Himself was a Jew—this mankind had forgotten. The Romans' share in the crucifixion of Christ had been forgotten long ago, but the collective guilt of the Jews had become the symbol of guilt, so that whenever people looked for a guilty man they found a Jew and they never ceased to crucify Jews in the name of mercy. The enemies of Christ were the enemies of the Jews; all the same, no Jew could do any more than Christ had done for mankind, but even if all the Jews were to die for mankind, it would be to no avail. "People will forget how many Jews you saved," he told his father. "They will only count the corpses of the French and Czechs and British and Belgians; mankind differentiates between dead men and dead Jews, you can't change that. A thousand Japanese who perish

in an earthquake count a thousand times more than a hundred
thousand dead Jews; people will count only the sacrifices inflicted on the world, not the Jews saved. If the German Christians want to sell the Jews to British or American Christians,
let them, but don't get mixed up with it, Father!"

The Professor recognized the truth in his son's words. It
would have been better if a Christian emissary could have
stood here, it would have been better indeed if the cause of the
Jews had been represented by Christians for centuries. The
Jews, he thought bitterly, should never have become involved
in their own problems. The Catholics and the Protestants and
the Mohammedans, the Germans and the British and the
Americans—they could all get involved in their own problems,
but not the Jews. It was religious freedom and patriotism in
one case, self-seeking in the other—every time the Jews stood
up for themselves it had ended in accusation, condemnation
and persecution. If they crept along by the wall they were
cowardly, if they stepped out of the shadows they were impudent; if they were thrifty with their money they were miserly,
if they were generous with it they were ostentatious; if they
strove to get on they were eaten up with ambition, if they behaved modestly they were lacking in courage; if they fought
it was to win honors, if they didn't fight they had no honor
—but where was the Christian who took up the cudgels on
their behalf, where was the Christian who took over their mission?

"You know that I was never a good Jew," he said.

"There are no good and no bad Jews anymore. A Jew is
anyone people take for a Jew."

"Don't you think that I would do just the same for others
who were in the same position?"

"No, I don't think so, but that makes no difference," said
Felix.

He regretted the harshness of his words, came closer, sat
down beside his father, looked into his face and had the feeling
that he would never see him again. He was a specialist in diseases of the ear, nose and respiratory tract, and did not consider
himself a great diagnostician, but he was sure that he could
distinguish between pity and diagnosis. The idea that he

would never see his father again suddenly seemed to him unbearable. He had spoken first about the world, then about the
mission, but he had done both in order not to speak about his
father. Was it too late to convince the old man that of all human
lives, he ought first to take thought for his own life?

"You're ill," he said. "You ought to come with me to Paris
and go into a sanatorium. . . ."

"I'm only tired," said the Professor. "I have a bad night and
a strenuous day behind me." He smiled. "And the pleasure of
seeing you again. . . ."

He was a little dismayed that Felix had spotted his illness,
but his son's concern warmed his heart. Even if Felix didn't
understand him, it was good that they had seen each other
again.

"It would be utter madness to go back into the witches' caul-
dron," said Felix. "One of your famous patients will be able to
get your wife and child out. I have good contacts with the
French Foreign Ministry . . ."

"It's too late. I have taken on this mission."

That was the truth, thought Felix. His father had taken on
the mission, now he regarded himself as a missionary; it was
too late.

"You should go to bed," he said. "I'll wait until you're in
bed."

The Professor had been overcome by a great weariness; he
was afraid of the room in which yesterday—now he knew—he
had almost died; he did as his son asked him. He slowly undressed, went into the bathroom, cleaned his teeth. He tried
to carry on an everyday conversation, to find out about Felix's
work; he sent greetings to Madeleine, the children, Professor
Lamartine. At the same time he thought to himself that he
had never before undressed in front of his son. Felix handed
him his pajamas. When the Professor was in bed Felix said:

"I'll leave you my telephone number here, in case you need
anything during the night. I'll drop in again tomorrow morning. What time do you get up?"

"About eight."

Then Felix left. At the door he switched off the light.

No sooner had Felix closed the door behind him than the

Professor lit the bedside lamp, reached for his dressing gown
and got up. He sat down in the armchair. He was afraid of
sleep.

During the early hours of the morning a thunderstorm had
broken out over the lake, the air had cooled and was pure and
clear. Although the Professor knew what lay before him, what
difficulties, unpleasantness, perhaps humiliation, awaited him,
he felt better than at any time since he had left Vienna. He was
to meet Herr Stechlein at eleven, but he set out for the town
an hour earlier.

The Rue Nationale was still quiet. Two old women were
gossiping outside the butcher's, the woman who kept the sta-
tionery shop was hanging up the tin frame filled with picture
postcards outside her door; a baker's lad cycled past with long
white loaves under his arm; outside the offices of the spa
administration an old man was sweeping the street cautiously
as though he didn't want to hurt it.

The Professor stopped in front of the shop in whose window
the green dress was still elegantly draped. He had probably
only taken this early morning walk in order to make sure that
the dress had not been sold yet. The fear that it might slip
through his fingers, might be snapped up from under his
nose by some purchaser quick to make up his mind, took on
superstitious forms. Secretly he had already made up his mind
to buy it and identified his return home with this piece of
fabric and silk, because in contradiction of all rational thought
he imagined he could not set out on the return journey, could
not see Bettina again, without the dress. After some hesitation,
after holding the door latch in his hand and letting go of it
again, he entered the shop, where he was received by a sales-
lady with excessively blond dyed hair and makeup that looked
grotesque in the light of day. This lady—who turned out to
be the owner of the shop—remarked that she had been watching the customer for a long time through the window, that
he had obviously and very understandably fallen in love with
the green dress, *"cette petite affaire charmante."* Ignoring the
Professor's question as to how much *"la petite affaire charmante"* cost, she first extolled the dress's unusual qualities,

the exquisite material, nor did she forget to pay adequate tribute to its family tree. It was a Paris model—*"En effet, votre
goût est parfait, monsieur"*—you couldn't find its like anywhere else in Évian—"Alas, the public isn't what it was"—the
size was just right too—"Slim, medium height, perhaps a little
smaller you said, didn't you, monsieur?" In short the price of
8,400 francs was not high, was in fact a bargain.

The woman, thought the Professor, must have seen the dismay that came into his face as she named the price. He couldn't
have thought of any role that suited him less than that of the
confidence trickster, but he had never learned to haggle, to
make excuses, to forgo a purchase because the price was too
high; so he decided, before making an irreparable mistake, on
a compromise solution—half confidence trickery, slightly sensible and very silly. The price was high, higher than he had
expected; he was waiting for money from abroad that had been
held up by the exchange regulations, in other words if Ma-
dame would accept a deposit of, say, twelve hundred francs he
was sure he would be able to collect the dress in a few days.
The couturière accepted the proposal more readily than he had
anticipated. She was very well able to distinguish between an
ordinary man and a "monsieur," she said; besides, she didn't
want to disappoint the charming gentleman and—she smiled
—"the little lady." She was already stretching out her hand
for the hundred-franc notes, had already written out a receipt
for them.

As the Professor left the shop he felt a mixture of joy and
self-accusation, the aftertaste that recklessness nearly always
leaves. He was glad that the dress was, so to speak, now his,
but he had a bad conscience about the large sum of money he
had spent; he finally reassured himself with the thought that
if the worst came to the worst there was nothing to prevent
him from adding a second act of folly to the first and forfeiting
the deposit.

On the way to the Hôtel du Léman, which stood in the same
street and where, Herr Stechlein had told him, he was to go to
room number eight, Heinrich von Benda could not help thinking that the man from the Gestapo had no difficulty in cir-

culating unhindered between Switzerland and France, whereas he himself could not even have gone to Geneva, since he had "used up" his unique Swiss entry and exit visa and now had only the transit visa, which he had to save for his return trip via Basel. How could the Conference end with even a half success, if a man was worth only so much as he was worth in his homeland, if that man alone was welcome as a guest who could return home and did not need hospitality? Since the law of the jungle was spreading, how could the jungle itself fail to spread?

He found the Hôtel du Léman, a very modest *hôtel meublé* on the corner of the Rue Nationale and the Rue de la Source des Cordeliers, a dilapidated and not very confidence-inspiring inn with narrow French windows many of whose shutters were closed. For a moment he wondered whether he shouldn't walk up and down outside the inn a few times inconspicuously, perhaps turn into a side street and then emerge from it again, so as to make sure his shadows were still with him and to shake them off, but the idea struck him as repellent and degrading. Was it not repellent and degrading enough to have been ordered to this hotel by the Gestapo agent? His contact with the Americans was no secret to the Germans, nor was his contact with the Germans any secret to the Americans; the only purpose was to make him play a part in a low "thriller" being enacted on the margin of the Conference.

The hotel had no lobby and no porter's lodge; a steep staircase led upward from the doorway. The Professor stopped at the foot of the stairs as if before a steep mountain path, considered for a moment whether to risk the ascent, but admitted to himself that he feared the coming conversation more than the physical exertion; if he could not bring himself to take the next few steps he would be capitulating less before the stairs than before his interlocutor. He started to climb, his breath grew short, he had to rest after the third step, went on, rested again. But with each step his anger grew, because the overlords were able to exercise their power over him even from a distance. When he finally reached the summit, or rather the first floor, he stood still again, waited, tested the regularity of his breathing. He did not want to meet the enemy in a state of breathlessness. Only then did he start searching along the almost completely dark corridor.

When, after knocking, he opened the door, he started back in dismay, thinking he had mistaken the room. Herr Stechlein was nowhere to be seen; an unknown man was standing by the slightly open balcony window. He was at once assured that he had come to the right place, however. "Please come in," said the man and introduced himself. His name was Megelein, he said, Josef Megelein—Stechlein, Megelein, thought the Professor, probably their real names were quite different. Herr Stechlein wasn't "free" today, but he, Megelein, was fully authorized to receive the Professor's information and "possibly" to answer his questions.

The Professor did not doubt the stranger's words, in fact after the first sentence he thought he knew why Stechlein had been replaced by Megelein. Without doubt the latter was a more important personage, not altogether devoid of natural intelligence and better qualified to reach independent decisions. Unlike Herr Stechlein he did not correspond at all to the he-man type now extolled in Germany. He was a small, narrow-chested man with black hair, so thin as to suggest ill health, indeed it could not escape the doctor that this emissary of the master race was in the early stages of Parkinson's disease, *paralysis agitans*. The masklike immobility of the face, as though it had been painted with some white substance, was all the more striking because the head was in constant, if not violent, movement; Herr Megelein seemed continually to be saying no, to be shaking his head; nor could he stand or sit in one place but ran to and fro with his body bent forward, tripping round the small room as though driven by an oscillating force.

The Professor sat down and lit a cigarette—the last that day, he silently promised himself. He had spoken to the American Ambassador, he began, and had at once come upon an obstacle which made all further negotiations difficult if not impossible. The United States, and hence no doubt all the other participants in the Conference, were willing to consider the Reich Government's proposal only if it was presented officially or at least by a mouthpiece of Berlin. Before she would even consider material measures, America demanded proof that the Reich Government was serious about handing over the Jews; understandably, the United States did not want to make an offer to purchase merchandise—he used and stressed this word—that turned out not to be for sale at all.

"In other words," interrupted Herr Megelein, "the gentlemen want to put Germany in the wrong. They want to force the Reich Government into the role of a supplicant whose request they will then publicly reject, probably with a great show of indignation. Well, we are not surprised. . . ."

"The Ambassador said nothing about rejection."

Here the Professor stopped, because a terrible suspicion had risen in him. Perhaps the representative of the Gestapo was not altogether wrong, perhaps this man, even if guided by evil intentions, was more at home in the domain of politics, perhaps America was really not concerned about the refugees, perhaps she only wanted to unmask the Germans as traders in human beings, without buying what they had to offer. Or, worse still, Herr Megelein thought he understood the intentions of the other side so well because, in reverse, they were Germany's intentions. The Reich wanted to unmask the participants in the Conference as dealers in human beings, without in reality having any thought of releasing the Jews.

"Did you tell the American that your mission was secret?" asked Herr Megelein.

"Naturally."

"Well, anyhow, you didn't start off very intelligently."

The Professor felt the blood rise to his face. The rendezvous with the representative of the traders in human beings, which he himself had asked for; the agent—or whatever he was—whose ailing figure aroused no pity but merely underlined the repulsive back-alley atmosphere of the whole affair; the dark, untidy room with the open bed, the stuffy warmth, the smell of stable, and now the tone in which the wriggling worm spoke to him—all this made Heinrich von Benda aware how easy it was to speak of inner dignity, but in the clash with a world that was organized to deprive man of his dignity, it broke down, was bound to break down.

"Herr Megelein," he said, straightening up, "if you wish to

continue this conversation you will kindly adopt a more polite tone. Perhaps you forget that you are now in a civilized country, but do not forget that I can at any moment announce that my mission has failed—mostly through your actions."

"You won't do that, Herr Professor," retorted Herr Megelein. "Not so long as your wife and your child are in Vienna."

"That is not all you are forgetting, Herr Megelein," the Professor continued, as though he had not heard the threat. "The other countries are not confronted by a trustworthy legal government but by the rule of tyrants—naturally they demand guarantees which they would not necessarily demand of another nation. The situation with which the Conference is faced is not one which the participating states have created but one created solely by Germany. However America, however Évian may react, it is a reaction to the unheard-of events taking place in your country."

Herr Megelein had meanwhile been sorting through his papers; now—with a polite gesture, as Heinrich von Benda noted to his surprise—he handed the Professor *The New York Times* which had arrived that morning. In a detailed story on the Conference the brief statement appeared that the world-famous Viennese surgeon, Professor Heinrich von Benda, had arrived in Évian as representative of the Jewish Community "with the permission of the Gestapo."

"What of it?" said the Professor, handing back the paper. "Everyone knows that I could not have left the country without the Gestapo's permission. Moreover the information probably comes from you. You are using my name in order to prove to the world that Germany is not unwilling to release its Jews."

Herr Megelein pulled his chair up closer, sat down and looked at his visitor, trying in vain to stop his head from swaying to and fro like a pendulum.

He was sorry, he said, if he had been somewhat rude just now. He personally had nothing against the Jews, he even had a good friend who was a Jew, a certain Dr. Pollack from Berlin, perhaps the Professor knew him, Pollack had escaped to Canada, which he, Megelein, greatly regretted—or rather, he didn't regret that Pollack had escaped, but this man had been his medical adviser and he would miss him. Precisely because he had nothing against the Jews, however, he would be sorry if the Évian Conference gave the Reich Government *carte blanche* to solve the Jewish question in its own way. Before the Professor could interrupt him, he explained:

"As I said, we were not surprised. When you telephoned we already knew what the score was. We are well aware that the Conference was not called to help the Jews, but to pass a moral judgment on us and to damage us politically. Heads I win, tails you lose. Nevertheless, the Reich Government does not wish to withdraw its offer; on the contrary, we have made up our minds to dissipate the other countries' distrust. Therefore I can inform you—and you may pass it on, unofficially, of course—that the Reich Governor in Vienna has been instructed, on the day the Conference breaks up without having reached a decision on our offer, to arrest forty thousand Jews and put them in concentration camps."

"That is pure blackmail!"

"You're wrong. Who could prevent us from doing the same thing without announcing it beforehand? Furthermore, you are empowered to inform the Americans—unofficially, of course—that we shall begin by regarding the arrested forty thousand Jews as a transport without a specific destination, as a freight that can be dispatched either in the direction of the concentration camp or in the direction of the frontier. If, by the first of August, ten million dollars, the price for the Jews, a mere bagatelle, has been paid into a Swiss bank to an account that will be indicated later, the Reich Government will look upon this as a sign that negotiations have been entered into. In this event the transport will immediately be dispatched toward certain frontier stations to be agreed upon. We cannot do more to show our goodwill."

"And if the money has not been raised by the first of August?"

"As I told you, I have nothing against the Jews," said Herr Megelein shaking his head, involuntarily it is true, but as though simultaneously denying what he was saying. "I have nothing against the Jews," he repeated, "—please don't make me think of what will happen to the forty thousand in the event of a refusal. Moreover," he went on quickly, "it would be a

mistake to count on German ingenuousness again. The ten million dollars must be paid in by one or more governments"—he
spoke as though reading out paragraphs from a code of laws—
"we shall not accept the sum from wealthy Jews. We are not
pursuing any political aims, therefore, unlike the Americans,
we do not demand an official approach from foreign governments, nor shall we approach them. We are prepared to compromise. It will be enough for us if they honor our goodwill by
as symbolic gesture. However—and you must expressly emphasize this—this payment by installments will be the first and also
the last, the rest of the amount must be paid in a lump sum." He
rose, tripped over to the table and began to rummage among
the newspapers piled up on it. Standing with his back to the
Professor, he said, "By the way, you have nothing to fear; it
will hardly be your fault if your efforts fail."

He handed the Professor five or six German papers and urged
him to read them. There was no change in the arrangements,
he added. The Professor could ring Herr Stechlein's Geneva
number whenever he considered it necessary. With these
words, and not without a certain formality, he conducted the
Professor to the door, where he attempted to bow. The only
result was a curious circling movement of his head.

As Heinrich von Benda left the hotel, the first thing he saw
was his day shadow, the young man of yesterday, who was apparently deep in the contemplation of a toyshop. The Professor
looked at his watch. Midday had just passed; in the Hôtel Royal
they would now be going to lunch. He had a vague feeling that
the newspapers he was carrying under his arm had not been
given to him at random, that they might hold the key to the
conversation in the Hôtel du Léman. There was a little bar
next to the hotel. He went in and sat down at a table in the rear.

He skimmed through the headlines of the newspapers.
MISERABLE BEGINNING AT ÉVIAN. THE JEW CONFERENCE CON-
DEMNED TO FAILURE, NOBODY WANTS THEM—and so on. First
he opened the *Danziger Vorposten* at an article marked in red
in which it said:

> The Jew Conference at Évian seems to be developing into an
> anti-Jewish conference, since it turns out that while everyone
> likes to feel sorry for the Jews, because feeling sorry for them

is linked with stirring up hatred of Germany, not one state is prepared to do away with the supposed "disgrace to civilization" in Central Europe by taking in a few thousand Jews. Thus the Évian Conference merely confirms the German attitude to Jewry. If even such states as have hitherto given hospitality to only a few Jews declare themselves "saturated" with Jews, who can reproach the German people, who have had Jews within their frontiers on a positively inflationary scale, for establishing laws in order to protect the nation's blood and property?"

Another article, in the *Deutsche Allgemeine Zeitung,* spoke an even clearer and more threatening language:

If 30 states are going to be called to an international Conference, greater account should be taken of the historical situation and a total solution should be worked for. Because what had taken place in Germany is imminent in many other states. Whether these other countries will exercise as much restraint as Germany in solving the problem is extremely doubtful.

And finally there was an article in the *Völkischer Beobachter* which seemed to the Professor to contain direct reference to his mission:

They weep crocodile tears over the Jews, but nobody is willing to make a sacrifice for these "unfortunates," since everyone knows what the Jew means within a national community. Thus it is impossible not to recognize the fact that those states who themselves refuse to take any Jews merely justify the German Reich's defensive measures against the Jews, measures which are in any case not yet sufficiently far reaching.

The Professor lit a cigarette, inhaled deeply. Could he ignore the signs that emerged from these newspaper columns? Justification—the Führer's own mouthpiece had uttered the word; the others, equally mouthpieces of the Führer, hinted at it. So long as there was no war—and, unlike his son, the Professor was by no means convinced that the world would respond to the next provocation with military measures—so long, then, as it did not come to armed conflict, to that contact which broke off all other contacts, Germany, even if it disregarded its laws, was part of humanity. The criminal who is about to break into a house tests the presence or absence of its occupants, perhaps their physical strength, the weapons they possess, the locks and bolts. The National Socialists attacked the Évian Conference, but it was not certain that they did not welcome it. They only had to look over the wall of Évian to see whether the house of humanity was occupied. An unguarded heart was like an unguarded house, a touchstone for the heartless; opportunity makes the thief. And what about himself? By casting all warnings to the wind, had he not become the tool of crime? Would not those who had given him his task be more pleased if his mission failed than if it succeeded? Would they not interpret the world's no as a yes to their deeds of horror? It was all the more important that his mission should not fail; all the more important that he should not give way to discouragement; all the more important that he should not weaken. He tried to convince himself that the conversation with the head-shaking representative of the Reich Government had also had its good side, had not been so hopeless, ill will did not necessarily mean an evil outcome. Forty thousand Jews threatened with extermination—that was less than the hundreds of thousands he had come to Évian to speak for, but it was also more, because the danger was immediate, could be seen with the eye and grasped with the hand; these people loaded onto trucks or crammed into cattle cars, on the way to the slaughterhouse or to freedom, could be imagined, perhaps even the diplomats in the Hôtel Royal, the Americans and Australians, the French and Canadians, could imagine them. And even these newspapers had their good side, because they disclosed, perhaps earlier than Berlin had meant, what Germany's intentions were. One side expected freedom from Évian, the other a free hand. A free hand? Justification? Was it one and the same thing if you threw hundreds of thousands into prison, or if you refused to pay the price for their freedom? Was it one and the same thing if a kidnapper killed his victim, or if you refused to satisfy the kidnapper's demands? And even if it were one and the same, the crime and toleration of the crime—was there such a thing as a *carte blanche* for crime, a justification for murder?

The Professor took the newspapers under his arm, paid and left. "Because what has taken place in Germany is imminent in many other states." This was a sentence that the gentlemen in the Hôtel Royal would understand. Forty thousand people. This was a number they must understand. If he had ever been a good doctor, then it was the odd combination of pessimism and optimism that had made him so—every good doctor was a pessimistic diagnostician and an optimistic therapist. It was the 7th of July and there were another twenty-five days till the 1st of August.

It was getting on for nine in the evening when the Colombian delegate—although only his government's legal adviser he bore the title of ambassador extraordinary and minister plenipotentiary—received the Professor.

The sympathies or aversions which two people feel for each other from the outset depend upon the most various circumstances. Mysterious reactions that one might almost describe as chemical play just as much part as physical externals, remnants of atavistic memories as much as involuntarily injured or instinctively spared vanities, similarities of education and culture as much as the sound of the voice or the modulation of the language; but almost equally important is the moment of introduction, the initial spark, so that love or hate at first sight are by no means unusual, indeed generally have a lasting effect that is difficult to change.

When Heinrich von Benda and the Colombian Minister met, conditions for this moment of introduction, this initial spark, were all the more favorable because their scholarly and scientific reputations helped them to find common ground. Even the appearance of the tiny sitting room where the Minister received his visitor was calculated to move Heinrich von Benda sympathetically. The room was in a state of the most pleasant disorder; books that had nothing to do with the subject of the Conference lay everywhere; the photograph of a beautiful woman, probably a pale-skinned mestiza, and another of three children stood on the mantelpiece; on a table a coffee percolator was bubbling, giving off a delightful aroma. The Minister was a man of modest height; his head was too large and seemed to demonstrate the importance of his brain by comparison with his body; his face had that pleasant ugliness that

sometimes characterizes artists and philosophers and betrays a
fine indifference to outward things, a changeable face which,
although it was turned inward, vividly reflected his environment.

The little man, whose soft, melodious voice hinted at a desire to help, whatever he might say, did indeed do his best to
help Heinrich von Benda. Instead of questioning the Professor,
forcing him to go into difficult and awkward explanations, he
himself repeated what he had been told by the American Ambassador. "I assume that you have come to see me," he said,
"because I am chairman of the committee whose task is to test
out Germany's intentions and possibly make recommendations
to the Conference for discussions with the Reich Government."

The Professor agreed, but immediately added that the situation had changed since his visit to the American Ambassador.
As the Chairman had wished, he had made contact with the
German Government; then he reported, several times interrupted by the Minister with questions, what Herr Megelein
had told him.

"That's monstrous," said the Minister, when Heinrich von
Benda had finished. "It's beyond human imagination."

"Is it beyond your imagination?"

"I don't know. Probably beyond mine too, but certainly beyond the imagination of most of those taking part in the
Conference."

"I have brought you the German newspapers. If people had
read *Mein Kampf* more carefully they would not have had to
strain their imagination unduly. In our era the Devil is so sure
of himself that he announces his intentions."

The Minister nodded, placed the papers on a shaky pile of
books, poured out coffee for himself and his guest. "I must con-
fess to you," he said, "that today's sessions, both of the plenary
assembly and of my own committee, have left me feeling deeply
depressed. And it is precisely this utterly hopeless lack of imagination that has depressed me. As a judge, I have sat in judgment over many murderers. It is hard enough to put oneself in
the place of a single murderer who has killed a single person.
If I tell my committee tomorrow of the planned deportation

of these forty thousand victims, do you think there will be one among them who will believe it possible?"

"Then the most serious crime ought to be punished the least severely?"

"Does that surprise you? War, the greatest of all crimes, is not considered a crime at all."

"In this case it is a war against the defenseless and innocent."

"That applies to all wars."

"A soldier isn't defenseless."

"He is not defenseless against other soldiers, but he is defenseless against those who press the weapon into his hands."

"Will the Conference permit the deportation of forty thousand innocent people?"

"We should ask ourselves whether the Conference will believe that they are in danger at all."

"Have you so little faith in the success of the Conference?"

"I am not a pessimist and not a skeptic, but I have no very high opinion of human imagination. It is strange that mankind, although it is not exactly good, is incapable of imagining evil in its ultimate form."

"How convenient for evil! Would the Conference take measures to save the victims if it could be convinced of Hitler's plans?"

"That's a difficult question. You see, the Catholic Church— I am a Catholic like most of my countrymen—speaks of seven deadly sins. Apathy of the heart or sloth is the last on the list, but I'm not sure it shouldn't be the first. Are pride, covetousness, lust, anger, gluttony, envy anything else than apathy of the heart? The delegates are human, therefore their hearts are apathetic. Not wicked, but apathetic. . . ."

"I wonder if there's any difference."

"You're right. But apathy and sloth are strange words; they imply inertia, and inertia has a double meaning. It is inertia if I do not set a ball rolling, but inertia also characterizes the rolling ball; the law of inertia is the law of continuation. The heart exhibits inertia by continuing to beat when it ought to stop."

"I didn't come to Évian in order to come to terms with inertia," the Professor said.

"Your task is so difficult because it represents imagination,
which wages a ceaseless battle against apathy and inertia. I
often think that imagination ought to figure among the cardinal virtues."

"I don't think posterity will judge the participants from such
an enlightened, philosophical standpoint."

"We are asking a great deal from the delegates. We are asking them to imagine both the intentions of a murderer and
the sufferings of a man condemned to death. There are no murderers among them and also no men condemned to death." He
stopped. "Don't misunderstand me. I don't want to discourage you. Trust me; assume that, as far as the ultimate aim is
concerned, we are animated by the same intentions."

"Will you inform your committee of the offer? Forty thousand human beings for ten million dollars. . . ."

Heinrich von Benda was a bad actor, or rather no actor at
all, since in the course of a happy life he had lost the art of
dissembling, that poor man's art which the successful do not
need. He had reacted to the Minister's religious philosophy
with a sober question, and it was not hard for the Minister to
read the disappointment in the Professor's face. This famous
Viennese surgeon, thought the Minister, had come to him to
find out whether he could persuade the governments to part
with ten million dollars, ten million dollars for a start. Like
everyone striving for a single goal, the Professor evidently
looked neither to left nor right but only to the front. Yet he
too, the Minister, had a goal in view, he had a plan and wanted
to convince his visitor of its merits.

"If you want me to be frank with the Committee," said the
Minister, "I will do so. But if you trust me we ought to ask
ourselves what the Germans are really planning, what lies behind their offer and their threat."

"They want to blackmail the other countries."

"It's not as simple as that. If the Germans only wanted the
money to oil their war machine, it would make no difference to
them where it came from. Why do they refuse to accept money
from charitable organizations, why do they insist upon the ran-

som money being put up by states, nations, governments? '*Non olet,*' said Vespasian when people objected that the money he had gained from the urine tax had a bad smell. Hitler is more than Vespasian: not only does he not care whether money smells, he actually prefers it to stink."

"Does the money of governments stink more than the money of private organizations?"

"If governments pay ransom money, they sanction the deeds of the government from which they are ransoming the victims."

Although he had been thinking the same thing a few hours earlier, the Professor shook his head. "The father who pays a ransom to the kidnapper to free his kidnapped child," he said, "is not sanctioning the kidnapper's deeds."

"The comparison, if you will forgive me, is as obvious as it is false. The father of the child has had no contact with the kidnapper before the deed and will never have any contact with him again. For his part the kidnapper attaches absolutely no importance to his social acknowledgment by the father of the kidnapped child. The states participating in the Conference all without exception have diplomatic and commercial relations with the German Reich. Up to the moment when they pay out a ransom they can delude themselves that they are dealing with a morally equal partner. But the moment when they bow to blackmail, accept the bargain and pay the ransom, international morality will demand that they break off relations with the blackmailer."

"Which they want to maintain at any price."

"That is a fact with which we shall have to come to terms," the Minister declared.

He rose and went to the window. On the terrace of the Hôtel Royal, as at the Hôtel Splendide, an orchestra was playing; they had just struck up the hit of the season that accompanied the dance of the year, the "Lambeth Walk." A crooner was singing: "*Every little Lambeth gal / With her little Lambeth pal, / You'll find them all / Doing the Lambeth Walk, oi!*" The night was sultry, the air in the room stood still, but the Minister closed the window.

"It is more important to be clear in our own minds as to what Hitler is planning," he said, turning back to the Professor. "You spoke just now about the Devil. In the primitive notion of hell, which with us in South America, in particular, is still very much current, the damned are tortured by a whole host of devils. But the Holy Scriptures mention only one Devil —where, then, do these devils come from?" He blinked his shortsighted eyes. "In reality the devils of whom the Devil disposes are identical with the lost souls. The lost soul assumes the shape of the Devil and in the cauldrons of hell the devils' own souls are boiling. The Devil, whose highest and most essential aim is to be like God, seeks to make man in his own image, and with the lost souls, indeed he succeeds in doing so; he recruits devils who from that moment on are condemned to pour boiling oil over their own souls. In other words, the Devil lends the damned the status of devils."

"Do you believe that Hitler thinks as far as that?" the Professor asked.

He found it difficult to overcome his impatience. Had he been wrong about the Colombian? This dark, mercurial man might be an idealist, an inexplicable fire burned behind the deepset eyes, but it was too late to strew tracts along the path of disaster.

"He certainly doesn't think in those terms," replied the Colombian. And as though to counter his guest's impatience he continued: "Don't imagine I am indulging in vain theories. I am examining Hitler's intentions. He has undoubtedly realized that even in politics, a pretty devilish trade, conscience plays a role, that even politics rests on a narrow foundation of morality, that absolute immorality doesn't pay, unless . . . unless he succeeds in changing the moral norms, in exporting his own immorality, in making the world collaborate in his crimes as his accomplice. You see, it is not a matter of indifference to Hitler whether the world maintains contact with him under the false and hypocritical condition of an existing morality or whether it maintains this contact even after it has recognized this immorality. Hitler reckons on our bargaining with him for human beings and nevertheless continuing our relations with him. Thereby—whether he hands over his victims to us or not—we shall have assumed the status of devils."

A heavy weariness, which is almost always caused by hopeless-

ness, came over the Professor. Yes, this Catholic, perhaps religious, certainly believing South American, married to a mestiza,
representative of the most democratic state on the Latin-American continent, an eminent jurist, was neither a racist nor an
anti-Semite nor an opportunist, he wasn't even a diplomat or a
professional politician—but how could the other participants in
the Conference even consider the proposal, if this intelligent
and, as it seemed to the Professor, warmhearted man rejected it?
One of them would find this excuse, another one that, but they
would all share the lack of imagination which the Colombian
had lamented. None of them knew what it meant when the
doorbell rang in the early morning and helpless men were
dragged away from their wives, when people packed in freight
cars like cattle were taken off to an unknown destination, when
blows rained down on bare backs and a man, deprived of his
dignity, ended without knowing the meaning of his end. None
of them had seen Fritz Grünwald die. Perhaps the Colombian
was right, perhaps only the small watershed of imagination divided humanity from inhumanity, perhaps man was only as
good as he was clearsighted, perhaps children at school should
be taught a little more imagination instead of mathematics and
virtue, instead of Latin and religion. But was not the Colombian's heart just as apathetic as the hearts whose apathy he casti-
gated as their cardinal sin? And he himself, Professor Heinrich
von Benda? Was he himself not thinking of his tired heart, and
was his tired heart not also becoming apathetic? The first of
August. He had no right to accept the law of inertia, hadn't
even the right to think. If he were to think, he might, who
knows, come to the same conclusions as this well-meaning jurist,
and that would mean that he had not thrown himself in front of
the cattle cars.

"I follow your train of thought," he said. "But it doesn't
convince me. Hitler has corrupted Germany, he wants to corrupt the world. But the world is corrupt because Hitler exists.
He would not have come to power without the complicity of
the world and could not exist without its complicity. It is possible that he wishes to test the world's power of resistance, but a
world that allows forty thousand people to perish is no less
immoral than one that ransoms them from the Devil. I know,"

he went on, "I shan't be able to convince you. My arguments
are not political. I am merely counting the days and thinking of
forty thousand Jews."

The Minister was once again blinking his eyes in that curious
way that had struck Heinrich von Benda at the very beginning
of their conversation. Without replying, the little man went to
the percolator. He asked whether he might pour the Professor
another cup. It was Colombian coffee, he said, the pride of the
country, just as tasty as Brazilian but lighter. The Professor
accepted gratefully. Throughout the evening he had smoked
one cigarette after the other; now, in order to deceive himself,
he produced the most amateurish arguments. Nicotine, he told
himself, constricts the blood vessels and hinders the circulation;
coffee, on the other hand, dilates them and accelerates the circulation, so that the hot drink would fulfill a welcome, indeed
wholesome, neutralizing function.

The Minister came back and sat down on the low, uncomfortable chair on which he had been sitting all the evening.

"I said I didn't want to discourage you, and now I have done
just that," he said. "I see a way out—listen." His plan had begun
to form as soon as he heard of the Professor's mission, but it had
only now, in conversation with the Professor, taken solid shape.
It was undoubtedly the right one. This very night he would
inform the American Ambassador of the Professor's conversation with Herr Megelein. The Conference would undoubtedly
last for another week, till the fifteenth of July, the participants
thought. If it proved possible—without prejudice to other, future plans, aims, possibilities, commissions, committees and
offices to be set up later, perhaps even with an unexpressed hint
that they had now done enough and cleared their consciences—
if it proved possible to persuade the participating states to take
forty thousand refugees immediately, then they could "hoist
Hitler with his own petard," could maneuver him into a fatal
situation. "Don't misunderstand me." Filled with enthusiasm
about his own idea he seized the Professor's hand. "The Conference would take charge of forty thousand Jews, but not the
same forty thousand; there must not be the slightest hint of sale
and purchase. Don't you understand? On the fifteenth of July
the Conference, the participating nations of Évian, declare the

gates of the world open to forty thousand new refugees—the scale of distribution is a minor matter, there will be no difficulty in solving such a limited problem with the aid of the United States. Just imagine Germany's position if she dared to arrest forty thousand Jews two weeks later! That would be impossible, an open provocation, a declaration of war on humanity. If Germany wishes to continue to create the impression that she really only wishes to get rid of her Jews, not to exterminate them, then the trains must move in the direction of the frontier."

The Minister jumped up, knocking over the little table that had swayed under the burden of books, newspapers and documents. He knelt down to pick up the scattered articles. The Professor also bent down, and the two men went on talking excitedly, one of them continually bending down to the floor, the other crawling about on the carpet almost like a child at play.

"Don't ask me what is to become of the other hundreds of thousands," said the Minister. "Good deeds like evil ones have the curious quality of fertilizing themselves. I shall inform the Conference of the immediate danger, and if necessary ask that you be heard in secret session." He set up the table again. "Naturally Germany will realize that the number of forty thousand, just this number, is the civilized world's answer to the offer of sale. An answer with which Germany did not reckon, the last answer it expected. We refuse the sale, but we stretch out our hands to the forty thousand unfortunates. No, no, nothing of this sort must be put into words. A wise policy"—he stood up—"always leaves one's opponent the possibility of retreat. We must not offend Germany; also it is in the interests of the participating states to ignore the offer of sale and maintain the impression of a voluntary gesture." He arranged the books in a precarious balance. "At the same time you must—" He broke off. "You were going to say something?"

Heinrich von Benda's eyes had grown moist; he had been seized by an emotion in which a certain feeling of guilt was mingled. He had judged the Colombian rightly at first, then wrongly afterward. "I understand you," he said. "But do you think . . . ? The whole quota of the United States for Germany and Austria totals a bare twenty thousand immigrants.

Why should it be possible to achieve now what hitherto appeared impossible?"

"Without the new threat, the latest offer, your mission would probably have failed. The danger was too vague, the numbers too great. Now I can come before the Conference with a concrete plan. I can say: By taking in forty thousand people you will save not only these, but also their brothers . . ."

"Their brothers . . . ?"

"Without unmasking himself as a blackmailer, Hitler cannot release forty thousand Jews and at the same time put hundreds of thousands into concentration camps."

For the first time in weeks Heinrich von Benda saw a ray of hope, but he feared that he was giving himself up to an illusion.

"And what about imagination and apathy?" he said. "Will the delegates . . . ?" He looked toward the closed window, through which the music of the "Lambeth Walk" could still be heard in a low key.

"We must believe in it," declared the Minister. "The Conference now has a clear, immediate aim that even promises political advantages. Imagination will be stimulated but not overburdened. I shall say to the gentlemen: If the Conference fails, if it cannot even fulfill such a small task, then we shall complain in vain that we did not invent evil, did not make inhumanity a law, did not bloody our hands. There was a man once before who washed his hands in innocence, but mankind has passed a terrible judgment on his apathetic heart."

Heinrich von Benda polished his glasses. "I know you won't play the part of Pontius Pilate," he said. "This is a happy hour."

"There is one more thing I must say to you," declared the Minister, and his voice suddenly had a different, sober ring. "You cannot return to Vienna."

"I don't understand."

"If my plan should be successful, they will know in Berlin that you betrayed the number forty thousand to us."

"Those were my instructions."

"Your instructions were to offer forty thousand Jews for sale— and even that only as a first installment. Your instructions were not to force the German Reich to set forty thousand Jews free.

The number betrays you, yet precisely this number is the important thing. It is our answer."

The Professor shook his head. "If I did not return I should be defeating your whole plan. Berlin would declare that there had never been any talk of arresting or releasing forty thousand Jews. My 'treachery' would be used as an excuse for reprisals." He smiled wearily. "You must have enough imagination to understand the laws of hell."

"I should be guilty of apathy myself if I sacrificed one man with certainty in order to save forty thousand perhaps."

"I must take responsibility for myself. But I promise you that I shall reach no decision without consulting you."

The Minister smiled. "You are beginning to employ a diplomatic vocabulary," he said. He looked at his watch and stretched out his hand to Heinrich von Benda. "It's late. I must try to get in touch with the Ambassador. I think he is being entertained by the British delegation."

Heinrich von Benda set off along the narrow path bordered by fir trees that led downhill from the Hôtel Royal to his own hotel. No artificial lighting was needed, for the sky was clear and starry and the moon was poised above the gables of the Hôtel Royal like a clock that had escaped from its tower and implanted itself in the sky. As he walked away from the hotel where the Conference took place the Professor could not see the moon, but the light of the moon clock turned the gravel into thousands of shimmering grains. A frosty silver had changed the firs into Christmas trees; they stood cool and alien in the summer night waiting for their winter's day. Although it was past eleven it was warm, but the warmth was of quite a different kind from Heinrich von Benda's homeland, where the warmth of summer nights was interwoven with a heavy, sweet, seductive fragrance, where nature seemed to be sinking into an amorous sleep. Here the sleepless mountains sent their warning messengers out into the country, the other seasons lay in wait around summer, and transience passed through the forests like a fleeing bird. When Heinrich von Benda stopped and looked up, he saw the peaks of the mountains on the other side of the lake; the moon had covered them with a blanket of snow, it was impossible to know whether these frozen, petrified waves were guarding the valleys or threatening them.

Heinrich von Benda thought of Bettina. Was she sleeping, or was she wandering about the silent house? Was she sitting reading in the library, or had she gone on tiptoe to the child's bed? Was she strong, was she afraid, was she thinking of him, did she know that he was thinking of her? The photographs of the woman and the children on the mantelpiece of the hotel room reappeared before him. It was one thing to set out from a safe harbor to help the shipwrecked, quite another to row to the help of the shipwrecked when one was helpless oneself. The lifeboat in which he sat was leaking. How would he act if Bettina and Heinrich were here? Was it really concern for the Jews that forced him to go home, or had inhumanity left him no other choice but to be humane? For an instant he gave himself up to dreams of a fine treachery, saw himself at the Paris railway station waiting for Bettina and the child, saw himself with the two of them on a steamer taking them away from Europe to the safe shores of America, saw himself in the bright operating theatre of a distant hospital, saw a new house somewhere in the valleys of New England, near Boston or Cambridge. For an instant he told himself that he had made up his mind not to go home—to go home, a mocking phrase. He visualized himself as if the great decision lay behind him and as he did so he felt, almost physically, all heaviness fall away from him. Now his only concern was how and when Bettina would leave the country, but that too would work out all right; he pondered which call he should answer, which invitation he should accept; he even thought of such minor details as whether some embassy would be able to get his books and porcelain out of Vienna— and although he had meanwhile realized that he was indulging in a mere daydream, a futile game with the future and an empty illusion, he nonetheless experienced a remarkable sense of relief; nothing final had yet happened, he could still throw his conscience overboard like superfluous ballast. He left a narrow crack open in the door of his conscience, as though to surprise himself later, in the end, with the weighty decision. Breathing more easily he went on his way, and as he walked other, happier thoughts came to him. After all, he told himself, the most im-

portant thing was that he would soon see Bettina again, he
would see her again soon whether he went home or waited for
her abroad. On this moment of reunion he hung his heart. He
remembered the hot summer night when they had begotten
Heinrich—although they couldn't possibly know, they had
laughingly agreed that it could only have been that night on
which they had suddenly decided to leave the house and go out
to Baden near Vienna and stay at a little inn not far from
Heiligenkreuz. In the morning, when the neat landlady had
brought them breakfast in bed, Bettina had said she felt that
during that night he had given her a child, because "Of course it
is men who give us children, not the other way around." Youthful vigor coursed through him at this memory, he walked faster
and faster, almost as though Bettina were waiting for him—
when he heard footsteps behind him, no illusion, they were firm
male steps, and he was seized by that eerie sensation that comes
over almost everyone feeling himself being followed by an unknown person in the dark.

Before the Professor had time to think, to become aware of
his fear and decide what behavior to adopt, he heard himself
addressed and already there stood in front of him the slim
young man whom he was in the habit of thinking of as his day
shadow.

"I hope I didn't frighten you," said the young man. "You do
speak English, don't you, Professor?"

Surprised, because up to now he had taken the young man for
a German—but he spoke with the easygoing drawl of the American West untinged by any foreign accent—the Professor answered yes. The shadow, bright and clearly visible in the moon-
light, quickly discharged the formalities. His name was James
K. Nelson and he was from Washington, not the capital, he
added, but the northwest coastal state of the same name.

He had been waiting for an opportunity to speak to the Professor *tête-à-tête*, he said, and again he apologized for accosting
him so late at night. He belonged to the American Secret Service, he explained, as simply as someone introducing himself as a
lawyer, an engineer or a bookkeeper; he had been given the
assignment of keeping an eye on the Professor in Évian. No, the
Professor shouldn't misunderstand him—"I'm not here to pro-

tect you"—on the contrary, his job was to see whom the Professor was in touch with, from whom he received his instructions
and whether his intentions were really those he had conveyed to
the American Government. But now—he stammered it out like
a man not fully conscious of his feelings and certainly not able
to put them clearly into words—he was entangled in a conflict of
conscience. "I don't know why I'm bothering you with this,
Professor, but I feel I have to and I beg you to listen to me." He
found it impossible to tail a man, possibly to denounce him, a
man whom he honored, admired, whose noble purposes and
courageous behavior in the face of enormous difficulties were
known to him.

James K. Nelson, like an accused man clumsily defending
himself, now embarked on a lengthy explanation, most of it of a
personal nature. He had been a medical student, but had been
forced by unfortunate circumstances to give up his studies.
Through a distant relative, an American vice-consul in a south
German town, he had been put in touch with the American
Secret Service and was now—"in for a penny, in for a pound"—
wedded to this repulsive profession that was so totally out of
keeping with his nature and character. When he was sent to
Évian he had been informed, naturally in the most general
terms, of the Professor's mission. "Since then I have been following you like a shadow, as you must long ago have noticed,
since I'm not very good at it." He drew a deep breath, as though
feeling relieved, and began to speak, contrary to every regula-
tion, of the real reason for his present action. The German Secret Service, he said, was also tailing the Professor, and with
these people you never knew for sure what they were after. "My
colleague"—he uttered the word with utter disgust—"is a dangerous man. You never know what he's up to." The abduction
of the two theatre people in Liechtenstein, the abduction of the
German journalist from Switzerland—"Perhaps you think that
what I'm saying doesn't make sense, but the things that happen
don't make sense either. One thing is pretty clear to me. These
people want to prevent you from staying abroad and perhaps
talking more than they would like." He, James K. Nelson, was
well aware that he was a wretched agent and unworthy of his
confidential position, but he didn't give a damn about that,

since his profession was in any case "vomit-making." In other
words, he was asking the Professor to make use of him and to
call upon him for help at any time, if the situation demanded it.
He would have to continue to keep the Professor under surveillance and also to report back truthfully to his chief, but the
Professor should nevertheless look upon him as a kind of guardian angel. "Although"—he smiled—"I don't look the part."

In reality James K. Nelson did look like a guardian angel. As
the Professor had turned around, the moon was shining in his
eyes and blinding him. The young man was facing him. In the
harsh blue light he looked even taller, even slimmer, even
younger, he was wearing a billowing white toga and the silver of
the pine forests in his hair. Heinrich von Benda didn't know
what to say, although he did not distrust the stranger for an
instant; only he became more conscious than ever of the unreality of the situation. Here he stood at night in a wood on the
hills of Évian-les-Bains, the stars were sparkling; through the
trees he saw the red and yellow window-eyes of the Hôtel Royal;
the Secret Service agent had turned into a guardian angel; from
the Hôtel Splendide, quite nearby, voices could be heard, the
Colombian Minister was even now talking to the American
Ambassador, there was a scent of pine trees in the air; Bettina
and Heinrich were on the other side of the frontier—and all this
was supposed to be real, was supposed to make sense.

Finally he succeeded in stammering "Thank you," after he
had already turned to walk away. He couldn't help thinking of
Peter Schlemihl, the Man without a Shadow. He was glad that
he had a shadow.

The lobby and lounge of the Hôtel Splendide were still
crowded and full of movement. A group of journalists stood
around the radio in the bar listening to the midnight news.
Chinese bombers had sunk Japanese warships in the Yangtse,
Germany's zeppelin idol had violently attacked the USA on the
subject of helium deliveries, the rebels in Spain had taken the
coastal base of Nules, Arabs had destroyed telephone cables and
railway tracks in Palestine. On a long table there were still some
Conference communiqués left over, but they were all jumbled
up as if they had been subjected to wind and rain. The young
monsignor was reading his breviary. Two Swedish married cou-

ples wandered in from the Casino slightly tipsy and drank some
of the Évian water which, as every night, stood on the sill of the
porter's lodge as a gift to guests. The refugees were sitting in a
corner of the lounge, Frau Lederer and her son among them;
they were listening to a speech by a small, bearded man. As the
Professor stopped hesitantly in the doorway, he spotted in the
group a Viennese industrialist whom he had relieved from troublesome kidney stones only two or three years before. Instinctively and because he himself could find no rest, he started off
toward the group, but he noticed just in time that the man
turned away and suddenly stared at the pattern of the carpet as
though hypnotized. If Heinrich von Benda had believed himself mistaken, that he was only imagining something that hadn't
really happened, he was immediately disabused; the young, or
actually not so very young, Lederer pretended not to see the
Professor approaching, and began to talk vivaciously and at random to his mother, who at first could not understand his torrent
of words but then herself convulsively engaged in conversation
with him.

At this moment, while the Professor came to a bewildered
stop, a woman came up to him, took him by the arm and, before
he could collect his thoughts, consent or resist, led him to two
plush easy chairs standing in the far corner of the lounge.

"Don't bother about those stupid people," the woman said in
a low voice, in German. "Sit down. I should like to talk to you.
My name is Selma Selig."

"Oh yes," said the Professor. "I've been wanting to talk to
you for a long time."

This was no mere figure of speech, no empty politeness. The
name Selma Selig had been known to him for a long time. As
always when one meets somebody of whom one has heard many
various and contradictory things, especially if that person enjoys
a kind of fame, the Professor tried to measure his preconceived
ideas against the reality, to harmonize what he had heard with
the actual person. Selma Selig had been much talked about in
Vienna. She was, as far as the Professor remembered, a Galician
Jewess, from Lemberg probably or Krakow, of a very well-to-do
family, who had lived since the end of the World War in
Geneva. There, since the founding of the League of Nations,

she had been one of that elite of conference interpreters of whom legends were told. This handful of men and women knew four, five, or more languages and knew them so well that each of them could translate long and complicated speeches simultaneously, while they were being delivered, translations good enough to be printed unaltered. These phenomena of mental agility were highly paid and highly honored, the League of Nations courted them and bestowed diplomatic status on them. It was all the more noteworthy, therefore, when Selma Selig, *prima inter pares,* one day three or four years ago said good-bye to the League of Nations and exchanged her secure, esteemed position for a highly insecure and doubtful one. She had founded the Comité International pour les Réfugiés Intellectuels Provenant de l'Allemagne, whose chairman she was and whose function, as the name implied, was to help intellectual refugees from Germany. The committee did indeed help them in a variety of ways: it obtained entry visas, distributed small sums of money, corresponded with universities, collected clothing, bought ship tickets, organized food handouts and published books. Selma Selig gradually became a legend, for she was as benevolent as she was troublesome, as unselfish as she was importunate according to circumstances. She used her old contacts and ruthlessly put pressure on embassies and civil authorities, spent her savings as though she were a millionaire, imposed a tax on millionaires, including emigrants, occupied theatres and lecture halls for her meetings, threatened the hesitant with social boycott and recruited assistants as though she were a commanding general.

To his surprise, the Professor observed that she looked exactly as he had pictured her. This woman of about fifty reminded him of all the suffragettes he had met a quarter of a century ago, when women marched out to acquire the rights of men. At that time, long before the coquettish bob, the short, boyish hair clinging to the ears had been the fashion, face makeup and all beauty aids had been anathema, and they had worn austere tailormade costumes in imitation of masculine suits. What had been so strikingly fashionable or even revolutionary then was bound to look old-fashioned twenty or thirty years later, and in fact there was something almost touchingly old-fashioned about Selma Selig; she looked like a Jacobin after the victory of Robespierre. The touching effect of her appearance was underlined by a physical deformity: one hip was considerably higher than the other, so that she dragged one leg; she had the walk of a person who had suffered an attack of infantile paralysis in her youth, but she seemed to have become accustomed to this weakness, indeed she moved faster, more agilely, more energetically than people with no impediment. When she spoke her pale little face was almost beautiful, and since it was a highly feminine, gentle face it seemed continually to be giving the lie to the masculine character which the aging spinster had assumed.

"Don't bother about those stupid people," Fräulein Selig repeated. "They haven't been outside long enough to know what methods the Gestapo uses here."

"The Gestapo?" asked the Professor and remembered his conversation with Mr. Nelson.

"One of those fellows approached me too. To warn me against you, naturally. There are dozens of them here whose only task is to spread distrust and dissension in the ranks of the refugees. No sooner had you emerged from the Hôtel du Léman over there than they all knew"—she glanced across at the whispering group of emigrants—"whom you had met. I can't enlighten them, nor can you."

The Professor lit a cigarette, looked at Fräulein Selig questioningly.

"The French Ambassador," she said, "with whom I have been friendly for many years, told me about your mission. You have an ally in me." She spoke in short sentences that sounded final. "The whole discussion about the moral justification of your mission is nonsense. It is morally unjustified, and it is necessary. In the autumn there will be war. If there is a war, Hitler will murder millions of Jews. A few million hungry mouths for which he has no use. We must get as many Jews out before that as we can bargain for with Germany. All other considerations must wait."

"Everything I have heard till now . . ."

". . . depresses you. You're right. You can't count on the governments. But there are a few dozen private organizations to

which we can turn. It will be enough if the Conference raises
the immigration quotas; we shall be able to find the money."

"Germany will refuse money from private sources."

"That's what the Germans say today, as long as they have a
prospect of getting the money from the governments. If Germany were not on the edge of ruin it would not make war. In
the end Germany will accept the money, even if it comes straight
from Rothschild's bank."

"I wish I could believe you. But today is the eighth of July,
and you said yourself that we are racing toward war."

"That's why there's not a moment to lose," said Fräulein
Selig, and she began to explain what she considered necessary
under these urgent circumstances. Some of Germany's most
prominent men, she said, were now abroad, Jews and Christians, scholars, writers, painters, poets, philosophers, musicians,
conductors, doctors, actors, producers; alongside these were the
great of other nations, the Italian conductor, the Spanish virtu-
oso, the Polish composer and now also Professor Heinrich von
Benda. From some of them, the Nobel Prize winner for litera-
ture and the Nobel Prize winner for physics in particular, she
had already received positive confirmation. If he, the world-famous surgeon who had just come out of Austria, would now
head the committee, if he would go to Paris, London, New
York, then, within a few weeks, millions of dollars could be
raised, then at least the Jews of Germany and Austria, five
hundred thousand in number, could be snatched from the
Flood.

Heinrich von Benda looked into the little woman's glowing
eyes, but the longer she spoke, the higher grew the wall that
rose in front of him. He was still not thinking of himself, not
thinking of the role which she had given him and which he was
not in a position to play. Should he tell her that what was at
issue here was not a few million dollars, that hundreds of millions of dollars were involved; that the German Reich was demanding foreign currency which, even if the money was raised
from private sources, the governments would have to approve
and release for export; that when it was a matter of millions the
magical names were not so magical; that now forty thousand
people were in immediate danger and that in three weeks nei-

ther the physicist with his theories nor the poet with his pen nor
he himself with his scalpel could work miracles? All at once it
seemed to him in the worst way self-evident that the idealists
had as little imagination as the realists, because while the latter
hadn't the courage to free themselves from the fetters of reality,
however loose they were, the former flew too high even to picture the misery and paralysis and wretchedness and obstacles
that lay beneath them. Goodness in all its magnitude was as
unimaginable as evil in all its magnitude: the Devil counted on
lack of imagination, and he knew what he was counting on.
Heinrich von Benda felt drawn to this lovable little woman, but
he could not overlook the fact that she too was standing in the
center of a small circle—a brave lion tamer in a cage who knew
nothing about the wilderness. What their national interests
were to others, the welfare organizations were to her; what the
apparatus of the state was to others, the glorious individual was
to her; what the law for everyone was to others, the law of the
few was to her. But she too believed only in her own ways, her
own means, her own solutions.

He didn't want to discourage her, therefore he spoke only of
himself. He was afraid, he said, that she misunderstood his mission. He could go neither to Paris nor to London nor to New
York, perhaps in no more than a week he would be on his way
back to Vienna; by then his mission must have proved itself a
success or a failure.

While he was trying to explain to her why he could not act
differently, the lounge had emptied. The emigrants had left,
slipping past him and Fräulein Selig while pretending to be
deep in a lively and uninterrupted conversation; only an old
lady was still sitting in one corner, moving her hands as though
she did her embroidery in her sleep, and the young monsignor
was still reading his breviary. It was suddenly as cold as it only
can be in a hotel lounge at night.

Fräulein Selig did not admit defeat, nor did she insist on
convincing Heinrich von Benda that day; she promised to return on the morrow to discuss the "unheard-of idea," as she
called the Professor's return to Vienna. With this she turned to
personal questions and inquired about the Professor's family.
As she did so, her face was transformed in a most pleasant way.

The tension lifted, it grew soft and much younger; indeed, as the Professor spoke of his young wife, something inquisitive, roguish, gossip-seeking appeared in her eyes. If he wanted to telephone his wife, she said, she could arrange that, and if he wanted to write his wife a letter the best possible opportunity was available this very day.

"One of our most reliable collaborators—an 'Aryan,' incidentally, as they say nowadays," she explained, "is flying to Vienna tomorrow. He can take the letter."

"Uncensored?"

"I can guarantee that. I'll send for the letter tomorrow morning around nine o'clock."

With quick, shuffling steps the Professor walked out into the lobby, where his nighttime shadow had taken up his duties. He was standing by the porter's lodge drinking the water extolled in advertisements for cleansing the kidneys.

It was two in the morning when the Professor entered his room. He stood by the open window and looked out into the invisible. An infinite silence had descended upon the chaos; it was impossible to imagine that this tangled, seething, burning, spitting, whirling chaos had become so still. Was God's hand lying upon the chaos, or were only the traces of a dead God—the mountains and the forests, the valleys and the rivers, the seas and the lakes—left in the chaos, the silent witnesses to a God who had died?

The Professor stepped back from the window, sought in his pocket for a last cigarette, found it to his relief, lit it and picked up his writing paper.

Between the Devil
and the Deep Blue Sea

*And the Lord shall fight for you, and ye shall
hold your peace.*

EXODUS xiv, 14

III

On the morning of July 9th there was no session. The delegates paid visits to one another in order to discuss behind scenes what they intended later to discuss in secret session.

During the night it had started to rain, and both the Swiss mountains on the far side of the lake and the Savoyard Monts du Chablais on the near side were veiled in mist; Évian-les-Bains seemed cut off from the world. True, the stubborn barometer in the lobby of the Hôtel Royal was firmly fixed on *Beau temps,* but the rain was streaming obstinately down the windowpanes, and the few privileged guests there for the cure, who had been permitted to stay in the hotel in spite of the Conference, sat disgruntled in the lobby or talked about the weather which, like women, provides all the more material for conversation the more trouble it causes.

His lordship, the British delegate, had called upon the American Ambassador shortly after breakfast. His lordship had problems which were apparently, but only apparently, of a technical nature. Over the question of whether the Conference—or more correctly the permanent Office for Refugees, whose establishment had been a foregone conclusion from the outset—should be incorporated in the League of Nations or function as an independent entity, the United States had adopted an absolutely rigid position. The delegate from Great Britain was now trying to make the Ambassador from America change his mind, to persuade him to work more closely with the League of Nations. Politely but resolutely, the American Ambassador refused. None of the British arguments—the reduction of costs, the convenience of using existing machinery or easier collaboration with existing organizations—could be dismissed out of hand, but the American had little faith in the machinery of the

League of Nations and even less in the intentions of Great Britain. In the great machine of the League it would be easy for a few wheels to idle unnoticed, and perhaps just the one that was at issue here; when a commission fails to achieve anything it sets up subcommittees, which in turn disintegrate into sub-subcommittees; all reports pass through the bureaucracy of the secretariat or come to a stop there. The delegate of Great Britain knew all this; and the American Ambassador asked himself whether his British colleague was not advocating use of the League of Nations because he was aware that bureaucracy was a means of achieving the smallest result with the greatest effort.

Where then, asked his lordship, recognizing the futility of his efforts, was the permanent commission for refugees to be set up? He had spoken to the French Ambassador the previous evening; Paris was ruled out as the headquarters of the new office. The French Ambassador had argued that the commission would attract refugees as a light attracts moths; although the office was by no means intended to cope with the problems of individual refugees, the refugees would nevertheless see the meeting place of the commission as a Mecca for their pilgrimages. The Republic would prefer it if Paris were not even considered as a possible site for the commission's headquarters and the host country at Évian was thus spared the necessity of refusing the flattering proposal.

"Very well," said the American Ambassador. "But it must be a European capital, and I'm afraid London is the only possible choice."

He could express no view on this suggestion without having consulted his government, replied the Englishman, but he must not conceal the fact—they were talking in confidence—that Britain likewise regarded the influx of Jewish refugees with mixed feelings. He took a newspaper cutting from his pocket—it was the leading article from *The Times* of July 6th. In this leading article the most respected newspaper in the British Isles condemned the German Reich's attitude to the Jews. "But please read the sentence underlined," said his lordship pointing to a passage which ran: "It may be admitted that the presence of a large number of Jews within the state presents difficult problems in certain countries, especially when they achieve an im-

portance out of proportion to their numbers." With this significant sentence the highly respectable *Times* was certainly not
advocating anti-Semitism, but German anti-Semitism was neither so incomprehensible nor so unpopular as it appeared.

"You see, we must look at things realistically, Mr. Ambassador," the Englishman continued. "The whole world condemns
the brutality with which Hitler puts his anti-Semitic theories
into practice, but I have long suspected that Herr Hitler is a
step ahead of us in his political thinking. We are used to entering German anti-Semitism on the debit side of German politics
—and indeed, looked at from the point of view of morality or
world history, which is one and the same thing, the persecution
of the Jews does stand on the debit side. But if we think politically, we must shift anti-Semitism from the debit to the credit
side of the page. I know I am expressing a paradoxical idea, but
I am not sure whether Herr Hitler really hates the Jews as
much as he pretends, whether he has not rather recognized anti-
Semitism as a skeleton key with which the gates of most countries—certainly the European countries—can be opened. Take
the example of Czechoslovakia. No one will say that the Germans are very much loved by the Czech people. Yet on the day
of the *Anschluss* the Czech Minister of the Interior hermetically
sealed his country's frontier with Austria; Austrian and German
Jews who crossed the frontier in spite of this were arrested and
handed over. Most of them, I am told, are now in the concentration camp at Dachau near Munich. The Minister of the Interior
is a Czech, but he is a passionate anti-Semite. Which is he the
more passionately, a Czech or an anti-Semite? In any case I
think one is justified in supposing that Herr Hitler's National
Socialist program contains a grain of internationalism, that in
effect its sole international appeal lies in its anti-Semitism."

This thesis advanced by his British colleague did not appear
to the American Ambassador in the least absurd, but he took
care not to concur with it, and hid his feelings behind a stony
mask. What did the Englishman mean and to what purpose was
he developing his theories? Were they to take the wind out of
Hitler's sails and tolerate or even silently foster anti-Semitism
outside Germany—oh, this fatal policy of taking the wind out of
someone's sails, by which one never avoids the storm but always

sails into the tempest. Or had the Englishman merely chosen this roundabout way of advising him against setting up the permanent office in London, on the excuse that it would prepare fresh ground for anti-Semitism in Britain?

His lordship looked at the window, down which the rain was crawling like a millipede. As though to answer the Ambassador's mute questions, he said:

"At the Conference the word war will never be uttered, but you and I know that the great decision is approaching us. Us, I say, because America will not be able to escape it either. We need allies, Mr. Ambassador. Is it inhuman if I ask whether we should throw away the sympathies of the Czechs, Poles, Hungarians in order to save thirty or forty thousand Jews from persecution? With the best will in the world the participating states cannot take more. I know that people look at Britain askance, because they suspect us of taking Arab interests in Palestine into account. We do consider the countries of Islam, certainly, but will not France tomorrow and America the day after tomorrow have to consider the European states or Latin America?"

Thus spoke, thus argued the Englishman. Meanwhile the representatives of some Latin-American states had gathered in the hotel bar, or rather in the Salon Vert, which was situated in the west wing of the hotel and offered a pleasant view of the rose garden.

The representatives of Ecuador, Guatemala, Costa Rica, Paraguay, Venezuela, Uruguay, Nicaragua, Peru, Chile and the Dominican Republic were on their own here, which greatly contributed to the frankness and honesty of their utterances. In particular the delegate of Venezuela, his country's ambassador to Paris, could at last give vent to the thoughts that were oppressing his heart. The American President's initiative, he said, reminded him of the North Americans' attitude during the World War, when they were always ready, with no regard for the sacrifice, to fight "to the last Frenchman or Englishman." The United States had no intention of raising their quota for refugees, and what this quota amounted to could be seen by a comparison with Argentina—in 1935 every time forty-eight Jews received an immigration permit for the USA, thirty-two immigrated into Argentina, although the population of the United

States was about eight times that of Argentina. Évian was demonstrating the traditional policy of the United States, which understood by American brotherhood only one thing: "The same
burden is to be placed on the small, weak brother as on the big,
strong one."

He didn't want to contradict his Venezuelan colleague, said
the delegate of Peru—likewise ambassador in Paris—he saw a
great deal of truth in what his honorable colleague had said, but
he strongly advised diplomatic caution. The United States was
the greatest power on the continent and their President, to put
it mildly, was an unpredictable man, possessed by that typical
North American missionary zeal which had found such disastrous expression in 1846 in the war against Mexico. He considered it not only foolish but also superfluous to raise objections
in principle, since concrete, tangible considerations intelligible
to everyone were enough to put a stop to the United States'
generosity at the expense of the Latin-American nations. Take
Peru, for example. Did Peru need to advance arguments of
principle against immigration, when in her modest industry of
625 factories a total of only 18,508 workers earned a total of
about 15 million sol? They couldn't expect pampered European
Jews to be content with the wages of illiterate Indians, while to
raise wages to a European level would spell certain economic
ruin for the country.

Very true, said Chile's representative, an eminent diplomat
who represented his country not only as ambassador in Bern but
also at the Geneva International Labor Office. He fully sub-
scribed to the remarks of the previous speaker, but they would
do better to focus their attention on constructive proposals.
That very day the *Journal de Genève* had reported that Germany had imposed on the Jews a refugee tax of $56 million, had
confiscated this sum and paid it into the state treasury, and
there were rumors that the confiscated capital actually
amounted to $196 million. A considerable sum, as everyone
must admit—enthusiastic nods confirmed the correctness of the
speaker's estimate—in any case a sum that would speak elo-
quently outside Germany too. If the Conference called upon
Germany to give every emigrant money to the value of only two
thousand dollars from the refugee fund, it would be making

that constructive suggestion of which he had just spoken—constructive in every sense, because a Jew with two thousand dollars in his wallet was by no means worthless, was worth precisely two thousand dollars; constructive also because by taking up such a position the Conference would be demonstrating its freedom from prejudice and, if Germany refused, would nevertheless have proved its goodwill.

The discussion in the Salon Vert continued into the afternoon. While other Latin-American delegates also did their best to produce constructive ideas, the chief British delegate had made his way to the suite of the Australian Minister for Trade and Customs, where the representatives of Canada, Ireland and New Zealand were already gathered.

Although a smell of pipe and cigar tobacco lay over the large salon, the air here was fresh and wholesome, for the windows were open and the scent of the rain-soaked woods mingled with the masculine aroma of English, Dutch and Cuban tobacco. After his lordship had taken a seat by the window, he informed his colleagues of the results of his conversations with the Chairman, not without frankly indicating the meagerness of his achievements. The American President's special envoy was a difficult man, very taciturn; moreover the Americans possessed an enviable capacity for draping a cloak of humanitarianism around their highly practical, if not selfish actions—their behavior had not changed appreciably since the War of Independence of 1775. They must not forget that in two years the President would have to face what would be probably the most difficult election of his life, in the course of which he had stood the test of so many elections; it was only natural that he should have one eye on the persecuted European Jews, the other on the numerous and economically powerful Jews of America.

The Jews of Europe—they had just been talking about them, remarked the Canadian, a professional diplomat who represented his country at the League of Nations. At the afternoon sitting of the committees—two new ones had been formed the previous day—the delegates of Britain, Ireland and the Dominions must press for a clear definition of the competence of all future Conference bodies. "You only have to go down into the lobby." He turned to his colleagues. "It's seething with Span-

iards and Italians. The Italian emigrants have brought their
country's greatest historian, the Spaniards their most famous
painter; our hotel would be a happy hunting ground for auto-
graph collectors today. During the next few years, if not the
next few months, unless all the signs are wrong, Czechoslovakia,
Rumania, Hungary and Poland will begin to migrate, to migrate like Macbeth's Birnam Forest; we are faced with a new
Migration of the Nations, and if we do not take precautions the
waves of this migration will swamp us. The further we extend
the limits of our competence, the less we shall achieve. At the
end of the Conference no doubt must remain that we came
together to help the refugees from Germany to the best of our
ability and conscience, but by no means to solve the whole
problem of the Migration of the Nations in the twinkling of an
eye."

The Canadian's remarks were not met with undivided approval. Certainly it was important to set intelligent limits on
the scope of the Conference, stated the Australian Minister for
Trade and Customs, but it would be scarcely just and certainly
not useful to emphasize the philo-Semitic tendency of the Conference or to offend the Italians and Spaniards. The United
States was quite right to distribute their immigration quotas
according to nationality or country of birth and to make sure
that the Nordic Anglo-Saxon character of their country
was not diluted by Slav influences or by the importation of
members of the yellow race. "The Migration of the Nations is
universal—are we to open our doors only to East and Central
Europeans, only to members of the Semitic race?"

The New Zealand delegate to the League of Nations had
shaken his head in disapproval. He found this discussion very
much beside the point, he said. The Conference was hastening
to its climax, they must stop indulging in theoretical arguments. He had heard that the South Americans, or some of
them, had gathered in the Salon Vert to consult together in a
common front. "I can assure you"—he smiled—"that my Secret
Service does not function too badly. If my information is correct, one of the South Americans will this afternoon put forward a very sensible plan, and I suggest that it would not be a
bad idea to forestall him. We should propose the formation of a

subcommittee responsible for so-called documentation. The subcommittee would have to ascertain what kind of refugees each country is prepared to accept, to establish the age of acceptable immigrants, the professional categories to which they must belong, the amount of capital to be demanded, the income that they may expect. In my opinion it would be unworthy of Britain and the Dominions to mention race or religion, and moreover unwise for a great colonial country to do so. On the other hand, no one can blame us for protecting our most elementary social and economic interests by making our quotas dependent upon whether the refugee is a farmer, a laborer, a craftsman, an independent businessman, young or old, poor or in possession of capital; the unfortunately excessive emigration of intellectuals should in any case be confined to those well-known figures who anyhow present no problem."

The proposal was accepted and the gentlemen—it was by now one o'clock—repaired to the dining room. They had to cross the lobby, which had turned into a buzzing beehive. Every delegate who emerged from the lift or appeared at the foot of the stairs was immediately encircled by correspondents demanding details of the morning's discussions, the program for the afternoon, the truth about resolutions and rumors. There were also numerous representatives of private organizations, who had come because they had heard that the Chairman had arranged for the leading personalities of these organizations to be heard. Each of them wanted to know whether his organization would have an opportunity of appearing before the Conference. The Canadian Ambassador had been right: many famous Italian and Spanish emigrants had also turned up, embarrassing visitors, because how were the delegates to shake off the old man who had written *Greatness and Decadence of Rome,* how slip past the famous Spanish cellist, how entirely avoid speaking to a former colleague, Italy's ex-Foreign Minister, the scion of an ancient princely family? The Jewish baron whose name was identical with high finance, the Austrian count who for years had fought for Pan-Europe, the once so powerful German newspaper proprietor, also wanted a few words with the delegates, which was all the more difficult because German agents, Hungarian journalists, the leaders of Sudetan German and Rumanian anti-Semitic organizations, Palestinian agitators, representatives of American women's clubs and spies from every country immediately joined groups engaged in conversation.

In the light, spacious dining room the delegates were at last alone again. Anyone entering the dining room at this hour of the day could not doubt that the thirty-two delegations took their mission seriously, didn't let a moment pass without important conversations and never lost sight of the purpose of their gathering. Whether the American Ambassador was the guest of his French colleague, whether Argentina's Ambassador in Paris had asked Chile's Ambassador in Bern to his table, whether the Danish Foreign Minister was entertaining the Belgian Chief of Police—the only topic of conversation at every table was the fate of the refugees. Nevertheless it would have struck even an uninformed observer that on this nineteenth of July conversations were not simply being continued, that an unusual excitement had gripped the dining room, and he would soon have discovered the direction from which this excitement came and what, or rather who, had caused it.

The Colombian Minister, who was sitting at a corner table with the Brazilian Ambassador and the representative of Holland, kept leaving his table, approaching other groups, waiting briefly for an invitation, pulling up a chair, addressing his colleagues with lively gestures, returning to his own table, swallowing a few mouthfuls, throwing down his napkin and setting out again, a human frog hopping from table to table.

In the morning the Colombian had called together some members of his committee in his suite and informed them, at least in part, of Professor Heinrich von Benda's mission. He had avoided mentioning the German Government's offer to sell dead souls for cash or attempting to persuade the nations to buy dead souls—a deal entirely to the taste of Gogol's Chichikov; he had avoided mentioning this indisputable impertinence, but he had implored his colleagues not to reject the German ultimatum conveyed by the Viennese Professor. Forty thousand Austrian Jews condemned to extermination—the Conference could not adjourn without at least giving asylum to these forty thousand "living corpses"; again he had quoted a Russian author. The Minister and jurist had pleaded for a limited goal, but he had urged that this goal should be achieved without fail and without delay; and although he had by no means gained the delegates' unconditional agreement, he had not met with unconditional refusal. They had declared their readiness to listen to the representative of the Austrian Jewish Community in secret session.

Now the Colombian Minister did not have the authority to put into effect such a decision of the committee without the agreement of the other participants in the Conference, or at least of the Chairman. It would also have been totally undiplomatic to confront the majority with a *fait accompli* through a surprising and unorthodox step, to anger them and push them into opposition through a mere error of competence.

No sooner had the Colombian spoken to the Chairman and the French Ambassador, no sooner had he disclosed the position to his table companions, the Dutchman and the Brazilian, than the rumor of the committee's proposal to hear Professor von Benda, of the *coup de théâtre,* as such unforeseen events are called in diplomatic language, spread from table to table, so that at the next table he visited the Minister scarcely had to explain the facts and could confine himself to his plea. Since diplomats exercise extreme diplomacy in dealing with other diplomats, no one took up a stand in relation to the "Colombian Plan," as it was immediately called; they confined themselves to questions of procedure, namely whether it was permissible, desirable and in the interests of the Conference to agree to Professor von Benda being heard.

If the jurist's proposal was vigorously discussed between the *hors d'oeuvre*—that day there was a wonderful tender pink salmon from Scotland free from any flavor of salt—and the tasty *poulet de Bresse,* between the main course and the *entremets,* a very digestible *crème caramel,* all interest turned to the table of the Chairman, who had meanwhile been joined by his lordship the British delegate, the Argentinian Ambassador and the High Commissioner for Refugees. People wondered what the delegation leaders of the Great Powers were saying, whether they were surprised, indignant or impressed, whether their expressions betrayed concern, disagreement or unity, whether it would be a good thing to support the project, to reject it out of hand or to maintain an attitude of wait and see.

By the time coffee was served—it was neither Brazilian nor Colombian coffee, but the very specific *café filtre*, strongly laced with chicory, preferred in France—it was definitely known that the American Ambassador had not opposed the idea of hearing Professor Heinrich von Benda, with the one proviso that the Jewish representative should not appear before the plenary assembly, but before the Colombian's committee.

By the time the waiters passed along the tables with a selection of sweet liqueurs—Cointreau, curaçao, crème de menthe and Benedictine—the Colombian delegate, the cause of this midday disturbance, was no longer in the room. He had gone off in search of Professor Heinrich von Benda.

The dream the Professor had dreamed stayed with him long after he had awakened. In the dream Bettina had lain beside him, her head had rested on his shoulder, she had pulled up her knee to her breast and over his stomach, he had felt the warmth of her loins on his skin; the neat landlady had come in and said that Herr Lederer, Herr Ludwig Lederer from Vienna, was waiting outside to apologize, but the sleeper had not known who Herr Lederer was or why he wanted to apologize; the rain had beaten on the windowpanes and Bettina had said they should breakfast in bed—they were still lying in bed when Herr Lederer came in, now he remembered him; Herr Lederer was carrying a tray, but on the tray lay little Heinrich; Herr Lederer stood by the bed and looked at the couple in bed sadly; he said the landlady didn't want to come in because the child was Jewish, and Bettina stretched out her hands to the child, and then the child lay between them, and dreaming on he felt only the warmth of the little body.

The flying carpet of dreams had brought Bettina even closer than, in spite of the distance, she had been before. Dreams have the remarkable capacity, as they themselves vanish behind ever denser falling veils, of causing certain outlines of reality to emerge more clearly, so that the disappearing dream leaves behind it a searing sense of the present. Évian, the hotel, his mis-

sion, seemed to the Professor that morning to have moved away
into the distance, Bettina and the child to be near enough to
touch.

Since he knew that no sessions were taking place he intended
to grant himself a rest; he breakfasted late and went into the
lounge to read the newspapers and the morning communiqués
giving the Conference's program for the day. As in his dream
the rain was beating against the windowpanes, the wind was
whistling through the trees in the garden outside the lounge
door. The dream disquieted him still, filled him with an inexplicable anxiety; dream images of varying degrees of intensity
flashed like the gliding lights of a lighthouse out of the mist.
When he laid aside his newspaper he caught sight of Herr Lederer, Ludwig Lederer from Vienna, who, wearing a raincoat,
hurried through the lobby behind his mother; although Ludwig Lederer was a good two heads taller than his mother, he
seemed to be running along behind her like a pet dog. The
Professor found it difficult to distinguish between the real and
the dream Lederer; because he had sprung from the Professor's
dream, Herr Lederer, insignificant himself, had suddenly
gained particular significance.

The Professor must have been sitting like this for half an
hour when the porter announced a visitor. A certain "Monsieur" Hubert Pichler wanted to speak to the Professor, said the
porter, and his expression indicated that he regarded Hubert
Pichler as an odd visitor and no "monsieur."

Hubert Pichler was not so odd at all, he merely looked it in
these surroundings. His hobnail boots and rough clothing that
was far too warm for the time of year emphasized the peasant
appearance of the visitor, who wore under an insect-bitten nose,
that projected like an enormous fingerstall, a tiny moustache
running exactly from the sides of the nostrils to the center of
the upper lip. This moustache, once common among Austrian
peasants, today looked provocative.

Pichler sat down hesitantly on the edge of a chair, looked
around, saw that there was no one within earshot and came
straight to the point. He had set out from his village during the
night, he said—it lay on the other side of the frontier, in Vorarl-

berg—to bring the Professor a letter from his daughter, Frau Elisabeth Berenson, who was staying with him, had indeed found a safe hiding place at his house.

The Professor was too moved to utter a word. Elisabeth was alive! He felt as though he had never stopped thinking about Elisabeth, had never been free from concern for her, from worry about her disappearance; at the same time he reproached himself for having suppressed the concern and worry, for not having thought about Elisabeth enough, not having done enough on her behalf, actually having grown accustomed to the unthinkable, so that the good news now came to him as an undeserved surprise. He stretched out his hand for the letter, but the man made no move to deliver the message.

"Frau Berenson is well," Pichler began. "The children are well. They've been with me at the farm for a fortnight, they like it there"—he was dragging out his report unnecessarily, repeating the same phrases over and over again—"only little Margaret, the smallest one, had measles, that was pretty difficult, I mean we couldn't call in a doctor, but she got over it anyhow, you know children get over things quickly, and doctors don't know any more than we do." Now the account became somewhat confused and did not keep at all to the chronological order. "Frau Berenson read in the paper that the Herr Professor was here, and Herr Berenson is already in Palestine, he's quite all right, the Herr Professor has nothing to worry about, but I don't know how Frau Berenson knows that, she can't get mail; the farm is about a mile above the village, the police don't come up there, only my wife gets a bit worried, not that she doesn't get on well with Frau Berenson, she's a thoroughly kindhearted woman, only a bit nervous"—he meant Elisabeth, not his wife.

These kindhearted people want to get rid of Elisabeth, of Elisabeth and the children, thought the Professor, and all at once his mission seemed to him unimportant beside the need to save Elisabeth. Yes, his conscience had been asleep, the fate of forty thousand or a hundred thousand or a million people was a good pillow; while his conscience rested on this pillow it slept away its duty to his own daughter. "Daddy will manage it"—this had been a favorite saying, a daily thought of Elisabeth's; and

now Elisabeth was virtually imprisoned in a Vorarlberg mountain village and Daddy could do nothing, Daddy was too busy
saving forty thousand Jews.

The peasant had folded his hands over his belly; he did it as
most people do whose hands are clumsy and hard and horny
from work, only the first joints of the fingers touched lightly, as
though the fingers were afraid of one another.

"Today, at the latest tomorrow," said the man, "we can bring
them over the frontier, only little Margaret is a bit weak on
her legs, but it'll be all right, I shall be there myself, of course
we shall have to be careful about it, it's pretty dangerous for me,
Frau Berenson has no visa, and unfortunately she hasn't any
money either; my wife keeps telling me to be careful; but when
people are in trouble you must help them, I always say. Of
course I shall have to have a few men to come with me, they
don't like doing it, the Swiss are as sharp as watchdogs, it's
pretty dangerous—"

Now the Professor understood why Pichler was beating about
the bush—the bush was money, Pichler was asking for money,
that was why he had come.

Only now did the peasant decide cautiously to pull out his
wallet and give the Professor Elisabeth's letter.

The letter, in Elisabeth's upright, excessively large handwrit-
ing so that although there was not much in it, it filled four
pages, confirmed everything the peasant had said. Elisabeth
wrote that she had managed to get out of Vienna with the four
children and make her way to the Swiss frontier; from here,
where no one knew her, she had hoped to get abroad, but she
had nothing but an out-of-date Austrian passport, there was no
question of obtaining a visa, and when she had slipped out of
Vienna under cover of darkness it had been impossible for her
to take more money than she had by now spent. From Oskar,
who had been in Italy at the time of the German entry into
Austria, she had received only a brief message from Palestine.
"He says he is trying to arrange for us to come to Palestine, but
you know how it is. . . ." Herr Pichler, she wrote, was a decent
man; he knew all the paths over the mountains, had already
brought a dozen refugees across the frontier. "It's only a question of money." What luck that she had read in a newspaper

that her father was in Évian as the representative of the Jewish Community. "I only pray that he finds you. With God's help we shall see each other soon."

Luck—the word cropped up in the letter more than once, and for Heinrich von Benda it changed into another word, no less beautiful and no less difficult, the word duty, for what children take to be luck is often nothing but the parents' duty: it begins with Christmas presents and can end with ransom money.

"If there were no children it would be cheaper," he heard Pichler say. Only now did the Professor become aware that the peasant had been watching him with mistrustful attention as he read. "The men are afraid," Pichler went on, visibly reassured. "They're afraid the children will give them away, or won't manage to climb, it's pretty hard, they ask a hundred marks for adults, two hundred for children, a head of course, nine hundred marks, let's say a thousand in all—I'm not asking anything for myself, it's only because of the fortnight, life is getting dearer all the time."

"You shall have the money, Herr Pichler," said the Professor. "And I thank you with all my heart"—but he didn't know, hadn't even the vaguest idea, how he was going to raise a thousand marks in so short a time.

While he entangled his visitor in a conversation, lulling him in the belief that he was now mainly concerned to know more about his grandchildren, even about the farm and conditions of life up there, in the villages and the pastures on the other side of the Swiss frontier, the Professor worked out in his mind how much money he had, how much he could save, how much he could pay at once and later replace, whether he could change francs into Reichsmarks or whether Herr Pichler would be content with French currency. Trying his hand at the unfamiliar trade of confidence trickster, he threw the sentence: "A thousand marks, that's about a hundred and four thousand francs . . ." into the conversation, as though casually; but he realized at once that his shot had not hit the bull's-eye, in fact was right off the target. French currency was out of the question, declared Pichler, foreign currency had to be reported over there, and he would have difficulty in explaining how he came to be in possession of French money.

"All right, then of course you can have it in marks," said the Professor—he was afraid of offending the peasant—only Herr Pichler would have to be patient until the afternoon, he had first to change the money; Herr Pichler should come back for the sum agreed at three or at the latest three-thirty.

The peasant said good-bye. His tone, it seemed to the Professor, had become somewhat cooler, there was surprise on his face, perhaps his suspicions were aroused again. Heinrich von Benda was alone.

He possessed only fifteen or twenty Reichsmarks. His total capital in French francs amounted to barely a thousand marks; it was impossible to change even one single franc into foreign currency. A few of his wealthy patients abroad occurred to him. Strangely enough it was the names of those he hardly new that he first remembered; but however well or little he knew them, none of them could lend him the sum demanded by three o'clock or at the latest three-thirty; anyone who was outside Germany was glad not to possess any German currency, and who in any case possessed a thousand marks? He would have felt no inhibitions about approaching anyone, a friend or a stranger, for money, to ask for a loan or a gift, he would have begged and implored without inhibition, but Professor Heinrich von Benda was so poor that he didn't even know where to turn in order to beg. A tyro in humiliation, the most peculiar ideas crossed his mind. He thought of the American Ambassador, the Colombian Minister, even his shadow, the young American. He thought of the twelve hundred francs that he had frivolously handed over to the *couturière* in the Rue Nationale, and he was ashamed of his thoughtlessness, although twelve hundred francs more or less, any francs more or less, would not have helped him, would not have meant anything. For a moment he was tempted to renounce the whole rescue attempt: its outcome was by no means certain, there were armed German and Swiss frontier patrols, there were the difficult mountain paths, many of them perhaps icy even in summer; Elisabeth was weak and her children small, Margaret had just got over the measles. It was only a brief temptation and a cowardly justification, but where was he to get the money? From Selma Selig, of course! Why had he not thought at once of the good woman who had helped heaven knows how many Jews to flee, who had funds intended to assist in precisely such cases, why had he not thought of Selma Selig whose influence with the Swiss authorities, once the escape had succeeded, might be of the greatest importance?

Fortunately Fräulein Selig had told him in which family *pension* in Évian she was staying; he sought and found her address and number on the way to the telephone booth; he asked the operator to put him through and waited with a pounding heart to see whether he would find Selma Selig at home. In a matter of seconds he heard the pleasant, deep voice, told Fräulein Selig of the visit from the peasant, explained his family circumstances to her, told her the deadline and did all this without feeling strange or ill at ease in his new trade of supplicant.

It was a large sum, commented Fräulein Selig, and she also asked the Professor not to say any more on the telephone; in no case must her part in the risky enterprise become known. "I'll be with you in an hour, and by the afternoon I shall have the money."

Heinrich von Benda heard nothing about the risk and the largeness of the sum, he heard only the last sentence, and as he heard it he was overcome by such a feeling of happiness that he could almost have cried; but this feeling spread and expanded, it took the Professor's whole mission under its wing, because anyone who had such luck in his own private affairs, anyone to whom such a fine and certain and rapid coincidence happened, for whom duty changed into happy coincidence and unexpected success, could also not fail as a missionary for others, for the unknown and despairing.

As he left the telephone booth the Colombian Minister, who had been waiting at the porter's lodge, came toward him. Heinrich von Benda greeted him with a smile, almost as though he had been expecting him.

In addition to Colombia, the committee was made up of Belgium, Ecuador, Bolivia, Brazil, Norway, Switzerland and Great Britain. Bolivia was represented by an ambassador, Brazil by an envoy, Belgium by the Brussels chief of police, Ecuador by a chargé d'affaires, Norway by a highly placed judge, Switzerland

by the Bern police chief, Great Britain by the deputy leader of
the delegation, a minister plenipotentiary.

Heinrich von Benda had to wait in the hotel lobby until he
was called. He had placed his briefcase on his knees; it contained for the most part statistical data and excerpts from German newspapers. Were these the written proofs for the defense
or was it the required reading for an examination, the Professor
asked himself; and he himself—was he an accused man to be
brought to trial, or an examination candidate about to appear
before his professors? He had often sat on the other side of the
table. How many students, anxiously aware of their shortcomings, had waited to be called before him to convince him of
their knowledge or delude him as to their lack of it—if only he
asks me this, if only he doesn't touch on that subject, if only it
were over . . . ! He had been invited from one hour to the
next, he was unprepared, and perhaps it was fortunate that at
least now he had some time to collect his thoughts. The Colombian Minister had informed his colleagues about the German
ultimatum, but had concealed from them the fact that Germany
was demanding money to release the forty thousand Jews; soon
the Professor would have to decide whether also to remain silent or to speak the truth. If he did not mention the demand,
how were the ten millions to be raised, and would Germany let
the forty thousand go without receiving the ransom money they
demanded? But if he revealed the number, if he named the
price besides the ultimatum, he would be stabbing the Colombian, his only friend, in the back, would perhaps make it easy
for the members of the committee to draw back totally and
finally with moral self-satisfaction, with horror, indignation and
anger. He would have to leave the decision to the impulse, the
inspiration of the moment, the spark struck by contact. What
sort of contact would it be? Before anyone else could examine
him, Heinrich von Benda examined himself, and he was surprised to note that he felt no humiliation, not even anger at the
length of time he was kept waiting, at the slowly passing hour.
Everything was an examination, whether you were a defendant
or a student, whether you were arming yourself for a joust or
embracing a woman, whether you were going to an operation or
receiving guests, whether you were delivering a lecture or em-

barking on a journey, but there were examinations in which only the examiners could fail. He had to prevent his judges from being condemned—it was not so strange, after all, that he felt no humiliation.

The Hôtel Royal was too small for the numerous committees and subcommittees that were meeting here simultaneously, so that the Colombian's committee had established itself in the hotel bar. As he entered, the delegates rose; the chairman introduced the Professor to them. The Professor had had time to study their titles; now he tried to harmonize the names and titles with the men, but the introductions went too quickly and only two or three people impressed themselves upon him—the overostentatiously dressed young delegate from Ecuador, the cumbersome, bucolic figure of the Swiss police chief, the little man with dark glasses whom he knew to be representing the Republic of Brazil.

They sat down at the green conference table, which, to be more exact, consisted of three tables, forming as it were an open gate. To the Professor's left sat the representatives of Great Britain, Brazil, Belgium and Switzerland; to his right the chairman, next to the representatives of Bolivia, Norway and Ecuador; but he was alone on the long side of the table, an isolated object of attention. At the moment, however, the delegates were still discussing a question that had evidently been preoccupying them before the Professor's entry; an intimacy from which he was excluded prevailed among them. Only the interpreter, a blond young Frenchman with curly hair, and the shorthand typist, a sad little creature, looked at him with a certain curiosity.

The Colombian Minister opened the proceedings by introducing the guest in flattering terms. The Conference, he said, intended to hear several delegates of private defense and aid organizations, but it was not by chance that Professor von Benda was the first to be invited, for he possessed information which it was the Conference's task, indeed urgent duty, to hear. Perhaps it would be helpful and would expedite matters, said the Minister, if he himself asked the first questions—and he immediately turned to the witness. "How many Jews, Professor, are still living in Austria now?"

"Between a hundred and eighty thousand and two hundred thousand," replied the Professor. "But it is impossible to say with certainty. The number of those regarded as Jews is rising daily, since the Nuremberg Laws are being applied more and more rigorously. It is said that in the whole Reich half a million Catholics are to be included under them."

"How many Jews have so far left what used to be Austria?" the Belgian police chief asked.

What used to be Austria, thought the Professor—of course, that which has been conquered has ceased to be.

"About fifty thousand," he said.

"Have these people taken any possessions with them?"

"The Austrians hardly. Up to the end of last year German Jews who had at least thirty thousand Reichsmarks, or a family of two who could together produce fifty thousand Reichsmarks, were allowed to take a modest proportion of their capital with them. The rest of the confiscated capital was supposed to be paid into a fund that would make certain loans to emigrating Jews."

"What do you mean by loans?"

"The loans are without practical significance. They are what is called 'demonstration money.' When an emigrant applies for a visa, the country he wishes to enter in almost all cases demands proof of a certain capital. Sometimes the German Government places this sum at his disposal, but the emigrant is not allowed to retain the money; it is taken away from him again after he has obtained the visa but before he has left the country."

Although he knew French, the Professor had been speaking in English; now the interpreter translated his answer into French. No sooner had he done so than the delegate from Ecuador—the overelegantly dressed young man, lithe as a Spanish dancer—burst out: "That is blatant fraud!"

"Undoubtedly." The Professor nodded. "The fund that is supposed to contain many millions of pounds of confiscated capital serves the purpose of fraud."

"That's not what I meant," the Ecuadorian chargé d'affaires said, turning to his colleagues. "The fraud is practiced on a single victim, the credulous host country, but it is practiced by two accomplices—or are you going to tell us, Professor, that the Jewish emigrant who produces the counterfeit coin knows nothing about the fraud?"

"*Monsieur le chargé d'affaires,*" the Professor replied with restrained exasperation, "the victims are the Jewish emigrants who have been robbed of their property, people in danger of their lives, and the fraud, if you want to use the word, is forced upon them."

He thought of Elisabeth. The Vorarlberg peasant was on his way back to his village with a thousand marks, and if the Lord who ruled over mountains, valleys and frontier patrols willed, tomorrow night, with His help but in disregard of the host country's laws, Elisabeth would cross the frontier into free Switzerland. She wouldn't even be able to show a counterfeit coin and would bring nothing with her but four hungry mouths.

"Has your own property been confiscated?" the Ecuadorian chargé d'affaires asked from the other end of the table.

"Apart from very small sums belonging to my wife my accounts have been blocked," the Professor replied and his face went red. He noticed that the delegates were smoking, and lit a cigarette. After the first deep inhalations he felt calmer; today as an exception—the thought passed through his head—since abstinence was bound to increase his nervous tension, he would not restrict his smoking.

"Gentlemen," he heard the chairman say, "we are not here to ask personal questions, but to gain information about the situation of the Jews in Germany." When he turned to the Professor there was the same sly yet encouraging twinkle in his eyes that Heinrich von Benda had noticed during their first encounter. "On what conditions do the Germans issue emigration permits?"

"In the case of a Jew whom they are prepared to let out at all, it depends in the first place upon his being able to produce an entry permit for another country."

"Assuming that a Jew cannot obtain such papers and makes his way to one of the German frontiers—say the Belgian, Dutch

or Swiss. Do the Germans let him pass—I mean, do they turn a
blind eye if the refugee tries to leave his homeland illegally and
enter a neighboring country equally illegally?"

The Professor thought he knew what the Colombian was
after. "On the contrary," he replied. "They hunt down illegal
emigrants and, if they catch them, they put them in prisons and
concentration camps."

"Do you know of any instance where the Germans have sent
large transports of Jews to one of the frontiers?"

"On the contrary, all places on the frontier are closed areas to
Jews."

"What do you conclude from that?"

"The conclusion is obvious," the Professor said. "But before
discussing it, I should like to show the committee these cuttings
from German newspapers. The *Völkischer Beobachter* of yesterday declares that the 'Jew Conference' is 'a Satanic game of
political agitation,' but 'thanks to the attitude of countries like
Argentina, who repudiate interference in their internal affairs,
it is condemned to failure.' The Vienna edition of the *Völkischer Beobachter* headlines its report 'No One Wants the Riff-
raff' and writes: 'Most of the government representatives refuse
to open the gates of their own countries to a gang who have
caused Germany's ruin.' The *Hitler-Jugend,* Munich, writes:
'One thing alone has emerged from this meeting of the unwanted. The Jews' lackey in the White House was making a
mistake when he speculated on the participants' tear ducts.' I
believe that these excerpts are the best answer to the chairman's
question. If Germany's sole purpose was to get rid of its Jews,
then the German Government would be bound to welcome this
Conference and do all it could to assist Jewish emigration. Germany does not want to get rid of the Jews but to exterminate
them."

The gray-haired delegate of Norway, who was also President
of the Nansen Office, raised his hand. "I should not like to allow
Professor von Benda's conclusions to go uncontradicted," he
said in a low voice, but with sovereign emphasis. "The expul-
sion of half a million Jews, even the attempt to smuggle them
out of the country, would on the one hand place before the
world the most serious problems and, on the other, would lead

to very serious international complications for Germany. The fact that Germany does nothing of the sort indicates a willingness to work together with other countries and by no means proves what the delegate of the Jewish Community, in his understandable excitement, has asserted. We have no reason to suppose that Germany intends to 'exterminate' the Jews—it is a long way from material persecution and even occasional acts of violence, regrettable as they may be, to 'extermination'; we should guard against regarding the latter as a fact, as an established certainty."

While he was asking himself whether it was merely apathy and lack of imagination, or the premeditated intention of turning this great hour into a quickly forgotten episode that was speaking out of the mouth of the Norwegian, Heinrich von Benda felt a heaviness in his left arm that began to weigh on his shoulders and oppress his heart. This time, it seemed to him, the cramp had not started in the immediate vicinity of the heart, had not spread from there; the pain was creeping in the opposite direction, from the shoulder over the chest toward the heart. The pain stretched out its claws toward the heart, drew them in again, stretched them out again. Like an anatomist bending over a body that has been cut open and dissected, he saw his heart, saw the calcified corona of arteries, saw the ring gripping his heart tighter and tighter, saw it open up only to close all the more tightly. He slipped his hand into his trouser pocket, found the box of nitroglycerin pills, opened it in his pocket, took out one pill, careful all the time not to betray himself with his gesture. This time he would not wait until he had no choice and had to take the pills; he would take them before an attack robbed him of his breath. Seized with panic, he noticed that his breath was becoming shorter and shorter. On the two sides of the table at which the delegates were sitting there stood a carafe of water with glasses, and in front of him too there stood a glass, but he would have had to lean over the table, would have to ask for the carafe, could probably not swallow the pill unnoticed. He did not want to arouse pity, must not do so, and who could tell whether in fact he would rouse pity at all, whether one or other of the delegates would not imagine that he was playing a mean game with the delegates' sympathy. The two carafes grew before his eyes, grew out of themselves and became gigantic, glassy mirages. He straightened up because, although experience should have taught him the contrary, he hoped that the pain would abate; the pain did not abate, but his glance fell on a carafe which, although it bore the advertisement of a whisky firm, was filled with clear water— the carafe stood on the bar just to his right, only a step from his chair. He rose, walked to the bar, poured water into one of the glasses standing in a row by the carafe, and standing with his back to the conference table, he managed to bring the pill that he was holding in the palm of his hand unnoticed to his mouth. As he turned around and returned to his place the carafes had been held out to him from both sides, but he merely said thank you with a smile and acted as though nothing had happened. He stubbed out the smoldering cigarette in the ashtray.

A murmur of approval had greeted the Norwegian judge's words; now the Brazilian with the green glasses turned to the Professor.

"Has there ever been any mention in the Jewish Community's discussions with the German Government," asked the Ambassador, "of whether such emigrants as the Évian member states would accept would be given more than ten marks, that is to say a sum at least halfway sufficient to provide them with a means of livelihood?"

The Professor looked for help at the Colombian chairman. Not a word had yet been said about the German ultimatum, the forty thousand had not yet been mentioned; any informed official of the League of Nations could have answered the questions so far asked. Why had he been called to appear before this forum, why was he here? Hitler was demanding two hundred and fifty dollars for every Jew, and around the green table at Évian people seemed to be interested only in how much each Jew was worth in hellers and pfennigs, or rather in dollars, and how they could close the frontiers to every Jew who was not worth anything.

"There is absolutely no possibility," the Professor said, "of the German Government departing from its ten-mark principle; for the last two months or so it has ceased even to provide so-called 'demonstration money.' "

The next question came from the left; there, at the end of the table, sat the Swiss police chief, who looked like any policeman, in Switzerland or elsewhere.

"What do the Jews plan to do," he asked, "after they have left the country entirely without means?"

"They want to work."

"You obviously haven't heard of unemployment," the delegate from Ecuador interposed.

"How high is the percentage of intellectuals among the Austrian Jews?" asked the Belgian, who looked like any policeman, in Belgium or elsewhere.

"About fifty percent."

"Have you counted businessmen as intellectuals?"

"No."

"In other words, the number of manual laborers is negligible?"

"Probably."

"And probably the number of young Jews is equally small?"

"It probably isn't high, because the young people were the first to leave the country. The older people are, the more attached they are to their homeland, the less able to believe what is happening in Germany and Austria."

The pain in Heinrich von Benda's chest began to give way to a dull weariness. He was familiar with the sensation he was experiencing now: first a warmth spread in which the pain became submerged, then a weariness that swallowed up the warmth.

As though from far away, he heard the voice of the Swiss delegate backing up his Belgian colleague. "At least eighty percent of the refugees would become a burden on public charity."

The Professor looked around. The Colombian Minister had immersed himself in his papers, as though he were looking there for the open sesame that would unlock hearts, or as though he were afraid to look at the Professor. There was the frank but worried face of the Bolivian, the pinched bureaucrat's face of the Belgian, the red petty-bourgeois face of the Swiss, there was the closed expression of the Englishman, who had not yet uttered a word, there were the veiled eyes of the Brazilian, and the cold eyes of the Norwegian, there was the provocative gaze of the delegate of Ecuador. To become a burden on public charity! Let not thy left hand know what thy right hand doeth. Charity that feels charity to be a burden. And how far what the gentlemen felt to be charity was from the demand that was going to be made on their charity!

At last the chairman raised his head, at last he said, "Is it correct, Professor von Benda, that forty thousand Austrian Jews are threatened with immediate arrest?"

"Such is my information, and it is undoubtedly correct."

"Where did your information come from?" the Brazilian asked.

"From the Gestapo."

"For what purpose did the Gestapo tell you this?"

"So that I might inform the Conference."

"Just a moment," the Bolivian Ambassador interrupted. "As far as I know, Professor von Benda has been accredited to the Conference by the Jewish Community of Austria. Is the Professor speaking in the name of the Community or of the Gestapo?"

"In the name of the Community," the Colombian interrupted quickly. "But the Gestapo did not give Professor von Benda an exit permit out of pure humanity, but because they think that at least over one point the interests of the German Government and the interests of the Jews coincide."

"Then it isn't true," the Ecuadorian delegate interjected, "that Germany wants to exterminate the Jews. Germany simply wants to dump them on other countries."

So this is the result of a half-truth, thought the Professor. The delegates were sitting at an inn on the edge of the jungle; every now and then someone appeared out of the jungle, but his stories sounded like lies and wild exaggerations; every now and then they heard the roaring of the beasts in the jungle, but in the inn they were sitting at copiously laden tables— "No one can be anyone else's comrade here." The Colombian's plan was bound to fail. If they didn't say that Germany wanted to sell the Jews, to sell or exterminate them, then the young man from Ecuador was right, it almost looked as though the interests of Germany and of the Jews were identical.

The Professor was about to speak when the Bolivian turned

to him. "Do you think Germany would dare to carry out such a mass arrest?"

The Bolivian—a dapper little man with gray temples, one of the early champions of the League of Nations, as the Professor now remembered—had intelligent, kind eyes: if you were a Jew you knew how to read other people's eyes. He had probably asked the question about the Gestapo to help the Professor.

"Yes," Heinrich von Benda replied. "Germany will dare that and more. Germany has kidnapped emigrants abroad and taken them back to Germany. The German Nobel Peace Prize winner, who by the way isn't a Jew, is dying from the aftereffects of maltreatment. Tens of thousands are being beaten and tortured in concentration camps—" He broke off. What was the use of repeating the unbelievable? "Why do you doubt," he asked, "that this regime is capable of arresting forty thousand innocent people—tomorrow forty thousand, the day after four hundred thousand, the day after that, if it can, four million?"

A look from the chairman told him that he had said too much. Evil must be presented on a reduced scale; in its true proportions it appears incredible.

"So to let in the forty thousand Jews," interrupted the Swiss delegate, "would be only a drop in the ocean." His hands lay on the conference table like two stones broken out of a column. "So our compassion is to be put to the test. If we go a step further, tomorrow Germany will indeed send us four hundred thousand Jews and the day after perhaps four million. I'm not a professional diplomat, I'm only a simple man who is used to speaking the truth. Reasonable compassion is one thing, the weakness of not being able to say no another. Germany is probably counting on our weakness and the emigrants who are illegally flooding the neighboring countries are certainly counting on it."

Only the delegate from Ecuador said, "Quite right!" Otherwise there was silence. Outside it had long ago stopped raining. A beam of sunlight came in through the heavily curtained windows and was caught up by the colored bottles standing on the bar. An elephant had crashed through the china shop and left it in smithereens. That had not been the idea. You could smash the china, the glasses, the bottles, the mirrors one by one,

slowly, carefully, one at a time; it was not only superfluous, it
was also contrary to diplomatic practice to smash all the china,
all the glasses, all the bottles, all the mirrors at once.

"I should like to point out to the honorable representative of
the Confédération Helvétique," the Colombian said, "that we
have not reached the stage of drawing conclusions. We are here
to put questions to Professor von Benda."

"Very well," the Swiss rejoined, offended. "In that case I
should like to inquire whether Professor von Benda negotiated
with the Gestapo on Swiss or on French soil."

"I happen to know that the Professor negotiated with the
Gestapo in Vienna," the chairman declared.

"Is it true that you yourself were in prison?" the Belgian
asked, coming to his Swiss colleague's aid.

"Yes."

"Were you maltreated?"

"No. I was released in response to the intervention of the
Duke of Windsor. A man was beaten to death in the next cell.
He wasn't lucky enough to have treated His Royal Highness."

"Did the Gestapo get in touch with you after your release?"
the delegate of Ecuador asked.

"Yes."

"Did you have the impression that you were released in order
to be entrusted with this mission?"

"I have already told you that the Duke of Windsor . . ."

"Have you a family, Professor?" the Belgian asked.

"Yes."

"Are they in Austria?"

"Yes."

"Did the Gestapo supply you with foreign currency?" the
Swiss asked.

Heinrich von Benda's gaze fell upon his hands. His hands
were white and they were trembling. He hid them under the
table. He heard the Colombian say, "I cannot permit that question. It goes without saying that the German authorities had to
issue a currency permit."

Heinrich von Benda heard this only as though from a great
distance. He began to speak and he now spoke without looking

to right or left, all he saw was occasionally the blond head of the interpreter and the mouse-colored head of the typist. At first he spoke in a low voice, then louder and finally loud. He felt no fatigue and no pain, like the wounded or shot, who may perhaps be dying but who feel no fatigue and no pain; no one tried to interrupt him, but he wouldn't have heard if anyone had tried to interrupt him.

"Gentlemen," he said, "I did not come here to answer questions that might just as well have been put to me by the Gestapo, but I am grateful to you for asking them because they teach me that the sickness that has fallen upon my fatherland is infectious; suspicion, ill will and prejudice need no passport, no visa and no foreign currency. Inhumanity, it seems, has no flag. A few days ago, when I set out on my journey to Évian, I seriously believed that I held the key to the salvation of hundreds of thousands of victims of undeserved persecution, illegal imprisonment, inhuman torture, hundreds of thousands of people marked off for death. I learned to be modest. Germany, I was told, would release forty thousand Jews in return for ten million dollars. I wanted to beg these ten million of you. Every day ten million dollars are spent on building roads—where are these roads to lead to, if we are approaching the abyss? Every day ships are built costing more than ten million dollars—are they to be ships without human freight? Every day ten million dollars are invested in agricultural projects—can the earth be fruitful if it is fertilized with corpses?"

Now he was resolved to betray his only friend in this circle; he had to betray him if he was not to betray forty thousand men, women and children.

"I was told here in Évian," he went on, "that I must say nothing about the price of the Jews, for in Évian people only want to know how much money the Jews can bring with them, why they don't go to another country, how strong the hands are that they bring with them, and how young the blood is that flows in their veins. Perhaps my friends are right, perhaps it would be wrong to yield to blackmail, perhaps not a single dollar is needed, perhaps a single act of mercy can open the prison gates. But one thing you must know. If this Conference breaks up without having opened a harbor of refuge to forty thousand people, then on the first of August forty thousand people will set out on the march to death."

For a moment he could not go on speaking, he could feel his heart growing weak, but greater than his fear of a fresh attack was his fear that he would be dismissed before he had said everything.

"How can I prove it to you?" he said. "Is there really nothing standing between life and death but my inability to make myself intelligible to you?" He drew a deep breath. "I have come here in the cause of the persecuted. To share my knowledge with you and, if necessary, to implore you on my knees. But I believe I am only acting in your own cause. The President of the United States has called you together here. You have heard his call. Nothing can ever erase the Évian Conference from the annals of history. When you entered your names in the register of the Hôtel Royal in Évian you unsuspectingly entered your names in the book of history. The pages will turn yellow, but they will not disappear. Évian will go down in history—as the place where good either laid down its arms or took them up. All evil takes place with the tacit connivance of the good; if they did not remain silent it would not happen. Nothing devilish in human history has ever happened without the Devil first testing the ground, stretching out his feelers, making sure of the complicity of the good. I have nothing more to say, no more questions to answer. I have only to ask you whether you want to share in the guilt."

The silence that followed the Professor's words had so many faces that it had no face. No one, and he least of all, could have said whether it was a silence of emotion or of disapproval, of reflection or of hostility, of understanding or of refusal to understand.

At last the chairman looked up. "I should like to thank Professor von Benda for his information," he said.

And the Professor rose, nodded awkwardly, turned and walked out of the silence.

Most of the lights in the White House had already gone out, so that looking at it from Pennsylvania Avenue one might have imagined that the Government of the United States lay in peaceful sleep. In reality, of course, things were different; the Secretary of State, who had arrived at seven, was still in the President's study.

The President and his Secretary of State, as had been for years the weekly custom, had been reviewing the most recent events of world politics. The picture was as confusing as it was depressing. In the Far East, which did not seem so very far from the West of their country, the Japanese had pushed their attack as far as the Hwang-ho; tension between America, which from the beginning had condemned Japan's onslaught on China, and the arrogant Japanese empire had increased alarmingly. Perhaps for the first time since the Thirty Years War, said the President, they were confronted by facts that demanded entirely new thinking. As at that time, the great powers were no longer acting exclusively according to considerations of power politics and economics, no longer on the basis of rational principles founded on objective fact or on the enhancement of prestige, usually predictable factors; so now the ideological element had been added, an almost religious fanaticism had spread. Blocs and axes had sprung up on the barren soil of similar or identical philosophies, everywhere the vain desire for crusades could be felt; but because the old interests were also in operation alongside the new, confusion grew to immeasurable proportions. Democracy was everywhere in a state of orderly retreat, if not of rout. In Spain the retreat had already become disorderly. To judge from the reports which the Secretary of State had placed before the President, the Spanish rebels would begin their great offensive against Catalonia in autumn, during the past week Barcelona had been heavily bombed and by the end of the year at the latest the State Department would have to decide whether it was prepared to recognize the victorious Fascist regime on the Iberian peninsula. Did recognition of the *fait accompli* mean approval of governments that had come to power by brute force and against the will of the people? This was not a new problem, to be sure, but since the new masters in Spain were at the same time enemies of America, the question arose in turn whether their regime was to be rejected for political or only for sentimental reasons. Here they were in the middle of

the irrational element within traditional political reasoning.
And what about Britain? The American observers in Palestine
could not keep silent about British brutality toward the Jews—
how could the United States seek support from the British in
their efforts to obtain more humane treatment of the Jews
within the rapidly growing German Reich, if the Germans
could point maliciously to British policy toward the Jews in
Palestine? Dress rehearsals for a war, a second world war perhaps—and in Germany they were already arming for the first
performance. Since February, when the Reich Minister of War
and the Commander in Chief of the Army had been dismissed
on the flimsiest of pretexts, Hitler had been in command of the
Army, the Wehrmacht had been entrusted to a lackey in officer's
uniform, the Foreign Secretary to a champagne salesman in
tails. The Chief of the German General Staff, the Secretary of
State had reported to his President, was considering resigning,
and the German experts in the State Department saw in this an
evil omen: obviously the megalomaniac corporal was preparing
to attack Czechoslovakia. "And what about us?" the Secretary
had asked. "We are living in a fool's paradise." And he had
meant that fool's paradise in which a flash of lightning is mistaken for a festive firework display and the thunder of artillery
for the salute of guns before a fiesta.

"The reports from Évian are no less worrying," said the President, opening a file lying in front of him labeled REFUGEES.

Yes, he had a report to make on that subject too, declared the
Secretary of State. He found it hard not to utter that "I told you
so" which small men so eagerly employ in their dealings with
greater ones. The Secretary was not a small man. The somewhat
sickly-looking, thin man with the bony shoulders that seemed to
be serving as a protection for his deepset head, with the sunken
cheeks, the foxy eyes and silky white hair, had for five years
been guiding the destinies of American foreign policy, guiding
them with great skill and in full awareness of America's coming
dominance; many people said he was the only man who knew
how to assert his will in his dealings with the self-willed President who surrounded himself with mediocrities. In the case of
the Conference on Refugees, however, the Secretary of State
had not been able to assert his will; if it had been up to him, the

invitation to the Évian states would never have been issued.
And yet the Secretary's objections were by no means of an in-
humane nature—the gentleman from Tennessee was a friend of
the Jews, he had a heart and understanding for the persecuted
and had also advocated for years a more liberal United States
immigration policy. His objections had been sober and realistic
—his sober and realistic point of view was what he now had to
put before the President.

The President's special envoy to Évian, he said, had today
asked in a lengthy cablegram for fresh instructions, and the
telegram seemed exactly like a message from a general in the
field asking the Chief of the General Staff for permission to
withdraw to a second line of defense. With a few exceptions—
among which were Holland, Denmark, Bolivia and Colombia,
and perhaps also Brazil in so far as refugees of the Catholic faith
were concerned—the nations meeting in Évian had shown little
or no understanding of the President's initiative. Of the two
great powers, France was playing a politely passive role, which
could not be said of Great Britain; Britain's well-organized sab-
otage action was being revealed more and more clearly every
hour. The appearance of Professor von Benda had caused consternation yesterday: the Reich Government, so he had informed a subcommittee, intended to sell the Jews of Germany
and Austria at two hundred and fifty dollars apiece, ten million
for the first delivery of forty thousand.

"After the committee had taken leave of Professor von
Benda," said the Secretary of State, "there were violent arguments. In general the view prevailed that Germany, far from
wanting to hand over the Jews—with or without money—was
aiming with its unofficial offer to torpedo the Conference. The
argument that one simply cannot talk to 'traders in human
beings' seems to be regarded by most of the delegations as a
very welcome let-out."

"Is this the Ambassador's view?" the President asked.

"He has done the most sensible thing under the circumstances. After he had been informed by the Colombian delegate,
the chairman of the committee, a committee of four, consisting
of the representatives of Colombia, Canada, Holland and Sweden, was formed at the suggestion of our Ambassador to con-

sider the 'Benda Project.' So we have a subcommittee of a committee—a usually effective way of avoiding serious discussion.
For the rest, the Ambassador is awaiting further instructions."

The President wanted to hear the State Department's opinion. The Secretary did not express himself immediately. For the
experts of the State Department there was only one thing more
difficult than a President who knew nothing about foreign policy: a President who knew a great deal about foreign policy,
that is to say about the so-called "broad outlines"—these broad
outlines always contradict the necessities of the day.

"First I should like to tell you about a dispatch we have
received from our Ambassador in Berlin, Mr. President," the
Secretary said. "The Ambassador reports that the plan to sell
the Jews is known to informed circles in Berlin, so it is not a
fantasy of the Viennese Professor's. In the Wilhelmstrasse, however, they have draped a cloak of decency around the project.
They state there that they wish to hand over the Jews on condition that they are settled in a particular spot as an isolated
group—preferably on the island of Madagascar, under no circumstances in Palestine. The idea is not unadroit from the German standpoint. A mass settlement of the Jews would mark
them as incapable of assimilation; Britain and the Arabs would
welcome a Jewish colony outside Palestine, and Germany would
have an excellent pretext for demanding a few hundred million
dollars for the organization of the mass exodus. Naturally
France would never dream of handing Madagascar over to the
Jews. I cannot deny that the Germans have shown a certain
ability to think historically."

"To think historically? I don't quite follow you."

"Through their unofficial offer, which, moreover, was delivered by a Jew, the Germans have maneuvered us into an extremely embarrassing situation. Obviously we cannot accept the
offer, because we should be supplying Germany with foreign
currency, thereby assisting their rearmament and, indeed, asking for war; also because we should in any case not be able to
find homes for the Jews. The other arguments I need not cite.
But if we reject the offer, history will reproach us with having
delivered up hundreds of thousands, perhaps millions, of peo-

ple to their executioners. We stand between the Devil and the
deep blue sea."

"The fact remains that Germany is the executioner."

"History, I fear, does not draw such fine distinctions. It
judges the executioner no more severely than the man who
delivers the victim to the ax. The situation is eerily paradox. I
doubt whether history will ever count Hitler's victims. History
very soon stops counting. But it will count every drowning person we have not taken on board. The inhuman monster is demanding of us a humanity that is not of this world. Is there a
price that is too high for a human life? That is what history will
ask, and what shall we answer?"

The President had had a great deal of practice in not showing
his surprise, particularly in his dealings with this man, who was
always surprising him. He looked toward the open window,
through which the pleasant coolness of the July evening was
entering the room. It was good, he thought, to have such a wise
man about one—wise was the man who did not forget morality,
even when he could make no use of it. The old fox evidently
had an idea that was in keeping with reality without infringing
morality.

"Your advice, Mr. Secretary . . ." the President reiterated.

"It falls into two parts. First, we must see how we can bring
the Conference to a decent end. Conference technique offers us
two possibilities that complement one another splendidly—ad-
journment and committees. So far as I can judge from the Ambassador's reports, no country will oppose the setting up of a
permanent refugee office; with a little pressure we can persuade
the British to give the office hospitality in London. We shall be
able to register a new refugee organization of this kind as a
success for the Conference. Furthermore Évian is well on the
way to setting up a considerable number of committees. This
creates no obligations and creates an impression of bustling activity."

"I must register my disagreement, but carry on."

"I have been thinking about Professor von Benda and his
mission and have also discussed the matter at length with my
heads of department. The reports of the secret service are exceptionally favorable."

"What do you call favorable?"

"So far as we can judge, Heinrich von Benda is an idealist who has not thought of combining his journey to Évian with any personal aims. It is true that he is under pressure from the Gestapo—he met the chief of the Swiss branch of the Gestapo in Évian—but he has not ransomed himself by promises and takes account of German interests only in so far as he thinks that they coincide with the interests of the potential Jewish refugees."

The President was so familiar with his Secretary's complicated trains of thought that he had already guessed what he was aiming at. Nevertheless he let him continue, because he believed in "political copyright," as he called it. Even his own ideas he frequently placed in other mouths—how much more were the ingenious entitled to copyright in ideas that really were theirs! There was no prouder paternity than that of ideas; politicians who are allowed to feel themselves to be the fathers of an idea see to it that their children walk early and do not develop bowlegs in the process.

The Secretary of State was developing the second point of his plan. The special envoy in Évian should be instructed to send for the famous surgeon and use every means—"The man's situation is desperate, and also his vanity can be appealed to"—to persuade him to desert. On the last day of the Conference—this date would be particularly desirable, because of the presence of the international press—Professor von Benda should state at a press conference the reasons why he did not intend to return to his homeland that had been annexed by the Germans. At this press conference Professor von Benda, the only credible witness to the monstrous proposal, should reveal to the world the traffic in human beings into which Germany had tried to inveigle the world. Thereafter the Professor should come to America, where any university—"I'm thinking of Harvard"—would welcome him with open arms. According to the secret service, the Professor had a wife and child in Vienna, but the secret service had declared its willingness to get Frau von Benda and the Professor's child out of the country by well-tried and entirely safe means, a fact which the Ambassador should be empowered to convey to the Professor in confidence.

"I don't think I need explain the advantages of this plan,"

the Secretary said. "Besides the news of the emigration of the great scientist and his revelation of the German traffic in human beings, reports of the very modest results of the Conference would pale; we should have saved face." He smiled unctuously like a Japanese. "In addition, the German proposal would have become a subject of public discussion, the world would condemn it; no one now or in the future could say reproachfully that we and we alone should have entered into the secret deal." He raised his small, almost feminine hand. "I know what you're going to say, Mr. President. The position of the Jews in Germany. I cannot believe the Germans would be so foolish as to undertake any reprisals, for they would be taken by the whole world as an admission that Germany really did want to sell its Jews. The German Government, which expects concessions from the world over the Sudeten question, can't afford that, at least not yet."

"A blessing in disguise," the President said. "That's how you see the Benda Mission. I don't know."

He looked at the little man with silver-gray hair who was sitting at the desk on his right, and all at once he felt the whole weight of the office that rested on his own shoulders. He who has no feeling for power should not become a politician, power gives herself only to those who passionately desire her, and he, the President, bore power a passionate love that was daily renewed. The only unfortunate thing was that once you possessed power you could not share it; even if you wanted to, you could not share it. The Secretary of State talked about responsibility before history, yet he himself would be mentioned in history at most as a name accompanied by the dates during which he held office. But he, the President? He had called the Évian Conference in order to shake the conscience of the world, to bring at least some of the unfortunates into safe harbor before the inevitable disaster broke. How magnanimous of the Secretary, whose advice he had ignored, to build for him a golden bridge across which to withdraw! Should he lie to himself and regard as a golden bridge what was in reality merely a dilapidated back staircase?

He rang for his personal secretary.

"Send our Ambassador in Évian a top-secret message as fol-

lows," he said when the secretary came in. "I consider it of great
importance that the Conference shall not be brought to a close
without"—he hesitated—"without visible results. Inform the
participants in the Conference"—he hesitated—"inform the
participants in the Conference in confidential conversations, but
in my name, that the United States is prepared to increase its annual immigration quota by exactly the figure that all the rest of
the member states together are prepared to take."

He asked for the text to be read over to him. "The dispatch
is to be sent via the State Department and not to leave earlier
than the instructions which Mr. Secretary will give the Ambassador tonight."

"Mr. President," the Secretary of State said when they were
alone, "to put it mildly, you astound me. You know as well as I
do that you cannot increase the quota by a single digit without
the consent of both houses."

The President's words had amazed the Secretary, but he was
even more amazed by the way the President looked. Since he
had dictated the dispatch the President seemed rejuvenated, the
wrinkles had faded from his gray, rather long face, there was no
fatigue to be seen in his eyes; he reminded the Secretary of the
times of the great election campaigns, when the semiparalyzed
man had traveled from place to place, stopping in every village,
shaking hands and delivering speeches, untiring, aware at every
hour of his magic, on the implacable hunt for power and yet
full of that gay charm which is normally alien to those with a
hunger for power.

The President laughed. "Listen," he said. "That is the difference between the power that is bestowed on one by one's office
and the power that is given one by an election. I appointed you
to your post and I shouldn't like to catch you bluffing. It is your
job to reduce risks to a minimum; it is my job sometimes to take
upon myself what military men call a calculated risk. If the
Évian states offer asylum to, say, a hundred thousand refugees—
we'll see whether the honorable Senator from Minnesota or
maybe Tennessee can prevent me from taking the microphone
in my hand and asking the American people to give hospitality
to a hundred thousand victims of persecution. The gentlemen

speak to the people over my head every day; I can speak to the people over their heads for once."

"And the Benda Mission?"

"I find your idea excellent. The Ambassador may do everything in his power to persuade the Professor to remain abroad. You see, Mr. Secretary, when we two converse it is never entirely fruitless."

In the middle of the night the Professor had taken a powerful soporific; it was past eight when he was awakened by the ringing of the telephone. Selma Selig's voice—she was ringing from Geneva—immediately revealed to him that she had good news. In fact a few minutes earlier her representative had rung her from the Swiss side of the frontier to say that Elisabeth and the four children were safe and sound and undiscovered on Swiss soil; indeed, borne by invisible hands, were already on their way to Geneva. When the Professor, his heart filled with excitement and gratitude, sought to find out more, the woman whom he now wholeheartedly regarded as his good angel interrupted him; he stopped at once, for he realized what a risk Selma Selig was running, how serious the consequences would be for her if it was discovered that she had assisted in the illegal crossing of the frontier, had paid for it out of her committee's funds and was resolved to make herself guilty of other infringements of the law. Briefly and factually, however, she stated that she would send a car to Évian around midday to bring the Professor to Geneva; passes issued by the Swiss and French authorities authorizing him to leave and enter the country and to remain for twenty-four hours on Swiss soil were waiting for him at the frontier post west of Thonon. Here no doubt she had made legal use of her contacts, but she nevertheless impatiently dismissed the Professor's thanks, either because she had already received too many thanks or because she feared the unsafe telephone.

It almost seemed as though one of those rare days was about to break that make even rationalists believe in fortunate constellations of the planets, because favorable events—as at other times unfavorable—take place without any intervention on the part of the subject, indeed seem mysteriously to multiply; rare days are these of which one says that on them nothing can "happen." No sooner had the Professor put down the receiver, overcome by emotion—for it is a human characteristic that it is not sad events, but on the contrary their happy undoing and resolution, that move the heart most deeply—no sooner had he reflected upon his happiness than the telephone rang again. This time it was the voice of the Colombian Minister, and he, too, sounded surprisingly cordial.

The Professor had spent the evening after his questioning in gloomy thoughts, as one does when one knows that one has disappointed a friend and is not sure whether there will be an opportunity to explain the compelling reasons for one's behavior. He had not expected a call, had actually feared that he would never again be received by the Colombian; he therefore felt it to be a double gift when the Minister assured him that although he had not approved of the Professor's impulsive utterances he had understood them. "I'm afraid that in your position and under these terrible circumstances I should have acted just the same," the Minister said, but his call proved that nothing final, nothing irrevocable, had happened. He was not empowered to inform the Professor of the committee's reactions, continued the Minister, but that same evening the full assembly had set up a committee of four to consider the problem of the forty thousand Austrian Jews and report back direct to the Chairman of the Conference. "Don't indulge in happy illusions," admonished the Colombian. "You have made matters incomparably more difficult for yourself and for me. We must talk about that before the committee meets tomorrow—by the way, it is made up of Canada, Holland, Sweden and Colombia." The Professor wanted to ask what favorable recommendations the new committee might make, whether it meant anything, what real, practical value it had and what influence it could exercise on the Conference, but he forebore to overdraw the bow and merely listened with gratitude to an invitation to dinner. This, however, he had to refuse, because he could not possibly get back from Geneva in time, which brought him once more into conflict with his conscience; he had not come to Évian on private business and this evening discussion with his understanding friend might have been of great, perhaps deci-

sive importance. However, this morning must have been exceptionally blessed, for the Minister showed neither surprise nor
anger. He invited the Professor to breakfast with him the following morning. This second invitation the Professor dared not
refuse; he resolved to return from Geneva under all circumstances, even if it were late at night.

By the time he had bathed and breakfasted—at last at peace
again and with a certain tranquil gaiety—it was ten o'clock, just
time to go to the hotel lobby and keep the appointment with a
prominent rabbi from New York, Samuel Milestone, which he
had made the previous day. The elevator was continually out of
order, so the Professor walked downstairs with a light step; his
thoughts were circling round his reunion with Elisabeth and
the children, especially with fourteen-year-old Marianne, his
declared favorite, and if he had to stop to listen to his irregular
heartbeat, it was only because he remembered Fräulein Selig's
promise. She was going to try to arrange a conversation with
Bettina, which might perhaps be possible from Geneva—it was
asking too much, certainly, but he must at all costs share with
Bettina his happiness at having found Elisabeth. The happy
turn of events had restored his self-confidence, for confidence in
oneself is fundamentally merely confidence in the alliance one
has made with destiny, a confirmation of the mutual love between destiny and oneself; also his relationship to Elisabeth had
always been a touchstone, her trust was his responsibility, not to
have disappointed it his happiness.

The next few hours, however, did not live up to the augury
of the day; the promise of the stars had not been binding.

He had seen the New York rabbi several times fleetingly, but
it had never occurred to him how little this American corresponded to the ideas one has in Europe of a Jewish preacher.
Although there were probably just as many young rabbis in
Europe as in the New World, people were accustomed to seeing
in the Jewish rabbi a wise man, a miracle worker. Rabbi Milestone, on the other hand, was not only a young man, he also
adopted the most youthful, indeed fashionably athletic appearance; with his black hair, large nose and black-rimmed spectacles he certainly looked what would be described as a Jewish
type, but he was no less an American type. The collar buttoned

down at the tips, the sloppy ready-made suit and the tie clip were as American as the free and easy gestures and the accent peculiar to the inhabitants of New York's East Side.

At this period circumstances had caused the world to enter into an entirely new relationship with the Jews, to acquire entirely new ideas about them—more absurd perhaps than it had anyway. More remarkable than this, however, was the fact that Jews developed new relationships among themselves and met one another with new, more conscious, and thus more prejudiced, preconceptions. The rabbi, an American Jew of East European origins, had his own preconceived ideas of what a Jew should be—an idea to which the completely Europeanized, completely Western Jew Heinrich von Benda in no way corresponded; and in Heinrich von Benda there was reawakened the old aversion to the emphasizing of an almost professional Jewishness. No wonder then that from the outset the Viennese professor and the New York rabbi could find little fellow feeling and even less common ground between them. Nevertheless, they would soon have overcome their spontaneous, instinctive, almost anachronistic prejudices if the subject that had brought them together had not at the same time formed an unbridgeable gulf between them.

In his matter-of-fact way—it was an unctuous matter-of-factness, a contradiction that the Professor found disturbing—the rabbi came straight to the point as soon as they had sat down under the chestnuts on the gravel terrace, or rather he spoke of the "Benda Mission," which, he said, was known in every detail to the Jewish organizations represented in Évian.

Heinrich von Benda remained silent. He had realized that his mission, of which a good dozen of the participants in the Conference were informed, could not remain entirely secret, but if the secret became generally known and was dragged through all the corridors, the press was bound sooner or later to get hold of it; this would finally destroy all prospect of a successful outcome.

The Conference, said the rabbi, had decided to hear the views of the most important Jewish organizations, in particular the World Jewish Congress, the Jewish Agency for Palestine and the American Joint Distribution Committee. He considered it incumbent upon him not only in the name of fair play, but also of Jewish solidarity, to warn and inform the Professor that, if asked, all the organizations would strongly oppose the "Vienna Project." Solidarity—this brought him, he continued, close to the heart of the matter. The fault did not lie with the Professor, who after all had devoted his whole life to science, but rather with the Jewish Community in Vienna. They ought to have had enough sense not to address the Conference over the heads of the existing organizations. The German and Austrian Jews possessed no overall picture; they didn't know, or didn't want to know, that for years the Jewish organizations had been working closely with foreign governments, the High Commissioner for Refugees, the Nansen Office and the League of Nations, that they had saved tens of thousands of Jews and ensured them a new life—work which the "Vienna Project" was likely to disrupt, if not to destroy. Understandably, the Professor had no idea of the complexity of the problem—"understandably," he said, interspersing his diatribe with mitigating phrases: "understandably" or "as I can well understand" or "which I don't blame you for at all." How could the Professor know that it was not only the German and Austrian Jews who were involved, but no less those of Czechoslovakia, Hungary, Rumania and Poland; that the prospects of saving the latter were far better, so that discussion must not be confined to the Germans and Austrians; that the name of the port of refuge was Palestine and that this had to be made safe before the ships in distress could be steered thither; that neither the financial means of the Jews nor the readiness of the various countries to accept refugees were inexhaustible, so that only negotiations between the governments and the whole body of Jewish organizations were capable of achieving a just distribution.

Like an icy wind blowing from the quarter from which one least expects it—that was how the rabbi's words affected Heinrich von Benda. Only because he hoped in the course of an urbane discussion to persuade the rabbi to act with discretion, did he speak politely and with restraint. "You mentioned solidarity, Rabbi," he said, "but I should like to know who is supposed to maintain solidarity with whom. Are half a million Jews in danger of their lives to worry about sparing the Jewish organizations unpleasantness? Ought not the Jewish organizations to cast aside all other considerations in order to save the Jews whose lives are directly threatened?"

"I'm afraid you've misunderstood me, Professor," rejoined the rabbi. "The aim is to save all our brothers. But as to the means, only those Jews can decide who are in safety and see the situation clearly."

"I can think of nothing more likely to blur vision than safety."

"I can understand your holding that view, but it is wrong. Just picture what would happen if the Jewish organizations backed your mission! How could we ever again criticize the relations of the civilized world with Hitler Germany, how could we call for a boycott of German goods, if at the same time we implored the governments to trade with Germany in human beings? I don't want to use big words like human dignity, although we shouldn't forget that either. Let the Christians trade in Jews among themselves—only the slave who acknowledges his servitude is really enslaved. But we needn't think so far ahead; let us think in practical terms! The task of the Jewish organizations consists primarily in arousing the conscience of the world. If the Évian governments ransomed ten or twenty thousand Jews they would pacify their consciences; they would have the feeling that they had done enough and more than enough—hundreds of thousands of our brothers would perish miserably."

The logic of these words filled the Professor with mounting disquiet. The whole world—Christians and Jews, ministers of state and simple people, men and women, warmhearted friends and cold egotists—it was impossible that everyone should be wrong and he alone right. And yet perhaps they were all wrong, because they had one thing in common, something outside religion, sex, status and character, something apparently insignificant and yet essential: their geographical position. They were all outside, and those whose desperate cause he represented were inside.

"Do you know," he said, "that the SA and SS will carry forty thousand people off to concentration camps if the Évian states do not take them over?"

"We are here to see that Germany does not dare to take this step. Have you read the German papers?"

"That is precisely what I have done."

"But, understandably, you have misinterpreted them. Don't you see that Germany is afraid of Évian? A proclamation of human solidarity—thirty-two states, Professor, among them the most powerful in the world!—would strike the murder weapon from Germany's hand. If we acknowledge the legality of the anti-Semitic measures, even indirectly, we are lost. Instead of rewarding Germany for her crimes we must call for a boycott of German goods, an embargo on deliveries to Germany, a boycott and embargo against all countries that trade with Germany. Yes—the world will negotiate with Germany, but only when Germany appears as a supplicant. Then we shall be able to lead not only the German and Austrian Jews out of Hitler's power, but the majority of our brothers—"

"All who are still alive, that is," the Professor interrupted him. "I used to think that only lack of imagination was dangerous, but it seems to me now that too much imagination may be just as critical. Has the course of the Conference so far—I'm told it is to be concluded in three or four days—convinced you that a proclamation of human solidarity is being prepared? What illusions you give yourself up to, Rabbi Milestone! And what makes you think that the psychology of the mass murderer is the same as yours and mine? If National Socialism cared about the opinion of the world, it would have strangled itself in the cradle. Are you a realist or are the men of the Vienna Jewish Community realists? Hitler cares nothing for the opinion of the world, the only things he does care about are dollars and cents."

The Professor's sharp tone angered the rabbi. He had always felt a distrust toward this famous surgeon, not so much because the emigrants had pointed out the links between the Professor and the Gestapo, perhaps the outcome of necessity, nor because the Professor was said to be married to a Christian, the daughter of an Austrian national painter, but above all because the rabbi had little liking for the species *Chamaeleo judaicus,* so common in Western Europe. It was remarkable that this old man, who imagined that he was sacrificing himself for the Jews, was not a good Jew, if a Jew at all; he had discovered his Jewishness late and under the pressure of events, like those who became God-fearing only during a storm; he was probably one of those German and Austrian Jews who, if Hitler had not prevented them, would have remained the most blatant nationalists—naturally such a man could have no relationship to Zionism, knew nothing of the common interests of the Jews, in fact had no idea that he would have acted just as enthusiastically in the cause of suppressed and persecuted protestants, Negroes, liberals or Botocudos. The rabbi pondered whether to retort to sharpness with sharpness or to appeal to the understanding of the blind Jew, but finally settled for a middle way.

"I requested this meeting," he said, "because it would have made an extremely bad impression if you had heard from a third party that the Jewish organizations were going to oppose the Vienna Project. But that doesn't mean"—he smiled warmly and leaned closer to the Professor—"that your mission is bound to have been in vain. If you could make up your mind to remain outside, one or more of our Jewish organizations would call a press conference at which you could disclose the monstrous commission with which you were entrusted. No one would doubt the word of Professor Heinrich von Benda. Your story would arouse a storm of indignation . . ."

"And the Jews in Hitler's hands?"

"That we are hostile to Germany, which has forced us to be so, is nothing new to Hitler. It is too late for compromise; strength is the only language the Germans understand."

This was what the rabbi was saying when the porter appeared in the hotel door, came over to the Professor and informed him that a car had just arrived from Geneva and was waiting for him.

Like his interlocutor, Heinrich von Benda too now asked himself whether he should say openly what he thought, should flatly reject the proposal that had obviously been carefully considered, prepared at length and finally uttered, or whether he should choose the diplomatic path. It would no doubt have been easier to tell the rabbi, who certainly knew it already, that he, Professor von Benda, quite apart from his convictions, had no choice, that he had a wife and child, but what did the rabbi care about the Christian wife and the little child? Or the Professor too could have said that he "well understood" the standpoint of the Jewish organizations and "didn't in the least blame them." But the bitterness that had overcome him was of a special making and different from anything he had felt before. Anyone who held a passport, even if he were a Jew, could not understand a Jew without a passport, so that the great inside and outside separated Jews from one another just as much as they were separated from other people; not even the blood-stained regime had succeeded in welding together the Jews, who were said to stick together like glue; there were German Jews and Palestinian Jews and Jews who had only been made into Jews by Hitler, and Jews who thought they represented all Jews; prejudices, differences of interests and convictions and methods made the Jews forget that the only thing that mattered now was to bring help to the drowning, without consideration for a future which only the shortsighted were sure they could see. Nevertheless the fear that a brusque refusal might lead to a conflict moved him to assure the rabbi that he would carefully consider the arguments he had just heard, would pass on to the Jewish Community in Vienna the objections that had been raised, although he did not agree with them, and would base his own attitude entirely on the instructions he received from Vienna—but he must make it a condition, and this was in their mutual interest, that both sides should exercise extreme discretion.

The rabbi assured him that, as up to now, he would naturally deal with the matter in confidence, but he seemed to have seen through the Professor's intentions, because he insisted on continuing the conversation, tomorrow afternoon at the latest, since the hearing of the first Jewish organizations was fixed for a secret session during the night.

As Heinrich von Benda walked toward the hotel door where a chauffeur was waiting for him, he had the feeling that the eyes of the rabbi were following him with searching interest. Probably Rabbi Milestone was asking himself what sort of car it was that had come to fetch the Professor, what the Professor had to do in Geneva and how it had been made possible for him to

cross the Swiss frontier without difficulty. He could no more tell
the representative of the Jews the truth than anyone else. He
thought of little Herr Steiner at the Basel frontier station.

In the first joy of reunion father and daughter spoke only of
Elisabeth's fortunate rescue.

Fräulein Selig had taken Elisabeth and her children into her
house. This house, a spacious villa in a side street off the Avenue de Champel, not far from the Parc Alfred Bertrand, was a
complete expression of Fräulein Selig's personality, although in
the good lady's soul the contradictions could certainly not be so
neatly separated from each other. The soul, so far as is known,
possesses no first floor and no second floor, whereas the house in
the Plâteau de Champel possessed both, so that Fräulein Selig's
active and busy soul was able to spread itself on the first floor—
where there were two offices, a conference room and a gigantic
store of clothes, canned foods, soap and other utilitarian objects,
all intended for the refugees under Fräulein Selig's care—while
the Fräulein's more private soul occupied the second floor. In
addition to the living room and dining room there were a bedroom and two guest rooms, all furnished very comfortably even
if somewhat incongruously—Art Nouveau tarsias, Biedermeier
furniture, awful family watercolors, and important work by
Klimt and some beautiful icons in the last analysis got along
together admirably. The two guest rooms had been put into
apple-pie order for Elisabeth and her children by an old maid-
servant who, incidentally, was the spitting image of her mistress.
Fräulein Selig wouldn't hear of the family living anywhere else
during their stay in Geneva. She found a convincing explanation for her hospitality in the illegality of their presence in
Switzerland—Elisabeth and the girls had no valid papers, to say
nothing of Swiss entry and residence permits. "If anyone is to
get in the hair of the Swiss police," commented Fräulein Selig,
"then it had better be me, from whom they don't expect anything but trouble and disregard of the law."

While the Professor was in prison, Elisabeth had been warned
by a corrupt and hence human police officer, who had previously done all sorts of business with Berenson, that she and the
children were to be arrested next morning and held on the

flimsiest of pretexts—namely alleged currency offenses by Berenson—as hostages for Berenson's return. That same night a friend of Berenson's had taken Elisabeth and the children to his hunting lodge at Payerback-Reichenau, near the Semmering Pass, where he had hidden them for several weeks under the most difficult circumstances, making it a condition that Elisabeth should not get in touch with anyone and least of all with her father, who was likewise persecuted and undoubtedly kept under observation. The treachery of a forester and imminent discovery drove Elisabeth and the children—she still had a little money—through the land; they spent a fortnight in a convent not far from Innsbruck, from which they were taken in the care of an old nun and under fantastic circumstances to Vorarlberg. Meanwhile Berenson had managed to get from Italy to Palestine. There, said Elisabeth not without pride, he had obtained an entry permit for his family, but for the time being this document was of purely theoretical value, since as far as the German authorities were concerned Elisabeth and the children had "disappeared" and could not be given an exit permit, indeed would have been arrested at the first police post. Thus the only way out was to flee to some foreign country, preferably neighboring Switzerland, from where it might be possible to travel on to Palestine. Since, however, Elisabeth had no passport, the Swiss consulate, which she had cautiously approached, had refused to allow Frau Berenson and the four girls into the country. Elisabeth's money was at an end and all her hopes, when she had almost reached her goal, had evaporated—when she learned from a brief report in a Bregenz Party paper of her father's presence in Évian, and persuaded the peasant to make the journey into Switzerland.

Elisabeth told her father all this in the presence of the four children—Margarete seven, Ludovica nine, Stefanie ten and Marianne fourteen—who sat around their mother and followed the story wide-eyed, in an attitude peculiar to children, whose own experiences are converted almost immediately into a fairy tale. Although only a few months had passed since the Professor last saw them, the girls seemed to have grown up in an almost uncanny manner; they all looked like the children in the pictures of Breughel the Elder, who, despite his genius, was unable to paint children and always portrayed them as small adults. The Professor asked himself whether the children, the two younger ones in particular, understood what had happened to them, what had suddenly and apparently senselessly turned them into outcasts and persecuted, made them hide and creep away, hurry along country roads, slip by night along mountain paths, deny their name, become a burden upon strangers whose favor they had to woo, and all this without guilt or condemnation, so that everything they had been taught must seem to them utterly absurd. He looked at them as they sat there—Marianne, pale blond with big dark eyes, in an armchair, her arm passed protectively around the seven-year-old, who for her part had vaulted onto the arm of the chair, Ludovica and Stefanie on a chest, these two girls almost exactly the same height, dark, looking like twins, well behaved and full of grave attentiveness —and the Professor was certain that they had understood in a deeper sense than the adults, the way the hunted understands as it flees in zigzag leaps from its pursuers and, obeying its natural instinct, seeks refuge in the forest. Elisabeth, who hardly concealed anything from the children—at this time parents could not help being frank with their children—recounted many episodes involving brave, even amusing behavior on the part of the girls. Thus in Hubert Pichler's house Margarete had suddenly declared that at last they were "at home," and had replied to her mother's astonished question that "at home" was where "the spinach tastes like at home." The others laughed at this story, although they scarcely understood what it meant, but they laughed a great deal altogether at the thought of the terrors they had lived through and survived, because in retrospect flight and danger and humiliation were linked with the discovery of a new pride, an early dignity that comes only to those whom others have early tried to rob of their dignity.

When father and daughter were alone—Fräulein Selig had enticed the children into the storeroom, where she entrusted them with all kinds of important tasks—Elisabeth's expression changed; the obligation which the mother had felt toward her children, the daughter did not feel toward her father; in his eyes she could show herself weak, to him she could reveal all her misery.

She looked at least ten years older than she was. At the best of times possessed of a very sensitive constitution and transparently pale, she had now been reduced to skin and bone; her narrow face was more than ever dominated by the huge dark eyes that had previously contrasted so pleasantly with the honey-blond hair, but now shone out like the last living things in a white mask. It was the strange, terrified and wandering look in these eyes that had first struck the Professor and profoundly worried him, but as time passed he grew increasingly perturbed as he was forced to realize that the eyes were only an expression of Elisabeth's strange, terrified and wandering soul. For minutes at a time she spoke with restraint, calmly and completely sensibly, but then she forgot what she had said, hesitated, repeated what she had already recounted at length, referred as though as a matter of course to names that the Professor had never heard, spoke of unknown places as though she had spent half her life there. The Professor could not help noticing that she had written in her letter distrustfully, indeed disparagingly, of Oskar Berenson's efforts to get her and the children to Palestine, but just now had mentioned his loving endeavors almost triumphantly. Thus, it obviously had not been for the benefit of the children but because her opinions, her relationship to others and her judgment changed grossly from one minute to the next. As he listened to her—the normally taciturn woman spoke a great deal and as though under compulsion—the Professor could scarcely understand how Elisabeth had succeeded in saving herself and the children, in outwitting the manhunters and at hopeless moments manifestly always doing the right thing; he could only suppose that in distress her understanding had functioned flawlessly, but under the superhuman burden of responsibility her reason had finally been suffocated. Now that she felt herself to be in a safe harbor and had laid aside her feeling of duty, the strangled reason that had lain beneath it came into view.

In a safe harbor? No doubt there was something wonderfully true about her superstitious trust in her father; she could have enumerated the miracles that she had expected from him, miracles that had actually taken place, like so many pieces of evidence. When she was in the greatest danger he had suddenly appeared, and beyond the frontier, in safety; when she needed money most urgently, he had sent it to her immediately, the very same day; when she stepped onto dry land an envoy of her father's, or at least someone she had reason to regard as such, had taken her under his wing and brought her to a hospitable, comfortable house, where her father had almost immediately come to see her. There are children who stop believing in fairy stories, but a day comes when every adult begins to believe in fairy tales.

Now he had to destroy the fairy tale. True, he was in Switzerland, but his stay came to an end next day; the money he had sent her had not been his own; the man who had gone to meet her, and the woman who had given her hospitality, were cogs in a mechanism of mercy; he had neither the means nor the power to get her to Palestine or even to guarantee that she would be able to stay unmolested in Geneva, and he himself, perhaps before the week was up, would have to return to Vienna. Certainly, the most important thing had already happened, and not without his help. She and the children were safe, as safe as a Jewish woman and Jewish children could be in Europe, and there was Fräulein Selig, the limping angel, who would conceal her until the visa for Palestine arrived and would then get her traveling papers, probably a Nansen passport, and pay for the journey out of the funds of her charitable committee.

The Professor spoke to his daughter straightforwardly, yet with gentle caution; but immediately, almost while he was still laboriously seeking explanations, his caution proved superfluous—perhaps the day really was blessed. Once more a transformation took place in Elisabeth. She begged her father not to worry about herself and the children—if she had survived the last months she would also survive the next weeks; after all, there was Oskar Berenson, who loved his children above everything. Only the Professor was disturbed to see the way in which, after accusing her husband of irresponsibility, adultery, even cowardice, she suddenly placed her whole trust for the future in him again. He was all the more surprised that she immediately grasped the significance of his mission, of which he informed her in a few brief words, and approved his efforts without hesitation or conditions. Of course, she said, he must go back to

Vienna whether his mission succeeded or failed, first because of Bettina and the child, second because if he did not an even more terrible fate would await the Jews, but also and above all because desertion was out of all keeping with his character. He compared her with Bettina and in his own mind reflected upon the various, contrasting, mutually contradictory expressions of love, which were nevertheless all expressions of love—in the wife care for his physical well-being predominated, in the daughter the fear that he might destroy the proud image which she had made of him since her earliest childhood. But as to everyone else he had met since his arrival in Évian, they were distinguished from Elisabeth by their lack of knowledge; they had not been "inside."

A knock at the door interrupted the conversation. Marianne asked her grandfather to follow her to the office, because Vienna might come through at any moment; Fräulein Selig had asked for the Professor's home number two hours ago.

On the stairs Marianne stopped still, took the Professor's hand and began to confide in him her worry about her mother's "strange behavior." This confirmation of his observations, the fourteen-year-old's concern, heightened the Professor's disquiet. He walked down the stairs hand in hand with the child toward Fräulein Selig's office. He tried to reassure the child, but he had made up his mind not to leave Geneva until he had spoken to a nerve specialist. Professor Richard Vuillemin—the name suddenly appeared to him as a faded visiting card falls into one's hand as one is rummaging through an old wallet. Richard Vuillemin, Genève, Place du Rhône; he could even remember the name of the street, only the house number had slipped his mind. They had met at medical congresses, for a time had even corresponded; an important and extremely charming man. True, Professor Vuillemin was a heart and lung specialist, one of the greatest in Europe, but a telephone call would be enough, Vuillemin would immediately refer him to the right man.

As soon as he was alone with Fräulein Selig in the office, he had asked after Professor Vuillemin—as would have occurred to any man of his age, he had feared for a moment that his colleague who was the same age, if not older, might be dead—and already Fräulein Selig was dialing the number of the doctor, who was well known to her. It must have been the day's lucky star; Professor Vuillemin was at home, although his surgery hour was over. He came to the telephone as soon as he heard Professor von Benda's name and greeted his Viennese colleague with exuberant cordiality. Of course he could recommend a nerve specialist, but first he must see Dr. von Benda personally. The Professor replied that he was only in Geneva for a few hours and had to return to Évian-les-Bains that evening, but it made no impression on the old doctor; he insisted that Heinrich von Benda should at least call to see him for a few minutes on his way to Évian.

"We won't occupy the line now," said Fräulein Selig, when the Professor had hung up. "Vienna should be through at any moment."

Heinrich von Benda lit a cigarette and did so this time without burdening his conscience, for the excitements of the day had been too much for him, and without the deceitful tranquilizer he would not have known how to stand up to further strains, which also included exceptionally joyful events. Yes, it was curious that he felt this excess, this accumulation of happenings, emotions, experiences, decisions and expectations, most acutely just at the moment when, after unexpectedly seeing his daughter again, he was about to have the joyful experience of hearing his wife. Almost like an alcoholic who already has too much alcohol in his blood and cannot tolerate another drop, the cup of his experiences was full to overflowing. He could measure the extent of his fatigue by a hitherto unknown phenomenon: excitement, that is generally a means of overcoming fatigue, even if artificially, now seemed to have lost its efficacy like a drug one has taken to excess; the greater his excitement, the greater became his fatigue. If fatigue were to continue to gain ground the second, more dangerous phase of the disease would be reached, the phase that can be described as indifference—that indifference which prevents soldiers from doing the only sensible thing, namely from running away, so that the most indifferent go down in history as heroes; the same indifference which prevents civilians from storming forward, so that the finest deeds remain unperformed through sheer weariness.

He struggled with his fatigue, fought against its threatened degeneration into indifference, and as he did so listened with only half an ear as Fräulein Selig returned to her project—the great collection from private sources, which he was to head. Tomorrow, she said, she herself was going to be heard by the Conference; for a start she would ask the participating states for a thousand visas for German and Austrian intellectuals, and she hoped to surprise the Conference with the shaming information that for each of these intellectual refugees a thousand dollars lay ready—a million dollars that "one single old lady from Geneva," as she called herself, had gathered together by begging.

The telephone rang, and once more Heinrich von Benda's excitement overcame his fatigue. After three or four minutes, which seemed endless and during which he had to make a great effort not to snatch the receiver from Fräulein Selig's hand, she said, "One moment, Frau von Benda," and passed it over to him. Before he had spoken a word the Fräulein rose and limped quickly over to the door, which she shut behind her loudly and unequivocally.

"How wonderful to hear your voice," said Bettina. "What are you doing in Geneva?"

"Elisabeth has arrived here. She and all four children are fine."

"What splendid news! Give Elisabeth my love . . ."

"She sends you a thousand kisses."

"Are you staying in Geneva?"

"No, I'm going back to Évian during the night. But how about you? And Heinrich?"

"We're fine."

"Really?"

"Really. Heinrich is healthy and happy. He laughs all day long."

"How about you?"

"Tell me about yourself."

"No, you tell me about yourself. Did you get my letter?"

"Everything is perfectly all right. But I'm worried about you, you know what you promised me?"

"Yes, I know."

"You will take the cure, won't you?"

"I don't know."

"You must, that's the most important thing. For Elisabeth's sake, too. You mustn't come back—before you've finished the cure."

"It's as though I hadn't heard your voice for years. And now you're so close."

"I think about you every minute."

"So do I. Are you alone a great deal?"

"No, everyone is taking care of me beautifully. Everyone hopes you won't break off the cure."

"I'll let you know."

"Are you well? Is your heart all right?"

"My heart? Of course."

"Isn't it too hot for you at Évian?"

"No, it's quite pleasant. Sometimes it rains."

"We're having marvelous weather. Heinrich spends all day in the garden. He's as brown as a berry."

Thus they talked away the fleeting minutes, talked only of personal, intimate, even insignificant things, as it must have appeared to an intrusive eavesdropper, but they didn't care about the intrusive eavesdropper, who was undoubtedly listening to them. They spoke that language of love which is simple and mysterious, because the words are intelligible to anyone but the meaning only to two initiates, spoke in a tone which would have offended a strange ear and which a third person, even the most benevolent, would have thought ridiculous, but from one mouth to one ear rang out in the purest melody, asked questions which they could have answered themselves but which they had to ask precisely because they already contained the answer, playfully found the transition from one idea to another which no one else would have found, but stopped because they had so much to say that nothing which came to mind seemed to them important enough—and in between fought continually against the moment when they would have to fall silent.

When the Professor had put down the receiver he remained sitting in Fräulein Selig's armchair and gazed for a long time at the strange office, looked around and asked himself how he had got here. At this moment he still knew what Bettina was doing and what Heinrich was doing and that in the Hietzing house, which he had occupied for over thirty years, everything was "all right." In a few minutes, when he had left this room, gone back to Elisabeth and lost sight of the telephone, he would no longer know. He delayed leaving the room.

On the way to Évian he stopped the car outside Professor Vuillemin's house. The house was situated in the Place du Rhône near the shores of the lake. It was already dark. The streets by the mouth of the Rhône as it ran into the lake were lit up, and on the tiny peninsula the monument to Jean-Jacques Rousseau was floodlit; the green of the foliage looked unnaturally green. On the opposite bank, on the Quai des Bergues, stood the hotels in whose halls and lounges history had been made for twenty years—hotels still, but already monuments of futility as well.

The old house had no elevator. Professor Vuillemin's apartment and surgery were on the third floor—a long, difficult way, paved for the Professor with doubts. To be sure, if he was not to go away full of disquiet about the fate of Elisabeth, he had to visit the doctor; but Benda the doctor had been seized with fear of Vuillemin the doctor. Since the first signs of his illness had shown he had not met a single doctor; he feared the diagnostic eye. When he reached the third floor he dared not ring at once, because his pulse was as irregular as if the two halves of his heart were two dancers who, having grown reckless or mad, had begun to dance two different dances; the back of his neck and his ears were glowing with heat, while a shiver ran over his body and the outlines of the stairs, the banister and the doors swam before his eyes. He remembered that once—it must have been a good twenty-five years ago—a man had collapsed and died at his surgery door. He had long since forgotten the incident and also the man, but now he saw him in his mind's eye as though it had only happened yesterday. He was a comparatively young man, hardly more than forty, reddish-blond with a comical mop of hair and a great many freckles; he had been holding the door handle in his hand when apoplexy overcame him, and his hand never let go of the handle, he hung on to it with the whole weight of his body; dead, he hung on to life, they had difficulty in loosing his fingers from the gleaming metal. The memory put the Professor in a panic, he touched the bell very lightly and waited, without taking hold of the handle, till the door was opened to him.

He noticed at once that Professor Vuillemin got a shock when he saw him. Vuillemin was older than he, seventy, perhaps somewhat more, but of a fresh appearance with a wreath of snow-white hair around his healthy-looking scalp, pink cheeks and merrily crafty pale-blue eyes behind rimless spectacles. The Professor remembered that Vuillemin was a famous huntsman and an amateur cellist of some reputation. Most doctors, heaven knows why, were either huntsmen or musicians or both; and Heinrich von Benda thought of the fact that he himself had never had time either for healthy sport or for healthy dilettantism.

The room was typical of the apartment of an elderly bachelor. It contained chiefly objects from distant journeys which he had grown fond of: elephant tusks, a Turkish smoking table, a leopard skin, Etruscan figures and treasures from Oriental bazaars. The viscous port wine stood ready, but the Professor merely sipped at his glass and quickly asked various polite questions. For the most part he let his Swiss colleague talk, because he was finding it more and more difficult to breathe and every longish sentence caused him difficulty.

The personal conversation immediately moved on to politics, as always happened at this period and as was particularly inevitable in this case; to the unimaginable things taking place in the neighboring country, to the occupation of Austria and the terror that now reigned there, to the dim prospects for peace and the lightning flashes of war. Of his own mission Heinrich von Benda disclosed nothing, but he mentioned that he was in Évian on official business, spoke of his imminent return to Vienna; and as he spoke he read the horrified astonishment in Professor Vuillemin's eyes.

Only now did he speak of the reason for his visit. He had persuaded Elisabeth to let herself be examined by Professor Vuillemin without, of course, revealing that it was the state of her nerves and mind that he was worried about; in the course of a routine examination, which itself could only be of value, Dr. Vuillemin was to decide whether he considered a consultation with a nerve specialist necessary. Breathing heavily, Heinrich von Benda described Elisabeth's childhood, the peculiarities which he had observed in her at an early stage, her difficult births, her marriage with its frequent crises, her flight and finally the disquieting symptoms that had struck him a few hours ago. "My fears may be exaggerated," he said, involuntarily clutching at his heart. "We doctors have a tendency to hypochondria as far as our own and our family's health is concerned. All the same, I shouldn't like my daughter to be subjected to fresh changes and excitements until we know whether it is a passing disturbance or a serious injury to the nervous system."

He was about to add that he didn't know when he would see Elisabeth again, but he was interrupted by Dr. Vuillemin's question: "And how is your own health?" This question torn out of the context of the conversation affected the Professor like an assault—moreover it seemed as though Vuillemin had been waiting to ask it ever since the beginning of the interview.

Heinrich von Benda tried to smile. He said that at the moment he "couldn't afford any hypochondria," but he had to admit that he hadn't had himself examined for more than a year, that he had continually put off going to see a doctor; he promised, as though apologizing, that he would go and see a specialist as soon as he was back in Vienna. Vuillemin wouldn't hear of this. "Come—let me examine you," he said, and said it with a determination that brooked no contradiction.

The order and the energetic gesture with which Dr. Vuillemin had risen frightened Heinrich von Benda all the more because he himself belonged to the dying species of the great diagnosticians who—although they do not trust their sixth sense unconditionally, utilize all the modern aids, machines, measuring instruments, chemical tests and electrical apparatus, and also recognize the virtues of specialization—have at the same time preserved something of the primordial instinct of the village and family doctor. Such diagnosticians still possess the ability to read from the patient's eyes, to draw conclusions from the texture of his skin, even to detect certain signs in the sound of his voice—or they only imagine all this and merely have at their disposal, because nature so wills it, the key to the secret store-house of diseases.

Professor Vuillemin paid no heed to his colleague's elaborate excuses and vigorously dismissed the assertion that it would be an unreasonable demand, an unprovoked assault. He took Heinrich von Benda by the arm and led him with gentle force into his consulting room to the accompaniment of humorous remarks. He told the story of an eminent medical man who yielded to the pressure of a young doctor and allowed the latter to examine him, greatly to the patient's discomfort, because the ambitious young doctor's face grew longer and longer and he finally forbade his eminent patient all the pleasures of life. The diagnosis made a deep impression on the eminent doctor, a man well on in his fifties, recounted Dr. Vuillemin while the Professor undressed. Depressed, he went back to his family doc-tor, a man getting on in years, who certainly observed the same facts—blood pressure too high, heart restless, blood sedimenta-tion rate not exactly wonderful—but who not only reassured but actually congratulated his patient. "When a man is over fifty, my dear Benda, he should go to a doctor who is older than himself and who is used to that fact that there are no miracles. A systolic blood pressure of two hundred and twenty is relative, relative to the doctor as well as to the patient. At my age one tends to wonder at the youthfulness of a man of sixty-five."

If Dr. Vuillemin had told this humorous story for psychologi-cal reasons, he proved in this particular case to be a psychologist who would have done better to have kept quiet, and it may well be that he very soon regretted his talent as a *raconteur*. After he had tapped the Professor's naked body, palpated the liver, brought stethoscope and reflex hammer into play and measured the blood pressure, his face took on precisely that expression which he had so vividly imitated while describing the young doctor in his story.

Heinrich von Benda opposed his colleague's wish to make an electrocardiogram only weakly, invoking the waiting chauffeur. Now he wanted to know the whole truth, although at the same time he behaved as an utter layman would have behaved in the same situation. He made a great effort to think of something unimportant or pleasant, so as to cheat the incorruptible apparatus; when he made deep knee bends he carried out the movement slowly and carefully, actually holding his breath as he straightened up in order not to betray the stubborn shortness of breath. But Dr. Vuillemin did not allow himself to be tricked nor was he content with the first stress test. After he had measured the time between the accelerated cardiac activity and the heartbeat's return to normal, he led the Professor to the door, asked him to go down to the second floor and then walk up again—the Professor was relieved to observe that Vuillemin meanwhile remained in the doorway and kept the door open—then took him back into the surgery and set about making a second electrocardiogram.

Only then did Dr. Vuillemin fold up the long narrow strip of paper that had slithered out of the electrical apparatus like a snake and take it with him into the adjacent study, while the Professor was glad to avail himself of the permission to dress. Finally he followed his colleague into the study and, since Dr. Vuillemin said nothing, indeed scarcely looked up, sat down beside his desk.

Thus the two old doctors sat side by side in the semidarkness of the study looking at the endless squares each subdivided into twenty-five smaller squares, on which a needle had traced darkly tremulous lines resembling a mountain chain, interrupted by thinner, pointed shapes going upward or downward, like oil derricks rising from the landscape or fountains spurting into the air. If the electrocardiogram before the stress test showed the telltale irregularity of the action currents, then the second picture, taken after stress, was more like a temperature chart showing fluctuations of temperature with extra sensitivity. The ventricle markings were squeezed together in an irregular sequence, the auricle markings no longer visible; at certain specific points the needle seemed to have skidded, instead of moving up and down more or less regularly it had described a clumsily drawn mountain ridge, a kind of recumbent, extended S. While Dr. Vuillemin slipped the narrow strip of paper across the desk, stopped, pulled the strip back again because it had unrolled over the edge of the desk, neither of the two professors uttered a word, because neither needed to decipher for the other what the other had deciphered equally well; as they sat there the thought came to Heinrich von Benda that it was a strange and sadistic burden to deliver the death sentence to a condemned man in code.

"I'm not surprised," he said at last, as though consoling the other, because he had the feeling that Vuillemin was reproaching himself for insisting on the examination.

"You're not surprised," Vuillemin said, and he spoke sternly because he supposed that a certain bluff sternness would give the impression that he was not too dismayed by the picture. "You're not surprised, but you act as though one could simply ignore a thing like that." He pointed to the cardiogram. "You talk like a pessimist and act like an optimist. That's the silliest thing you could do. You know as well as I do that no ECG looks like another and that the next need not be half so bad—if you act sensibly. I'll see that a pleasant room in the Canton Hospital is made available for you, we'll call in Jacquinot, a first-class man . . ."

The Professor listened, but all he was thinking was how to escape from the gentle tutelage and leave the consulting room and the house without giving too much offense to this well-intentioned man who, moreover, was speaking the truth and giving the right instructions. The verdict had not taken him by surprise, and even if the white serpent with the pattern of curves on its smooth skin was more venomous than he had anticipated, nevertheless he had not imagined the pattern very differently; what he had known an hour ago but had not taken cognizance of, he must not take cognizance of now that it happened to lie before him in black and white. Laymen thought that doctors did not believe in miracles, but he had been a doctor for so long that he had learned to believe in miracles. If he had not seen the cardiogram he would have gone on living as before, he would have waited till the end of the Conference and would have gone back to Vienna. Only the optical picture had changed; it would not influence his decisions. Once in Vienna, however, he would take a rest, he would go immediately to his colleague Hostelmann—no, not to Hostelmann, he had been one of the first Party members, not to Hostelmann then but to Röchling or someone else—he would keep to his bed for a fortnight, perhaps three weeks . . . now all that mattered was to find a good excuse to console the overenthusiastic Vuillemin. What did Vuillemin imagine anyway! His Swiss residence permit came to an end tomorrow morning, his pass became invalid, the good Vuillemin was talking of a bygone age when you simply decided to take a room in the Canton Hospital . . . but that wasn't the right excuse, because naturally Switzerland would make an exception for Professor Heinrich von Benda, particularly with such a fine medical report as Professor Vuillemin's, angina pectoris, threatening myocardial infarction, I refuse to accept responsibility . . . only he had no desire to make use of his contacts, to invoke medical reports, to claim the privileges of exception. Moreover he had come to Vuillemin on Elisabeth's behalf, and it was possible that in any case, if his fears were confirmed or merely if the papers from Palestine were delayed, he would have to appeal to the kindness of colleagues, to claim privileges for his daughter.

A lie was the easiest way out. Stressing his gratitude, he said that he could not make up his mind so quickly, that he had to return to Évian, but he would take his respected colleague's remarks to heart. He would change his way of life at once, give up smoking, get plenty of sleep, go to bed early and avoid excitement. Then, when the Conference was over, which could only be a few more days, he would come back to Geneva—"Yes, the Canton Hospital is excellent and I believe I know Jacquinot personally."

Professor Vuillemin let him go reluctantly, under protest and with many admonitions—he also assured him more emphatically than before that he would look after Elisabeth—but he did not insist on his suggestion because he did not want to cause Heinrich von Benda fresh excitement, against which he had most urgently warned him.

The chauffeur, a jovial German Swiss, whose car Fräulein Selig hired from time to time, talked affably and loquaciously throughout the journey. Heinrich von Benda was astonished to find that he was able to follow the other's thoughts, to answer him, even to ask him questions every now and then. Did everyone at death's door take his fate so lightly? Perhaps, but only because to be at death's door did not necessarily mean to be admitted. Everyone believed that for him the door would not open. No one really took death lightly, it was simply that no one believed in it; the most certain thing in existence was also the most unbelievable. From birth onward man gives himself up to an illusion. True, man is the microcosm of the macrocosm, but he considers the macrocosm to be part of his own microcosm. Atman and Brahma are identical; since the "great world" does not cease, the "little world" cannot cease either. In the house on the Place du Rhône, in Professor Vuillemin's somber, overloaded study, when the strip of paper bearing the electrocardiogram had run through the fingers of the two learned gentlemen, Heinrich von Benda had believed that his own fate meant so little to him because it seemed to be submerged in the universal fate, in the great dying—for such is man that the manner of his death is not a matter of indifference to him and he dies more easily with others—but it wasn't that. What had happened was that incredulity, like the safety rope of a cable railway, had been switched on at the same instant as the mechanism broke down. He knew all that and yet did not believe in death, or it had only taken him an hour to get used to living with death. Excitement—what was more exciting than to receive the death sentence? But the inadequacy, the incapacity for clairvoyance, the ignorance of medicine, were shown at precisely this moment; the Professor felt neither oppression nor shortness of breath nor pains. The cardiogram knew nothing of human willpower, knew nothing of a mission that had to be fulfilled.

It was getting on for midnight when the car reached the city boundary of Évian and turned down by the English Garden into the Quai. In front of the Casino the gamblers' cars stood in close rows, and the chauffeur drew his fare's attention to the many foreign license plates. The summer night was pleasantly warm and a jazz band was playing on the terrace.

Apathy of the Heart

And when Pharaoh drew nigh, the children of Israel lifted up their eyes, and, behold, the Egyptians marched after them; and they were sore afraid: and the children of Israel cried out unto the Lord. And they said unto Moses, Because there were no graves in Egypt, hast thou taken us away to die in the wilderness? Wherefore hast thou dealt thus with us, to carry us forth out of Egypt? Is not this the word that we did tell thee in Egypt, saying, Let us alone, that we may serve the Egyptians? For it had been better for us to serve the Egyptians, than that we should die in the wilderness.

EXODUS xiv, 10, 11, 12

IV

IN the morning at eleven the Conference reassembled for a public session, for one of those progress reports which it seemed to believe it owed to that powerless, and yet curiously enough feared, anonymous authority known as "public opinion." Heinrich von Benda had also been admitted to this public meeting.

He had breakfasted that morning with the Colombian and saw the meeting from the viewpoint of their conversation. The Colombian Minister had not been exactly optimistic, but far from defeated. "The problem is apparently simple," the Colombian had said. "That is precisely why it is so enormously complicated; it is easy to define, not so easy to solve. We can summarize it by saying that the question is whether we—you and I and a handful of well-intentioned delegates—will succeed in persuading the Conference to accept forty thousand refugees, to work out a quota rate for them, or whether we shall adjourn in a few days with theoretical expressions of goodwill. By our answer to the question of whether we are prepared to grant asylum to forty thousand refugees, Germany will judge whether we are serious about the whole refugee cause." The Colombian had arranged for discussions between the Professor and the members of the committee of four—apart from himself, who was sufficiently familiar already with the Professor's views, the representatives of Sweden, Holland and Canada; these discussions, he said, could take place immediately after the public session. He had asked the Professor most emphatically not to mention again the question of paying Germany ransom money but merely to convince the other members of the committee of the German ultimatum. "Along with many other factors," he had said, "we are now involved in a race with time. I believe that

with your help I can persuade the majority of my committee to
support immediate action; but if this is not taken by tomorrow
at the latest, the Conference will take note of our recommendations and refer them to the permanent commission, which will
probably be established in London. No one knows when the
London commission will be set up and when it will actually
begin to function. Meanwhile the impression of human solidarity which, in spite of everything, Évian has created, will pale,
Germany will resume the persecution of the Jews which for the
duration of the Conference—not least thanks to your mission—it
has ceased. War may even break out. London, as usual, is
shrouded in fog," he had added with a bitter laugh.

Now Heinrich von Benda was once more sitting in his seat in
the back row and watching the Conference at work. By contrast
with the opening session, the men who had taken their seats
around the horseshoe-shaped table were no longer a mass of
anonymous heads. He thought that he could distinguish between friend and enemy. Mexico was to him no longer the
country of the Sierra Madre where archaeologists dug for treasures of the Aztecs, Norway no longer the land of the fjords and
the 150,000 islands, Peru was not the land of the royal city and
the Incas; to him they were only countries that would sooner or
later grant asylum to a greater or a smaller number of refugees.
As he listened to the speeches he found no difficulty in distin-
guishing between the words that were intended for world opinion, which is always moral, and those aimed at groups with
special interests, which are always narrow-minded.

The session began in a monotonous fashion. The Conference
resolved to take note of the reports of the subcommittees, without these reports being read out. The number of subcommittees
was astounding. There was the new committee chaired by the
Colombian which—so it was stated in official language—was to
decide "on the possibility of negotiations with the German
Reich"; there was the subcommittee whose task was to ascertain
the views of the refugee organizations and actually to listen to
one or two representatives of the refugees, though of course the
time taken up was to be "limited"—this committee, under the
chairmanship of the chief Australian delegate, consisted of Belgium, Great Britain, France, Mexico, Peru, Cuba, Nicaragua,

Costa Rica, Venezuela and the United States; there was the *Sous-Comité Technique,* chaired by the Norwegian judge, whose members were Brazil, Canada, Chile, Great Britain, France, Haiti, Holland, Switzerland and the United States and which was called upon to establish documentary evidence regarding the capacity of individual states to take in refugees, the categories of refugees they would welcome and the question of passports. Useful, indeed indispensable institutions all of them, if it had been merely a matter of importing goods, of overcoming tariff barriers, of the transport, preservation and deterioration of foodstuffs, if it had not been a matter of human lives.

The American Ambassador opened the discussions proper. The results achieved so far could be described as "most encouraging," he said; through the reports of the subcommittees the Conference had been able to gain information not hitherto available to the nations; in particular he praised the "spirit of humanity" that animated all the delegations.

The next to speak was the delegate of Chile. He expressed himself in the almost unintelligible French spoken by Spaniards —it sounded like pure Spanish, because nothing is more difficult than to speak intelligibly in a foreign language one imagines to be related to one's own; he changed every closed French "u" into an open Spanish one, so that the words, spoken from the front part of the mouth, sounded round and primitive, like the language of African natives who impart to every foreign language the rounded sounds of their own. What Chile's ambassador to Bern had to say, however, was by no means primitive; here spoke a philosopher of sober realism who made no secret of the fact that "the question of migration is simply and solely one of production and unemployment: it would be rash and contrary to the interests of the workers of every country to raise the demand for workers and hence increase production, especially if then no consumers could be found for the products." Before the man of goodwill, said the philosopher, "there rise the walls of reality"; the intelligent man must always take these into account.

If the Chilean delegate was a philosopher, the delegate of Peru proved to be an historian of deep knowledge. The little man in whom politeness seemed, as it were, innate, for he always carried his left shoulder slightly thrust forward as though, listening attentively, he were opening or leaving free a path for a greater, more important person on his right—the Peruvian turned to the Chairman and began to laud the United States as the model for the American nations. The formation of a middle class, in particular a class of small landowners, had finally become the aim of the Latin-American states, the states bordering the Pacific Ocean; in the case of Peru this was coupled with the imperative need to incorporate the Indians in the life of the state, a life which, he emphasized, revolved around "a Spanish nucleus" and must be "kept Catholic and Latin." "Furthermore," the polite historian continued, "the United States has provided us with an example of caution and wisdom. Up to 1890 they opened their gates to all immigrants without exception, unperturbed by possible consequences. Since then far-seeing laws have halted the stream of immigration, the first passed in 1921, the second in 1924. What was the United States aiming at with these limitations? Above all to ensure that immigrants could immigrate safely and without harm to themselves, but at the same time"—he raised his voice—"to defend their Nordic heritage and the Anglo-Saxon race. The title of a pessimistic book by Madison Grant says a great deal on this subject. The book is called *The Passing of the Great Race,* meaning the twilight of precisely that race which the United States and its greatness have created. America's future would look discouraging if that great country pressed too many representatives of alien races to its bosom."

The sweat broke out on Heinrich von Benda's forehead. Not only did he now know many delegates, many also knew him, to most of the observers from foreign countries and from Jewish organizations he had become a familiar sight, and all the representatives of the press knew of his presence. He had the feeling that during the Peruvian envoy's speech he had to withstand a cross fire of eyes. As a matter of fact this was not at all the right expression, for many eyes merely swept past him quickly and as though by chance; others, after looking at him, were swiftly hidden under lowered lids. There must have been many here who were ashamed of the Peruvian, but not a single one who rose to oppose him. The Professor was aware of this impression;

he was not so certain whether the Peruvian had looked at him, but he felt as though the polite historian were speaking to him personally, as though he were saying that not only were the mass of the unwanted unwanted, but that he who represented them was equally unwanted.

After the philosopher and the historian it was the economist's turn—the Swiss police chief, whose statements surprised the Professor only in so far as this honest man did not employ any smoother, any less frank, any more diplomatic language here, in full view of the public, than he had employed during the questioning of Heinrich von Benda. True, the delegate from Bern was able to quote many moving examples of the Confederation's historical humanitarianism—had they forgotten that during the World War Switzerland had taken in 150,000 children? —but he emphasized that Switzerland had 100,000 unemployed, that his country was spending over 160 million francs a year on the poor and the out of work, that is to say no less than 40 francs per head of the population! Many Swiss, he lamented, had been forced by the economic situation to emigrate; there were about 355,000 foreigners, nine percent of the population, on Swiss soil; two or three thousand Swiss citizens were stranded in Spain—two or three thousand who had first claim on their care! "We cannot therefore permit the refugees to remain in our country," he said, "but we will nevertheless treat them with consideration."

A similar language was spoken by the representatives of New Zealand, Ecuador, Paraguay, Mexico, Ireland and Venezuela, a rather more warmhearted one by the delegates of Sweden, Denmark, Uruguay and the Dominican Republic, but because Heinrich von Benda's ear had become sharpened, he was not so much aware of the variations in the personalities and their arguments and tones, as of the fine unity which they proclaimed as members of the Conference. This is how those jury verdicts come about that always surprise laymen; no sooner have twelve people the same dignity and the same office than they also have the same views and the same sovereign power over the lives of others. During the opening session it had been a matter of course—only to him, who had come here with high hopes, had it not seemed so natural—that each one should clearly state his position, his own or that of his country, a macabre variety performance consisting of individual numbers, a string of monologues. But now, a week later? Did not the word conference mean bringing together, discussion, consultation, exchange of views, persuasion, did it mean *conférence* in the French sense of the fluent announcement of entertaining attractions? What the delegates were saying now, they might just as well have said on the first day of the Conference—did each one wish to speak only for himself and not with others, had no one convinced anyone else, moved him to see things differently and inspired a change of heart? The Professor had often thought of Fritz Grünwald, rarely of the Nazi Governor. Delight in others' misfortune was alien to his character, therefore he was not depressed by other people's malicious satisfaction, but he now saw the Governor, saw the glassy figure in the rococo bed in the Leopoldine Wing; he thought he knew what the Governor would say next morning at breakfast, when the Évian reports were placed before him, knew with what gesture he would hand the newspapers to his entourage, with what words he would register the despicableness of a world that left nothing unattempted in order to become in the twinkling of an eye as despicable as the despicable expected them to be.

"In an atmosphere of tense expectancy," the newspapers would write, though in reality it took place against a background of dreary monotony, the High Commissioner for Refugees—or, as his official title had it, *le haut Commissaire de la Société des Nations pour les Réfugiés venant de l'Allemagne*—rose. This Englishman spoke with a hesitant uncertainty as though the sentences were snakes stretching out their heads or snails putting out their feelers and then quickly drawing these organs of touch and sight back into their shells again. For the last two years, he said, he had everywhere been welcomed with politeness and encouragement but had everywhere received the same answers, answers dictated by necessity. Three conditions must be fulfilled before the problem of emigration could be successfully solved. It required cultivable land, money, and fundamentally it also required different refugees—the present refugees were, so to speak, the wrong ones, since their professional qualifications did not correspond at all to the demands of the host countries. The European was speaking through the mouth of the High Commissioner when he emphasized, not without a certain reproach toward the other great continent, that before the World War some 100,000 Jews a year had emigrated to the countries of North and South America. After this thrust, however, he withdrew his feelers—he did not consider it opportune to ask why the involuntary emigrants, the persecuted and hounded, were received less hospitably than the voluntary ones had been. Then he uttered a figure; the Jewish organizations, in agreement with his own estimate, had confirmed that a family of emigrants cost a thousand pounds; this was the sum required to settle a single Jewish family on the other side of the ocean with the prospect of a useful development. A thousand pounds, the Professor repeated to himself, that would be about three thousand dollars. The Reich Governor had asked a thousand dollars per family, very easy terms, as it was called in business language; the number of children would not be counted, this too made the terms easy. Obviously human life was not yet quoted on the Zürich stock exchange, there was no standard international exchange rate, it fluctuated; anyone familiar with the stock exchange knew that there were always two rates of exchange, one for purchases and one for sales.

The High Commissioner's statements had left a deep impression—or at least so the papers would say; no one wanted to speak after him. Nevertheless a document lay before the Chairman. He wished to read it out, he said, and this time it seemed to Heinrich von Benda as though the American Ambassador gave him a brief look, an apologetic look; that the Chairman "wished" to read out the document was doubtless a mere figure of speech.

The honorable representatives of the countries of Nicaragua, Costa Rica, Honduras and Panama had signed a joint declaration intended to remove all misunderstandings and make their position quite clear. The declaration was brief, consisting of only four points; the Chairman read it out in English. In Point One the four governments declared themselves united in the desire to give "the magnanimous initiative of His Excellency the President of the United States" their "moral support" and to work with the Conference for the fulfillment of the "grandiose task." In Point Two the four states declared their agreement with the establishment of a permanent refugee organization, "on condition that this organization does not defend the cause of those refugees whose entry is contrary to the laws of the undersigned states." In Point Three the four states declared themselves united in their willingness to assist the future Commission by the supply of travel documents where the refugees had been refused such documents by their home country. In Point Four, finally, the four governments declared unanimously that "none of the four states would accept financial responsibility for the settlement of any refugee" so that "every refugee must settle at his own risk and expense" and that above all "merchants and intellectuals," since the four signatory states were "saturated with these elements," "must be categorized as undesirable."

The interpreter was still droning out the declaration in French when pages of the Hôtel Royal in their chic uniforms—in their white leggings they looked exceptionally cute—drew the heavy curtains, so that the Conference hall was suddenly flooded by the noontide sun of the radiant July day. It was as though a cinema performance, a matinee, showing a somber, depressing film that portrayed reality in far too gloomy colors, something that was fundamentally not realistic at all, had come to an end and the audience was now able to disperse and turn to more cheerful reality. The doors were opened; the public, journalists, interpreters, shorthand typists, male and female secretaries spread out over the terrace and the lawn, and this, of course, distinguished the Conference from a cinema performance, for here the actors, major and minor, were present in person, had descended from the screen as it were, had become flesh and blood and three-dimensional; but they bore very little resemblance to the parts they had been playing. They now looked thoroughly human.

The Professor too had gone out into the park. He was surprised how little effect the depressing morning with all the demands it had made on his nerves, how little effect the stuffy heat in the hall, the merciless sun and the gross variations of temperature had had upon him. Since his visit to Professor Vuillemin he had neither felt pain nor experienced the terrifying shortness of breath that had previously descended upon him from time to time. Without vanity, but with a certain satisfaction, he observed that he had become a part of the Conference; true, he was not a cog in the works of the great clock, but perhaps he was the dial that shows the hour. Correspondents came up to ask his views, which he formulated circumspectly and noncommittally —this too, the art of uttering sentences that meant nothing, he had quickly learned; diplomats nodded to him as they hurried by, although to most of them he had not been introduced—it was a fraternity that needed no introduction; in the conversing groups one or the other delegate would turn toward him for an instant, as though they had just been discussing him. All the more clearly, however, did the Professor feel his own passivity, all the more did he fear that the psychological moment might slip through his fingers. It went against his grain to join a group of strangers, to grip an unknown by the lapel or the button of his jacket, but this was not the moment to think of dignity or rank or prestige; he must look around for the Canadian, Swedish and Dutch delegates, must engage these members of the committee of four in conversation. It no longer cost him a great effort to plant himself in the vicinity of the group that had formed around the Canadian delegate to the League of Nations, watching to see if the Canadian would take his leave and their eyes would meet; he waited patiently till the high official of the Dutch Foreign Ministry at last made his way alone toward the dining room, and while he was talking to the Dutchman his eyes were seeking the chief Swedish delegate.

Before the pleasant-sounding bell in one of the hotel's curious wooden towers rang for lunch, he had spoken to the Colombian's three colleagues, had told them what he knew of the German Reich's intentions, had mentioned the planned arrest of the forty thousand, had urged, implored, argued, had even cautiously interwoven one or two threats in the name of world opinion, had flattered, admonished and besought the delegates, had arranged an evening meeting with the Swede and agreed to continue the discussion. As he made his way, bathed in sweat, toward the porter's lodge to order a taxi—he no longer felt capable of walking to the Hôtel Splendide—he had the feeling that this morning of July 12, 1938, had not been entirely wasted.

Bearing in mind the promise he had given Professor Vuillemin, after a frugal lunch Heinrich von Benda had lain down for a brief rest, but he could not sleep, could scarcely close his eyes. The end of the Conference, although no day had been fixed, was drawing ominously closer, and the end of the Conference meant the end of everything; it seemed to be admonishing, driving, spurring and tormenting him. He had come here to set hundreds of thousands of Jews free, to lead them out of slavery, to save them from even worse, had jettisoned his profession and his own destiny, had almost forgotten his responsibility toward his own family, a voice had bidden him leave his past and even his character behind him by the wayside like useless ballast. For better or for worse, the right mission or the wrong one—he couldn't judge, didn't want to rack his brains over this question, for the right is never entirely the right and one cannot defend it if one thinks about the wrong that lies within it. Moses too had not thought like the Jews, otherwise he would have been merely a Jew and not Moses, but he did also think as a Jew, that is to say differently from those who were not Jews—for better or worse, he could not sell the Jews, because no purchaser could be found to take them, even if only as merchandise. Very well then, no ransom money, not hundreds of thousands, no ransom money and only forty thousand. But if the force of his conviction, his knowledge of what already was happening "inside" and of the worse to come, were to prove insufficient even to achieve such a small, such a limited objective, if they were unable to overcome the apathy that was spreading everywhere—what then? Was he overestimating his strength? The emigrants who eyed him with such suspicion were right: he had come to Évian as the emissary of the Reich Government, indeed of the Gestapo, its executive and most characteristic organ. But they were also wrong—to whom could he explain the paradox and what did it matter if no one understood it?—for equally he had come as the representative of the Jewish Community, and what did the original purpose matter, since he no longer represented the German interests and still represented those of the Jews?

These he must represent to the end, he must not weaken, must not cease to support the good man whom Providence had sent him, the man from Bogotá, must give him all the help he could, to bring his plan, modest and restricted as it was, to fruition. If the plan succeeded they would hold him responsible in Vienna, but this too was a thought he must not think. He had omitted to inform the Gestapo; he was resolved to continue not to do so. It would be worth while for the sake of the forty thousand, but it must be forty thousand; he alone could convince the Conference of the danger that hung over them. Had he done everything, had he done enough? He still believed—and this was not just a vague notion, it was a feeling, as sure as for decades his diagnostic instinct had been—that the key lay nearby, like the hidden slipper that children hunt, hot, cold, cold, hot, hotter, hot, and that it was his fault if he could not find it. Therefore after his return from the session he had spoken to the monsignor whom he had run into quite often ever since his arrival, the Vatican's observer, as he was generally described in the newspapers and elsewhere; yes, it had been above all the German newspapers that had led him to take this bold step. They wrote that the monsignor was not confining himself to the task of observer, that he was stirring up trouble, egging on the delegates, informing and influencing the press, in short acting in a manner entirely in keeping with the "diabolic conception" of the Church, its "senile doctrine of Christianity" and its "universalist principles." The observer of the most powerful Church in the world and he, sent as an observer by the most powerless minority—they must talk together, perhaps it was the key of Peter that was capable of opening the prison gates. He did not rest, did not close an eye, for he had made an appointment to speak to the monsignor at four and must not at any price fail to keep the rendezvous.

The heart is so constructed that it is capable of standing very high levels of both heat and cold, but is intensely sensitive to gross fluctuations of temperature. That afternoon Heinrich von Benda was to be subjected to just such sudden changes of climate; the thermometer began its vertical dance, its rise and fall, when the telephone on his bedside table rang for the first time.

After the Professor had put the receiver to his ear, he immediately recognized the thin voice of the man who had called himself Megelein; like the little man's head, his voice too seemed continually to be oscillating. The Professor, Megelein said coming straight to the point—he had not considered it necessary to give his name—was to come punctually at five on Friday to the Casino, was to sit down in the big roulette room close beside the mirror facing the entrance and wait there for a stranger, the emissary, who would introduce himself as Herr Stechlein. "Don't forget to bring your passport with you," said Herr Megelein, "you'll need it for your entry card." With these words he hung up, without waiting for the Professor to reply or object. In fact the Professor had wanted to object; first, because he had no wish to meet a representative of the Gestapo again on French soil; second, because the place and circumstances of the rendezvous reminded him of those cheap spy stories which the secret services evidently took as models for their equivocal reality; finally, because the mention of his passport filled him with uneasiness. The sadistic motive behind the time chosen for the call did not escape him either, for it could not have been by accident that Herr Megelein or his chief had elected to give him instructions a good forty-eight hours before the meeting; for two whole days he was to be in a state of anguished apprehension, stretched on the rack.

He lifted the receiver fearfully when the telephone rang again only a few minutes later, but this time a warm voice flowed over him like a warm wave. It was Professor Vuillemin, and he had good news, or at least not bad news, to give him. The examination of Elisabeth—as a precaution Dr. Vuillemin had arranged for a nerve specialist to be inconspicuously present—had admittedly confirmed that Elisabeth was undergoing a severe nervous crisis, but had not revealed a total nervous breakdown or any irreparable or even dangerous disorder; in fact it would have been a miracle if such a crisis had not arisen. On the other hand her condition could not be ignored, they must call a halt to a psychological development that might be dangerous, must take steps to clarify her mental confusion; Elisabeth could be given outpatient treatment, but it was urgently necessary to avoid further excitement, further disturbances of her equilibrium. Therefore Dr. Vuillemin had already been in touch with Fräulein Selig. "I'm not an influential man," he said with growling modesty, "but Fräulein Selig and I have found ways and means of obtaining a fortnight's extension for Frau Berenson and persuading the authorities to shut one eye, if not two. We shall legalize her status retrospectively; should the Palestine visa take longer to arrive, we shall find some way around the difficulty. I wanted to let you know that at once, Professor von Benda, so that you shall not suffer any unnecessary worry— excitement is poison, not only for your daughter, remember that."

Professor Vuillemin brought the conversation to an end almost as abruptly as Herr Megelein, though by no means for the same reason, leaving the Professor in a state of gratitude and emotion. Involuntarily, he could not help thinking of the Swiss delegate to the Conference; one did well not to judge nations by a single representative, least of all by a policeman.

He had gone into the bathroom to freshen himself up, for by now it was five to four, when the telephone rang again.

This time it was Fräulein Selig, whose chief purpose was to tell him what he had already learned from his Geneva colleague; but Heinrich von Benda pretended that he was hearing the good news from her for the first time. Naturally this was not the only reason for her call. The following Saturday, she said, a charity concert for refugees was being staged by her committee at the Grand Théâtre in Geneva, to which the Professor could lend special brilliance by his presence. This would also be a fresh opportunity to see his daughter and grandchildren again; therefore she had already obtained an entry visa and a limited residence permit for him. Here again the Professor did not want to dim the Fräulein's joy; he concealed from her his fears that the Conference might come to an end on Saturday. There was a general wish to start the homeward journey over the weekend; in all likelihood, therefore, he would in any case be on his way back to Vienna and would be able to use his transit visa for this unorthodox purpose.

It was already four-fifteen when he entered the hotel lounge, and he had to apologize to the monsignor for his lateness. The room was empty, for the few hotel guests present preferred the garden at this time of day. The two men found that the quiet-

ness of the room was admirably suited to their conversation;
they also found that the coolness of the lounge—the green roller
blinds had been lowered—was preferable to the afternoon heat
outdoors.

The apology which he had had to make placed the Professor
in an unfavorable position—for the fact of having waited always
gives the one who has waited a certain superiority—but even
without this the monsignor was no easy man to talk to.

If the priest represented, even if only as an observer, the holy
Roman Catholic Church, the mysterious world power that
ruled so dominantly from such a small base, the great intermediary between heaven and earth, he bore no sign of the importance of his office—a young man, little more than forty, a
poorly dressed village parson with big feet in ugly lace-up boots,
incessantly smoking a short pipe and ignoring the ash that fell
from time to time on his cassock. His narrow face was dominated by a slightly crooked nose whose septum continued well
below the nostrils and far down the lower lip; his features were
irregular, as though badly drawn, yet not unpleasant. What
took the Professor by surprise, however, was the priest's language. The taciturn man was a German, a German from the
northwest, and like all educated Westphalians he spoke without
a marked accent but with a distinctness that lent every word a
self-contained if unvarying importance and in its cool clarity
was reminiscent of the stage German of the Vienna Burgtheater.

The Professor had made up his mind to tell the Vatican's
representative everything, including the real reason why he had
come to Évian in the first place. Now that he was sitting facing
the monsignor he recalled what Elisabeth had told him of the
help she and the children had been given in an Austrian convent, and it seemed to him that it was this quite fortuitous,
quite personal yet indirect experience that had led him to speak
to the monsignor. Why had he not thought of it earlier, and
why was he here if not to utilize such opportunities? Did the
Vatican know that human lives could be saved with money, and
would the Vatican not intervene if it did know? Had he himself
not given way to resignation too quickly?

They were both in Évian as observers, he began—the monsignor gave no sign of agreement—but their missions were of a different kind, since he, Professor Benda, had to the best of his ability to influence events.

No sooner did he start to speak of his mission than the monsignor interrupted him. "We had been informed of your mission, Professor, even before the Reich Governor called you to the Hofburg."

"I could understand," said the Professor, feeling his way, "that the abasement of man to merchandise which such a purchase would, in a sense, sanction is contrary to the principles of the Catholic Church."

"That is not the point. In the churches of the Middle Ages the alms bag was shaken vigorously to collect for the pirates—or rather, for the unfortunates who had to be ransomed from the pirates."

"Do you know, Monsignor, that among the unfortunates who are now called 'Jews' there are about half a million Catholics?"

"That is not the point either. 'Spiritually, we are Semites,' the Holy Father declared recently to some Belgian priests. His last encyclical is directed against anti-Semitism; you may not know this, but it was distributed among the German clergy by secret couriers during the night of Palm Sunday. Bishops who dared to print it were persecuted, the printing presses shut down. In his most recent broadcast the Holy Father quoted the case of a rabbi who came to the aid of the persecuted Spanish Catholics; like the rabbi, the Holy Father identifies himself with all persecuted innocents, all of them."

The conversation came to a halt. Even before the Professor had spoken to him, the monsignor had set himself a goal, a difficult goal. The Church, which for centuries had spoken of the Jews as the murderers of Christ, had rendered itself partly guilty of the anti-Semitism whose seed was now sprouting, like blood spurting from the Devil's herb as it swelled and grew. Rome had to beat a retreat, and the aged Pope was determined to do so; that was why he had sent the monsignor to Évian. The task was to convince the world that the Roman Church condemned anti-Semitism and race phobia—not without satisfaction had the monsignor read in the German press the rumors of his own biased attitude, which he had himself spread with great tact and skill—but the retreat must be carried out as carefully as the gradual disavowal of the Inquisition that had been taking place since the seventeenth century.

The Professor too was uncertain what he ought to say. "That is not the point"—twice the monsignor had used this phrase. What, then, was the point? He must not waste this moment, must not worry as to whether he was offending the monsignor, whether the priest might consider him an impudent Jew.

"Why, Monsignor," he asked, "did the Vatican refuse the invitation to take part in the Conference?"

"How can the Vatican take in refugees? The Church possesses no other territory than that of love."

"You know about the forty thousand Jews whose lives are in immediate danger. The Vatican has no territory, but the Church is wealthy. Can it not ransom these people from the pirates?"

"I used the simile, but it is wrong. The pirates were acting from greed, which is at least a human motive. The number of prisoners was small."

"Is it the dimensions of the crime from which the Church recoils?"

"The Church is a spiritual power. It cannot enter into such a bargain."

The monsignor felt how unsatisfactory his answer was. All answers would be unsatisfactory if he did not confide in the Professor the whole truth. For a week he had been watching the Professor, had seen how the old man hurried from one delegation to the other, how he avoided the press and put up with the suspicion of the emigrants, how he had clung to an illusion with the courage or the desperation of a drowning man. Should he open his eyes? It was bad enough to be a blind Jew with illusions, even worse to be a Jew who sees clearly.

"If we had met earlier," he said, "I should have implored you to abandon your mission from the outset. It sprang from a Satanic conception. Inhumanity does not begin where we think it does, that is to say with the destruction of human lives. Whoever regards another human being as worthless—an insane person, a cripple, an old man, a criminal, a savage or the member of an alien race—already carries murder within him, in fact is already a murderer. In any case, his power of resistance is paralyzed; he may not carry out murder, but he will not oppose it. So long as passive anti-Semitism has not been eradicated, it is no use assailing active anti-Semitism. You think I am indulging in empty rhetoric? I am speaking of your mission. You have been sent to Évian to confirm the worthlessness of the Jews, precisely what millions of people in the world believe or feel. From the declaration of the worthlessness of human life to its destruction is but a step."

As he spoke the last words he had lowered his voice, had moved his chair closer to the Professor's. The Professor, who was sitting with his back to the door, turned around. One of his two shadows, the blond German agent, was standing in the center of the lobby talking to a page.

The Professor too now spoke in a low voice, almost whispering. "By paying the ransom the Évian states could have proved that human life is not worthless, that not even the life of a Jew is worthless."

"There was never a chance."

"How do you know, Monsignor?"

"We know."

"Do you mean that anti-Semitism has such deep roots?"

"I mean that Hitler has good reasons to bank on it."

"Why does not the Church speak out against anti-Semitism?"

"It does so."

"But not in deeds."

"The aged Pope Benedict XIV," the monsignor said, "already spoke of the 'martyrdom of neutrality.' "

Heinrich von Benda's hands grew moist. In words which he himself could hardly have found, the priest had spoken against anti-Semitism. The Church condemned anti-Semitism, but it escaped from the protest into the "martyrdom of neutrality."

The monsignor noticed the Professor's emotion. "If nothing else convinces you," he said, "one thing must convince you. A Church which accepted the idea of race as a concept superior to that of religion would condemn itself to death."

"What good would it do if you convinced me?" Heinrich von Benda retorted. "The world will not judge the Church otherwise than—as an accomplice."

"The Church will have to suffer that." He said it without acerbity, without repudiation, with a sad resignation. "You are right. One day people will ask who were the accomplices, and who knows whether the complicity of silence will not be judged more harshly than guilt itself? I should have had to face the problem even if I had not been a priest—I am a German. There is no collective guilt, because there are no collective sources of guilt, but there is a collective complicity, and although guilt and complicity are not the same, we cannot expect the world to distinguish between the two. Incidentally, you have misunderstood what I meant by the 'martyrdom of neutrality.' There is a comfortable and there is a suffering neutrality; this distinction cannot be a matter of indifference to the Church, nor will it be a matter of indifference to history. The apparent neutrality of the Church is a suffering neutrality. What I want to convince you of, is not the philo-Semitic outlook of the Church, but . . ." For the first time he seemed to be searching for words. "In pursuance of a tradition from which it cannot break away without abandoning itself, the Church must seek the roots of evil before it can proceed against evil. This tradition is in keeping with the nature of the Church; where the symptoms of an epidemic appear, they cannot be cured without combating the epidemic. I don't know, I doubt, whether you will understand me. The Church cannot save the Jews and then combat anti-Semitism. It must go about it the other way around."

"Even if hundreds of thousands are exterminated?"

The priest did not reply.

"Why," said the Professor, "has Pius XI not excommunicated Hitler?"

What was he to tell the old man? thought the monsignor. That the excommunication of Hitler had been decided upon, but that a myriad objections and impediments stood in the way of the great deed, a medieval act in the midst of the modern world; that the wheel of the Church turned slowly and lethargically; that if the Church was to intervene in history, as it had once done with dubious success, it must be certain of victory and that it was not certain; that only the ignorant world looked upon the Roman Church as a unity, but that no cardinal and no country priest looked upon it as such; that the Pope was eighty-

one and ailing, one foot in the grave, and that no one knew who
would follow, or if it would be a man determined to act in the
spirit of Pius XI.

"Hadrian VI," he said, "once remarked, 'Alas, how much
depends upon the period within which even the excellent man
exercises his influence.' The Church, responsible for four hundred and fifty million Catholics, must wait for the historical
moment before taking a step of such enormous significance."

The Professor's eyes fell on the long table in the middle of
the room, on which copies of the communiqués of the Conference had accumulated like dry rolls in a closed Automat. The
states of Évian believed they could not ransom the Jews because
they were worldly powers, dependent upon trade with Germany, which, if they bought human lives from Germany, they
could not continue; and the Vatican believed it could not ransom the Jews because it was a spiritual power that could not
dirty its hands with ransom money. The first thought only of
today and tomorrow, the other only of centuries to come, believed perhaps in divine justice, which in the end had always
manifested itself; perhaps it would manifest itself this time—in
the end, but certainly not before August 1, 1938. Or was it even
simpler? Would the envoy of the Vatican also talk about the
"historical moment," for which the Pope had to wait, if it was a
representative of the Spanish priesthood who stood before him,
if "the point" had been to ransom forty thousand Catholics?

No purchase then, no ransom money and also no excommunication, said the Professor, without hiding his bitterness.
But the voice of the Vatican was mightier than that of any
temporal government, very definitely mightier than all the Jewish organizations put together. There could be no doubting
Germany's word, not on this point: on the 1st of August forty
thousand Jews would be carried off. He was surprised with what
fiery passion and with what ever new words he was able to
reiterate his appeal, which he had already uttered heaven knows
how many times. How else than as weakness, as silent toleration of the horrifying, as indifference and worse could the German Reich judge the absence of the Catholic Church from
Évian? Had the monsignor at least done everything to indicate
to the representatives of the governments here in Évian, in par-

ticular the Catholic ones, the believing and church-fearing
South Americans, the Irish and Belgians and French, that the
Vatican was contemplating excommunicating Hitler, was simply waiting for the "historical moment"? "The word observer,
Monsignor, can mean many things; it can also mean standing by
and letting the wheel of disaster roll on without throwing oneself between the spokes."

The monsignor chewed at his pipe that had long since gone
out. There was no emotion to be seen in this curious face—curious because in it intelligence and inexpressiveness were inexpli-
cably combined—and yet it did not strike the Professor as
offended or cold or hostile; so far as lay within him, this dry
man seemed to be concerned; only it was impossible to say
whether he was concerned for the Conference, the Jews, the
refugees or merely the dilemma of the Church.

"We are trying harder than perhaps you may believe," the
monsignor said, "to persuade the governments to take immediate action."

"Why do you not make this appeal publicly?"

"First because any such intervention in the affairs of the governments would only arouse the spirit of opposition—in the so-
called Catholic states more than elsewhere. Second, because Hitler is already talking about a Catholic-Jewish plot and the consequences for the Jews as well as for the Catholics would be
unpredictable. And finally because the standpoint of the Church
is known without this. For centuries it has been advocating
compassion."

"Do you mean that its voice has become worn out?"

"When the Church raises its voice in worldly affairs, it must
do so with some prospect of immediate success."

"Did the man whom you call the Son of God, whom we Jews
honor as one of our greatest rabbis, think of immediate success?"

"We are not divine, Professor."

"But do you not strive to emulate the divine?"

"We proclaim love, but we are powerless when our voice goes
unheard."

"In the case of the Jews it would not go unheard," the Professor said, mastering his agitation only with difficulty. "The

Church has so rarely raised its voice to advocate love for the Jews that this voice, if it ever spoke for the Jews, would not be worn out. It would be unexpected and hence doubly loud."

A slight blush passed over the monsignor's face. "You force me to tell you something which I wished to spare you," he said. "The Vatican has information not available to anyone else." He was now speaking in such a low voice that the Professor could barely hear him, and he did not seem to be doing so on account of the agent, who had long since vanished from the lobby. "The German Reich never intended for an instant to release the Jews, neither for two hundred and fifty dollars a head, nor for ten times that nor for a hundred times. The game that Germany played with you was decided upon months ago in Berlin— they were waiting for a favorable opportunity to set it going. Germany, absent from Évian, announced through your mouth that, far from giving the Jews a pfennig more than ten marks to take with them, it actually demanded material sacrifices for the release of the Jews. By these means Germany set out to paralyze the Conference. That it did not entirely succeed should give us grounds for hope."

The Professor clutched at his heart, but he did not do so because pain had gripped his heart; on the contrary, it was as if with this gesture he wanted to test his incomprehensible heart that had neither been convulsed nor threateningly drawn attention to itself. He became aware that he was almost longing for an attack, for the terrifying separation from men that it brought with it, for the sense of isolation in the antechamber of death. Although no pain oppressed him, he felt the same sensation that came over him after every attack: a withdrawal from himself and his environment, so that his ego seemed to break free from him and float away from him almost like the fluttering "spirit" in the trick photographs of spiritualists. He saw the young priest from a distance, from a bird's-eye view, a little black spot with an even smaller purple spot; the cool room with the lowered blinds, through which the afternoon sun was seeping, seemed to him unreal, and the empty feeling of unreality was intensified by the shadows of the trees that were dancing in the room like falling autumn leaves.

He pulled himself together and asked, "Why do you tell me

that?"—a question which the monsignor probably did not understand; he was bound to suppose that the Professor was inquiring after his motives for giving him this information, whereas Heinrich von Benda really meant: Why do you have to strike this blow at me?

"I did it reluctantly," the monsignor replied. "You accused the Church. The Church is not guiltless, but its guilt goes back for centuries and the time it will take to wipe it out will be inexorably long. I know what you are thinking. A fortnight and the Church is thinking in centuries. And it would not console you if I told you that although love needs centuries in order to gain victory, hate does not triumph in the meantime. Hate goes bankrupt every twenty years. But it should console you that your mission was successful because it failed. One day you will understand me." He leaned closer. "Furthermore the President of the United States has taken a fresh initiative. He has offered the Évian governments a last opportunity not to be accomplices. While there's life there's hope."

The Professor took his leave and went. He had scarcely heard the last words, only the no. One day . . . In an hour he would be facing the Swedish delegate. Would he still be able to advocate his cause—and what cause? The monsignor was right. He had clung to his mission, yet the monsignor had overestimated him—he had done so not only for the sake of the Jews, he had also done so because without this belief his own existence would have been senseless. He was intimately bound up with his mission, even though he detested it. He could not permit himself to believe that he had been nothing but a pawn pushed to and fro by unseen hands, pulled by unseen hands on unseen wires. Not only did the lives of the Jews depend upon his mission, his own life also depended upon it.

On this 14th of July, 1938, the representatives of the international press telegraphed to their newspapers and cable agencies that the session of the plenary assembly called for ten in the morning had suddenly been canceled without explanation; nor were the various committees going to meet, at least not in the morning. The announcements were limited to the news that the Chairman of the Conference had called a number of leaders of delegations for "private consultations" in his hotel apartment.

The American Ambassador had good reasons for postponing the plenary session. In addition to detailed instructions from the Secretary of State, dealing among other things with the Benda Mission, he had received a cable from the President stating America's willingness to take as many refugees from the German Reich as all the other participating states, thirty-one in number, would take together. In reply to a query telegraphed by the Ambassador, the State Department had sent a telegram making clear that of course this referred to new quotas—the United States would increase its immigration quota only by the number of refugees to whom the participating were willing to give asylum over and above the existing quotas. Nevertheless, the magnanimous offer which he now had to pass on to his foreign colleagues seemed to the Ambassador of a highly dubious character. The Constitution did not give the President the right to raise the immigration quota, and although the Ambassador fully credited the sorcerer in the White House with the ability to win over the Congress, it was at the moment a daring, if not reckless, promise.

As always when he was faced by the alternative of following his instincts and disavowing the President, or suppressing his feelings and doing his duty, the Ambassador acted like a good civil servant: he resolved to carry out his instructions. Once he had reached the decision, he went to work as intelligently and cautiously as long experience had taught him. If you took on a task, however reluctantly, no third party must notice or even guess that it had only your conditional approval. This was demanded by intelligence; but caution demanded that he should not bulldoze people, should in this particular case avoid a *fait accompli* which many participants in the Conference would interpret as a condemnation of their attitude to date. Therefore the Ambassador had invited a certain number of important leaders of delegations to come and see him in his apartment for "private consultation."

The Bolivian Ambassador was the first on the list. He was taken into the Chairman's sitting room at ten-fifteen.

The Chairman imagined that with the Ambassador of the third largest Latin-American state, the first among the nations of the Southern Hemisphere to have accepted the President's invitation, he could speak frankly. This Bolivian descended from the ancient Spanish nobility was a man of high culture and as a delegate to the League of Nations one of the most striking figures to appear on the floor at Geneva.

"Excellency," said the Bolivian Ambassador when the Chairman had finished, "I cannot conceal my consternation at the President's plan. May I speak quite frankly?"

"I should be grateful if you would."

"The Latin-American states will not regard the North American offer as generous, but as boastful. A country that declares its willingness to take in as many refugees as all other participating states together is demonstrating that it is as rich, as large, as powerful as thirty-one other states rolled into one. I don't think one ought to suggest that, even if it is in accordance with the facts. Moreover"—he smiled his subtle smile—"if the United States is in a position to sign a blank check, then their bank account must be inexhaustible. Why then do they not increase their immigration quota independently of collaboration of other countries?"

"Because we would like to double the number of those saved."

"Excellency, try to put yourself in the position of the Latin-American states. My own country, for example. Of all countries in the world we have the smallest number of Jews—three or four hundred. Last year we came to an agreement with the German Reich authorizing the immigration of three thousand Germans —provided they are Aryans. Furthermore our laws restrict the immigration of Russians, Poles, Arabs and Jews, they forbid the immigration"—he ran through the list quickly and in a bitter tone—"of Chinese, Negroes, half-breeds, sick people, cripples, degenerates, criminals and Communists. In 1936 we permitted the immigration of certain German Jews. Bolivia is closed to Jews from Eastern Europe."

"I didn't know that," the Chairman said, dismayed.

"I mention it because, while the idea of the different value of different races may appear absurd to you and me, it has brought Germany and the South American states closer together. The further Germany moves away from Europe and the closer the United States moves to Europe, the closer Germany, in moving away from Europe, moves to the South American continent. Primitivism forms a link, Excellency."

The Latin cynicism with which the Bolivian Ambassador spoke sarcastically of his own country, his own continent, left a divided impression on the Chairman. He knew how closely allied honesty and cynicism could be, and he valued his visitor's frankness, but he did not doubt that the diplomat would speak differently in the plenary session.

"In Argentina," said the Ambassador emphatically, "there are already two hundred and seventy thousand Jews; that only amounts to two percent of the population, but of the most recent twenty-one thousand immigrants no less than ten percent were Jews."

"That was not a voluntary immigration."

"No, but the victims of the Spanish civil war are not voluntary immigrants either, and it is only natural that Argentina should prefer the Spaniards. The Brazilian laws stipulate that eighty percent of the immigrants shall be agricultural workers. Since the establishment of the National Socialist regime in Germany Brazil has given asylum to a total of seven thousand Jews, but new legislation requires that not only must every application for a visa be accompanied by a certificate of baptism, but also the immigrant has to answer the question whether he is an Aryan, a Semite or a Mongol."

He continued to review the immigration policy of the Latin-American states. Venezuela, he said, demanded that immigrants should deposit a thousand bolivars, Peru two thousand sols, Uruguay six hundred gold pesos, which, however, were returned to the immigrant at the rate of fifty pesos per annum. Chile accepted immigrants only if the father was not over forty, Ecuador would only take agricultural workers; only last year Ecuador had extradited within thirty days all foreign Jews who were not working on the land.

"You know," the Chairman interrupted him, "That Germany is threatening to arrest forty thousand Jews on the first of August."

"During the last few days," rejoined the Bolivian, "Germany's pressure on our delegates has been intensified. Certain foreign diplomats—can I count on your discretion?"

"Of course."

"The Hungarian observer is acting as Germany's unofficial representative. Germany is threatening to break off economic relations with all Latin-American states who prove themselves at Évian to be 'friendly to the Jews.' "

"If there was any logic in Germany's Jewish policy, the Reich ought to welcome a successful conclusion to the Évian Conference."

"On the contrary, Germany knows perfectly well that the world is not in a position to take all the German and Austrian Jews, let alone those of Eastern Europe; hence it could at best be a partial solution. But any significant increase in the quotas would represent a declaration of solidarity with the Jews. Germany has uttered the threat to carry off forty thousand Jews only to prove that the world will not take in the Jews even when they are in danger of their lives."

The American Ambassador looked surreptitiously at his watch. The conversation had been protracted, and the Ambassador of France was waiting.

"I should like to thank you for your friendly advice," he said to his visitor. "Would you consider it a mistake to inform the Conference officially of the President's offer?"

"An intensification of North American pressure would drive South America into the arms of the Germans." The Bolivian rose. "I doubt, Excellency, whether Évian has helped the Jews," he said wrinkling his brow. "Most of the Latin-American countries were in the process of building up their trade both with the United States and with Germany. These states—I need hardly tell you that this is not my own opinion—now regard the Jews as the nigger in the woodpile who is forcing Latin America to choose between Germany and the USA. Anyone who is a Jew compels the world to declare itself—perhaps that is the kernel of anti-Semitism. But that would take us too far. . . ."

In the anteroom, to which the Chairman conducted his guest, the French Ambassador was waiting.

After the Chairman had offered him a glass of sherry—the Ambassador declined with thanks—the host came at once to the President's proposal. As he spoke, it struck him that he was presenting it in a different, less apodictic form than before; what he had previously conveyed as a decision he now clothed in the form of questions, and although he had less confidence in the French Ambassador than in the Bolivian, he adopted a more confidential tone.

No trace of surprise was to be seen on the narrow face of the French Ambassador, on which every vein was clearly drawn; he looked like a greyhound, or rather as a greyhound would have looked if it were intelligent. The Ambassador was a diplomat of the old school who would have agreed with Sir Henry Wotton that "an ambassador is an honest man sent to lie abroad for the good of his country"; he possessed the ability to keep his thoughts hidden behind flowery language and not to embark upon any path without assuring himself that all his escape routes were secured.

"I am convinced," he said, "that the President's proposal springs from the noblest humanitarian motives. At the same time, I fear that most of the participating states will not so interpret it. When they accepted the President's invitation, they believed that they would remain masters of their own decision. Then Germany came forward with the threat—this is how we must interpret the Benda Mission, I think—that we must unconditionally and without delay give asylum to forty thousand Jews. This threat—it would be no exaggeration to speak of blackmail—has had a deterrent effect which has its good side. With this threat Herr Hitler has not exactly made himself popular even with those—and I fear there are many—who are favorably disposed toward him. He showed his hand; today he wants to burden the world with forty thousand Jews, tomorrow with perhaps double or ten times that number. I think the Great Powers should not fail to point out the German blackmail; it will be useful to us later when Herr Hitler employs similar methods over the Sudeten question."

The Chairman took care not to agree. Throughout the Conference France had warned against any offense to, even any judgment upon, Germany. The Ambassador must have definite reasons, not as yet clear to the Chairman, for using such harsh words.

"Through the President's proposal," declared the Ambassador, "which will be adjudged by many to be a provocation, the United States—far be it from me, Excellency, to give you advice; I am only putting into words what any honest friend of America must feel—the United States is losing its comfortable and popular role as the victim of blackmail. For our part, in view of coming political developments, we in France are almost as concerned about America's popularity as about our own."

Now the Chairman knew what his French colleague was driving at. He could have cut the conversation short and saved the Frenchman a protracted and involved exposition.

If America, the French Ambassador meanwhile said with surprising frankness, now put pressure on the Conference, her methods would not be appreciably different from those of Germany, indeed the Conference could not help gaining the impression that Germany and America were working hand in glove to impose the refugees on the rest of the world.

The Chairman interrupted him. "I hope you do not mean to say, Excellency, that it is the same thing whether one tries to coerce the world with a mass deportation, perhaps a mass murder, or to compel it to mercy?"

"I am not expressing my own opinions," replied the Ambassador imperturbably, "not even my country's. I am trying to analyze the reactions of the rest of the participating states. They themselves have used the word coercion—need I say that in politics no distinction is made between coercion to evil and coercion to good? Independent states do not wish to be coerced into anything."

"And what about our duty to help these unfortunate people?"

"Let us phrase it differently. Did not Plautus already say that the shirt is closer than the coat? You speak of these unfortunate people, just these and not others, and although charity is an undeniable law of civilization, nevertheless everyone prefers to come to the aid of those who are closer to him rather than those who are farther away. To the South Americans the Spaniards, or even the Indians, are closer than the Jews, to the British the colonial peoples are closer than the Jews, to the agrarian states the peasants are closer than the Jews—all of them shirts, Excellency. The Jews, I fear, are the world's coat."

"People may perhaps not think like that when they find out in a future war how little Hitler thinks of human life—not only of the lives of Jews."

The Ambassador shrugged his shoulders. "King Ferdinand of Aragon said that little birds of prey do not notice another bigger bird of prey that is soaring above, waiting to take them by the throat."

The Chairman rose. "What attitude would France adopt in the Conference to the American offer?"

The direct question did not seem to have taken the French Ambassador by surprise. "I shall immediately get in touch with Paris, but I think I can say now that my government will be forced to adopt a wait-and-see attitude. I am speaking as a private citizen and your friend when I say that I would prefer not to have to express any opinion at all on your President's proposal. Should we succeed, with the aid of a kind Providence, in averting war, this will only happen if the German Reich is convinced in time of the solidarity of the Great Powers—over every question, even the smallest, even over the question of the refugees. Hitler is in many respects a genius, but his lack of political experience is a mortal danger. He doesn't know that powers which are in total disagreement in minor matters may be in complete agreement over major questions; he will misinterpret our disagreement at Évian and it may, who knows, encourage him to take some reckless step over Czechoslovakia."

The Chairman took leave of his visitor, although the answer was on the tip of his tongue. Must Hitler really be convinced of the disunity of the powers, could not Évian have served rather to convince him of their unity—even over such a "minor" matter as the refugees?

As he led the Canadian delegate into the lounge, he thought back over his almost forty years in the service of the state, of his almost thirty years in diplomacy, and he asked himself how often he had succeeded in persuading someone to change his mind. Only in novels and plays did conversations end differently

from the way in which they had begun, only in books and on
the stage were there dramatic changes within the space of a few
minutes, were opinions really exchanged in the true meaning of
the word, that is to say in such a way that the one accepted what
the other had to give him. Political conversations, political discussions, were like railway trains running on parallel lines,
sometimes side by side, mostly past each other, making for one
ultimate destination, but stopping at different stations.

His conversation with the Canadian—and his subsequent conversations with the chief Swedish delegate, with the chairman of
the Nansen Committee and with the High Commissioner for
Refugees—ended no differently from the way they had begun;
in none of them was the President's proposal greeted with enthusiasm, approval or even benevolent assent. Some regarded
America's compassion as arrogant, others warned against the
effects of a moral ultimatum, some actually expressed the view
that this might very well be bluff, with which the United States
was merely trying at the last moment to salvage the Conference, or rather their own prestige; all were agreed, however,
that if America so wished she was entitled to lead the way by
example, but not to impose action upon other smaller and
poorer states.

At one-twenty, when his last visitor had left, the Ambassador
decided in favor of an orderly retreat. After consulting with the
members of his delegation, he sent the President a cable in
which he described his discussions in the necessary detail and
asked him to forgo his magnanimous offer.

The day had been sultry and the evening brought no real relief.
Although the American Ambassador had asked him to come
and see him at ten, an unusually late hour, the Professor had
gone to the Hôtel Royal at eight o'clock because he hoped that
on the heights, where the hotel of the Conference looked down
into the valley, the air would be cooler and more pleasant. Such
hopes, such illusions, were not new to him. During the last few
days he had continually wished himself away from where he
happened to be—out of his bedroom into the lounge, out of the
lounge into the garden, from the street into the hotel, from the

hotel into the street, out of solitude into company and out of
company into solitude.

Now he had dropped into a deck chair on the garden terrace,
a strange piece of furniture—strange because this brightly
striped object, intended for comfort but in reality exceedingly
uncomfortable, was meant for a sunny day, not for the night,
and looked thoroughly out of place on the lawn at evening.
When he looked to the left he could see the hotel, which was lit
up from top to bottom and almost unnaturally lively, like a
festive house on the stage; the doors of the dining room were
open and busy waiters could be seen coming and going behind
the thin curtain; the doors of the bar and the lounge were shut,
here discussions seemed still to be in progress. Between the trees
on the right one could see the lights of Évian-les-Bains, a French
spa singled out by history and completely unaware of its New
Status. Darkness lay over the lake like a blanket woven of haze
in which the tired day had wrapped itself. The scent of the pine
woods mingled with the moldering, warm odor of the rose garden. Here and there voices reached the ear of the man in the
deck chair, and it struck him that they were exclusively male
voices. In a day, or at the latest two days, things would be different; the delegates would leave, gamblers and people taking the
cure would once more occupy the illuminated bird cage, the
voices of women and perhaps also of children would be heard,
all the doors would open and all the terraces be populated, the
village beyond the trees and the hotel on the hill would grow
together again. The Évian Conference would be a vanished
ghost.

He breathed deeply—it really had grown cooler now. Had the
day been in vain?

During the night, in which, in spite of sleeping tablets, he
had slept little, he had succeeded after a stubborn struggle in
breaking out of the torpor, in mastering the paralysis that had
come over him after his conversation with the envoy of the
Vatican. Had the Germans been using him as a chess piece? He
remembered—a curious association—a ballet at the Vienna
Opera House in which the chess pieces had been portrayed by
ballet dancers, castle and bishop and knight and pawns and king

and queen were male and female dancers. When chess pieces came to life, became human beings of flesh and blood, they could escape the hand that guided them, make themselves independent, carry out surprise moves and act according to their own judgment. It might very well be that he had taken on an unworthy mission and that the governments were wise to reject the dishonest German offer, but they had no reason to boast of their rejection. Most attempts at blackmail only failed if the person offered for ransom did not seem to the victim of the blackmail worth rescuing. With the strength of despair he had spent the whole day hurrying from delegation to delegation, trying to convince the participants in the Conference that they could at least thwart the intentions of the despisers of human beings by a symbolic act, the acceptance of the forty thousand. The origins of his mission had been dubious, but at least he had withdrawn himself from the guiding hand, whereas the others, although not compelled by superior forces, had turned into rigid figures of ivory. Nothing prevented the world from proving to the despiser of human beings that human beings were not as despicable as he believed—nothing but themselves.

In the morning the Colombian had received him again. He had treated him like a man with heart trouble, though naturally the Minister could have known nothing about Professor Vuillemin's diagnosis, and had no electrocardiogram at his disposal. The committee of four, the delegate had said, would recommend the provision of visas and residence permits for forty thousand. The Conference would have no time to discuss this recommendation, however, but would refer it to London, where the permanent bureau was to be set up; when it would meet, the Colombian could not say. Shamefacedly the Minister had spoken of the "success," which he himself had described as a failure twenty-four hours ago—shamefaced, but as if it were not his own, but only Heinrich von Benda's mission that had failed: a stranger who for a week had been no stranger, but a stranger nevertheless. Forty thousand Jews, the first of August; well, Germany wouldn't be so precise about its ultimatum, the Colombian had said reassuringly. The fact that the Évian countries were setting up a new organization would make the German dictator think, would perhaps paralyze the executioner's

hand. Perhaps. It was nice to believe in miracles, nice and com-
forting; and he who was tired of building a house built castles
in the air. Lowered eyes, a handshake, good wishes—the Colombian had done his best; he had not been a hypocrite nor apathetic, only tired.

Lunch with the rabbi from New York. Heinrich von Benda
had told him that he was going back to Vienna as soon as the
Conference adjourned. There, behind the drawn curtains of the
bar or the lounge, the hearing of the private organizations,
principally Jewish, was now being concluded, and the Rabbi
had disclosed to the Professor what they were going to say. Palestine had sent a woman delegate to Évian, an important
woman who, it was said, was destined to play a great role in the
Jewish state, when there was a Jewish state. What sort of state?
A state that cultivated its graveyards even before it could till its
fields. Selma Selig was being heard, the little limping Fräulein
who was determined to save the best Jews, as though the lives of
the best weighed more than the lives of the others, who were
not quite so good. And other Jewish organizations were being
heard, ready to pay ships' passages, to furnish all sorts of guarantees and affidavits signed by a citizen of the receiving countries
for an immigrant, undertaking that the Jew would not be a
burden upon state welfare, only upon other Jews. Sworn assur-
ances—the only question was, who for; the only question was,
would the dead really not be a burden upon anyone? But everyone, the rabbi had left no doubt about that, would speak out
against the Benda Project, this unethical and moreover imprac-
ticable project of a solitary fool. Did the representatives of the
organizations not know that the thirty-two delegations had already packed their bags, that they were in the process of leaving
Évian to the sick and the gamblers, that they were only listening
out of politeness and with half an ear, as the hotel manager
listens as he says good-bye at the door—"I hope you enjoyed
your stay, we look forward to seeing you again"; but he would
never see them again—didn't they know that the Conference
secretariat was already drafting the final resolution and that
perhaps by tomorrow thirty-two lifeboats would put out to sea
again, without having taken a single shipwrecked person
aboard?

The lights of the hotel fell upon the lawn; in one of the lounges the curtains were drawn back. The Professor looked at his watch: it was nine-thirty.

What had the Ambassador to say to him, why had he sent for him so late in the evening? It was hard to believe still, but to abandon all hope was also hard. The Colombian had indicated that the participants in the Conference would reject without discussion a secret American project, thrown into the arena by Washington at the last moment. Was it the project of which the monsignor had spoken, upon which the Vatican's envoy had hung his faint hopes? And ought he, Heinrich von Benda, not to admit to himself that his mission had failed, that it had been from the outset without purpose and without meaning? He thought back on his life and the balance sheet did not seem to him so unfavorable, so devoid of purpose and meaning as his mission. Fortune, which had been true to him for more than sixty years, a whole human life, had stored up great powers in him; evil chance, the raging torrent of general destiny, the humiliation of the hour, had not been able to destroy them totally. Everyone upon whom misfortune falls tries to fathom the meaning of the misfortune, finds it, becomes resigned or quarrels with God; but has anyone ever tried to fathom the meaning of good fortune? In misfortune he had to seek for the meaning of his former good fortune and might perhaps find it. Good fortune had bestowed upon him that high courage which was able to bear humiliation with humility, had lent him that stubborn spirit which refused to be suborned by petty doubts, had given him the sure hand which did not tremble even during a hopeless operation.

Or was he wrong? Would the final judgment against which there was no appeal be passed during the coming hour? Had he been a solitary fool?

He looked up at the clear, starry sky. "Blacken thy heavens, Jove, / With thunderclouds . . ." How did the passage go in *Prometheus*? He had learned it by heart at school; it was a long time ago, but now the words came back into his mind: "Who helped me / When I braved the Titans' insolence? / Who rescued me from death, / From slavery? / Hast thou not all thyself accomplished, / Holy-glowing heart? / And glowing young and good, / Most ignorantly thanked / The slumberer above?" Oh no, his heart did not glow young and good; it had accomplished nothing. Should he curse the slumberer up above? Shylock, Prometheus, Moses. It happened in the course of the centuries that the sleeper awoke and became aware of what was being made of his world, and inflamed with wrath uttered the words: "And I will be honored upon Pharaoh, and upon all his host"; he who was to see could already see the lightning in the "dark cloud," and could already see that the armies of the Egyptians would follow the armies of the refugees, the persecutors would follow the persecuted, obeying a secret compulsion, across the frontiers and into foreign countries, and that the armies would go in after them, "all Pharaoh's horses, his chariots and his horsemen, into the midst of the sea," and that the Lord would fight for Israel and "against the Egyptians." But he was still asleep, the sleeping God, he was still not awake, had still not spoken to Moses.

The Professor rose laboriously from his deck chair and walked toward the hotel. It was five minutes to ten.

The American Ambassador was sitting by the window and saw the Professor coming slowly toward the hotel. The hearing of the private and Jewish organizations had been concluded only a few minutes ago; they had all without exception spoken out against the Benda Mission, and although he had been from the beginning an opponent of this audacious mission, he could not suppress his pity for the old man. On his desk lay the report of the agent who had been keeping the Professor under surveillance. It told him of the flight of Elisabeth Berenson and the Professor's trip to Geneva. The Ambassador felt a little ashamed that he knew more about the Professor's private life than Heinrich von Benda had confided in him or intended to confide in him. They were both old, the Professor and the Ambassador; a year ago they had both been "eminent," the Professor more eminent than the Ambassador. Position, prestige, fame, were probably the only antidote to old age; not a real antidote, since they could neither prevent hardening of the arteries nor dilate the veins, but a proved cosmetic remedy all the same: famous old men do not look quite as old as they are. Professor von

Benda must have grown very old since he had been sitting in
the anterooms in which in the past people had waited for him,
since his name was not even sufficient to open the gates of a
country to his grandchildren, since he had been dependent
upon pocket money from the Gestapo.

Curiously, the end of this train of thought reassured the Ambassador. It did not happen often in the life of a diplomat that
he could do something good, something good in that true sense
in which it ought to be understood, the human sense. Now he
could convey to the Professor the invitation from Harvard, offer
him the professorship in his department, open the gates of
America to him, promise him American citizenship and, more
important, guarantee the rescue and liberty of his wife and
child. The Professor need only reach out his hand and Heinrich
von Benda's human dignity would immediately be reestab-
lished; after a humiliating episode which had been thrust upon
him from outside and for which he was in no way to blame, he
could become himself again, and if that happened, happened in
this one single case, the Évian Conference would not have been
entirely in vain.

The Professor was announced from the porter's lodge. The
Ambassador looked at his watch, and as he did so other, less
pleasing thoughts came into his mind. Was he yielding to illusions, was he deceiving himself, was he wrapping opportunism
in the cloak of humanitarianism? There were strings attached to
his offer, hidden conditions. Humanity to the boundaries of
politics, politics when nothing could be achieved by humanity.
The hour of politics had come. The task was to lay bare the
inhuman regime in Germany that had refused to listen—undoubtedly a laudable task and an honest start, but nevertheless
a political maneuver in which Heinrich von Benda's role was
that of a chess piece. His human dignity was to be restored, but
not unconditionally, not out of dignity and humanitarianism
alone; human dignity hung by the string of politics.

The Professor entered the room; he was cordially received by
the Ambassador. The American approached his goal by a
roundabout route. First he informed his visitor of the results of
the Conference, which he described as satisfactory, holding the

Apathy of the Heart

promise of positive developments in the future. He tried to
buttress his forced optimism with details. Only then did he
speak of the Benda Mission, about which he had been skeptical
from the start, which he had regarded as having no chance—
"and it is better that you have apparently met with no success;
you will soon realize that when you see the effect which the
Conference's final communiqué will have on Germany."

The Professor asked himself whether the Ambassador had
summoned him for such a late hour in order to console him for
the failure of his mission. He studied the Ambassador and observed that he had visibly aged since their last meeting. He did
not only look old, he also looked tired and ill. He spoke in a low
voice, slowly, interrupted himself, breathed heavily, little beads
of sweat stood on his forehead, a few drops of sweat were glisten-
ing above his thin upper lip; it was as if stone were sweating.
The Professor did not know what moved him, in the middle of
this highly political conversation, to inquire after the Ambassador's health; it must have been his diagnostic eye, the long years
of habit or what the French call *la déformation professionelle*.

"Yes, I must admit I'm somewhat tired," the Ambassador
said. "It was a strenuous day, I've been on my legs since eight."
He smiled. "One doesn't get any younger. . . ."

"It's the heat," the Professor said.

"It goes on and on." The Ambassador looked at the window.
"Not a breath of air. Do you also find that you suffer more from
the heat every year?"

"One grows increasingly sensitive to the temperature. You
should take off your jacket, Excellency."

"You don't mind?" the Ambassador asked with relief.

He wiped his forehead and hung his jacket over the back of
the chair, while he invited the Professor to take his jacket off
too. The Professor did so, although he seemed to be quite un-
affected by the heat, this particular nocturnal sultriness; once
more he became aware that since his visit to Vuillemin he had
been feeling better, experienced no pain, no shortness of
breath, especially now that he had begun involuntarily to concern himself with the health of another. Of course, he knew that
his advice could be of little help to the Ambassador; it was

neither old age nor the heat that had changed the Ambassador.
The old man was suffering from failure; nothing is more tiring
than failure.

"You should send for some lemonade," the Professor said.
"Made with three or four lemons. It's a household remedy, but
it's extraordinarily effective, more effective than vitamin C. You
can't trick nature."

The Ambassador rang his secretary and ordered two *citrons
pressés* made with three or four lemons.

"I shall tell them at home that Professor von Benda pre-
scribed me lemonade," he said. "Not everyone can boast of such
a distinction."

"I went to the doctor myself yesterday," the Professor said
with a touch of embarrassment.

To Professor Vuillemin, Place du Rhône, Geneva, thought
the Ambassador; it was in the agent's report. But all he said
was: "You have a great deal of excitement behind you. You
should have come to me about your daughter; naturally we
should have taken steps to help her."

The Ambassador had not thrown this remark into the conversation unintentionally, and he was surprised that the Professor
did not seem to be in the least taken aback. He had to convince
the Professor that the United States could not only feed half the
world, produce guns and airplanes, strengthen or undermine
the Zürich stock exchange, but could also, if it so wished, conjure Frau von Benda and the Professor's little son out of Germany.

"You had other things to worry about than my family," the
Professor said.

"Don't say that," the Ambassador replied and began to steer
toward his goal. Now that the Benda Mission had failed, he said,
at least in the sense that no government in the civilized world
would be willing to buy Jews like merchandise, to trade with
the Germans in human lives, there was no point in the Professor returning to Vienna. Indeed it was impossible and—before
Heinrich von Benda could interrupt him—he went on. "I have
a personal message for you. Both the President and the State
Department have expressly authorized me to make this statement to you, and as soon as I have done so you will see how

immense is my country's faith in you. In my whole diplomatic career I have never before found myself in a position to give a foreigner such confidential, indeed strictly secret information—I have your word, Professor?"

The Professor nodded; the Ambassador went on:

"You are doubtless aware of the existence of the secret services, a necessary evil. People are always talking about the deeds of the British Intelligence Service—pure fantasy, or at least a completely out-of-date idea. The American secret service outdid the legendary Intelligence Service long ago. There is almost nothing, if I may say so, which it cannot do, and in this particular instance one cannot even speak of an evil. In short, the President has the secret service's word, and I have the President's word, that our agents in Austria will"—he searched for a word—"convey Frau von Benda and little Heinrich unmolested across the Swiss frontier within ten days and from Switzerland straight to the United States." That the Professor himself, he added, was more than welcome in America—Harvard or another university, the Professor could take his choice, he need hardly say; he avoided appealing too blatantly to the Professor's vanity.

Now the sweat broke out on Heinrich von Benda's forehead as well. He felt the drops of sweat on the back of his neck, felt them running down his back and making his shirt wet. Now temptation was assailing him. Bettina, Heinrich and himself in freedom! What good would it really do the Jews if he returned to Vienna empty-handed? Did he expect the Germans to celebrate him as a hero because he had played their game to the bitter end, to call off the persecution of the Jews for his sake? Did the barbaric regime need a pretext to persecute the Jews, to deport them, perhaps to kill them? Did it not express its dark intentions daily and hourly in newspapers, in speeches and in deeds? He had wanted to return for the sake of the Jews, but was it shameful that he had also wanted to return for the sake of Bettina and Heinrich, and would it be shameful if he changed his decision, now, when the President's special envoy promised freedom for his wife and child? It was a conditional death sentence that Professor Vuillemin had passed, but after his return it would change into an unconditional one. Had he not a right to a hospital bed, in Geneva or New York, and was it not his duty to Bettina and Heinrich to remain alive? He suddenly remembered a name, Erwin Dartin, an actor at the Burgtheater, eighty-one years old, for many years his patient—Dartin had been barely forty when the heart specialist passed sentence of death on him more than forty years ago, and a few weeks ago Dartin had played the old Moor in Schiller's *Räuber*.

The waiter brought the lemonades, placed them on the table between the two old gentlemen in shirtsleeves and left. Each of them cautiously took a sip of the cooling drink.

"I didn't come to Évian to save myself and my family," the Professor heard himself say—does one really sometimes say things before one has thought them, as though by a courageous word to set up an insuperable barrier in front of a cowardly thought?

The Ambassador felt this sentence to be a fortunate dispensation; all day long, even while he was listening to his colleagues, conducting negotiations and hearings, he had pondered how he could show his visitor the string on which the Benda family's rescue, and the Professor's own rescue, hung without making it overclear, without drawing the link between rescue and condition, between humanity and politics, in overemphatic lines.

The Professor's safety was not the only thing at stake, answered the Ambassador. The most important thing of all was to save the Benda Mission, in a higher and better sense than would have been achieved by the purchase of Jews. The Mission had not been in vain nor should it really be described as a failure. There was universal indignation over the German proposal, even among the delegations who were distrustful of the refugees and could not exactly be looked upon as philo-Semitic; in the course of the Évian Conference the general attitude toward the German Reich had changed most unfavorably, unfavorably for Hitler that is; there were even voices calling for a boycott of Germany, for sanctions such as had been imposed upon Italy during her invasion of Abyssinia. It hadn't come to that yet, not by a long way, but what was the use of the indignation of two dozen diplomats if the world, public opinion, heard nothing about the unexampled blackmail, a blackmail which was typical, which had served the blackmailer well in the case of Austria and which there was reason to fear he might employ again in the Czech and Polish questions? To appeal to Hitler's humanity would be like trying to draw tears from a stone; the Germans understood no language but that of strength. No country—the United States was no exception on this point—thought of going to war for the sake of the Jews, but the treatment of the Jews was symptomatic, and it could not be made clear too soon to the Czechs and Poles and Russians and Yugoslavs what faced them in the event of war. The United States—now he spoke it out, presented it as a concession to the Professor, almost as a favor to him—the United States was prepared to reveal the secret of the Benda Mission, to mobilize the world press on American soil and introduce Heinrich von Benda to them as witness for the prosecution, to lay bare the traffic in human beings and throw the weight of their moral indignation into the scales.

"And what about the Jews in Germany, the Jews in Austria?" the Professor said.

How often had he repeated this sentence during the last few days, how often had he met with the deafness which, like a secondary symptom, arose as a sequel to apathy! He heard the Ambassador's reply and much of it sounded almost convincing— that Germany would want to prove the opposite of what it was reproached with; that the persecution of the Jews could not be continued in the midst of universal indignation; that the fate of the Jews could in any case not get worse, could only get better; that Germany might even declare itself willing to give up the Jews, demonstratively and without compensation. He heard the Ambassador's reply, but as he listened he saw not a hundred thousand Jews, not forty thousand, he saw only two, Dr. Schönglas and Armin Silberstein.

"You must give me time to think it over, Excellency," he said.

"Certainly," the Ambassador assured him quickly. "Washington was thinking of a press conference at Évian, but I refused at once; nothing must happen before your wife and child are in safety."

Since his visit to Dr. Vuillemin, the Professor had not

smoked, but now he began to feel for a cigarette with trembling hands. The Ambassador noticed and handed him a packet of American cigarettes.

"Before I was called to the Reich Governor," said the Professor, "I was in prison. I didn't mention it . . ."

"I know."

"One of my cellmates was beaten to death. Another, a Jewish lawyer, Dr. Hugo Schönglas, was released when I expressed my willingness to undertake the mission. On the day I speak to the press, or word of my flight leaks out, they would arrest him. They would beat him to death."

"Would they not equally arrest him after your return? And you yourself?"

"The head of the Jewish Community was also my cellmate."

"Herr Silberstein will be arrested as soon as they no longer need him."

"He would be held responsible for my actions."

"At most for the failure of your mission. But the first person whom they will hold responsible can only be you, Professor von Benda. If you don't think of yourself and your family, don't forget what you mean to a world of sick people."

Still not a breath stirred. The shirt was sticking to Heinrich von Benda's body; he was afraid of catching a cold, took his jacket and put it over his shoulders.

"Many people believe that," he said in a low voice. "My wife believes it, my son told me so. But . . ."

"I didn't know you had a son."

"He is a doctor in Paris."

"You see!"

"I don't know, Excellency, whether a few years, a few months ago, I might not have saved my family and myself first from a sinking ship. I should have found a good excuse, should have thrown the value of my life into the lifeboat. I still don't think that all men are of equal value, only their lives are of equal value. That is strange, perhaps a contradiction; I would have to be a philosopher to explain it."

"You are proceeding from the false premise that you could save a single human life by returning."

"Suppose the premise is correct?"

He looked across the low table at his host, who had likewise put on his jacket again. How was it that barely a week ago he had had the impression that he was separated by an abyss from the other old man, and now the same man seemed to him almost like his reflection in the mirror? He no longer hesitated to ask the Ambassador a personal question, and said, "What would you do in my place, Excellency?"

"That is hard to say," the Ambassador said hesitantly. "I lost my wife while I was still a young man and did not marry again. I have no children. Since my youth I have devoted myself to the state, without ever getting very far in the civil service. No, don't contradict me—I was always too conscientious a civil servant to be a good diplomat, and too conscientious a diplomat to feel comfortable as a civil servant. I became an ambassador relatively early and have always held posts where there was not much to lose. It is possible that I was sent to Évian because there was not much to lose here either. I'm not an important man, but I have some experience, though of course that isn't much use now, since we are confronted by a world that functions according to new, unprecedented laws—that is probably the reason why old men are so useless. All the same, I am incapable of thinking in any other way than politically, but that means that I am used to seeing only the wood and not the trees. If I were in your position I could still not act in any other way than politically, so I should undoubtedly abandon a ship that would go down just as much with me as without me. Don't think I am evading your question. Only it is hard for me to put myself in your position, because with the first person whom you saved from death you did more than I have done in my whole long life. I have always envied men like you, Professor von Benda, therefore I cannot understand your wanting to leave the operating room, where you can save a single individual with some certainty, to serve mankind that has made martyrs of all its prophets."

"I am not thinking of mankind," the Professor said. "I see the faces quite clearly before me. . . ."

Thus the two men talked for almost another hour, spoke of themselves, the Conference, Germany and America, the coming war, the mission, the heat, old age, sickness and weariness. And the longer they spoke the less Heinrich von Benda could make up his mind, so that in the end he asked for twenty-four hours to think it over; and the more vacillating the Ambassador became because on the one hand, since he had achieved nothing with humanity, he at least wanted to achieve something with politics, on the other he felt a silent triumph, a belated triumph over the President and the Secretary of State, who had appropriated the Benda Mission to themselves and their political ends, who were so sure that they could count on human weakness, that is to say could trade in man, in anonymous man, the commodity.

When Heinrich von Benda had left, erect, with a springy step, the Ambassador gazed after him, and it seemed to him as though the incarnation of human dignity had just left the room. He no longer felt tired; the heat no longer oppressed him. He was a great doctor, indeed—Professor von Benda, the Ambassador reflected. Their talk had refreshed him.

When the Évian Conference met that morning for its closing session, the hall was not as full as it had been for other public meetings. The text of the resolutions had already been distributed to the delegations and the press in the early morning; it had to be voted upon, but its acceptance was a mere formality. Many journalists, some subordinate officials and most of the camp followers had left; secretaries whose presence in the Conference room was not indispensable were in the apartments sorting out the papers and packing the cases. This time the Professor had found a seat in the first row behind the delegations.

He had put away the copy of the resolutions in his briefcase; he would have time enough to study them in detail on his way home. The final resolution consisted of six statements of fact and six recommendations. Point Three of the statements of fact emphasized that "involuntary emigration has assumed such proportions as to prejudice the improvement of international relations and increase international tension"; Point Five stressed that "a reasonable solution" of the problem confronting the Conference "demands the collaboration of the country of origin, for which reason the participating states were "convinced" that "the country of origin will contribute to the success of the enterprise by permitting the involuntary emigrants to take their property with them and emigrate according to a systematic plan"; Point Six expressed the thanks of the Conference to the President of the United States as its initiator, and to France as its host. Clause A of the recommendations proposed that the Conference, which regarded itself as a permanent institution and intended to continue its deliberations, should concern itself not only with those refugees already in flight but with all those "forced to leave their country of origin by reason of their political outlook, religious faith or racial origins"; Clause B recommended that "strictly confidential information relating to the refugee problem shall continue to be exchanged"; Clause D declared that "the governments of the countries of asylum are not willing to undertake any obligations toward financing involuntary emigration"; Clause E stated that where the refugees were refused regular state documents by their country of origin the countries of asylum would accept other documents, but only such as answered the "demands of their laws"; Clause F, finally, outlined the functions of the permanent bureau in London—it was to have a president, four vice-presidents and a director. The main and final resolution included the recommendations of the subcommittees as well as an account of the expenses of the Conference. The expenses amounted to 16,000 Swiss francs. Of this sum the United States and Great Britain had contributed 3,024 francs each, France 2,240 and Canada 980 francs. The states of Guatemala, Honduras, Nicaragua and Paraguay had each contributed 14 francs to the costs of the Conference. The payments collected by the secretariat amounted to 15,988 francs. Who had met or would meet the deficit of 12 francs was not clear from the document.

The pages of the Hôtel Royal had not drawn the curtains as carefully as they usually did, so that the Conference hall lay in twilight produced by the contrast between the sunlight entering from outside on the one hand and the electric light on the other. The weather on this day was fine, but the sky was not cloudless, and when a cloud darkened the sun the artificial lighting became more intense; when the cloud had passed, the light of the chandeliers paled.

The Professor, in the front row of the spectators, doing his best to see between the backs of two delegates sitting in front of him, attentively watching what could scarcely produce any surprise now, could not help thinking of an afternoon in the house of the Viennese court singer Terrina, a woman given to buffoonery, who had specified in her will that after her funeral the guests should gather in her Hietzing villa and, over a good cup of coffee, excellently made as usual by her old housekeeper, should chat as gaily and unconstrainedly as they had done during her lifetime in her famous salon that was held twice a month, on the first and the fifteenth. Had Frau Terrina really been indulging in buffoonery, or had she merely been extraordinarily clever? In any case, the gaiety could not have been more unnatural; in the midst of the unconstraint commanded by the will everyone's thoughts were concentrated on the death of the aged beauty whom they had just borne to the grave.

"Thanks to the spirit of cooperation that animated all the participating states," the American Ambassador began his speech, "the Conference has succeeded in setting in motion machinery which will contribute to improving the lot of the unhappy human beings with whom we have been dealing here." He enumerated the considerable number of "confidential reports" that had been presented by the countries of asylum to the grateful Conference; they would form a basis for a greater movement of emigration "within the framework of the law."

The Chairman had spoken for less than three minutes; when the Professor, who was sitting facing him at the other end of the hall, thought that he would embark upon his speech proper, he had already sat down.

His lordship the chief delegate of Great Britain spoke at all the greater length. If up to now he had seen himself in the role of the strict judge who reduces the exaggerated demands of the plaintiff to their true, considerably smaller proportions, his closing speech was now more like the plea of a defending counsel, though it was not so much the refugees as the United Kingdom which he felt called upon to defend. Great Britain, he said, had always fulfilled its mandatory obligations to support Jewish immigration into Palestine and to ensure its systematic progress; the number of Jews who had entered Palestine of recent years amounted—"if I am not mistaken"—to forty thousand in all. At the last moment, so to speak, he was also able to give the Conference a piece of good news: the crown colony of Kenya had expressed its willingness to take certain Jews, "of course only a limited number."

This statement, as was only to be expected, was greeted with lively applause. It was all just as jolly as at court singer Terrina's posthumous coffee party, perhaps even jollier, since people really seemed scarcely to remember the funeral; and the delegates would have parted in the best of moods, or at least with a feeling of relief, if the Colombian delegate, to everyone's surprise, had not risen to speak once more. He was sitting directly in front of the Professor, so that his back was turned to him; Heinrich von Benda could not see him, could only hear the warm, friendly voice.

It was by no means the wish or the task of the Republic of Colombia, said the Minister, to disturb the mood of satisfaction that prevailed everywhere on this last day of the historic Évian Conference. Great things had been planned in Évian and important things accomplished. It would, however, be a mistake, indeed one might say a crime, if they were to forget that the human sufferings with which the Conference had been concerned and which it was able to alleviate only to a very slight degree were not the consequences of a natural disaster, that they had been "inflicted upon human beings by human hands." Colombia was an unimportant country by comparison with colonial powers like Britain, France and Holland, nevertheless Colombia could say that in spite of changing regimes Colombia had never put a single political prisoner behind bars throughout this whole century. As the representative of this country, and a man who had been throughout his life concerned with international law, he must point out that the Institute for International Law, which was attached to the League of Nations, during its one and only meeting on the soil of free America, had drawn up a resolution consisting of many paragraphs of which at least two must be quoted and called to mind.

An irritated, angry mood had come over the room. They had eaten and drunk Terrina's coffee and cakes, the singer lay under the soil, the command of her will that they should make merry had been fulfilled—what moved this little man from the distant

River Magdalena to mention the dead, perhaps even to embark
on a tactless graveside speech?

The Colombian put on his glasses and read: "Article One: 'It
is the duty of every state to grant every individual the same
right to life, liberty and property and to guarantee the full and
undivided protection of the law to all who live within its territory, irrespective of sex, race, language and religion.' Article
Five: 'This equality must not be nominal, it must be real. No
discrimination, of either a direct or an indirect nature, will be
tolerated; in particular, no state will be permitted to deprive
any of its citizens of the right to citizenship on the grounds of
race, language or religion.' The civilized states of the world,"
continued the Minister, "Gave their assent to the Declaration
long before the Évian Conference. Colombia attaches importance to the fact"—now he raised his voice—"that the resolutions of the Conference on Refugees supplement these resolutions but in no way cancel them. We must never forget who has
broken the laws of humanity, but the infringements of moral
law that are taking place in many parts of the Old World, are
spreading over the earth and are in the process of rendering this
planet uninhabitable, are no excuse for the rest of the world—
the passive complicity of others does not exonerate evil, but nor
does the activity of evil dispose of complicity. The Christian
religion speaks of forgiving, it says nothing about forgetting,
neither forgetting the evil deed nor the innocent victims. If we
forget a single one who has stretched out his hand to us, we have
been here in vain. Évian," he concluded, "is a good, a hopeful
beginning—the question of where the path we have embarked
upon will lead remains open. At the end of this Conference, as
at the beginning, I salute the greathearted initiative of the President of the United States of America. The problem is vast, it
must be solved. Colombia refuses to believe that two thousand
years of Christian civilization are to end in disaster."

The applause was polite, meager and a little impatient; midday was approaching, the hotel bills had to be paid, the cars
were ready outside, the railways trains and airplanes were waiting, the timetable was threatening.

The French Ambassador now delivered a speech that was

perhaps shorter than he had originally intended; as the representative of the host country and honorary chairman of the Conference he had now—as custom demanded—taken over the chair, which the American Ambassador had vacated with a little smile, a well-concealed little sigh of relief.

The French Republic, he said, would remain true to the historic tradition of help for the persecuted and international brotherhood, but at this hour he did not wish to speak of his own country; it was his welcome duty to thank the representatives of the thirty-two states who were gathered together on French soil. In a language worthy of Corneille and Racine, he praised the American Ambassador, the High Commissioner for Refugees, the Chairman of the Nansen Committee, the chairmen of the subcommittees, the Secretary-General of the Conference and his assistants, above all he praised the press which had performed its difficult task discreetly and with great restraint. *"Messieurs les journalistes, vous êtes les rois de l'opinion: c'est vous qui la faites."* Finally he proposed that a telegram of thanks should be sent to the President of the United States.

The telegram to the White House was approved unanimously, the other addresses of thanks were approved unanimously, the resolutions of the subcommittees were approved unanimously, the resolution of the Conference was approved unanimously. There was no discussion; and what could it have achieved, since the resolutions had long since been most carefully duplicated, since indeed they had long since been neatly stowed away in the diplomats' trunks?

Heinrich von Benda was late in noticing that the participants in the Conference had risen, that they were bidding one another good-bye, surging toward the door. To his left and right the row of chairs was empty; he hadn't noticed that either, because he had been busy polishing his glasses. During the Colombian's speech he had been overcome by tears, since then he had seen everything through a veil that seemed again to be made of tears; and it was little use polishing his glasses, the lenses were perfectly clear. Only now, when he put his glasses on again and picked up his briefcase that he had rested against the leg of his chair, did he become aware that up to the last moment he had hoped, had still hoped during the Frenchman's speech; there was nothing in the world more ridiculous than an optimist.

He rose and felt his way between the empty rows of chairs. The pages in their white leggings were drawing the curtains and a few secretaries were still standing around the conference table gathering up their pages; in the budget of the Conference the expenditure on paper, pencils, mimeographic pads and duplicating ink amounted to 1,500 francs. The doors were reopened; over the green table grains of dust were dancing.

The picture presented by the lobby had changed. It was almost empty, this gilded hall whose architecture and interior decoration had for nine days almost disappeared under masses of people. On both sides of the swing door leading into the semicircular courtyard there were piles of trunks, briefcases, overnight bags; outside the door stood a chatting group of liveried chauffeurs; black-clad receptionists were handing out bills to departing secretaries, and by the elevator waited a beautiful Indian woman who had just arrived with a large retinue.

The Professor also walked toward the elevator, more quickly than was his wont, because he had caught sight of the American Ambassador, who was just shaking hands with some of the South American delegates. The eyes of the two old men met over the heads of the South Americans; the Ambassador quickly, almost rudely, got rid of his colleagues; he did not keep the Professor waiting but came toward him with outstretched hand. He said good-bye to the Professor, wished him a good journey and "all the happiness in the world." He did not repeat the question he had put to him the previous evening.

Heinrich von Benda looked at the case that he had packed in the course of the last hour, with some effort and continually stopping to rest; and now, as he lay down on the bed, having taken off his shoes but otherwise fully dressed, he couldn't help smiling, smiling about himself and his strange character. The case lay open and betrayed the almost pedantic tidiness of the man who had packed the papers, suits, shirts, socks and underclothes in a highly amateurish manner, but with the greatest care, into such a small space. In the General Hospital, whose

most famous department had for almost twenty-five years borne
his name, his colleagues had once poked fun at the young assistant's almost pathological love of order. One grew old but one
did not change, or at most changed in the sense that with age
the raw material of nature became more visible, good and bad
emerged more clearly, every characteristic was intensified, because more strongly marked and a caricature of itself; it also
seemed that the character was indivisible, was not expressed in
this or in that, but in everything, the small as well as the great.
He thought of the meeting that lay ahead of him, that would
take place in two hours, at five in the afternoon, the meeting
with the representative of the Gestapo, Herr Stechlein—Herr
Stechlein, but not the Herr Stechlein he knew; and he was
scarcely surprised anymore to note that he was not afraid of this
meeting, that he faced it without fear and actually without dismay. It might have been his sense of order that had freed him
from fear; his mission was completed, his case packed, and since
there must be order it was doubtless also necessary that he
should meet those who had bestowed his mission on him, represented by the anonymous men with the false names, that, as the
political expression has it, he should return his mandate to
them. Or was it something else? People say the Jews can stand so
much, more than other people, and they don't always say it in
their praise, they often say it disparagingly, as though the Jew
were simply impossible to kill, whereas it is really his duty to
end with rather less resistance—they merely forget that the resistance of other sufferers, men in prison, the victims of an
earthquake, the patients in a hospital, also increases inexpli-
cably, unimaginably and immeasurably as soon as their suffering
is shared with others. But every Jew suffers in the great community of the sick, the imprisoned and the victims. Since he had
become a Jew—for one did not merely suffer as a Jew, one could
also become a Jew through suffering—Heinrich von Benda's destiny had been submerged in the destiny of the Jews. The fine
indifference toward his own fate had been granted him and
with this indifference resistance; a single Gestapo agent could
not strike terror in him.
If something betrayed his state of nervous tension, it was his
wish for a cigarette, that itching in the hand, that dryness in the

mouth, that continuous subconscious preoccupation with the forbidden object.

He stretched out his hand for his wallet which, also in the tidiest manner, he had placed on the bedside table. It was an expensive black crocodile wallet that the patients in a hospital ward had given him for one of his early birthdays; he hoped that none of them now regretted it. He took from the wallet all the bank notes it contained, smoothed them out and began to count them. Since his return from the final session the thought of Bettina had not left him, just as one first begins to look at the photograph or the picture of a person one loves at the moment when one knows that one will soon see him again, will meet him in person. With satisfaction, indeed with a certain pride, he noted how thrifty he had been—not much less than eleven thousand French francs. He had paid down twelve hundred for the green dress, so he needed seven thousand two hundred, and he would still have around three thousand eight hundred left over.

As he smoothed his trousers and put his shoes on again—he had learned to do this slowly and cautiously, since precisely this insignificant movement caused him the greatest difficulty, seemed every time to restrict his heart—his conscience made itself felt and caused him to pause. Selma Selig had spent large sums for Elisabeth's flight and keep, her committee would have to spend more still before the ship left for Palestine, also he could have given what remained to Elisabeth and the children, but he found various excuses—it was extremely difficult to change French francs into Swiss, Fräulein Selig would never have accepted the money, Elisabeth was already provided for, there was still enough left to give the children a few small presents—but the decisive argument was the frivolous thought that he had earned this loan from the Gestapo and by this light-minded purchase he would be cocking a snook at them.

Shortly after four he made his way to the Rue Nationale. As on the first day, when he had gone from his hotel into the town, he heard at his back the footsteps of his American companion, but the sound no longer worried him, partly because he had grown used to it, partly because he was thinking of his rendez-vous with Herr Stechlein and was at bottom very glad that even in the Casino he would evidently be protected from the unknown man. He was all the more dismayed to observe that in a few days, although he had not wished to admit it, his condition had appreciably deteriorated. On the one hand he had for economy's sake not taken a taxi, on the other he regretted having started to walk, because this time the distance seemed twice or three times as great as before; he had to keep stopping for breath, and every time he started off again the rhythm of his heart became more restless, more jumpy, as though his heart were trying to keep in step with him.

The sky, obscuring the sun, hung heavy over the town. A stream of cars was passing down the Rue Nationale in the direction of Geneva, whirling up the dust as they passed. On the corner of the Spa Management Offices the Professor had to stop and wait because ten or twelve truckloads of French soldiers were driving past; the soldiers were wearing winter uniforms and steel helmets from the World War and gazing without interest at the sleepy street. Heinrich von Benda hurried past the Café Muratore because he caught sight of Frau Lederer sitting on the terrace eating an ice, while her son was immersed in a French newspaper.

The dress was no longer in the shop window and the Professor feared that the *couturière* had sold it to a customer for ready cash, on the pretext that the purchaser had not reappeared. This fear proved mistaken and the heavily made-up lady proved herself an excellent judge of character. She had not only saved the dress, she had already wrapped it up, so sure had she been that she "could count on Monsieur." An extremely pretty box was handed over to the Professor. The cardboard bore a picture of old thirteenth-century Évian, capital of the Pays de Gavot, and when he touched the box it gave off the rustle of an extravagant quantity of tissue paper. The Professor regretted that he could not take the box with him, could not hand the dress over to Bettina in this festive and coquettish container. At the same time it occurred to him that he would have to try his skill as a smuggler. Both the export and import of luxury goods were forbidden; there would be nothing for it but to fold the green dress and slip it in between his suits and shirts.

The idea of telling Bettina about his smuggling exploit filled

him with a certain gaiety, all the more so as he remembered
their brief trips abroad, which had always given rise to comical
difficulties. Like most women, Bettina regarded the customs as a
ludicrous and irritating institution which must at all costs be
dodged, to deceive which was a thoroughly legitimate female
privilege. Although the parcel was light he held it cautiously in
his right hand, because he had found that every burden placed
on the left side of his body had an unfavorable effect; but he
swung the parcel joyfully in his right hand, almost like a schoolboy swinging his satchel, proud of his possession and probably
also of the recklessness by which he had let himself be carried
away. Only as he crossed the Rue Nationale in the opposite
direction and came to the Quai did it dawn on him that he
would undoubtedly be refused entry to the Casino carrying a
parcel, since casinos rightly fear that gamblers, anticipating
anger at their losses, might bring a bomb or a bundle of high
explosives in with them.

In fact as soon as he had entered the Casino he was invited by
a gold-braided commissionaire to leave the suspicious object in
the cloakroom, in which apart from the parcel there were only
two umbrellas and a sleeping poodle. After he had shown his
passport and convinced the receptionist that the visitor had
never been inside the Évian Casino before and hence could not
be subject to any prohibition to re-enter it, he was handed his
entry card and went into the main hall, clearly the one described to him by Herr Megelein.

Contrary to what the empty cloakroom had led him to expect
—but after all, it was summer—the room, even now in the afternoon, though not exactly packed was astoundingly busy. Play
was going on at two tables, silently and with a minute attention
such as is only seen in casinos during the afternoon, when they
are not occupied by the smart world eager to see and be seen,
but rather by the world of genuine gamblers out to win money
and exercising the most intense concentration. Most of the gamblers were immersed in their cards, in diagrams of the gaming
table and the wheel of chance which they supposed would disclose their chance of winning; a few poorly dressed elderly ladies reached with pointed, hesitant fingers for their modest sup-

plies of counters; the croupiers announced in bored voices and as though absentmindedly their "Rien ne va plus," but just because the crowd intent on the game was not dense the Professor immediately spotted two or three delegates whom a few hours ago he had seen in the conference hall of the Hôtel Royal. This brought his thoughts back to himself, to the curious and dubious role he was playing here. He walked toward the mirror with downcast eyes, like the child who believes that if he does not look he cannot be seen. What would people think of the delegate of the Austrian Jews if they discovered him in this superficial environment so soon after the Conference had come to an end? There was as yet no one sitting on the silk-upholstered bench under the mirror, and he dropped onto it with a feeling of relief, as though he had come into a safe harbor. None of the gamblers, their eyes riveted to the white ball, seemed to pay any attention to him, even to have noticed him.

Only when he had sat like this for a considerable time, for the first time fully aware of the disturbing proximity of the site of the Conference to the Casino and also foreseeing that life, or what was called life, would pass on over the refugee conference, that the gilded and melancholy brothel of the gambling passion would weather this period just as it had since human memory triumphed over reason, always looking as though it belonged to the day before yesterday but always attracting new generations— only then did he notice the young American, his shadow and guardian angel, who had taken up a position nearby, with his back to him, behind a player seated at the roulette table. Immediately afterward he caught sight of a man who had appeared in the doorway, looked around in search of something and then came toward him.

He was Herr Stechlein, said the stranger, sitting down beside the Professor—a coarse-looking man of about forty, immediately recognizable as a German by his almost clean-shaven head with the short tufts of hair over his forehead, a true caricature of a Gestapo agent and as such grotesquely misleading.

"I have only one thing to tell you," Herr Stechlein, the second Herr Stechlein, declared in an undertone without looking at the Professor, "but I am giving you a serious warning. Don't make light of it, don't disregard it. You will return to Vienna tomorrow. Any attempt at flight will be immediately and ruthlessly punished."

Heinrich von Benda was seized with a desire to laugh, to laugh in the agent's face. He had contemplated every possibility except this; it had not crossed his mind that the agent's purpose could be so primitive, the warning so innocuous, the threat so superfluous. So the omniscient secret police of the German Reich were so ill-informed that they imagined that now his mission had failed he would seek safety in flight or emigration, would utilize the offers from abroad—if the Gestapo knew of these at all—and leave his wife and his child in the hands of the executioners. At the same time as the desire to laugh he was also seized by the childish and fruitless, but irresistible desire to irritate and mislead the second Herr Stechlein and to watch his reactions.

"I shall not return tomorrow," he said, without explaining further.

"You will," retorted the agent, staring in front of him.

"No, not until the day after tomorrow," said the Professor. "I still have a few things to do in Geneva. There is a concert in Geneva I intend to go to."

Now Herr Stechlein involuntarily turned to him, and his expression betrayed that he didn't know what to say next, for his instructions had been tomorrow, not the day after tomorrow; he did not possess the authority or the flexibility to negotiate over this twenty-four-hour stay of execution. He did not reply, but turning away from the Professor again began to drone the words that had obviously been dinned into him in Geneva. They possessed precise information regarding the Professor's intended flight, he declared threateningly and as though boasting of his knowledge; they were aware that he had utilized his stay abroad to bring his daughter, a notorious currency smuggler, to Switzerland, that he had also made arrangements for the flight of his wife and child, that he had got his son to obtain a French residence permit for him, and finally his contact with Professor Vuillemin was no secret to them. Under no circumstances would the Reich Government accept any, obviously fake, medical certificate; they would reject it out of hand as a mere excuse. Here at last Herr Stechlein found the link with the Professor's declaration; the joyful recognition that he had seen through the other showed all over his face. "That's what you have to do in Geneva," he said. "But don't delude yourself, we know everything."

"You don't know everything," retorted the Professor. "I am going to Geneva today, where, for your information, I shall be staying at the Hôtel de l'Écu, at the cost of the Gestapo, incidentally, as I was promised; tomorrow evening you will be able to see me in the Grand-Théâtre, and on Sunday I shall set out for home."

With these words he rose and made his way to the door, without any leavetaking. He admitted to himself that he had behaved like a reckless schoolboy who sticks out his tongue, but the temptation to act for the last time as a free man—as recklessly and senselessly, as thoughtless of the consequences, as free men always act when it pleases them—the temptation had been too great, he had not wanted to resist it.

He collected his parcel, ran his hand tenderly over thirteenth-century Évian, forgot to take his change, and immediately afterward was standing at the foot of the broad steps outside. He felt a stabbing pain in his heart and his arms grew heavy—the right arm holding the parcel also seemed to be pulling him down—so that he decided to avoid any further strain and call a taxi. Several cabs drove past, but they were all occupied. He was wondering whether to return to the Casino café and wait there, or to risk the journey on foot after all, when he heard a voice beside him.

"Wait here, Professor," said Mr. Nelson, the American secret service man. "I'll get you a taxi."

The Homecoming from Évian

*Thou in thy mercy hast led forth the people
which thou hast redeemed: thou hast guided
them in thy strength unto thy holy habitation.*

EXODUS XV, 13

V

THE Professor had asked the porter of the Hôtel de l'Écu to send all the major newspapers up to his room in the morning, and now there were more of them than he wanted to see or read. A mountain of English, American, Swiss, French and German papers were heaped up on his breakfast table.

He started with the German papers, as was only right for a brave man who wanted to get the worst over first. The report given by the *Völkischer Beobachter* under the heading ÉVIAN JEW CONFERENCE DISCREDITS THE INTERNATIONAL HYPOCRITES occupied four whole columns in a prominent position. It was subtitled: THE TOTAL RESULT: A COMMITTEE. The "VB's Own Report" began with the words: "It is perhaps merely a coincidence that the Évian emigrant Conference, at which the Jewish element was by far the most strongly represented and the one which received the greatest consideration, terminated today in good time for the Sabbath rest. It was, however, not a purely Jewish conference," the report continued, "but a conference of governments who wished to clarify the problem of what to do with the Jews who had emigrated from Germany. That the Catholic Church was represented at the Conference by a cleric named Father Odo, who enthusiastically supplied information to the international press working against the German Reich, was manifestly only an incidental fact that made no difference to the true character of the Conference." The reporter then expressed his satisfaction at the "failure of the Jew Conference." "The majority of the government representatives, it must be said to their credit, adopted a negative attitude to these goings-on and were careful, in their own utterances, to avoid all polemics against Germany as the country of origin of the majority of Jewish emigrants."

A leading article in the *Völkischer Beobachter* exhibited no less satisfaction. The whole thing, it said, "was a complete debacle," as might have been expected from the outset. Instead of taking in the Jews, the governments "took steps to protect themselves against an influx of Jewish immigrants, because they clearly saw the disadvantages of Judaization. . . . There remained one possibility: the Soviet Union. But this Jew-run state did not even take part in the Évian Conference. Why did not Lazarus Kaganovich send Litvinov-Finkelstein to Lake Geneva? . . . In Finland too the question is regarded in exactly the same way. Thus 54 Jews who recently tried to immigrate into Finland from the Reich were allowed to land in Helsinki only after great precautions had been taken."

The Professor laid aside the swastika-decorated *Tageszeitung* from Nuremberg, which, heaven knows why, was sold in Geneva, after reading the headline BREAKDOWN OF THE JEW CONFERENCE and the first sentence printed in heavy type: "The Jewish delegations left the French tourist center on Lake Geneva cursing savagely." On the other hand his eye was caught by a lengthy leading article in the *Münchner Neueste Nachrichten* that was headed BALANCE SHEET OF THE CONFERENCE and ended with the sentences: "Germany was naturally not represented at this curious conference. Nor are we concerned about the resolutions that were passed at it, because in our country the Jewish problem is being systematically attacked and will be solved step by step." The words "will be solved" were printed in italics—a statement of incontrovertible fact and an unconcealed threat. The article ended: "If they care so much about the Jews in Germany, they can have them. We shall be glad to get rid of them and won't even ask anything in return."

No foreign newspaper seemed to contradict the German reports in any essential respect. Certainly, the tone of these reports was different, as though from another world, dignified, regretful, compassionate. They sought their own and other countries' guilt. The London *Daily Herald* spoke out vehemently: "Responsibility has been evaded and placed on London"; *The New York Times* lamented: "If thirty-two nations

that call themselves democracies cannot agree on a plan to save
a few hundred thousand refugees, then there is no hope left that
they will ever succeed in reaching agreement over anything,"
but as to the failure of Évian, the "great flop," the "disaster for
the hypocrites," the "total debacle," as the German press called
it, the newspapers from Paris to London, from Geneva to New
York, were in complete agreement with the press of the German
Reich—and this was what most depressed Heinrich von Benda.
This time the German papers did not need to lie, could invoke
the testimony of foreign countries, only needed to provide a
malicious commentary on it.

The Professor spent most of the morning, midday and the
early afternoon with Elisabeth and the children—an unadulter-
ated joy for Marianne and her sisters, with whom the Professor
went for a walk in the Parc Alfred Bertrand and actually ven-
tured into the magic world of the big store in the Rue du
Rhône. He could not see any improvement whatever in Elisabeth's condition, but Professor Vuillemin, to whom he spoke on
the telephone and confessed his intention of returning home,
counseled confidence, calm and patience. In one single, entirely
selfish respect, he was relieved that Elisabeth was not quite herself; otherwise he could not have explained her apparent lack of
concern over his imminent return to Germany, from which she
herself had escaped under such difficult circumstances. The
nervous crisis of which Dr. Vuillemin had spoken—an expression, incidentally, which the surgeon and kidney specialist
Heinrich von Benda regarded with skepticism, because everything to do with the nerves, at least in the psychological sense,
reminded him of the mutually canceling positive and negative
effects of electricity, which we can observe, register, even put to
use, without knowing what matter, what energies we are really
dealing with—Elisabeth's nervous crisis did not express itself
eruptively, but in a total withdrawal, a total encapsulation, or
one might even call it a self-centeredness, from which her children were excepted.

Although the hours were precious, were growing ever more
precious, he returned after lunch—which the family had taken
with Fräulein Selig in the Bavaria, that widely famed restaurant
where framed drawings of all the great figures of the League of

Nations hung in rows on the walls—to his hotel, for he had been overcome by the weariness that announced an imminent attack. He tried to tell himself that the weather was to blame for the heaviness in his left arm, the burdensome and unremitting pressure on his chest; in the early morning a thunderstorm had descended upon the lake, but the sky had not cleared afterward, and a warm, continuous, resigned rain had been falling ever since. He lay down on the bed, but without undressing, for just as during the Conference he had always been afraid of missing something, he now feared to meet pain in an unarmed state; he felt his clothes to be a coat of armor in which he was ready to meet the attacker. This behavior was all the more foolish because lying in bed he could perfectly well call for help, while everything he wore—trousers, shirt, tie and shoes—constricted him; the armor protected him less than it weighed upon him. On the other hand his life instinct, the mechanism of self-defense and self-preservation, seemed to be functioning astoundingly well. He was actually able to avoid thinking about his return to Vienna, about the account that would be demanded of him there, about the consequences of the failure of his mission and of his behavior. He thought only of seeing Bettina again, of the first kiss, the first hours; thought of the morning, when Heinrich would creep into his bed and lie between him and Bettina.

He still felt unwell, though somewhat rested, as he changed his clothes, because Fräulein Selig had promised to call for him and take him and Elisabeth to the Grand-Théâtre by car.

The theatre, situated not far from the hotel in the beautiful Place Neuve, where the new town with its lively, metropolitan air passes over imperceptibly into the almost perfectly preserved old town, was festively illuminated; the elegant arc lights were mirrored on the wet asphalt, and the elaborately dressed audience crowding into the hall with its rich stucco decorations betrayed nothing of the concert's purpose, a benefit for those unfortunates that one newspaper had characterized that morning as "people who could not remain in certain countries and could not enter others." The poster disclosed that it was a "charity concert"—an expression by which the Professor had always been strangely moved, since on such occasions the charitable are meant to forget why they have come and the recipients of charity have neither the money nor the opportunity to take part in the festivities. As the Professor sat down in the first and best box between Elisabeth and the little Fräulein, he could not help thinking of the oddness of his own role: today he was still a promoter, a subject, a kind of poster for charity, of which tomorrow he might be the object and beneficiary.

A famous emigrant had placed himself at the service of the Geneva Symphony Orchestra for the concert, a conductor of worldwide reputation whose name was taboo in Germany because he, a German even according to Hitler and his absurd laws, had left his homeland "without reason," as they said—in reality he had had very good reason to abandon his nation which in his name too, but without his permission or consent, was behaving so shamefully.

It went almost without saying that on this evening Beethoven's Ninth Symphony in D Minor, Opus 125, was to be played; never, at any other time, had so many appeals been made to the testimony, precisely this testimony, of the man who had proclaimed, with a power unequaled before or ever to be equaled again, the victory of light over darkness. It was a hundred and fourteen years since Ludwig van Beethoven, after nine years of work, had finished his symphonic monument to joy in life. One had to sail back a hundred and fourteen years in the ship of time to find the hope that triumphed in the fortissimo outburst of the fourth movement—yes, triumphed, because Beethoven's Ninth did not sing the song of chance happiness, of joy bestowed as a gift, of inborn love, but of the liberation from coercion, the mastery of relapse, of peace achieved through effort.

The old man in the box at the Grand-Théâtre believed that he could remember all the performances of the Ninth Symphony that he had ever heard: in his youth, in the pit of the Vienna Konzerthaus, later with his first wife, Elisabeth's mother, then during the thirteen years of his widowhood, finally two or three years ago with Bettina. He remembered the conductors—the great Italian who now, as a protest against the regime in his country, had emigrated to America, the Jew who had left Germany just in time, the other conductor who had

made his wretched peace with the monster—and his heart beat
with gratitude toward the fair-haired sturdy man who was today
conducting the orchestra; one day perhaps they would thank
those who had carried their homeland away with them on the
soles of their shoes. One day . . . In this music, in this *allegro
un poco maestoso* of the first movement, one could already feel
"the great hand" of which Moses had spoken, "which the Lord
showed upon the Egyptians." The old man in the box of the
Grand-Théâtre wanted to surrender himself to artistic enjoyment, but had he any right to such enjoyment, could he think
for even an instant of anything else than what had been domi-
nating him for months? Could he see, hear, experience anything
in a different context, and was what the majority of the audience were taking as artistic enjoyment intended as artistic enjoyment at all, was it not rather—yes, was it not the blood bank
prepared for the coming, imminent, inevitable bloodshed? A
long path, lost laurels, the walking behind one's own coffin,
one's own guilt, collapse into chaos, the apostle's betrayal and
punishment, Golgotha and Mount Calvary, the struggle of love
with hate—anyone who wished to hear could hear in the simple
tunes of the oboes the joyful melody which later would swell to
a positive transport of happiness, to the ecstatic jubilation of the
just victory.

The old man in the box of the Grand-Théâtre looked across
the hall, every seat of which was occupied. He could clearly see
certain individual faces: an old lady with a velvet band around
her throat, a young man with his mother, three delicate girls
with their father, a student listening with closed eyes, a couple
holding hands. It seemed to him a banal thought that they had
all paid for their tickets—not merely for pure artistic enjoyment,
but also in order to help the cause which the little Fräulein here
on his right bravely and resolutely stood for. But then it did not
seem so banal, for what was money, and was it bad in itself, and
what was bad in itself, and what was more capable of transformation than this human invention, and could not the thirty-
two nations who had been meeting a few miles from here, on
this same lake, have elevated the bad into the good, have transformed naked currency into the golden anchor?

He shifted his chair back a little and saw the little face that

was transfigured into an obstinate beauty, the face of the brave
Fräulein, and saw the noble, pale profile of his daughter, which
showed no trace of emotion. Elisabeth was wearing a black velvet dress done up to the chin which Fräulein Selig had hired for
her and which had been hurriedly altered to fit her that afternoon; the Professor thought that no other dress had suited her
better. Of the storms that had raged in her there was no sign;
her sick soul was resting like a dead sea. Too much had happened to her; nothing more could happen to her. He knew that
he would not see her again, but his sorrow was drowned in the
music, not because the melodies now demanded his whole ad-
miring attention—he listened, heard the recitative of the basses
and the pianissimo of the violins, but the music did not banish
his thoughts, rather it brought them turbulently to the surface—
his sorrow was drowned in the perfection because it was perfect, the expression of human potentialities and the certainty
that, although it did not by any means look like it, God really
had created man in his own image. In the turbulence of the
thoughts that came rushing in upon him, the human beings
who had stretched out their hands to him and whose hands he
had grasped passed in review—an operation by the early light of
dawn, a child on the operating table, a young assistant's mistake
prevented just in time, war wounded, an old monarch, an urgent journey through the snow, the sick orderly, the assaulted
lawyer, his own daughter—and although he was going from defeat to defeat, an unfamiliar feeling of satisfaction with what
had been achieved came over him, with that which was incomplete yet slowly coming to a conclusion.

Now the soloists had stepped forward and at the rear of the
stage the male and female choristers, who had been waiting in
reserve, clad in black and white, like confident angels, also came
to life. The language of music had not been sufficient for the
composer, the song of joy had to be proclaimed by human
voices: *"Auf des Glaubens Sonnenberge / Sieht man ihre
Fahnen weh'n, / Durch den Riss gesprengter Särge / Sie im
Chor der Engel steh'n."* Had the poet really written this two
hundred and fifty years ago, the composer set it to music over a
hundred years ago? *"Festen Mut in schwerem Leiden, / Hilfe,
wo die Unschuld weint, / Ewigkeit geschwor'nen Eiden, /*

Wahrheit gegen Freund und Feind, / Männerstolz vor Königs-
thronen,— / Brüder gält' es Gut und Blut— / Dem Verdienste
seine Kronen, / Untergang der Lügenbrut!"

An almost solemn stillness reigned after singers and orchestra
had fallen silent, and the applause first broke out when the
conductor, who had quickly left the stage, reappeared. This
applause, however, had the character of a demonstration, which
visibly confused the famous refugee; quickly recovering himself,
he turned to the box into the background of which the Professor had withdrawn, so that it was impossible to say with certainty whether he wished to pass on the harvest of applause to
the great surgeon or the little Fräulein.

Fräulein Selig had planned a simple supper in a nearby restaurant to follow the concert, at which both the Professor and
the conductor were to be present. Heinrich von Benda asked
the Fräulein to convey to the conductor his admiration and
gratitude, but he dared not spend the rest of the evening in
company. The Fräulein and Elisabeth brought him to his hotel.
Quickly he embraced his daughter, quickly he thanked the little
Fräulein, who insisted on sending a car to take him to Basel
next morning.

When the two women had gone, he decided, because of his no
longer new but ever renewed fear of the confinement and lone-
liness of his room, to spend a little while longer in the hotel
lobby. The lobby too was empty. He mastered his desire for a
cigarette, sat down by the window and looked out at the wet
quay along which the cars were peacefully gliding, as they had
glided yesterday and would glide tomorrow.

The departure from Évian-les-Bains, the day and a half in Geneva, had still been part of the mission which Professor Heinrich von Benda had received on that memorable June night
from the hand of the man of glass in the Vienna Hofburg; but
now, as he entered the car to set out on the journey home, the
magic strength derived from the duty he had assumed forsook
him. A feeling of emptiness had taken possession of him as soon
as he left the beautiful town, once more sunny this morning—or
rather a feeling of hollowness, since the emptiness was accompanied by a sense that something was missing which till now he

had possessed, and at the same time that which was missing was also present. He resembled the man who had undergone an amputation and still feels pain in the severed limb. With every mile the car left behind it, the Professor came closer and closer to himself, and the closer he came to himself the closer came fear, the more conscious he became that only his mission had stood between him and his fear. His orderly mind tried to break down his fear into its component parts in the hope that, like the works of a clock when they have been taken apart, it would cease to tick and to strike. There was the fear of going back into prison, which was already opening up on the other side of the Swiss railway station of the city of Basel and, like a Chinese box, seemed to consist of many larger and smaller prisons fitting one into the other. There was the fear of having to meet the prison warders who likewise, large or small, were basically alike, but also the fear of looking into the eyes of those who had remained behind, Silberstein and Schönglas and the nameless Jews to whom he had promised help. There was the fear of the house in which, although Bettina and Heinrich were waiting for him, he was awaited also—and at best—by silence, by hopeless passivity, inactivity and uselessness, superfluousness and hence old age. There was the fear of illness, of an illness that might paralyze him, might reduce him to a cripple. And there was the fear of death, which was in turn broken down into several fears, into the fear that death might come upon him at the wrong time and in the wrong place—as though there was ever a right time and a right place for death—into the fear that it would be an ugly and unworthy death, into the fear that before he died he would learn finally and unmistakably how useless his efforts had been and how useless the crafty game he had played with death. Worst of all, however, was the fact that he did not succeed in silencing his fears by dissecting them, but rather that, like the nine-headed hydra, two new heads grew for every one cut off; that he did not succeed in getting down to the stumps of the heads and, like Hercules, burning them out.

The farther the fast car went from Lake Geneva, the more the fears agglomerated into one single all-powerful fear, the fear that he would not reach his starting point, would not be able to get back to Vienna. At the same time, however, everything he

feared most seemed an indispensable necessity: the meeting
with the warders, the meeting with the betrayed, the meeting
with his own old age. The feeling of annihilation, which was
supposed to be symptomatic of his illness but which he had not
perceived and diagnosed during any of his attacks, now appeared, curiously enough without his feeling any pain—rather
he could say with certainty that the pain appeared only in the
wake of the feeling of annihilation. He asked the driver to stop
at the next village and the first inn he saw. While the unsuspecting driver swallowed a cooling beer, he asked for water, hurriedly swallowed two nitroglycerin tablets and sat down for a
short rest at a table by the window.

They had stopped at a charming little village in the vineyard
district of Neuchâtel. The village spring was splashing in the
midday heat. They could hear the cautious footsteps of the peasants on the cobblestones; the shutters of the little shops, which
looked as though they had been put there for the future production of some comic opera, had been lowered; ladies in their
Sunday best were coming from church; there was a smell of hay
and fertilizer; the flies sat lethargically on the windowpanes as
though sure no one would harm them. The Professor could
measure how homeless he had become by his almost irresistible
longing to stay in the village, of which he didn't even know the
name, to remain and settle there; only the homeless make a
home of every alien spot.

On their way to the parked car, he asked the driver how many
miles separated them from Basel, and when the driver told him
the number he was again assailed by a many-headed fear—fear of
the distance, of the trials he would have to endure in order to
get there, of the constricted space and suffocating air in the
closed car, but also fear of the speed. In two or at most two and
a half hours they would reach the frontier town, where the
prison train was waiting. Thus on the one hand he wanted to
speed up the car, on the other to delay the journey, but he gave
expression to neither, not only because his tongue had grown
heavy but also because saliva kept gathering in his mouth con-
stantly, preventing him from speaking. As far as the nameless
village he had sat next to the driver, but now he quickly made
an excuse to change his seat and move to the back of the limou-

sine; here he could stretch out his legs more comfortably, till he was almost lying down, with his head resting on the upholstered back of the seat. He very soon had to abandon this attempt to relax, however, because when he leaned back his head began to spin, the roof of the car seemed to descend upon him and the sound of the engine, in reality a steady low hum, grew into an unbearably loud whirring and hammering.

The midday heat had not yet abated when they reached the main railway station of Basel. If the Professor had been looking just then for a good omen—and it would not have been surprising if he had, for misery breeds superstition—he could have found no better omen than now appeared to him in the shape of the American agent James K. Nelson. He had been fearing— one fear among many—the hour he would have to spend alone on the station. The prospect of seeing a familiar face had been almost hopeless, but there stood the young American outside the station building, and his first gesture revealed that he had no intention this time of playing the part of a shadow. With a firm hand he took the Professor's case and overnight bag, waited, almost like a professional porter, till the Professor had pressed a tip into the driver's hand, then led the way into the station. Immediately the Professor's mood changed into the optimism natural to him. For a moment he imagined that Mr. Nelson was going to accompany him to Vienna, to protect him, in some inexplicable, mysterious way to stand by him and Bettina and Heinrich.

This illusion, of course, melted away as quickly as it had appeared. "I'm to make sure you really do board the Vienna express, Professor," said James K. Nelson. "An utterly stupid thing to have to do, but my instructions are to keep you under surveillance till the very last moment of your mission, and I thought I might at least lend you a hand. Incidentally, the train will be leaving forty-five minutes late."

They went to the station restaurant. The Professor asked Nelson to hand in a telegram to Bettina, which he had written out on a form obtained from the hotel. Nelson took the slip of paper but remained seated.

"Won't you think it over, Professor?" he said, looking around with professional caution. He winked his left eye slightly, which gave his in any case boyish face a touch of the urchin. "I could arrange a little accident that would prevent you from boarding the train."

"I have no choice, my dear friend."

"I think it would be possible to get Frau von Benda and your son . . ."

"Two of my friends are hostages in the hands of the Germans. Their names are Silberstein and Dr. Schönglas." He thought for a moment. "But if one day there should be a chance of getting all three of us . . ."

"I shall pass on your wish." He rose to send the telegram.

While the motherly Swiss waitress brought the tea, the Professor continually watched the door through which James Nelson had vanished. The agent's presence had reassured him; now that the young man had gone he was gripped by fear again, but this time it had one single, clearly defined face. In ninety minutes the train would move off, in three and a half hours he himself would change into the sleeping car; he would not be in Vienna until tomorrow. The hours that lay ahead of him seemed to him endless, the distance seemed to him endless, and as he pictured the distance his longing for Bettina grew endless. Nothing that awaited him in Vienna now filled him with terror; he did not think of anything that might happen to him, he thought only of Bettina's arms that would be placed round his neck, thought of the lost security that she would restore to him. For a few hours he had felt no pain—in the past he had measured the pain-free periods in weeks, then in days, now he measured them in hours—but his left arm had gone to sleep, had grown as devoid of feeling and numb as if it hung dead from his shoulder, and all over his body he felt under his skin a prickling sensation like thousands of ants, as though the ants were moving under a blanket, suppressed but present. With his right hand he touched the box of nitroglycerin tablets which for safety's sake he carried in his right pocket, from which he could most easily take it out, but he knew that for several hours he must take no more tablets, least of all now when he needed a clear head. He remembered his childhood promises, those deals with the invisible, remembered the bargains he had offered the Almighty in desperate predicaments, in secret but aware that he would not keep to them; he was tempted to make the Almighty a promise, so that he would bring him safe and sound over the frontier and home to Bettina, but he couldn't think of anything he could sacrifice, anything he could renounce, anything he could pledge.

Nelson came back and sat down at the table without a word. He refused the money which the Professor offered him; the telegram, he said with a bitter smile, would be sent "at the expense of the U. S. Government." The Professor wanted to give him a present too, so he said, "You can report to your superiors that you have found out details of my conversation with the Gestapo. The man who met me in the Casino, who called himself Stechlein, came to drop threatening hints as to what would happen if I refused to return to Germany."

"I hope that's not why you're going back?" replied Nelson. "The power of the secret services cancels each other out; they're completely worthless."

"No," said the Professor. "It's because of the Jews. If I can't help them, at least I don't want to harm them."

"Do you know that the London *Daily Express* contains a report on your mission today?"

"On my real mission?"

"It hints at it. Under the heading 'The Duke's specialist pleads for the Jews. Nazis watch him.' Incidentally your watch dog has left you. At least I haven't seen him anymore."

"They trust me. What do the papers write about the Conference?"

"Nothing. The President has issued an appeal for general disarmament."

The Professor paid, and they went out onto the platform, which was black with people. Nelson asked whether he could get the Professor something—newspapers, books, sandwiches. The Professor declined with thanks; he wanted to try to rest, moreover he had been told there was a dining car. Nelson wouldn't even let him carry his light overnight bag. "No," he said, "let me do something useful for a change."

The train was standing in the Swiss station; nobody knew why it was leaving late. Nelson climbed in and stowed the Professor's luggage in the luggage rack above one of the two

window seats. The Professor thought that he was lucky; after all
he had a guardian angel who watched over him, even if this
guardian angel was a secret agent, and in Vienna Bettina would
be waiting for him on the platform.

Nelson had lowered the window because it was hot and stuffy
in the compartment. There was no one else in it yet. The
Professor stood at the window. On the platform, besides Swiss
officials and frontier police, there were also French frontier
guards, and he also saw uniformed German railway officials
walking along the train tapping the flanges, brake blocks and
axle bearings with great thoroughness; they didn't seem to trust
the Swiss railways. The Professor leaned out of the window and
told the agent he could go home if he wanted to. Nelson shook
his head. He was going to wait until the train left. Perhaps he
thought the Professor might still change his mind.

Two passengers had taken seats in the Professor's compartment.
One, to judge by his speech, must have been a North German,
from Hamburg or Bremen perhaps, a slim shaven-headed man
with angular movements, probably an officer from the World
War; he held his briefcase under his arm like a saber. After
turning to the financial page of the *Deutsche Allgemeine* he
tried to immerse himself in it, but was prevented from doing so
by the other passenger, who seemed to be in a thoroughly good
humor and ready for lighthearted conversation. The first few
sentences uttered by this traveler were enough to disclose that
he was a wit such as, oddly enough, one meets more frequently
on trains than elsewhere—a big, fat man from Bavaria, director
of a mustard factory, as he announced unasked, who had been
traveling on business and was now glad to be going home; he
passed a number of humorous comments on the shortcomings
of foreign countries.

The train started off, the blond head of James K. Nelson,
from Washington, D. C., disappeared. "By all means leave the
window open," said the ex-officer in a friendly tone to the
Professor. "It's suffocating in here."

The Professor sat down. In a few minutes his two traveling
companions would learn that he was a Jew, then the relaxed
atmosphere would probably change and give way to tension, a

circle of embarrassment or hostility would form around him; but Heinrich von Benda consoled himself with the thought that it would only be for a few hours, then he would change to the sleeping car. Nevertheless he almost felt something like nostalgia for Évian, the distant spa that had now returned to the summer, where although he had been staying there was a representative of the Jews, no one had looked at him askance, except other Jews; for a lifetime nobody had looked at him askance, now he would have to get used to it. Perhaps he should have told the two gentlemen that he was a Jew; they might feel resentful toward him because of their failure to recognize him as such. In fact neither of them seemed to be aware of the invisible yellow star, because the wit, having been patronized, almost snubbed, by the ex-officer, turned to the Professor. "But you're not English; I just thought because you were speaking English with the gentleman." In order to give some sort of answer, the Professor said that his companion had been American; as he spoke, he regretted not having bought a newspaper in which he could now have immersed himself and so avoided a conversation. For his part the mustard manufacturer revealed himself an acute philologist; he had guessed at once that the Professor was a Viennese—oh well, north of Frankfurt am Main they confused Viennese with Bavarian, but that couldn't happen to Viennese and Bavarians themselves; they could tell at once whether someone had been born on the Isar or on the "beautiful blue Danube." "By the way, do you know the story of the Berliner who came to Vienna . . . ?"

The train, which was moving only slowly and as though hesitantly, was still on Swiss soil, the Rhine had not yet been crossed, the Baden station, only a few yards away, had not yet been reached; in fact they had just rattled across the Rhine bridge—the mustard manufacturer had disclosed the point of his story, in which the loudmouthed Berliner had come off pretty badly, had meanwhile also taken out of his waistcoat pocket a round Party badge and fixed it in his buttonhole—when the train stopped with a violent jerk as if it had changed its mind. Reversing at an astonishing speed, it steamed off back to the Swiss station. The man with the shaven head looked over

his glasses out of the window and assured the Professor that
they would not change direction, this was just a bit of that
irritating shunting to and fro which one always had to put up
with in this "damn station."

The ex-officer could have no idea that the train's perfectly
natural and evidently foreseen maneuver had almost the effect
of a shock on the Professor; he was tempted to see in this rapid
reverse, this return to the Swiss station, an omen, a warning,
writing on the wall, a sign from fate. Perhaps it was not too
late, perhaps he ought to get out, leave the station, seek salvation and asylum on the soil of free Switzerland. The train
stopped just short of the station, half of it still on the open
track, but the town was once more visible from the window,
particularly a building doubtless put up at the turn of the
century, whose mighty architecture, meant for eternity, seemed
to symbolize the self-confident certainty of the Helvetian Confederation. The mustard manufacturer looked down over his
double chin at his Party badge, as though wondering if he had
not decorated himself prematurely and should make this em-
blem of his allegiance, which was still not exactly popular
abroad, vanish into his waistcoat pocket again, but he decided
against this ignominious retreat and instead opened the *Völkischer Beobachter* with a vigor that made the paper fairly
rustle.

The Professor leaned his head back against the upholstery
behind him, because the brief, jerky movements of the carriage
had given him a feeling of nausea that had occurred before
following an attack, but never with such overwhelming sud-
denness, never with such vehemence. The train traveled a few
yards forward, then backward again, then forward again, and
Heinrich von Benda felt himself more and more transported
back into his childhood nightmare . . . while he was living in
the chemist's house, when he was ill and feverish, an invisible
figure had come up behind his bed, had stood behind him, had
shaken the bars of his bed. It had been an invisible figure, but
one he could imagine; the child had pictured him very clearly,
and the old man could still remember what this creature of his
imagination looked like: a head that consisted only of forehead
and chin, the long, smooth forehead continued into the long

smooth chin, a horrible mask of a face without eyes, nose or mouth, yet with large projecting ears. The invisible figure made up of forehead, chin and ears was now sitting at the back of the train and on the locomotive in front; he was pushing the carriages first forward, then backward.

The Professor straightened up, turned around, looked out. He secretly hoped to catch another glimpse of James K. Nelson, but the American had long since left; the whole station, which he could see quite clearly in the distance, had emptied; obviously nobody had foreseen that the train would approach it again. It was at this moment that an idea, like an obsession, insinuated itself into the Professor's brain: the train had returned for good, by chance or through a concatenation of circumstances over which he, Professor von Benda, had no control, or because a higher power so willed it, was not going to leave; he would not see Bettina and Heinrich, would not be able to save Silberstein and Schönglas and the forty thousand Jews. Save? The more the obsession took possession of him, the clearer it became to him that he had been mistaken, had intentionally deceived himself when he thought that he had finished his mission in Geneva or Évian; it was not finished until he was back, and it might be that it was just beginning at this moment. Moses had gone out with the Jews and had camped with them at Pi-hahiroth, between Migdol and the sea, over against Baal-zephon; he had not gone without them, had not passed without them into a foreign country, had not been separated from them by the Red Sea, but had gone down into the Red Sea before them, and before his eyes, not behind his back, the bitter water had parted.

The train was shunted to and fro, backward and forward, from one line to another; at every change of track the carriages were shaken up. For the first time the Professor lost his self-control; as though in despair he muttered to himself, "Is this train never going?" Astonished by such impatience on the part of the old gentleman, the two others looked at him, and the mustard manufacturer said reassuringly, "Don't worry, the damned rattletrap will go eventually." The Professor smiled apologetically, wishing his nervous outburst had never happened, but he would really have liked to jump out, to leave the train, walk along the line to the German frontier station and hurry through this into the country itself. Pain constricted his heart, his heart was a tiny object that vanished into pain like a wretched little coin in the fist of an evil sorcerer; he wondered whether to make his way to the dining car and take another tablet after all, just one that would give him some relief. Panic, born of the fear that he would die before they had crossed the frontier, made him forget his pain for an instant. He must not move, must hide from his heart and from death; he must not die before they had crossed the frontier; if he died before, they would arrest Bettina and take Heinrich away and torture Schönglas and Silberstein and kill the forty thousand; the fate of the Jews was not yet sealed, it depended upon whether he returned, completed his mission or reported its failure; he refused to admit that the idea of flight had ever occurred to him, no thought was further from his mind, no thought appeared to him more absurd; he was ready to give death a promise of willing submission and compliance, if it would let him out of its clutches for a few minutes, would give him a period of grace, allow him to cross the hated frontier.

While the invisible figure made up of forehead and chin and ears pushed the train this way and that, the Swiss customs control had reached the Professor's compartment. First the passports were subjected to a rigorous examination, then the officials looked at the four or five cases in the luggage rack, which, however, was a pure formality, since they had long ago decided to concentrate their attention on the luggage of the man with the Party badge. One of them slipped his practiced hands into the case, fished out three bars of chocolate, went on searching, found nothing else forbidden, explained in unequivocal Swiss German that only two bars per person could be taken out duty-free, set about claiming the duty on the third bar at the cost of a great deal of paper, carbon paper and writing.

While the Swiss officials were still at work the train had once again, and this time apparently finally, decided to move. The railway lines spread out endlessly on either side, the mountains of coal towered up, the piles of dirt stood high on the lines, the workers' houses seemed to be asking ill-humoredly what they were doing on the embankment and so close to a foreign country, old railway carriages slept forgotten on the edges of the railway tracks. The Professor was still wondering whether he dared go to the dining car, which however was now impossible because the train had entered the Baden station and stopped there. Suddenly there was a great deal of noise around the carriages. Whistles blew, words of command could be heard from the platform, boots drummed on the stone floor; officials in civilian clothes and uniforms, SA men, frontier police, crowded into the train as though expecting a victim and equipped to finish him off. Before the Professor's eyes there reappeared that day when men in black uniforms had taken possession of the prison on the Rossauer Lände and Fritz Grünwald's screams had echoed from the next cell. "Are you feeling ill?" he heard the voice of the mustard manufacturer ask beside him. He shook his head.

Now he was on German soil and became aware of the grotesque fact that he was glad to be on enemy soil, but his nervousness did not subside; perhaps the Baden station was considered international, his passport still hadn't been stamped, his return had not been officially confirmed.

"German Passport and Customs Control!" The frontier officials and SA men flooded the compartment. Would the man with the beery face appear in the doorway, the SA man who had said good-bye to him with the meaningful *"Auf Wiedersehen!"* No, the beery-faced SA man was not present, was not on duty today; they were other faces, only the voices seemed to be the same. One of the officials was already examining the ex-officer's suitcase, when another asked to see the Professor's passport—Heinrich von Benda had been sitting by the window and hence was the last to be dealt with. As before, a hundred years ago, when he had gone to Évian, his passport went from hand to hand, so that the attention paid to it could not escape his traveling companions; it was not imagination, it was a fact, that the control authorities had been informed of his arrival. He answered all the questions, which were asked sternly but correctly—"Have you any foreign currency?" "How much have you in marks?" "Was your second Swiss visa stamped abroad?"—truthfully; only when a uniformed official asked whether he had any presents, any valuables purchased abroad, did he answer with a lie: no, he had only articles of personal use in his case. For a moment his heart pounded in his throat as the consequences of the possible discovery of the article he was smuggling became clear to him; but the customs officer seemed not to be a psychologist and did not ask to see the contents of his suitcase.

Exhausted, the Professor sat down again by the window, which one of the officials had shut with an angry gesture. The train traveled on, although the officials had not yet left it, traveled on out of the covered station into the cloudless July afternoon. Heinrich von Benda had to close his eyes because the light dazzled him, but he opened them again; if he concentrated on himself, the pain became unbearable. The chimneys of the factories—immediately across the frontier they entered a highly industrialized district—stood like stone watchmen by the railway lines. Only gradually did the train free itself from the constriction of backyards and gain the open country, gardens, fields, woods; now, as though set free, it traveled faster and faster—all this the Professor observed as though through a thick veil, a veil had also fallen between him and the ex-officer, between him and the mustard manufacturer. The ex-officer was looking for a match, the mustard manufacturer reading his newspaper.

Heinrich von Benda bent forward, pressed his hand against his heart, sat up again, tried in vain to find a place for himself in his seat. He thought of Bettina, without feeling that he was coming closer to her; she was moving farther and farther away, and the farther away from him she went, the more desperately he clung to the wish to grasp her hand. He had saved her, and he could not understand why she did not save him. Now he could go to the dining car and take the drug that would bring him relief, but he did not stand up yet because the distance seemed to him too far, the risk too great. He did not know where the dining car was, how many cars separated him from it; on the iron footboard between the cars he would be shaken to and fro; before his eyes the rubber shock absorber took on the shape of the invisible figure, the faceless one with a forehead and a chin; he would have to force his way past human bodies, past policemen and SA men; perhaps it wasn't necessary to go to the dining car, he could just as well bend over the tap in the WC and take the tablet.

He admonished himself to think clearly. If excitement had caused the attack, fear of the frontier control, fear of coming home, the fear that he would not come home, then clear thinking ought to calm his nerves, relax his heart muscles. His passport had been stamped, the officials could testify that he had crossed the frontier, the train was traveling fast, eating up the miles, through Germany; he had done everything in his power; he had offered the Jews for sale, had haggled over the price; had not thought of the difficulties where difficulties multiplied, had ignored the hopelessness of the undertaking up to the last minute, and even after that had refused to recognize it, had not lost heart, had fulfilled his mission.

He must not lose heart now either. He would stand up, but he would not go to the WC—he would not go to the WC because he did not want to die in the WC of a train, because that was no death for Professor Ordenarius and Hofrat Heinrich von Benda; he would go to the dining car and stay there till the time came to change cars.

He rose, took a step forward, stretched out his hand to the door handle, took fright at the door handle, lost his balance, staggered back and sank into the seat by the door.

"He is ill," said the wit, folding his newspaper and bending over the Professor.

The ex-officer also bent over Heinrich von Benda.

"I think he's dead," said the ex-officer.

"We must call a doctor," said the mustard manufacturer.

He opened the door. The guard had just approached the carriage, took in the situation, began to look around for a doctor.

The ex-officer felt the Professor's heart and pulse.

"He's dead," he said.

The guard had not found a doctor; he came back with one of the frontier police. Immediately afterward SA men and officials came and looked into the compartment.

"That's Benda," said one of the SA men.

"An American brought him to the station at Basel," said the wit. "He wasn't feeling well then."

The ex-officer closed the Professor's eyes.

The frontier policeman who had been the first into the compartment looked up at the luggage.

"Open it up!" he said.

A second policeman lifted the case down, opened it. For a moment no one bothered about Professor von Benda, they were all looking curiously at the suitcase.

The frontier policeman rummaged about among the papers that lay on top, the duplicated records of the refugee conference at Évian-les-Bains. Then a scrap of green material came into sight.

"The Yid was smuggling a lady's dress," said the frontier policeman.

Documentation

1. AUTHOR'S COMMENTARY

The "Benda Mission," as it is called in this book, was reported, so far as I know, by three newspapers altogether, and all three only hinted at it. These were *The New York Times* (July 7, 1938), the London *Daily Express* (July 12, 1938) and the *Prager Tagblatt* (also July 12, 1938).

The *Prager Tagblatt* report was written by myself. I had been the League of Nations correspondent of this big German-language Prague newspaper since 1935, and as such accredited to the Évian Conference.

My knowledge of events, of which for understandable reasons I could make only limited use in my report, came almost entirely from the man whom in this novel I have called Heinrich von Benda.

About this there is a story.

When I was fourteen years old—thirteen years before the events described—I was operated upon by "Heinrich von Benda." The Professor was a friend of my family. The Professor had few acquaintances among the participants in the Conference and was totally inexperienced in press matters. We were living next door to each other in the Hôtel Esplanade. Although I was only twenty-seven, he took me into his confidence; we spent hours, indeed many half nights, together. I was something like a press officer in reverse: it was my job to shield him from the press.

This does not mean that this novel is "authentic" in every detail, that it is intended as a "factual report." We are accustomed to regarding a "historical novel" as one whose action takes place in the distant past. But there are also historical novels to which a breath of the present still clings; they are "historical" because they are based on an historical event, but nevertheless they remain novels. This is such a novel.

For more than twenty-five years I have been carrying my knowledge of the Conference at Évian-les-Bains and the "Benda

303

Mission" about with me like a burden and a duty. I have preserved the private notes of my conversations with the Professor, as well as part of the documentary material relating to the Conference. For the supplementary material I owe thanks in particular to the Library of the United Nations as successor to the League of Nations, the archives of *The New York Times*, the Public Library of New York, the Wiener Bibliothek, London, the Tasiemka Archives, London, the editors of *Aufbau*, New York, and the management of the Hôtel Royal, Évian-les-Bains. Far more than the facts, however, what preoccupied me during these past years, for almost a generation, was the figure of the Professor. Only in a novel could a monument be erected to him.

Since, however, this is a historical novel in the sense outlined above, I believe I have a duty to give the reader certain explanations.

1. The course of the Conference (July 6 to 15, 1938) is described almost exactly as it took place. Several public sessions have been condensed, but in essentials they were exactly as described here. Almost all the speeches have been taken verbatim from the minutes, even if some have been split up and others joined together. Public and confidential sessions have in places been treated as one.

2. All quotations from newspapers are literal transcriptions of the reports or articles in question. Only in two or three places has the date of publication been slightly changed, but always within the period of the Conference.

3. The descriptions of the participants in the Conference— particularly as regards their outward appearance—have been set down from memory and conform, so far as that is possible after a quarter of a century, to reality.

4. Where resolutions of the Conference are quoted, they are taken verbatim from the minutes or from newspaper reports.

5. The immigration conditions cited and the demands made in this respect by individual states are accurate in every detail.

6. The concert described in the last chapter was conducted by Fritz Busch.

7. The Conference was not continued as regards any of its significant functions. It petered out into nothing.

8. The Professor's family circumstances and all the events connected with them are pure inventions. Private conversations between the Professor and participants in the Conference, as well as those of various participants among themselves, have been reconstructed from my notes, but naturally they have not the same authenticity as speeches delivered in public sessions.

I hope I have made it clear in this novel that I do not identify myself with the Professor's special mission. To pass judgment on its human and moral justification, in so far as that is possible at all, has been left to the reader. During the Conference itself the mission was the subject of lively discussion in informed circles; at that time, many years before the Hungarian Eichmann episode, in which human beings were once again the subject of bargaining, few people took it seriously. I cannot decide whether the "monsignor's" information was correct and the German Reich had no other purpose than to torpedo the Conference, but on the basis of my experience I tend to this view. There can be no doubt that the German Reich offered forty thousand Austrian Jews for sale and set August 1, 1938, as the date for the expiry of the ultimatum. This was reported by the international press, above all by the London *Daily Express*. These are facts.

I repeat: it was not my intention to make sensational disclosures, but to portray the positively superhuman conflict of a man who was the prisoner of history. This man, whom I have called Heinrich von Benda, was convinced that there was no other salvation for the Jews under the dominion of the monster than either the "purchase" of the victims or acceptance of the Colombian rescue plan. For the novelist, who seeks the truth in man, this had to suffice.

My book raises the question whether the man whose heart is too apathetic to throw himself against the wheel of destiny is guilty of complicity.

I have answered this question in the affirmative.

2. ÉVIAN AND WORLD EVENTS

July 6, 1938: The Refugee Conference meets at Évian-les-Bains on Lake Geneva in the Hôtel Royal.

On this day the Japanese attack on China is a year old. The

Japanese have conquered an area of 775,000 square miles, the number of dead is given as 510,109.

The American Government announces that the United States economic crisis is finally over.

July 7, 1938: The American special envoy, Myron C. Taylor, is elected Chairman of the Refugee Conference. The secret discussions begin.

Alfred Rosenberg violently attacks the Évian Conference.

On the Transjordanian frontier of Palestine the first clash involving Britain and Arab troops. Two British cruisers set sail for Haifa.

Czechoslovakia considers further measures against the "illegal emigration" from Germany and Austria.

Admiral Horthy, Regent of Hungary, assures Hitler of his loyal support.

A violent strike breaks out in Los Angeles.

July 8, 1938: Numerous private organizations, especially Catholic ones, appeal to the Conference. *The New York Times* reports that the establishment of a permanent refugee organization has already been agreed between Britain and America. A memorandum from Archbishop Rummel of New Orleans is placed before the Conference. Important personalities arrive in Évian as observers, among them the President of the Pan-Europe Union, Count Richard N. Coudenhove-Kalergi, the exiled Italian politicians Nenni and Count Sforza, the historian Guglielmo Ferreno, the representative of the Jewish Agency of Palestine, Dr. Arthur Ruppin, the Secretary-General of the League of Nations, Joseph Avenol, and the New York rabbi Jonah B. Wise. The subcommittees set up by the Conference begin their discussions.

A spokesman of the German Reich Government describes Évian as "pure propaganda," at the same time denying reports that the majority of the Austrian people wish to emigrate. He claims that they have accorded the Führer an "enthusiastic welcome."

In Barcelona the Government admits that the town of Nules has fallen to the assault of the Fascist rebels. The latter are shelling Barcelona and advancing along the Teruel-Sagunto line.

The British Ambassador in Rome, the Earl of Perth, confers with Foreign Minister Ciano on the possible withdrawal of Italian troops from Spain.

America decides to withdraw citizenship from American volunteers fighting in Spain.

The National-Socialist German-American Bund demonstrates in Albany, N. Y.

July 9, 1938: The Refugee Conference meets at eleven in the morning for a plenary session. It listens to statements from the Colombian delegate, Professor Y. M. Yepes, as well as from the High Commissioner for Refugees, Sir Neill Malcolm. The observers from Yugoslavia and Greece, Ambassador Fotitch and Ambassador Politis, have arrived at the Hôtel Royal. So have Count Apponyi from Budapest, Baroness Philippe de Rothschild from Paris and His Royal Highness the Crown Prince of Bikaner.

The leader of the Sudeten German Party, Konrad Henlein, declares that his party has achieved a "record membership."

The disturbances in Palestine compel Britain to dispatch the 11th Hussars, a light tank unit. Figures for the day: 12 Jews and 52 Arabs killed, 24 Jews and 145 Arabs wounded.

President Franklin D. Roosevelt delivers political speeches in Oklahoma and Arkansas and speaks of the birth of a "nation with a soul."

Reich Marshal Hermann Göring in a Berlin speech calls upon the people to stay on the land and resist the temptation of the big cities.

Multimillionaire Howard Hughes sets out on a flight around the world in a single-engined Lockheed.

July 10, 1938: Secret meetings of the Évian Conference. An anti-Fascist politician who calls himself Giovanni Bianci, who has arrived in Évian, is expelled by both the Swiss and the French police.

The world press deals at length with Évian. Reading articles appear in the London *Times,* the *Manchester Guardian,* the

Daily Telegraph. The leading article in the *News Chronicle* is headed "Now Is the Time."

The Czechoslovakian Government has met in Prague to consider reports of the activity of disguised German SS men in the Sudeten and of acts of provocation.

Reich Chancellor Adolf Hitler has received the leader of the Sudeten Germans, Konrad Henlein, in Munich in the presence of the Foreign Minister Joachim von Ribbentrop.

In Shanghai cholera is causing up to 70 deaths a day.

July 11, 1938: All the Conference meetings are secret. The chief British delegate the Right Honorable Earl Winterton, M.P., Chancellor of the Duchy of Lancaster, gives a dinner party in honor of the head of the American delegation. Évian reports the arrival of the Palestine observer Mrs. Golda Meir.

Joseph Stalin reports that the Soviet Union will harvest 130 million tons of wheat, a record.

During the opening of the Zeppelin Museum in Friedrichshafen, Dr. Hugo Eckener makes a vigorous attack on the American Secretary of the Interior, Harold L. Ickes, who has refused to deliver helium on the grounds that it is a war material.

Germany announces that in order to save foreign currency it will in future employ human hair, chiefly women's hair, in the manufacture of carpets. Hairdressers are instructed to collect it.

July 12, 1938: While the negotiations of the Refugee Conference are continued behind closed doors, the Conference secretariat, under the chairmanship of the Secretary-General Jean Paul-Boncour, is drafting a resolution. According to *The New York Times* the three powers Great Britain, France and the United States have decided to formulate the resolution in such a way that "the possibility of negotiations with the German Reich remains open."

The Berlin *Politische Diplomatische Korrespondenz* declares that the aim of the Conference is to prove that the "sympathy of the member states for the Jews" was meant seriously.

A spokesman of the German Ministry of Propaganda, Josef

Stertin, declares in Vienna that the former Austrian Chancellor, Dr. Kurt von Schuschnigg, has been condemned to vigorous imprisonment because it has emerged that he was responsible for the execution of thirteen National Socialists.

Berlin announces that German unemployment has been further reduced; more than twenty million people are now in employment.

Barcelona reports further bombing of the city by Generalissimo Franco's air force with German and Italian support.

The organ of the Rumanian Government, *Vitorul,* writes that German pressure on Rumania has been intensified, but that Rumania is neither "Germany's vassal, nor a substitute for the lost colonies of the German Empire."

July 13, 1938: Over the Refugee Conference's further deliberation hangs the shadow of economic sanctions, with which the German Reich has threatened in particular the South American countries and Germany's small neighbors. The South American states have drafted a strongly worded resolution opposing the plan of "general immigration." Among the important personalities who have arrived in Évian are the Spanish cellist Pablo Casals and the former editor of the *Vossischezeitung,* Georg Bernhard.

Anglo-American economic negotiations going on in Geneva, and dealing especially with currency matters, run into a serious crisis.

Attacks on Jews in various German provincial towns.

July 14, 1938: At 5 P.M. a semipublic meeting of the Évian Conference attended by all delegates, but not open to the public. Discussion of all reports from subcommittees and their draft resolutions. A dinner given by the American special envoy in honor of the French delegation. A speech by Mrs. Golda Meir from Palestine for invited guests and the world press.

The *Völkischer Beobachter* launches a fresh attack on the Conference and especially condemns the behavior of the Vatican observer, Father Odo.

The Chinese claim to have sunk 22 Japanese warships.

In Geneva a Spanish Government protest against alleged secret negotiations being conducted by certain states with Franco meets with a cool reception.

At a meeting organized by Jewish organizations in the New York Astoria Hotel attention is drawn to German plans to "leave the streets open to the anti-Semitic mob."

Skeptical surveys of the results of the Évian Conference by the press in Washington.

July 15, 1938: Final public meeting of the Conference at 11 A.M. Acceptance of the resolutions, final speeches, telegram of thanks to President Roosevelt. Departure of the delegates.

President Franklin D. Roosevelt appeals to the world for disarmament and underlines the danger of a Second World War.

3. THE DELEGATIONS AT ÉVIAN

The complete list of the delegations to the Évian Conference —official title: Intergovernmental Committee for Refugees— runs as follows. (Remarks in parentheses are the author's. The order is not alphabetical in English, as it has been taken from the French Conference records.)

Australia

Lieut.-Colonel the Hon. T. W. White, D.F.C., V.D., M.P., Minister of Trade and Customs.

Mr. Alfred Stirling, from the Foreign Ministry, London.

Mr. A. W. Stuart-Smith, Australia House, London.

Argentine Republic

Dr. Tomás A. Le Breton, Ambassador in France.

M. Carlos A. Pardo, Secretary-General of the Permanent Delegation to the League of Nations.

Belgium

M. De Foy, Director General of Public Safety (police), honorary magistrate.

M. J. Schneider, Director in the Ministry of Foreign Affairs and Foreign Trade.

Bolivia

M. Simon Patino, Minister in France.

M. A. Costa du Rels, Ambassador, Permanent Delegate to the League of Nations.

United Kingdom

The Right Hon. the Earl Winterton, M.P., Chancellor of the Duchy of Lancaster.

Sir Charles Michael Palairet, K.C.M.G., Minister Plenipotentiary.

Advisers:

Sir John Shuckburgh, K.C.M.G., C.B., Undersecretary of State at the Colonial Office.

Mr. J. G. Hibbert, M.C., Director at the Colonial Office.

Mr. E. N. Cooper, O.B.E., Director at the Home Office.

Mr. R. M. Makins, Assistant Adviser on League of Nations questions in the Foreign Office (secretary of the delegation).

Secretaries to Lord Winterton:

Captain Victor Cazalet, M.P.

Mr. T. B. Williamson, Home Office.

Brazil

M. Helio Lobo, Minister first class.

Expert:

M. Jorge Olinto, Permanent Delegate, First Secretary of the Brazilian Legation.

Canada

Mr. Hume Wrong, Permanent Delegate to the League of Nations.

Expert:

Mr. W. R. Little, Commissioner for European Emigration in London.

Chile

M. Fernando García Oldini, Minister in Switzerland and Representative at the International Labor Organization, with the rank of Envoy Extraordinary and Minister Plenipotentiary.

Colombia

M. Luis Cano, Permanent Delegate to the League of Nations, with the rank of Envoy Extraordinary and Minister Plenipotentiary. (Only present at the opening sessions.)

Professor J. M. Yepes, Legal Adviser to the Permanent Delegation to the League of Nations, assistant delegate. (The real head of the delegation with the rank of Envoy Extraordinary and Minister Plenipotentiary.)

M. Abelardo Forero-Benavides, Secretary to the Permanent Delegation to the League of Nations (secretary).

Costa Rica

Professor Luis Dobles Segreda, Chargé d'Affaires in Paris, sitting by virtue of his diplomatic office.

Cuba

M. Juan Antiga Escobar, Envoy Extraordinary and Minister Plenipotentiary in Switzerland, Permanent Delegate to the League of Nations.

Denmark

M. Gustav Rasmussen, Ministry of Foreign Affairs.
M. Troels Hoff, Ministry of Justice.

Dominican Republic

M. Virgilio Trujillo Molina, Envoy Extraordinary and Minister Plenipotentiary in France and Belgium.

Dr. Salvador E. Paradas, Chargé d'Affaires representing the Permanent Delegation to the League of Nations.

Ecuador

M. Alejandro Gastelu Concha, Chargé d'Affaires.

United States of America

The Honorable Myron C. Taylor, Ambassador on Special Mission.

Mr. James G. McDonald, Adviser, President of the "President Roosevelt Consultative Committee for Political Refugees."

Mr. Robert T. Pell, Technical Adviser, Division of European Affairs, State Department.

Mr. George L. Brandt, Technical Adviser, formerly head of the Visa Division in the State Department.

Mr. Hayward G. Hill, Secretary of the Delegation, United States Consul in Geneva.

Mr. George L. Warren, assistant to Mr. McDonald, Executive Secretary of the "President Roosevelt Consultative Committee for Political Refugees."

France

His Excellency M. Henry Bérenger, Ambassador.

Experts and secretaries:

M. Bressy, Minister Plenipotentiary. Deputy Director of the International Unions at the Ministry of Foreign Affairs.

M. Combes, Director in the Ministry of the Interior.

M. Georges Coulon (no rank stated).

M. Fourçade, Head of Department in the Ministry of the Interior.

M. François Seydoux, official of the Bureau for European Affairs in the Foreign Ministry.

Baron Brincard, official of the Bureau for League of Nations Affairs in the Foreign Ministry.

Guatemala

M. José Gregorio Diaz, Envoy Extraordinary and Minister Plenipotentiary in France.

Haiti

M. Léon R. Thébaud, Commercial Attaché in Paris, with the rank of Minister.

Honduras

M. Mauricio Rosal, Consul in Paris, with the rank of Envoy Extraordinary and Minister Plenipotentiary.

Ireland

Mr. Francis Thomas Cremins, Permanent Delegate to the League of Nations.

Mr. John Duff, Assistant Secretary in the Ministry of Justice.

Mr. William Maguire, Second Assistant Secretary in the Ministry of Industry and Commerce.

Mexico

M. Villa Michel, Envoy Extraordinary and Minister Plenipotentiary in Holland.

M. Manuel Tello, Chargé d'Affaires representing the Permanent Delegation to the League of Nations.

Nicaragua

M. Constantino Herdocia, Minister in Great Britain and France, with the rank of Envoy Extraordinary and Minister Plenipotentiary.

Norway

M. Michael Hansson, former President of the International Mixed Court of Appeal in Egypt, President of the International Nansen Office for Refugees. (Was at Évian in a double role—as Norwegian delegate and as President of the Nansen Office. In the same year, 1938, his office received the Nobel Prize for Peace.)

M. C. N. S. Platou, Director-General in the Ministry of Justice.

M. Finn Moe, journalist, representative of the private organizations for refugees in Norway.

Adviser:

M. R. Konstad, Director of the Norwegian Central Passport Office.

New Zealand

Mr. C. B. Burdekin (no rank stated).

Documentation

Panama

Dr. Ernesto Hoffmann, Consul General in Geneva and Permanent Delegate to the League of Nations, with the rank of Envoy Extraordinary and Minister Plenipotentiary.

Paraguay

M. Gustavo A. Wiengreen, Envoy Extraordinary and Minister Plenipotentiary of Paraguay in Hungary.

Holland

M. W. C. Beucker Andreae, Head of the Legal Department in the Ministry of Foreign Affairs.

M. R. A. Verwey, Director of the State Insurance Office for the Unemployed in the Ministry of Social Welfare.

M. I. P. Hooykaas, Adviser in the Ministry of Justice.

Peru

M. Francisco García Calderón, Minister in France, with the rank of Envoy Extraordinary and Minister Plenipotentiary.

Sweden

M. G. Engzell, Head of the Legal Department of the Ministry of Foreign Affairs.

M. C. A. M. de Hallenborg, Head of Section in the Ministry of Foreign Affairs.

Secretary of the Delegation:

M. E. G. Drougge, Secretary at the Ministry of Labor and Social Insurance.

Switzerland

Dr. Heinrich Rothmund, Head of the Police Division of the Federal Department of Justice and Police. (After the Second World War he was the object of intense criticism, especially from within Switzerland itself.)

M. Henri Werner, Lawyer, Police Division of the Federal Department of Justice and Police.

Uruguay

Dr. Alfredo Carbonell-Debali, Delegate Plenipotentiary.

Venezuela

M. Carlos Aristimuño-Coll, Envoy Extraordinary and Minister Plenipotentiary in France.

OTHER PARTICIPANTS IN THE CONFERENCE

High Commission for Refugees from Germany:

Sir Neill Malcolm, K.C.B., D.S.O.
Lord Duncannon.
M. K. Erim, member of the Political Section of the Secretariat of the League of Nations.

General Secretariat of the Intergovernmental Committee:

M. Jean Paul-Boncour, Secretary-General.
Mlle. G. Boisseau, Assistant to the Secretary-General.
M. J. Herbert, interpreter.
Mr. Lloyd, interpreter.
M. Muller, translator.
Mr. McAfee, translator.
M. Mézières, treasurer.

PRIVATE ORGANIZATIONS REPRESENTED AT THE CONFERENCE

International Christian Committee for Non-Aryans (London)
Central Bureau for the Settlement of German Jews (London)
Association de colonisation juive (Paris)
Committee of Aid for German Jews (London)
Society for the Protection of Sciences and Studies (London)
Comité d'aide et d'assistance aux victimes de l'anti-sémitisme en Allemagne (Brussels)
Comité d'assistance aux réfugiés (Paris)
Comite voor Bijzondere Joodsche Belangen (Amsterdam)
Schweizer Hilfszentrum für Flüchtlinge (Basel)
Central Committee for Refugees from Germany (Prague)
Fédération internationale des émigrés d'Allemagne (Paris)

Service internationale de migration (Geneva)

Service universitaire international (Geneva)

Comité international pour le placement des intellectuels réfugiés (Geneva)

The Joint Foreign Committee of the Board of Deputies of British Jews and the Anglo-Jewish Association (London)

Agudas Israel World Organization (London)

American Joint Distribution Committee (Paris)

Council for German Jewry (London)

Hicem (Paris)

Association of German Scholars in Distress Abroad (London)

German Committee of the Quaker Society of Friends (London)

Bureau international pour le respect du droit d'asile et l'aide aux réfugiés politiques (Paris)

Jewish World Congress (Paris)

New Zionist Organization (London)

Emigration Advisory Committee (London)

Alliance israélite universelle (Paris)

Komitee für die Entwicklung der grossen jüdischen Kolonisation (Zürich)

Internationale ouvrière et socialiste (Paris and Brussels)

American, British, Belgian, French, Dutch and Swiss Catholic Committees for Aid to Refugees (no address)

"Freeland" Association (London)

"Ort" (Paris)

Centre de recherches de solutions au problème juif (Paris)

League of Nations Union (London)

Jewish Agency for Palestine (London)

Comité pour la défense des droits des Israélites en Europe centrale et orientale (Paris)

Union des Sociétés "Osé" (Paris)

Royal Institute of International Affairs (London)

Fédération des émigrés d'Autriche (Paris)

Société d'émigration et de colonisation juive "Emcol" (Paris)

THE WORLD PRESS

The international press was represented by about 200 correspondents—chiefly the League of Nations correspondents of the leading daily and weekly newspapers and of the news agencies.

The most eminent among them were the chief correspondent of *The New York Times* in Geneva, Clarence K. Streit, who later played an important part in American politics as President of the Union Now Society, an organization for close Anglo-American cooperation, and Robert Dell of the *Manchester Guardian*, the doyen of the correspondents accredited to the League of Nations. Other newspapers represented included *The Times* (London), *Daily Telegraph* (London, by the well-known diplomatic correspondent Noel Panter), *News Chronicle* (London, by the future liberal M.P. Vernon Bartlett), *Daily Express* (London), *Daily Herald* (London), *Reuter* (London), *Le Temps* (Paris), *Journal des Nations* (Geneva), *Journal de Genève, Tribune de Genève, Gazette de Lausanne, Neue Zürcher Zeitung, Dernière Heure* (Brussels), *Berlingske Tidende* (Copenhagen), *Aftenbladet* (Oslo), *De Telegraaf* (The Hague), *Amsterdamsches Handelsbad, Nieuwe Rotterdamse Courant, Prager Tagblatt, Lidove Noviny* (Brno, by the nephew of the President of Czechoslovakia, Bohus Benesh), *Prager Presse, Ujság* (Budapest), *Magyar Távirati Iroda* (Budapest), *Adeverul* (Bucharest), *La Stampa* (Turin), *Corriere della Sera* (Milan), *New York Herald Tribune, Chicago Daily News* (by the world-famous correspondent H. R. Knickerbocker), *Chicago Tribune, La Prensa* (Buenos Aires), *Osservatore Romano* (Vatican). There were a particularly large number of accredited German correspondents, led by the League of Nations reporter of the *Völkischer Beobachter*.

THE BUDGET OF THE CONFERENCE

	Unit	Swiss francs
United States	108	3024
Argentina	23	644
Australia	23	644
Belgium	19	532
Bolivia	2	56
United Kingdom	108	3024
Brazil	23	644
Canada	35	980
Chile	8	224
Colombia	5	140

Costa Rica	1	28
Cuba	5	140
Denmark	12	336
Dominican Republic	1	28
Ecuador	1	28
France	80	2240
Guatemala	0.5	14
Haiti	1	28
Honduras	0.5	14
Ireland	10	280
Mexico	13	364
Nicaragua	0.5	14
Norway	9	252
New Zealand	8	224
Panama	1	28
Paraguay	0.5	14
Holland	24	672
Peru	5	140
Sweden	19	532
Switzerland	17	476
Uruguay	4	112
Venezuela	4	112

The expenses of the Conference amounted to 16,000 Swiss francs. The total sum raised as above came to 15,988 Swiss francs, leaving a deficit of 12 Swiss francs.